THE UNAUTHORIZED BACK TO THE FUTURE CHRONOLOGY

By Greg Mitchell and Rich Handley

Layout and Design by Paul C. Giachetti

Cover and Interior Illustrations by Pat Carbajal

Foreword by Dan Madsen

HASSLEIN • BOOKS

Writers: Greg Mitchell and Rich Handley
Layout and design: Paul C. Giachetti
Cover and interior art: Pat Carbajal
Foreword: Dan Madsen

ISBN-13: 978-0-578-13085-9
Library of Congress Cataloging-in-Publication Data
First Edition: October 2013
10 9 8 7 6 5 4 3 2 1

CONTENTS

ACKNOWLEDGMENTS◄▪▪▪▪

It's That Time Again

"Hell, I'm in it with you and I don't even understand it."
—**Marty McFly,** *Back to the Future Part III*

"**H**ey, wouldn't it be cool if there were an exhaustive guide to the *Back to the Future* universe?"

Ah, that's how these things always start. Some starry-eyed butthead (in this case, me) has a bright idea he'd love to see made into reality, but of course he wants someone else to do all the work. In this case, I wanted **Rich Handley** to do it, and that's why I approached him back in 2009 with my heavy idea of making a *Back to the Future* timeline similar to his stellar work on *Timeline of the Planet of the Apes*.

Little did I know, at the time, that he would approach me to bring this dream to reality.

It has been a herculean effort on the part of many, over the course of three years, to bring this book to life. But I want to thank my editor and co-writer Rich Handley for trusting me with this assignment in the first place (seriously, what were you thinking?) and giving me the opportunity to be a part of this amazing project.

I, of course, must also thank my wife **Meghan** and our daughters, **Jo Beth** and **Dani**, for their endless patience. I missed a lot of family time over the past few years, and was often "someplace else," even when at the dinner table. But they stuck it out with me, and now I can begin the process of repaying them. I sense many trips to buy ice cream in my immediate future…

I also would like to thank, in no apparent order:

- **Paul C. Giachetti**, Rich's partner-in-crime at Hasslein Books, for his willingness to bring me onto the team and the painstaking work he took to organize, format and design this book. An encyclopedia can easily be a bit of a bore to thumb through, but Paul brought a level of panache that makes it a joy to turn every page.

- **Pat Carbajal** (patart-pat.blogspot.com), the amazing cover and interior illustrator for this book. I first discovered Pat's work through *Timeline of the Planet of the Apes* and promptly explored his blog, being constantly stunned by his sketches. Anytime I received a letter in my inbox telling me Pat had just turned in a new illustration for the book, I was immediately excited and couldn't open the mail fast enough. It's been such a treat to see him take images only communicated through the cartoon or video game and bring them to photorealistic life.

- **Stephen Clark** (BTTF.com), who is the man. I knew of Stephen for many, many years as, for the longest time, he seemed to be the only one keeping *Back to the Future* alive in the heart of fandom. I remember back when he ran BTTF.net, and was very excited to see him first unofficially and then officially adopted as the online home of *Back to the Future*. Stephen provided a veritable treasure trove of rare scripts that not only greatly enriched this book, but also satisfied and delighted my own personal fanboy curiosities.

- **Dan Madsen**, the president of the *Back to the Future Fan Club* long before I knew such a thing existed. It's been a true honor to have him on board to write the foreword and reflect on his experiences with *Back to the Future*. I'm the new guy on the block, and it's humbling to share page space with a man who was there from the beginning.

Others I'd like to thank include "the Two Bobs"—Mr. Bob Gale and Mr. Robert Zemeckis—who envisioned this endearing trilogy that has forever left its imprint on popular culture. That thanks also extends to the hardworking cast and crew of the trilogy, with a special note of thanks to Michael J. Fox, Christopher Lloyd, Crispin Glover and my favorite cinematographer, Dean Cundey.

Thanks to the cast and crew at Telltale Games for putting together a great game and a loving homage to the series, and for taking me back to Hill Valley all over again. Lastly, thanks to Johnny Dodd for re-introducing me to *Back to the Future* in high school and, after I hounded him for more than a year, finally parting with his original VHS copy and imparting it to me, as I was too cheap to go buy my own.

— **Greg Mitchell**

After Greg's fitting tribute, it's tempting just to write "What he said" and go about my merry way. But I can't do that.

Wait, can I?

Hmm… "What he—"

Naah. I can't. So…

First and foremost, I thank **Greg Mitchell** for the incredible amount of work he put into writing the initial draft of this chronology. Although Greg invited me to be his co-author once it became clear that writing a *Back to the Future* timeline was a much bigger task than we'd anticipated (which is why I'd assigned it to him—like Greg, I wanted *someone else* to do all the work), I can't stress enough that this book would simply not exist without him. It was his idea to produce a *Back to the Future* book, let alone two, in the first place, and I am therefore in his debt—not only for *Back in Time*, but also for the companion volume, *A Matter of Time: The Unauthorized Back to the Future Lexicon*, published in 2012.

I enthusiastically reiterate Greg's praise for **Paul Giachetti**, **Pat Carbajal**, **Dan Madsen** and **Stephen Clark**, for all the reasons listed above and more. Paul and I have come to realize we're basically the same person… so the fact that we work so well together may reveal our innate narcissism. Pat's work speaks for itself—no, really, it actually *talks*. Dan is a pioneer of fan-club magazines (I wrote a number of articles for *Star Wars Insider* and *Star Trek Communicator* magazines while he was still running the show, in fact), and

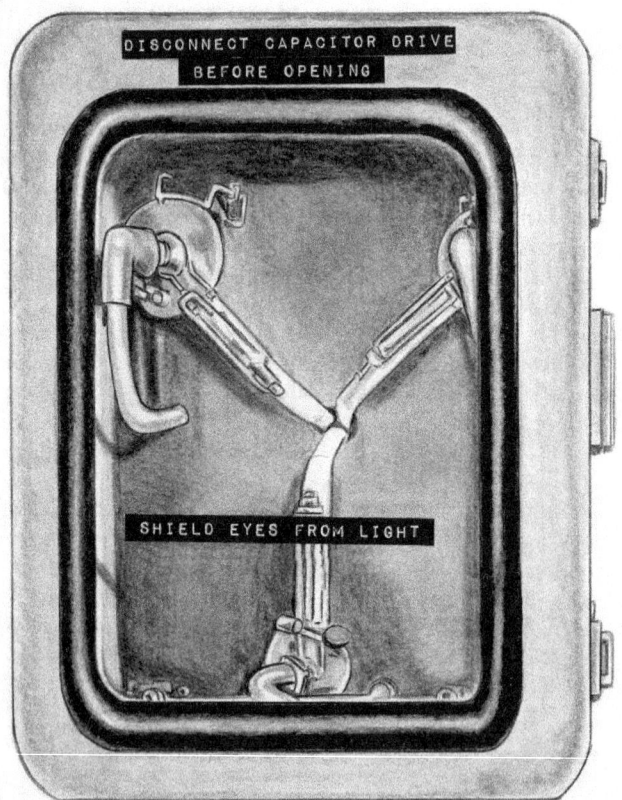

it's our honor to have him aboard. And Stephen very graciously shared his private collection with us and reviewed the manuscript to make sure we didn't do anything ridiculous, like claiming Doc was once a superhero.

Wait… what? He was? Oh. Never mind, then. (See page 68.)

I'd especially like to thank **Bob Gale** and **Robert Zemeckis**, not only for Mr. Gale's praise of the *BTTF* lexicon, but also for generously (and without being asked) sending me a *BTTF* poster signed by both of them. That was an unexpected delight, and it made my millennium. Thanks also to the amazing casts, crews and creative teams who brought *Back to the Future* to life in the films, cartoons, comics and video games.

In addition, I must recognize the contributions of several other individuals, including:

- **Joseph F. Berenato** (atomicwanderers.com), who once again rose to the challenge of proofreading an absurdly detailed manuscript. Joe is currently writing or co-writing two upcoming titles for Hasslein Books—*It's Alive: The Unauthorized Universal Monsters Encyclopedia* (with Jim and Becky Beard) and *Something Strange: The Complete Unauthorized Ghostbusters Encyclopedia*—and I, in turn, wrote an essay for *New Life and New Civilizations: Exploring Star Trek Comics*, a Sequart book edited by Joe. Paul and I are lucky to have him on the Hasslein team.

- **Paul Simpson** (scifibulletin.com), for pitching in on the proof-reading end. An accomplished writer and editor (who also wrote for *Star Wars Insider*), Paul is currently co-writing a *Doctor Who* essay book for Hasslein Books with Brian J. Robb, and generously offered to proofread this and other manuscripts for us. Between Paul and Joe, this book is in great hands.

- **Steve Cafarelli** (monkeygripmusic.com), a close friend for almost 20 years now, for maintaining hassleinbooks.com for us (a site he beautifully redesigned last year), and for that time he anonymously left a bag of Circus Peanuts on my doorstep, knowing my great love for that particular confection. Thankfully, Steve and I do not live in the Citizen Brown dystopian timeline, in which Edna Strickland denied Hill Valley's citizens of that divinely inspired banana-flavored, neon-orange-colored, peanut-shaped candy. (See page 112.)

- **Steven Greenwood**, for creating Futurepedia (backtothefuture. wikia.com), the amazing *Back to the Future* Wikia, an invaluable resource during the creation of both this book and the lexicon. Steve has been very supportive of both *Back to the Future* books. If you haven't checked out Futurepedia, you're missing out!

Finally, thanks to my loving wife **Jill** and our children, **Emily** and **Joshua**, who put up with my frequently hiding in the basement with my laptop while putting this volume together. I'm rejoining the family, guys! Well… until the next book goes into production.

— **Rich Handley**

FOREWORD

…to the Future!

by Dan Madsen

"If you put your mind to it, you can accomplish anything."
—Jennifer Parker, Marty McFly and George McFly, *Back to the Future*

In 1985, when I was 23 years old, I was given the gift of *Back to the Future*. Sitting in that darkened theater and watching Marty McFly's time-traveling adventure with Doc Brown was one of the top-five magical movie moments of my life. Every frame of that film kept me entertained and my eyes glued to the screen. It was, and still is, one of the best movies ever made—full of comedy, drama, action and adventure, along with great writing, storytelling and acting! I went back to see the film in '85 at least 15 times, and dragged my parents, friends and anyone else I knew to see it.

I have always loved sci-fi and especially time travel. As a die-hard *Star Trek* and *Star Wars* fan, I launched my own fan club business in 1980. It eventually evolved into a company called FANtastic Media, where I locked down the exclusive licenses from Paramount and Lucasfilm to run the Official Fan Clubs for both *Star Wars* and *Star Trek*. It was on the strength and success of that business that I was approached by Universal about an official *Back to the Future* Fan Club. I had heard that *Back to the Future Part II* and *Part III* were going into production back-to-back in the late '80s. After several meetings with Universal licensing, we agreed upon the details and decided to launch the club during the timeframe in which *Parts II* and *III* were opening.

To say I was thrilled is an understatement, because it was yet another chance to work with one of my favorite movie adventures. Here was an opportunity to visit the sets, meet the actors and behind-the-scenes talent, and write about the past, present and future of Marty and Doc's worlds. Interviewing the elusive Christopher Lloyd was a highlight for me, but talking with Michael J. Fox, Thomas F. Wilson, Lea Thompson and the lovely Mary Steenburgen for the official *Back to the Future* Fan Club magazine was a special treat. Chatting time travel and the evolution of the films with Bob Gale and Robert Zemeckis was pretty cool, too. I was responsible for most of the interviews and design for the BTTF fan club and its magazine.

My love for the *BTTF* movies has never wavered over the years, even though I have moved on to do other things. So I was thrilled to be asked to write the foreword for Greg and Rich's *Back in Time: The Unauthorized Back to the Future Chronology*, as it allowed me to step "back in time" myself and revisit all three films. After reading the manuscript, I learned a lot more about the timeline(s) and world(s) Zemeckis and Gale created, including the residual cartoons, novels, games and, to be honest… things I wasn't even aware of! The amount of time, research and effort that went into this book you now hold in your hands is truly amazing—even Marty and Doc would be impressed with how Greg and Rich followed the arrows of time through all of their various adventures... as well as their ancestors and descendants, too!

The way I see it, as Doc Brown might say, "If you're going to build a chronology book about the *BTTF* films, why not do it with some style?" Greg and Rich certainly have!

— **Dan Madsen**
August 2013

INTRODUCTION

Thinkin' Fourth-Dimensionally

by Greg Mitchell

"What if they say, 'Get outta here, kid, you got no future?'"
—Marty McFly, *Back to the Future*

Marty McFly's fears of failing as a creative aspirant echoed my own as I set out to write the book you now hold in your hands. But we'll get to my tangle with anxiety just a bit later. First, a good dose of gushing about one of the greatest franchises in cinema history.

As with any child growing up in the 1980s, the reach of *Back to the Future* was inescapable for me. The first time I saw the original movie, I was probably ten years old and watching it on television. I remember Leslie Nielsen introducing the film and hosting a behind-the-scenes special about *Back to the Future II* afterwards. Robert Zemeckis made a joke that hoverboards were real, and that Mattel lent them an experimental prototype for the film's production. As a ten-year-old, I was convinced that he was telling the truth, and for the next couple of years, I waited for the day that the hoverboard would show up at my local Wal-Mart. Sadly, that day never came. I watched *Back to the Future Part II* at a friend's house one summer afternoon on VHS, and was blown away by the paradoxical Western Union ending. I went to see *Part III* in the theater on opening night and had the front row all to myself.

After that night, though, *Back to the Future* sort of faded from my young mind. I'd catch one of the films on television occasionally, but it wasn't until I was in my later high school years that the movies became precious to me. Even now, I don't know what set it off. I recall that I was an angry, disaffected youth in 1996, looking for an escape from my teenage drama. I was a dud with the ladies, and an aspiring science fiction writer with very little faith in myself. Time travel became a source of fascination for me—the idea of going back into my own past and fixing things that I perceived as missteps. I daresay I became obsessed with returning to the carefree, less-complicated years of my childhood, which led me back to *Back to the Future*.

That was almost twenty years ago now so I can't say for sure, but I wonder if I saw something of myself in George McFly, who just needed a little boost from a rock-n-roll rebel. *Back to the Future* became my movie during high school. I prayed for a real-life Johnny B. Goode moment, when I took center stage and proved to the world that I was a valid human being (what teenager doesn't?).

After graduation, my love for *Back to the Future* grew exponentially. I first purchased the movies on VHS, and had periodic Trilogy Days when I'd watch all three movies uninterrupted, discerning new insights with each viewing. As I grew into my angry, disaffected twenties (he says with a wink), I adored *Back to the Future Part II* for its dark observance of our own mortality and the tragic outcomes of our misguided pursuits. *Back to the Future II* is an ominous, bleak movie, and totally spoke to me as I was still shaking out of my rebellious funk. Plus, the movie had higher stakes than its predecessor, introducing viewers to the Biffhorrific timeline. Whereas the first film concentrated on Marty preserving his own existence, the sequel broadened Marty's self-centered focus as he sought to move space and time to prevent his father's murder and rescue his family from their self-made hells. The film was tense, powerful and poignant.

It's funny. Now I'm in my mid-thirties, married with kids. I'm entering a new phase in my life, far removed from my high school insecurities and the brooding mentality of my twenties. These days, I gravitate toward *Back to the Future Part III*, with its return to a quieter pace of life, and simple acts of kindness within community, friends and family. *Back to the Future III* is a gentle installment in the trilogy—heartwarming, even, as we see Doc Brown discover that there's more to life than his career and his obsessions. There's love. Family. I think the standout star of the film is Michael J. Fox for his portrayal of Marty's ancestor Seamus McFly, who takes a stranger into his home without condemnation, but teaches him important lessons about life and standing true as a man; he even lends him a hat. That's a lesson that resonates for me now. There really is something for everyone in those movies, at every stage of life.

That's the short end of a very long love affair between me and the *Back to the Future* trilogy. As I write this, I recall each movie memory fondly, including the time my wife and I went on vacation early in our marriage to Universal Studios Florida. As the gates parted for us and we were beckoned by the swell of Alan Silvestri's rousing score, my wife, Meghan, looked to me and told me I'd come home. It certainly felt that way. I treasured each second of *Back to the Future: The Ride*, and I admit I never wanted to leave.

When I learned that a guy named Rich Handley, who wrote *Star Wars* tie-in fiction with which I was familiar (and let's not even get me started on my affections for that other franchise), wrote an exhaustive guide to the *Planet of the Apes* universe, I thought it would be cool to see *Back to the Future* receive the same treatment. I wrote to Rich, out of the blue, to tell him about my idea, and he surprised me by replying that he'd had the same notion of late. I was thrilled, and even more excited to help him collect the various tie-ins for the series, such as the comics, novelizations and cartoons. I was more than content to receive a "Special Thanks" when he finally finished the book, and was in no way prepared for the day when I received an actual phone call from him, asking me if I wanted to write the *Timeline* while he handled duties on the *Back to the Future Lexicon* (now available—order your copy today!).

I was floored and immediately agreed, having no clue what I was doing. I'm a screenwriter and a novelist. I'd never tried my hand at a journalistic-type approach to non-fiction. But, I thought "Ah, why not?" The chance to work with Rich, publisher/designer Paul Giachetti and the brilliant artist Pat Carbajal proved too great a temptation. I dove into the source material, never needing much of an excuse to watch the movies for the billionth time. What was most exciting was that Rich and I were able to lay hands on things I'd never seen before, such as unused scripts and rare comics, commercials, and that atrocious *Earth Day Special*—things I would never have seen had I not signed up for the job. It was a wonderful time of discovery as I realized that, though I'd been a longtime fan, there was still so much I'd yet to learn about the series.

But, as the months wore on, and the work increased, doubt and anxiety set in. What had I gotten myself into? What if I'm not up to the task before me? Complicating matters (though in a good way), my writing career really took off. In the time that it's taken me to write the *Back to the Future Timeline*, I've seen the release of four novels, short stories in numerous anthologies and one straight-to-

DVD movie, and I have another script in development for a major network. I've been overwhelmed by work, and some days I feared that, despite my love for the franchise, I wouldn't be able to finish.

But I am so thankful for Rich and Paul, who were there with me every step of the process, encouraging me, sometimes pushing me, but also generously extending my deadline so I could work on my various other projects. I am eternally grateful to Rich, who came in as my editor, then as my co-writer, helping to pick up the slack and raising the awesome factor of this book tenfold. More than anything I've ever worked on, this has been a group project, a labor of love.

What's been most rewarding about the process is that I can still pop in *Back to the Future* and watch it with glee, remembering that ten-year-old boy I used to be, who had no idea he would one day contribute to the series—in however small a manner—that he loved so dearly.

Thank you all for picking up the book. I hope you'll find it as illuminating as I did while writing, but not nearly as stressful.

And to Bob Gale and Robert Zemeckis, the visionaries who gave us this trilogy, what do you tell men who brought magic into your world, inspired you to create your own fantastical stories, and brightened your darkest days with visions of Michael J. Fox shredding guitar to Johnny B. Goode? That's exactly what the Two Bobs did for me. What can you say, at the end of the day, but thank you?

So, thank you, Mr. Gale and Mr. Zemeckis, for giving us magic and, even now, still transporting me back in time.

Oh, and I'd still like that hoverboard you promised.

— **Greg Mitchell**
May 25, 2013

ABBREVIATION KEY

Unlocking the Code to Time Travel

"And that's when you came up with the idea for the Flux Capacitor, which is what makes time travel possible!"

— **Marty McFly,** *Back to the Future*

This chronology draws information from not only the *Back to the Future* films and TV series, but also a variety of other sources, many obscure. For each entry, four-character codes indicate the source. Some codes also feature lower-case suffixes, denoting that an entry was culled from the script, novelization or comic book adaptation of a film or episode. In addition, codes for entries related to the animated series, comics and Telltale Games video game contain an episode or issue number.

Some view the films and their spinoffs as taking place in the same universe, while others consider them separate. This chronology does not take a stance on that debate, utilizing an all-inclusive approach: If it occurred or was noted in the cartoons, comics, games or novels—or in a commercial or music video containing *BTTF* elements—it's covered here. This includes early-draft scripts that differed greatly from the final product. For the purpose of this book, the events of such drafts are treated as alternate histories.

Since all entries indicate their sources via the four-letter codes, readers are free to reject any aspects of the franchise they prefer not to acknowledge. By way of example, **[BTF1-s1]** would indicate that an entry originated in the first film's draft-one screenplay, while **[BFAN-17]** would signify that the source was the animated series' 17th episode.

The symbols and codes are detailed below. To avoid redundancy, notes accompanying the entries use shortened forms of the film titles (*BTF1, BTF2* and *BTF3*), while *Back to the Future Part II* and *Back to the Future Part III* often drop the word "Part" for brevity's sake. What's more, the franchise's name as a whole is often shortened simply to *BTTF*.

Detailed information about particular characters, inventions or locations, as well as a complete episode guide, can be found in *A Matter of Time: The Unauthorized Back to the Future Lexicon*, available at hassleinbooks.com, amazon.com and BTTF.com.

CODE	STORY
ARGN	*BTTF*-themed TV commercial: Arrigoni
BFAN	*Back to the Future: The Animated Series*
BFCG	*Back to the Future: The Card Game*
BFCL	*Back to the Future* comic book (limited series)
BFCM	*Back to the Future* comic book (monthly series)
BFHM	*BTTF*-themed McDonald's Happy Meal boxes
BTFA	*Back to the Future Annual* (Marvel Comics)
BTF1	Film: *Back to the Future*
BTF2	Film: *Back to the Future Part II*
BTF3	Film: *Back to the Future Part III*
BUDL	*BTTF*-themed TV commercial: Bud Light
CHEK	*BTTF*-themed music video: O'Neal McKnight, "Check Your Coat"
CHIC	Photographs hanging in Doc Brown's Chicken restaurant at Universal Studios
CITY	*BTTF*-themed music video: Owl City, "Deer in the Headlights"
DCTV	*BTTF*-themed TV commercial: DirecTV
ERTH	*The Earth Day Special*
GALE	Interviews and commentaries: Bob Gale and/or Robert Zemeckis
GARB	*BTTF*-themed TV commercials: Garbarino
GETV	*BTTF*-themed TV commercial: General Electric, "The Future Is Now"
HUEY	*BTTF*-themed music video: Huey Lewis and the News, "The Power of Love"
LIMO	*BTTF*-themed music video: The Limousines, "The Future"
MCDN	*BTTF*-themed TV commercial: McDonald's
MITS	*BTTF*-themed TV commercial: Mitsubishi Lancer

CODE	STORY
MSFT	*BTTF*-themed TV commercial: Microsoft
NIKE	*BTTF*-themed TV commercial: Nike
NTND	Nintendo *Back to the Future—The Ride* Mini-Game
PIZA	*BTTF*-themed TV commercial: Pizza Hut
REAL	Real life
RIDE	Simulator: *Back to the Future—The Ride*
SCRM	2010 Scream Awards: *Back to the Future* 25th Anniversary Reunion (broadcast)
SCRT	2010 Scream Awards: *Back to the Future* 25th Anniversary Reunion (trailer)
SIMP	Simulator: *The Simpsons Ride*
SLOT	*Back to the Future* Video Slots
TEST	Screen tests: Crispin Glover, Lea Thompson and Thomas F. Wilson
TLTL	Telltale Games' *Back to the Future—The Game*
UNIV	Universal Studios Hollywood promotional video

SUFFIX	MEDIUM
-b	*BTF2*'s Biff Tannen Museum video (extended version)
-c	Animated series credit sequence
-d	Film deleted scene
-n	Film novelization
-o	Film outtake
-v	Video game print materials or commentaries
-s1	Screenplay (draft one)
-s2	Screenplay (draft two)
-s3	Screenplay (draft three)
-s4	Screenplay (draft four)
-sp	Screenplay (production draft)
-sx	Screenplay (*Paradox*)

THE TIMELINE

By Greg Mitchell and Rich Handley

"Suddenly, the future's looking a whole lot better."

— **Dr. Emmett L. Brown**, *Back to the Future* (deleted scene)

THE DELOREAN
NEARLY BECOMES
A TYRANNOSAURUS'
NEXT MEAL

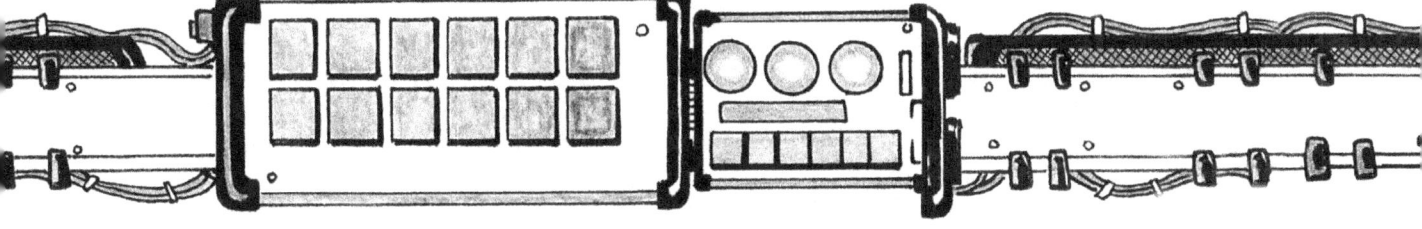

CHAPTER I:
PREHISTORY TO 1 B.C.

Mesozoic Era (252,200,000 B.C. to 66,000,000 B.C.) or Cenozoic Era (66,000,000 B.C. to Present)

- Emmett Brown worries that he and fellow time-traveler Marty McFly could find themselves stranded in one of these geological eras after the DeLorean's time circuits become damaged in 1931. Engaging the circuits, he fears, could throw the vehicle drastically off-course, sending them to the Cenozoic era—or, worse, the Mesozoic [TLTL-4].

   NOTE: Doc's fear of ending up in the Cenozoic era is nonsensical, since that is Earth's current Phanerozoic geological era—Doc himself is from the Cenozoic era.

Sometime Between 154,000,000 B.C. and 150,000,000 B.C.

- Desperate to find something spectacular to bring to his elementary school class for show-and-tell, Verne Brown steals his father's time-traveling DeLorean and, with Marty McFly along for the ride, "borrows" an unhatched dinosaur egg from a female *Apatosaurus*. Verne befriends the dinosaur and, once it hatches, names it "Tiny." After some misadventures in 1992, the Browns return Tiny to his mother in the Jurassic Period [BFAN-26].

   NOTE: Scientists date the Jurassic Period as lasting from 199 million to 145 million years ago, with the Apatosaurus species believed to have lived around 154 million to 150 million years ago. Verne claimed they were traveling a "zillion" years into the past, but since that is not a real number, it is unknown what year they'd have ended up in had he actually tried to enter such a destination into the Flux Capacitor.

Sometime Between 85,000,000 B.C. and 65,000,000 B.C.

- Jules and Verne Brown arrive from 1991 A.D. to explore the past. While elder brother Jules studies geological formations on the terrain, Verne horses around in a gyro-beanie cap. The two temporal intruders are discovered by a red-skinned *Tyrannosaurus rex*, but are saved from becoming the dinosaur's next meal by their father, Emmett L. Brown, who parks his time-traveling DeLorean on the beast's head. Verne and Jules, sporting a pair of rocket boots, hurry inside and return with Doc to their own era [BFAN-c].

   NOTE: Although no date was provided for this encounter, the Tyrannosaurus rex is generally believed to have walked the Earth between 85 million and 65 million years ago.

October 25, 64,000,000 B.C.

- Biff Tannen, having stolen Emmett Brown's DeLorean from the Institute of Future Technology, arrives at the "Dawn of Time" while evading a group of so-called "time-travel volunteers" following him in a special eight-passenger DeLorean. Taunting his pursuers, Biff flies the car past a *Tyrannosaurus rex* and into an active volcano's lava flow. When the stolen vehicle malfunctions due to Biff's rough piloting, Doc instructs the volunteers to accelerate their DeLorean up to 88 miles per hour while bumping Tannen's vehicle, thereby creating a time vortex and slingshotting both cars back to 1991 [RIDE].

   NOTE: The eight-seat DeLorean's time circuits displayed "8888" during the encounter with the Tyrannosaurus, as the chronometer's four-digit limit made it impossible to show the actual year. The ride's Sub-Ether Time-Tracking Scanner display, however, indicated the Gale-Zemeckis Coordinates to be "-64(10[6]) BC," translating to 64,000,000 B.C. (It should be noted that this would still be about a million years after the species' accepted extinction period.)

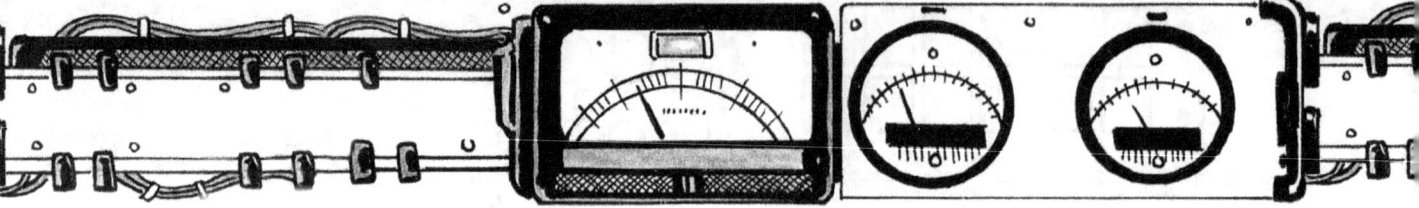

Wednesday, October 10, 3,000,000 B.C.

- Emmett, Jules and Verne Brown visit Hill Valley's Cretaceous Period to test out Doc's latest contraption, the Proprietary Ultrasonic Subatomic Molecular Redistributor. The trio are immediately caught in the path of a ravenous *Tyrannosaurus rex*, but are saved by the timely intervention of a *Pteranodon* that Verne affectionately dubs "Donny" [BFAN-3].

  > *NOTE: Since the* **Tyrannosaurus rex** *is believed to have become extinct 65 million years ago, while* **Pteranodons** *are thought to have died out around 80 million years ago, it is unknown how the Browns could have encountered such creatures in 3,000,000 B.C. Moreover, the Cretaceous Period, which lasted from 145 million to 66 million years ago, was long over by that point.*

- Delivered to safety by the friendly dinosaur, Doc prepares to test his invention, but Jules detects what he believes to be a shooting star. Upon closer inspection, Doc realizes that it's a meteor headed for Earth. With only seconds to save himself and his family from the flaming debris, the scientist reroutes power from the DeLorean's Mr. Fusion to the Molecular Redistributor and disintegrates the meteor in space, saving the world from cataclysm. The trio then prepares to go back to the future, unaware that Doc's intervention has created a parallel dimension in which the Dinosaur Age never ended.

  Doc and his sons return from a parallel 1991 A.D. in which, due to their meddling, dinosaurs evolved into Earth's dominant civilization. The Browns arrive seconds before their prior departure point, but the damage they have caused to the timeline is beginning to catch up to them—molecule by molecule, they are disappearing from history. Resolved to repair his mistake, Doc uses his Proprietary Ultrasonic Subatomic Molecular Redistributor to recreate the meteor that would have killed the dinosaurs. Verne has grown attached to his friend Donny, but his father drags the boy to the DeLorean as the meteor tumbles closer to Earth. The dinosaur looks on in tears as the vehicle vanishes mere seconds before the rock crashes into the planet, causing an Ice Age, and eradicating Donny and his fellow dinosaurs [BFAN-3].

Sometime Between 2,588,000 and 12,000 B.C.

- Thanks to an April Fool's Day prank perpetrated by his sons, Emmett Brown believes he has used up all but 0.01 percent of his brain power. Worried that the demands of modern life will rob him of his remaining intelligence, Doc flees to the Pleistocene Period to live with prehistoric humans, whom he teaches simple tricks, such as starting a fire. He soon realizes that living in the past would be a constant temptation to invent modern marvels, however, and thus returns to his own era [BFAN-12].

  > *NOTE: Jules and Verne, of course, later admitted to their prank.*

October 25, 1,000,000 B.C.

- Biff Tannen arrives in Hill Valley's Ice Age after stealing Emmett Brown's DeLorean from the Institute of Future Technology, pursued by a group of so-called "time-travel volunteers" in a special eight-passenger DeLorean. The volunteers chase Biff through a shifting glacier, but he escapes to October 25, 64,000,000 B.C. [RIDE].

Circa 40,000 to 60,000 B.C.

- A pool of natural asphalt begins forming at the future site of Hill Valley, California, that will later be known as the Hill Valley Tar Pits [TLTL-4].

  > *NOTE: The era in which this occurred was unspecified, but the La Brea Tar Pits are believed to have formed approximately 40,000 to 60,000 years ago. Since Hill Valley is in the vicinity of Los Angeles (where La Brea is located), both cities' asphalt lakes would likely have formed around the same time, due to simultaneous submersion under water and subsequent leaking of subterranean bitumen to the surface.*

Circa 30,000 B.C.

- Neanderthals, a subspecies of the genus *Homo* closely related to modern humans, become extinct. Rogue Neanderthal genes persist in human DNA, particularly manifesting in the Tannen blood line, causing many of its members to be rude and abusive [TLTL-2].

  > *NOTE: Or, at least, that is Doc Brown's theory.*

Sometime Between 2000 and 1500 B.C.

- Stonehenge, a prehistoric monument containing a ring of standing stones set within earthworks, is constructed in England's Wiltshire county [BFAN-2].

    NOTE: This dating is according to Doc Brown. Most archaeologists, however, believe the monument was built between 3000 BC and 2000 B.C.

1009 B.C.

- The Brown family visits ancient Egypt aboard the *Jules Verne Train* for a little sightseeing. Things go awry when Verne Brown plays a prank on the Egyptians by sculpting a giant Groucho Marx nose and glasses, and placing them on the Sphinx. Pursued by angry soldiers, Verne and his father, Emmett Brown, reach the locomotive and lift off, but not before a soldier hurls a spear, piercing the Flux Capacitor and sending the train—with the Brown family inside—to August 1692 [BFAN-4].

753 B.C.

- The city of Rome, Italy, is founded when Romulus and Remus—brothers fighting in the Trojan War—escape to a small village, which they lay claim to and take by force [BFAN-5].

    NOTE: Although Doc Brown cited this as the city's origins, this account actually originated in Roman mythology and is not accepted as fact by historians.

VERNE BROWN'S PRACTICAL JOKE PROVES UNPOPULAR IN ANCIENT EGYPT

MARTY MCFLY RACES
BIFFICUS ANTANNENY AT
THE CIRCUS MAXIMUS

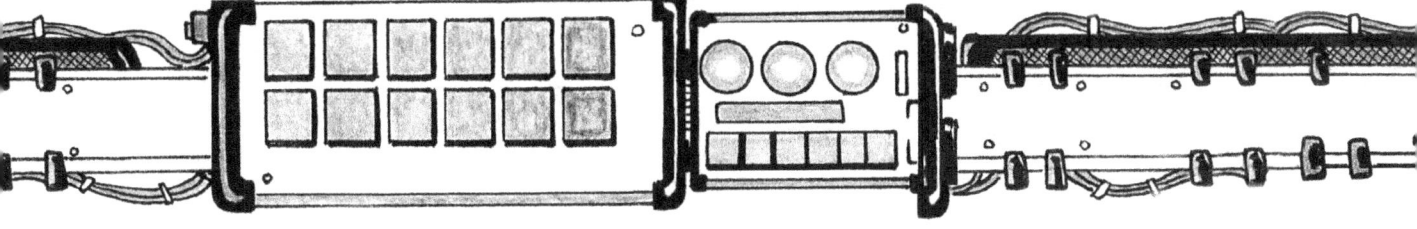

CHAPTER II

0000 TO 1800 A.D.

December 25, 0000

- Jesus Christ, the central figure of Christianity, is born, according to Emmett Brown [BTF1].

    NOTE: In BTF1, Doc considered visiting this date to witness Christ's birth. Since the so-called "Year Zero" is a nonexistent calendar year, it is unknown when he would have ended up had he done so. Moreover, Jesus' birth is generally believed to have occurred a few years B.C., and not in December—so even if there were a "Year Zero," Doc would have missed the birth by entering such a destination date. BTF1's DVD commentary revealed this to be a joke, not reflecting any real-world dating system.

4 A.D., 6 A.D., 8 A.D., 12 A.D. and 18 A.D.

- After meeting the Queen of Apocrypha and Tannen the Barbarian in 2,991,299,129,912,991 A.D., Doc and Marty return to 1992 in the recently damaged *Jules Verne Train*, "bouncing" off a number of other years along the way, including these years [BFCL-3].

Sometime in or Before 36 A.D.

- Emmett Brown travels to ancient Rome to borrow a collection of scrolls for personal study [BFAN-5].

- Gattaca Pellenon writes a book called *Caesar*, about the Roman emperor. A copy of the book ends up in the city's underground catacombs, in the hands of a person who dies reading it [BFAN-5].

36 A.D.

- Emmett Brown visits ancient Rome with Marty McFly to return a collection of scrolls he'd borrowed for study during his last trip to the 1st century. Doc's sons, Jules and Verne, have stowed away in the DeLorean's back seat in order to see Rome's arcades, which they

misperceive as being similar to 20th-century video game arcades. As Doc and Marty go about their business, the Brown boys enter what they believe to be a mall, but what is really a bathhouse.

Inside the bathhouse, a Roman citizen is being massaged by his Hebrew slave, Judah Ben-Hur. Unsupervised, the boys begin roughhousing, inadvertently causing the slave-owner to fall into a bath. Outraged, he blames Judah and prepares to beat him—but Verne intercedes, saving Ben-Hur and humiliating the Roman nobleman. Soldiers give chase, but Jules slips away to notify his father.

Marty peruses the marketplace, accidently spilling food on the breastplate of Bifficus Antanneny, the captain of Caesar's guard. His honor tarnished, Bifficus demands retribution and orders Marty arrested and sentenced to compete with him in a chariot race.

Doc comes to his children's aid. As he explains the harsh reality of slavery to the boys, however, nearby citizens perceive his criticisms as declarations of rebellion, and Doc is arrested. Jules and Verne plot to rescue him, grateful when Judah offers to guide them through the catacombs beneath the city and into the dungeon where their father is being held. After breaking Doc out of jail, the trio learns that Marty is in danger as well. They sneak into the Circus Maximus, where Doc heavily modifies Marty's chariot for his race against Bifficus.

Marty is determined to win the race and prove his bravery, but Doc informs him that he must lose for the sake of preserving history. Bifficus, Doc explains, must not lose his popularity with the Roman Empire, as he will eventually make way for Gaius Julius Caesar Augustus Germanicus—more commonly known as "Caligula"—to rule. Caligula's reign, he notes, will lead to the Roman Empire's downfall. If Marty wins the race, cementing Bifficus' shame, the Empire will never fall and the timeline will be dramatically altered.

Marty barely survives the chariot race, but despite the odds against him, the youth almost wins, throwing the race at the last second to restore Bifficus' honor and keep the timeline intact. As Antanney basks in applause,

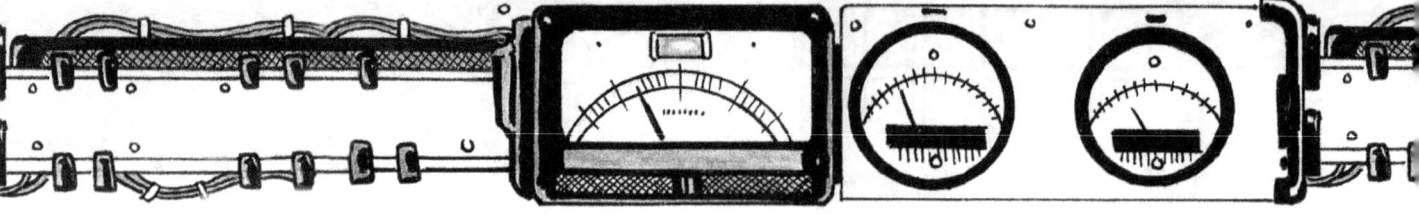

Marty and the Browns leave in the DeLorean, to drop off the scrolls before heading back to the future. As a parting gift, they give Judah Ben-Hur the modified chariot, enabling him to escape enslavement [BFAN-5].

> **NOTE: Judah Ben-Hur was a fictional character in Lew Wallace's 1880 novel, Ben-Hur: A Tale of the Christ, and in the 1959 Charlton Heston film based on that book, simply titled Ben-Hur. The Back to the Future version adopted Heston's appearance and speaking pattern. This episode was adapted in Harvey Comics' third issue.**

• While visiting ancient Rome, circa 36 A.D., Jules and Verne Brown inadvertently break off the Venus de Milo's arms while its sculptor is still creating it. Though at first angered, the artist is pleased upon seeing how the statue looks without arms [BFAN-5].

> **NOTE: The Venus de Milo is believed to have been sculpted between 130 and 100 B.C.—more than a century before the Browns witnessed its creation during the animated series.**

127 A.D.

• After stealing the DeLorean in order to turn a profit, crooked science TV show host Walter Wisdom—known to fans as "Mr. Wisdom"—escapes to ancient Egypt, in the year 127, hoping to elude Emmett Brown, his sons and Marty McFly. In his haste, Wisdom knocks over an inverted pyramid under construction, turning it point-up. This careless accident inspires the pyramid's Egyptian designer, who realizes his initial concept was flawed and that this new design holds much more promise. Unaware that he has shaped history, Wisdom escapes to the year 1883 [BFAN-15].

267 A.D. and 328 A.D.

• After meeting the Queen of Apocrypha and Tannen the Barbarian in 2,991,299,129,912,991 A.D., Doc and

Marty return to 1992 in the recently damaged *Jules Verne Train*, "bouncing" off a number of other years along the way, including these years [BFCL-3].

1295 A.D.

• Marco Polo, upon returning to Italy after a visit to China, brings along some noodles, thereby introducing Italians to pasta for the first time [REAL, BFAN-5]

> **NOTE: Emmett Brown believed this popular legend to be true. It is unknown whether he traveled to 1295 to discern the truth for himself.**

Sometime in or Before 1367 A.D.

• Lord Biffingham, the Earl of Tannenshire, obtains a "knight light," shaped like a horse and armored knight, which he activates each night at bedtime [BFHM].

> **NOTE: The lamp seemed to be electrically lit, but given the medieval setting in which the earl lived, it's possible it was actually candle-powered.**

1367 A.D.

• Emmett Brown brings his family to medieval England. Clara and the kids believe they are on vacation, but Doc has actually brought them to a simpler time to break their unhealthy reliance on modern technology. Upon discovering the truth, Clara storms off angrily. In her fury, she snaps at a man on horseback—Lord Biffingham, Earl of Tannenshire—who mistakes her for a common woman and orders her to get back to work. When Clara stands up to his bullying, Biffingham is impressed with her strength and seizes her. Doc, while admiring Stonehenge with his sons, hears his wife's cry and challenges the earl to a boxing match. However, he is captured in the process.

Alone, Jules and Verne and their dog, Einstein, follow Lord Biffingham and their captive parents toward Castle Biffingham. En route, they are ambushed by Harold

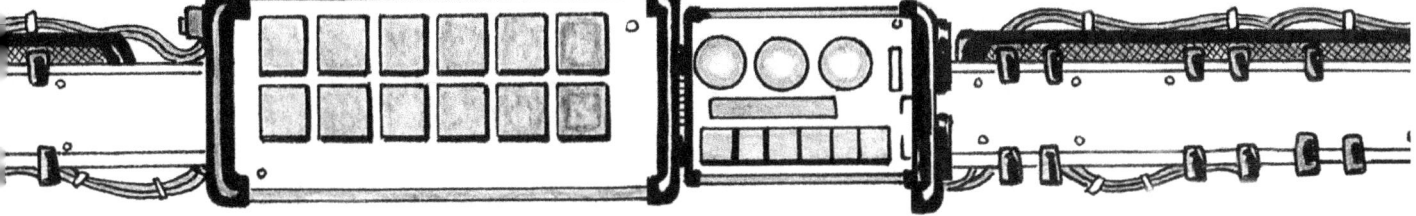

McFly of the Sussex McFlys, a farmer on a quest for revenge against Biffingham for kidnapping his lady love, Jennivere. Realizing they have a common enemy, they decide to work together to free their loved ones. Harold enters the castle posing as a minstrel, with the Brown boys as his clowns.

Lord Biffingham announces his intention to marry Clara, as soon as he kills her husband in a joust. Thanks to the intervention of Harold and the Brown boys, Doc wins the tournament, but he and his "aides" are sentenced to death by beheading. Clara and Jennivere escape the castle by assembling a hot-air balloon out of Oriental silk gowns that Lord Biffingham had intended for his bride-to-be. Clara saves her family from the executioner's axe [BFAN-2].

> *NOTE: The first documented hot-air ballon flight in the real world occurred 416 years later, in 1783.*

• Once free of the castle, Harold and Jennivere are reunited and decide to relocate to Ireland, at Doc's suggestion. The Brown family climbs into the DeLorean as Lord Biffingham arrives, seeking retribution. Clara, however, refuses to let Doc into the car until he admits that he was wrong to call his family "slaves to technology." He confesses, Clara lets him in and the family journeys back to the future [BFAN-2].

1532 A.D.

• Emmett Brown and Marty McFly visit Peru to seek a cure for Marty's Athlete's foot fungus. They search for a rare toad—the *Bufo marinus*—said to secrete an acid that can remedy Marty's ailment. Doc has brought along a tuning fork to agitate the *Bufo marinus*, which has a high hearing range. Once the fork is activated, the toads emerge from their hiding places, making them easy to capture. During the hunt, the time-travelers run afoul of Biffando de la Tanén, a Spanish conquistador who has set his sights on ruling South America. Tanén captures Doc

and Marty, but releases them on good terms, believing they are, like him, in search of the legendary City of Gold. He secretly tells his men to follow the duo, in the hope of being led to their prize.

Doc's and Marty's luck goes from bad to worse when they are next captured by Incan natives and taken back to the City of Gold, to be offered up as sacrifices in a pagan ritual. The Incas prepare to throw them into a pit filled with *Bufo marinus* toads. In small doses, the amphibians' acidic secretion can be helpful, Doc says—but in such high proportions, the chemicals will prove fatally toxic. As the natives commence the ritual, Doc sets off his tuning fork. The toads go wild, jumping free from the pit and overrunning the city. The Incas, revering the outsiders as powerful gods, turn to them for protection once Biffando de la Tanén—who has been following the time travelers—arrives at the city gate.

Tanén and his men storm the City of Gold, but Doc uses the tuning fork once more, unleashing a plague of toads on the invading Spaniards. With their enemies repelled, the Incas owe a debt of gratitude to the "wizards" who have rescued them. All Brown asks in return is a few specimens of *Bufo marinus* to take with him. At the behest of the Incan leader—whom Marty dubs "King Chicken-Head," for the brightly colored bird worn on his head—Doc destroys the rock bridge leading to the city, isolating it from the jungle and ensuring that it remains "lost" to other invaders. The time travelers then return to their own era so Doc can cure Marty of his Athlete's foot problem [BFAN-7a].

1631 A.D.

• In an effort to aid a team of experts in the year 1990 A.D. in discerning how to preserve the Earth's environment from total devastation, Emmett Brown begins traveling through time. His journey begins in 1631 when he visits the Mississippi River, marveling at its clear sparkling waters, still untouched from the pollution it will one day endure [ERTH].

NIKE	*BTTF*-themed TV commercial: Nike	SCRT	2010 Scream Awards: *Back to the Future*	**SUFFIX MEDIUM**		**-s1**	Screenplay (draft one)
NTND	Nintendo *Back to the Future—The Ride* Mini-Game		25th Anniversary Reunion (trailer)	**-b**	*BTF2's* Biff Tannen Museum video (extended version)	**-s2**	Screenplay (draft two)
		SIMP	Simulator: *The Simpsons Ride*			**-s3**	Screenplay (draft three)
PIZA	*BTTF*-themed TV commercial: Pizza Hut	SLOT	*Back to the Future* Video Slots	**-c**	Animated series credit sequence	**-s4**	Screenplay (draft four)
REAL	Real life	TEST	Screen tests: Crispin Glover, Lea Thompson	**-d**	Film deleted scene	**-sp**	Screenplay (production draft)
RIDE	Simulator: *Back to the Future—The Ride*		and Thomas F. Wilson	**-n**	Film novelization	**-sx**	Screenplay (*Paradox*)
SCRM	2010 Scream Awards: *Back to the Future*	TLTL	Telltale Games' *Back to the Future—The Game*	**-o**	Film outtake		
	25th Anniversary Reunion (broadcast)	UNIV	Universal Studios Hollywood promotional video	**-v**	Video game print materials or commentaries		

MARTY AND THE
BROWNS ESCAPE
LORD BIFFINGHAM,
THE EARL OF
TANNENSHIRE

Sometime in or Before 1692 A.D.

- Gertie Magoo, a Puritan in Salem, Massachusetts, dances indiscreetly in public. Disgusted, the townsfolk deem her and her cat to be witches, severely punishing them both [BFAN-4].

- The Puritan children of Salem conceive of the game "Seen and Not Heard," involving a contest to see who can stand still and silent for the longest span of time [BFAN-4].

Late August 1692 A.D.

- The Brown family arrives in Salem, Massachusetts, following a mishap with the *Jules Verne Train*'s Flux Capacitor in ancient Egypt. Emmett Brown attempts to repair the locomotive, but when that effort fails, he begins building a sophisticated robotic mail-delivery system, capable of sending a message to Marty in the year 1991. For a month he toils, in the meantime purchasing a house for himself and his family in Salem [BFAN-4].

Friday, September 23, 1692 A.D.

- After spending a month in Salem, Massachusetts, with his family, Emmett Brown sends a postcard to 1991, asking Marty McFly to travel back with the DeLorean and a spare Flux Capacitor. Marty arrives to discover that Doc has been living as a garbage man, as a means of studying the Puritan culture. He has also instituted an early form of recycling, doing his part to keep the Earth clean.

    The Browns make plans to attend the Puritans' weekly town social and invite Marty along, introducing him to the locals as Doc's nephew. There, Marty notices a vivacious redhead named Mercy. She notices him as well, and makes strong advances toward him, which Marty is all too happy to reciprocate… until learning that Mercy is Goodman Tannen's daughter. Wanting nothing to do with any Tannens, Marty spurns the woman's favor, inciting her wrath. She tells her father a fabricated account of their conversation, leading Goodman Tannen to believe that the stranger in their midst is a witch. Tannen promptly has Marty arrested and thrown in the stockade.

    While Doc and Jules work feverishly to repair the time train, Marty is tried in court for witchcraft.

Unable to tell his side of the story, Marty is convicted and sentenced to the "water test," by which he will be thrown into the bay. If he floats, he will be pronounced a witch and burned at the stake, but if he drowns, he'll have earned his innocence—though he'll be dead [BFAN-4].

Saturday, September 24, 1692 A.D.

- Despite Clara Brown's appeal to reason, Marty is bound and thrown into the bay. Before he can drown, Doc arrives in the DeLorean—which has undergone a floatation conversion—and rescues Marty underwater. Believing him to be dead, the Puritans declare him innocent of witchcraft. Marty and the Browns reunite and, with the DeLorean and repaired time train, head back to the future [BFAN-4].

Sometime in or Before 1697 A.D.

- Pirate king Mac the Black befriends fellow pirate Captain Hook, and has the man's signature tattooed on his chest [BFAN-14].

    ***NOTE: Captain James Hook was the primary antagonist of J. M. Barrie's play* Peter Pan; *or, the Boy Who Wouldn't Grow Up *and its novelization, **Peter and Wendy.**

1697 A.D.

- On a quest for independence—and an earring—Verne Brown steals his father's DeLorean and journeys back from 1992 to the Caribbean Islands, in 1697, to set sail with pirates. Along for the ride is Marty McFly, fresh from a breakup with Jennifer Parker due to his constant lying. The duo masquerade as pirates and, while Verne goes off in search of a place to have his ear pierced, a rebounding Marty seeks out a new girlfriend. He is instantly attracted to Señorita Maria, a mysterious beauty longing for the appearance of pirate Mac the Black. Seeing an opportunity for romance, Marty poses as Mac the Black in order to win Maria's affections. His charade, however, catches the attention of local authorities, as well as a band of surly pirates eager to swear their allegiance to him. The crew whisk Marty away to their ship, crowning him their new leader.

    With no money in hand, Verne fails to get an earring. Unaware that his traveling companion has just been

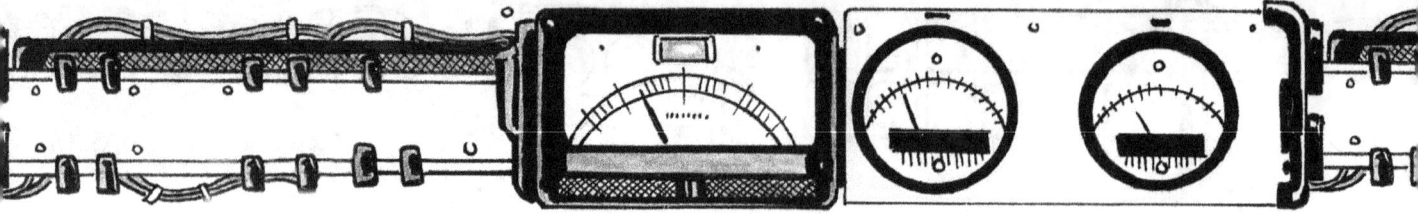

drafted into piracy, the child wanders the town and discovers an advertisement calling for a cabin boy aboard a pirate ship. Since one of the perks is a free earring, Verne jumps at the chance. The boy happily carries out his chores aboard ship, only to discover Marty acting as captain. Marty hopes to return to their own era before getting into further trouble, but Verne is not yet ready to leave—not until he has an earring.

Things take a turn for the worse when the crew sets sail for Smilin' Skull Island to rendezvous with Mac the Black's crew—and Mac himself. Revealed as an imposter, Marty makes a run for it with Verne, the real Mac and his pirates hot on their heels. Verne and Marty pose as women to throw the pirates off their trail—a move that backfires when Mac the Black becomes smitten by the "maiden."

Unwilling to admit the truth, Marty continues the charade, even to the point of walking down the aisle to marry the pirate king. At the last minute, Marty's identity is revealed. Humiliated and heartbroken, Mac the Black vows to execute Marty, who is only saved by the direct intercession of the Spanish Armada and Señorita Maria. A special agent for the armada, Maria is part of a sting operation set up to root out and destroy Mac the Black's pirating business.

Marty vows to make things up to Jennifer upon returning to his own era, having learned a valuable lesson about lying. Verne, meanwhile, decides against getting an earring—though he *does* get a tattoo of a pirate ship on his stomach [BFAN-14].

Wednesday, September 2, 1752 A.D.

- Verne Brown runs away to Philadelphia, in 1752, after Jules' teasing causes him to believe he is adopted, and that his real father is Benjamin Franklin. Verne interrupts the inventor's kite experiments, inadvertently preventing him from demonstrating the relationship between lightning and electricity. Despite Franklin's protests, Verne clings to the man, vehemently claiming to be his son. The experiment's failure results in an alternate timeline in which mankind fails to harness the power of electricity [BFAN-6].

> *NOTE: Historically, Franklin's kite experiment actually occurred on June 15, 1752, not September 2.*

- Determined to set history aright, Emmett Brown travels back in time with Einstein and Marty McFly, but their explosive entry into the past garners the attention of a British soldier, who mistakes them for colonial conspirators plotting a revolution against King George II. Marty leads the guard on a chase, allowing Doc to search for his son. Doc tracks his wayward child to Franklin's home and confronts the boy, but Verne, still angry, escapes into the night.

During a foot pursuit, Doc collides with the Liberty Bell, changing history by becoming the source of its famous crack. Verne hides inside an old state house (later known as Independence Hall) and nearly falls off the roof. Doc rushes to save him, and Verne, upon realizing how much his father loves him, accepts that Emmett really is his father. Their family reunion is cut short, however, when both are caught on the clock hands and end up in danger of falling. Marty saves them by flying the time train beneath them, moments before they would have plummeted to their deaths [BFAN-6].

> *NOTE: Historically, the Liberty Bell actually did crack in 1752, while being tested. It was recast, but was reportedly again cracked in 1835 while tolling the death of Court Justice John Marshall. This second crack then widened when the bell was struck in 1846 to honor George Washington.*

- The time travelers attempt to rectify the timeline and save Ben Franklin's doomed kite experiment. Utilizing a variation on Francis Hauksbee's frictional electricity machine, Doc generates an artificial lightning storm. Franklin gives his experiment another go, this time with successful results [BFAN-6].

Thursday, July 4, 1776 A.D.

- The signing of the U.S. Declaration of Independence signifies the American colonies' succession from the British Empire and the birth of the United States of America [REAL, BTF1].

1783 A.D.

- A hot-air balloon created by brothers Joseph-Michel and Jacques-Étienne Montgolfier makes its maiden voyage, becoming the first such contraption flown in recorded history [REAL].

NOTE: Emmett Brown had traveled in a hot-air balloon nearly 400 years prior, during the second episode of the animated series.

1790 A.D.

• Frankie and Sidney, two bank robbers who stole the DeLorean in 1991 as a getaway vehicle, arrive in Sydney, Australia, in 1790, after the car's voice-activated time circuits mistake their conversation for a destination. Einstein, who'd been asleep in the back seat, struggles with the criminals for possession of the DeLorean, but is thrown from the car. Baffled by the DeLorean's intricate controls, and disoriented by time travel, the crooks inadvertently crash into the HM Prison.

Warden Mungo P. Tannen arrests the thugs and assigns them to hard labor. Einstein later retrieves the DeLorean, sneaks into the compound and incites a breakout. Frankie and Sidney escape during the chaos, pleading with Einstein to let them return with him to the 20th century, and promising to turn themselves in to Hill Valley authorities [BFAN-7b].

Thursday, December 15, 1791 A.D.

• The United States Congress ratifies the Bill of Rights, the first ten amendments to the United States Constitution, intended to protect the natural rights of liberty and property. A local Hill Valley newspaper, the *Daily Megaphone*, covers the story [REAL, BFAN-9].

DOC BROWN CRACKS THE LIBERTY BELL

EBIFFNEZER TANNEN MEETS A HOVERBOARD-RIDING GHOST OF CHRISTMAS

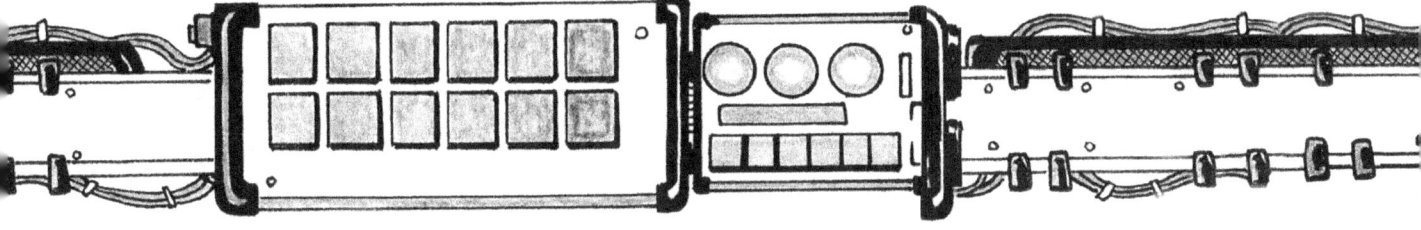

CHAPTER III

1801 A.D. TO 1884 A.D.

1804 A.D.

• The world's first rollercoaster, known as the Russian Mountains, is built in Paris, France [REAL, BFAN-25].

1820 A.D.

• Cold-hearted miser Ebiffnezer Tannen sees the completion of his very own wing at Debtor's Prison, a correctional facility in England [BFAN-10].

Friday, February 8, 1828 A.D.

• French science fiction author Jules Gabriel Verne is born [REAL].

> *NOTE: Verne's writings profoundly influenced Emmett Brown, inspiring him, at age eleven, to devote his life to science. Brown even named his sons after the author, as well as his time-traveling train.*

Circa Mid-1800s A.D.

• Tired of being picked on by school bullies, Verne Brown travels back to the 1800s with Marty McFly, hoping to convince Jules Verne to change his name so that Verne will eventually receive a different name as well. After repeated failed attempts, Verne resorts to Plan B: traveling to October 29, 1888—his own birth date—to urge his parents to name him differently [BFAN-21].

Tuesday, December 19, 1843 A.D.

• English author Charles Dickens' novella *A Christmas Carol* is first published by Chapman & Hall [REAL]. By 1845, it will become well-known in London, England, even by the likes of Ebiffnezer Tannen [BFAN-10].

Wednesday, December 24, 1845 A.D.

• Following a hot July afternoon of irritable bickering, Emmett Brown loads his family, Einstein and Marty McFly into his stretch DeLorean and visits 19th-century England for some cool weather and Christmas spirit. Once there, Jules Brown pleads with his father to let him hold the DeLorean's keys, presently attached to Grandpa Clayton's pocket watch. Realizing Jules is eager to prove himself a responsible young adult, Doc agrees.

Marty's wandering eye for the ladies leads the family to Fedgewick Toys. Doc recognizes many of the toys he owned in his youth—which, in this era, are brand-new. While he and Clara reminisce, a young pickpocket named Reginald steals the DeLorean keys from Jules. Verne and Jules give chase, leaving their family behind. Doc realizes the boys have gone, advising Clara to remain at the toy store until he and Marty return.

During their absence, landlord Ebiffnezer Tannen arrives, demanding retribution against the Fedgewick family for their late mortgage payment. The old miser orders them thrown into the Debtor's Prison's Tannen Wing. Clara catches Tannen's eye and he makes advances toward her—which she spurns, slapping him. Humiliated, Ebiffnezer angrily has her arrested and taken to the Tannen Wing as well.

Jules and Verne follow Reg to the boy's hideout, where they discover he is under the thrall of a criminal named Murdock, who trains children as thieves in order to profit from their crimes. Murdock offers the boys a job picking pockets, and Jules accepts, hoping this will put them in a position to retrieve the stolen car keys. Murdock and Reg take the boys out to begin their first lesson in thievery.

Doc and Marty return to the toy store empty-handed, and are surprised to find the place closed down, its owners—and Clara—thrown into prison. A local troupe of carolers alerts Doc to what has happened to his wife and sons. He and Marty split up, with Marty going after Clara, and Doc seeking to rescue his boys.

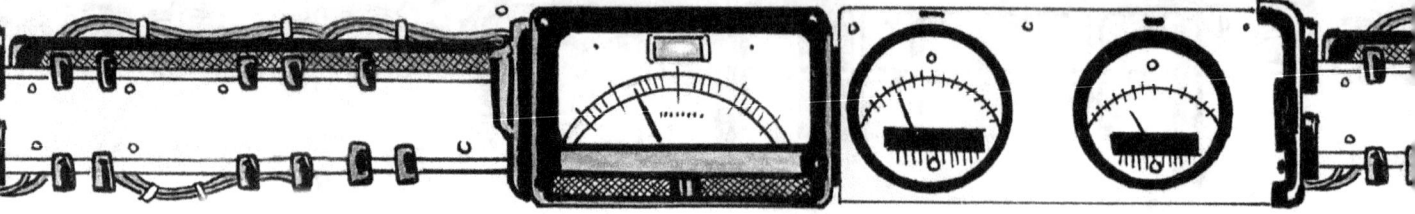

Doc stops at a pub, where he meets Murdock's fence, a one-eyed man named Wilkins. Claiming to be Reg's friend, Doc convinces Wilkins to take him to their hideout. Once there, however, Reg denies knowing the man. Suspecting him of being an undercover policeman, the criminals tie Doc up.

Later that night, Jules and Verne get to know Reg and pity him for not having a proper family. They convince him to help them retrieve the DeLorean keys, promising, in return, to help him start a new life away from Murdock. The boy agrees, and the three youths locate the keys, saving Doc Brown in the process. Awakened by the escape, Murdock and Wilkins race after their prisoners, but thanks to some quick scientific thinking, Doc turns the tables on the thugs, catching them just as the authorities arrive.

Failing to fast-talk the guards at Debtor's Prison into releasing Clara, Marty devises another scheme. Disguised in a dark robe and riding his hoverboard, he visits Ebiffnezer Tannen's bedroom, posing as the Ghost of Christmas. Marty abducts the miser and takes him on a whirlwind tour of London, showing him the plight of the poverty-stricken. However, even upon seeing the struggles of those under his thumb, Tannen's heart remains cold and unmoved.

It is only when a portable holo-movie projector falls out of Marty's pocket and plays a terrifying scene from a *Godzilla*-esque movie on Tannen's wall that the scrooge fearfully repents of his misdeeds. At Marty's command, he gladly releases twenty-five years' worth of prisoners from the Tannen Wing, including Clara and the Fedgewicks. The Fedgewicks take Reg into their home and family, while Tannen turns over a new leaf, out of fear that his greed and cruelty will incur the wrath of a giant, rampaging lizard [BFAN-10].

Sometime After 1845 A.D.

• For many years thereafter, the Brown family visits the Fedgewicks for Christmas dinner each July, a lasting bond uniting the two families [BFAN-10].

Sunday, March 3, 1850 A.D.

• In the original timeline, pioneers Martha O'Brien and Daniel Clayton are married while traversing the Oregon Trail [BFAN-13].

• The O'Brien-Clayton nuptials are inadvertently delayed when Verne and Jules Brown visit this era, along with Marty McFly, to photograph the boys' pioneer grandparents in order to impress Verne's future classmates during show-and-tell. As fate would have it, the time-travelers touch down seconds before a stampede of buffalo make their charge, damaging the DeLorean. They are rescued by Verne's rough-and-tumble ancestor, Martha O'Brien, and are taken in by a caravan of covered wagons traveling the Oregon Trail.

Bringing up the caravan's rear is Daniel Clayton. Verne is disheartened to learn that his grandfather-to-be is a "wimp," with a healthy interest in insects and his nose buried in a book, while Martha is the pioneer hero—roles that Verne had grown up believing were reversed. However, his personal disappointment is nothing compared to the paradox set into motion when Martha lays eyes on Marty and becomes infatuated with *him* instead of Daniel.

That night at the camp, the boys work hard to make Daniel presentable as a worthy suitor of the ornery O'Brien, while Martha goes to great lengths to become ladylike and win Marty's affections. The matchmaking is interrupted when Wild Bill Tannen arrives without invitation, demanding food. Fearing the stranger, they welcome him into the camp, but it doesn't take long for Tannen to discover the group's cash box. When Martha catches him trying to steal it, Wild Bill kidnaps her. Verne is the only witness to the crime, but instead of alerting the others, he takes off on his own to rescue his grandma.

Not long thereafter, Emmett Brown and Einstein arrive in 1850 aboard the time train. Doc informs Jules and Marty that their temporal tampering is having dire repercussions—their mother, Clara, is slowly being erased

from existence in 1991. Their only hope to ensure her birth is to convince Martha that Daniel is the man for her. An alert is raised in the camp as the pioneers learn that Wild Bill has nabbed Martha and fled into the wilderness. With Daniel Clayton in tow, the Browns and Marty set out to rescue her.

Tannen brings Martha to his camp and ties her up. Verne attempts a rescue, but is captured as well, though he is able to trick the kidnapper into blinding himself with a 20th-century flash camera. With Wild Bill out of commission, Martha unties herself and the boy—but their troubles increase when they must fend off a bear that has wandered into camp. Fashioning a glider out of wagon tarp, Doc and Daniel swoop to the rescue, saving Martha and Verne from the animal's clutches. In that moment, Martha realizes she is smitten with the insect enthusiast [BFAN-13].

Monday, March 4, 1850 A.D.

• As night turns to morning, Martha and Daniel are married one day after their original wedding date, though a misprint on the buckboard plaque still reads March 3, preserving that initial date for posterity. During their wedding, Daniel discovers a new breed of butterfly and names it after his bride: *Lepidoptera martha* [BFAN-13].

1855 A.D.

• Clarabelle "Clara" Clayton is born to Daniel Clayton and Martha O'Brien-Clayton [BFAN-13].

> ***NOTE: Clara's full first name, Clarabelle, was revealed in the animated episode "Brothers."***

1850s to 1860s A.D.

• Clara Clayton grows up in New Jersey, enjoying an active childhood, and frequently engaging in climbing and horseback-riding [BTF3-n].

1864 A.D.

• *A Journey to the Center of the Earth*, written by influential science fiction author Jules Verne, is first published in French [REAL].

> ***NOTE: The novel's first English translation would be printed in 1871.***

Thursday, February 11, 1864 A.D.

• Confederate General Beauregard B. Tannen poses with his regiment for a photo, one day before the soldiers' slaughter by the Union army [BFAN-1].

• Verne Brown visits Chattanooga, Tennessee, arriving via DeLorean in the pre-dawn hours. Eager to prove himself in his family's eyes, Verne sets out to become a man and is drafted into the Confederate Army by General Beauregard Tannen. Later that day, Verne stands with his new brothers-in-arms for a photograph, and befriends a young drummer boy named Jimmy, who teaches him the trade. Verne doubts they will be in any danger since they're "just kids," but Jimmy reveals the grim reality of war: No one is safe.

By daylight, Emmett Brown arrives via time train, along with Jules Brown, Marty McFly and Einstein, from 1991. Doc and Jules search for the runaway Verne, leaving Marty and Einie to watch the locomotive. The teen and dog are taken prisoner by Confederate soldiers, however, and—along with the train—are escorted to camp to stand before General Tannen. Doc and Jules are ambushed by Union soldiers who mistake the Browns for fellow combatants gone AWOL. The soldiers "return" them to the Union regiment, under the leadership of Clara's uncle, General Ulysses S. Clayton.

That night, Verne dines with the Confederates around a campfire. Jimmy laments running away from home to join the war, and Verne realizes his home life wasn't as bad as he'd believed. Marty and Einstein, meanwhile, are presented to Beauregard as Yankee prisoners and are thrown in the brig.

At the Union camp, Jules attempts to convince General Clayton to call off the battle, claiming his own niece's son, Verne, is in danger of being killed. Since Clara is only nine years old at the time, the general dismisses the boy's story. Doc notices a traveling scientist's "electrical magnetical machine" inside General Clayton's tent, used to cure the officer's rheumatism, and devises a plan to save his son [BFAN-1].

Friday, February 12, 1864 A.D.

• In the original timeline, General Beauregard Tannen's Confederate troops are killed by the Union army in the so-called Battle at Chattanooga [BFAN-1].

• In the new reality caused by the time-travelers' presence, Doc and Jules arrive with a homemade electromagnet made from railroad beams, a cannon's wheels and the "electrical magnetical machine." Jules cranks the magnet's wheel, causing the weapons of both armies to be yanked out of the soldiers' hands. Peace seems attainable, until something goes wrong with the magnet.

Troops on both sides take up arms, preparing to fight, with Jules and Verne caught in the middle of the battlefield. Fearfully, the brothers hold each other tightly. This simple act of brotherly love—one boy in Union blues, another in Confederate greys—prompts the armies to recognize that they are fighting against brothers, cousins and friends. Generals Tannen and Clayton resolve their differences peaceably, the battle is called off, and Marty and the Browns return to 1991 [BFAN-1].

CODE	STORY						
ARGN	BTTF-themed TV commercial: Arrigoni	BTF1	Film: Back to the Future	CITY	BTTF-themed music video: Owl City, "Deer in the Headlights"	HUEY	BTTF-themed music video: Huey Lewis and the News, "The Power of Love"
BFAN	Back to the Future: The Animated Series	BTF2	Film: Back to the Future Part II			LIMO	BTTF-themed music video:
BFCG	Back to the Future: The Card Game	BTF3	Film: Back to the Future Part III	DCTV	BTTF-themed TV commercial: DirecTV		The Limousines, "The Future"
BFCL	Back to the Future comic book (limited series)	BUDL	BTTF-themed TV commercial: Bud Light	ERTH	The Earth Day Special	MCDN	BTTF-themed TV commercial: McDonald's
BFCM	Back to the Future comic book (monthly series)	CHEK	BTTF-themed music video: O'Neal McKnight, "Check Your Coat"	GALE	Interviews and commentaries: Bob Gale and/or Robert Zemeckis	MITS	BTTF-themed TV commercial: Mitsubishi Lancer
BFHM	BTTF-themed McDonald's Happy Meal boxes	CHIC	Photographs hanging in Doc Brown's	GARB	BTTF-themed TV commercials: Garbarino		
BTFA	Back to the Future Annual (Marvel Comics)		Chicken restaurant at Universal Studios	GETV	BTTF-themed TV commercial: GE	MSFT	BTTF-themed TV commercial: Microsoft

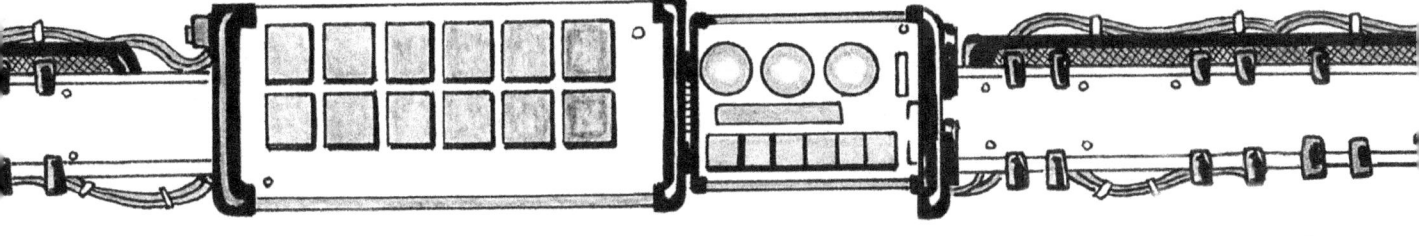

Sometime After February 12, 1864 A.D.

- History books thereafter reflect the altered timeline, recording that Beauregard Tannen's Confederate regiment never see combat throughout their careers [BFAN-1].

1865 A.D.

- The settlement of Hill Valley is incorporated into the state of California [TLTL-3, TLTL-v].

  *NOTE: The unused first draft of **BTF2's** screenplay cited William "Bill" Hill as Hill Valley's founder, but no date was provided for this historic event. By 1985, a statue of Bill Hill with a pack mule would be erected as a monument, and would stand at least 30 more years beyond that point.*

Sometime Between 1865 and 1910 A.D.

- Emmett Brown enjoys a day of frog-hunting with author Samuel Clemens (a.k.a. Mark Twain) in California's Calaveras County [BFAN-7a].

  NOTE: This adventure may have spurred Twain to write his short story "The Celebrated Jumping Frog of Calaveras County."

1866 A.D.

- At age 11, Clara Clayton contracts diphtheria and is quarantined for three months. To keep her occupied, her father, Daniel Clayton, buys her a telescope so she can see everything through her window. This evolves into a lifelong passion both for astronomy and for the works of Jules Verne, including *From the Earth to the Moon* [BTF3, BFAN-13]. Clara often gazes at the Moon, and nicknames the Copernicus crater "Little Sunshine" [BTF3-n].

Mid to Late 1800s A.D.

- Sarah Lathrop, Emmett Brown's future mother, owns a rag doll as a child that she calls Emma [BTF3-s1].

  NOTE: Apparently, Sarah later named her son after this doll.

1869 A.D.

- James Strickland arrives in Hill Valley and begins a career in law enforcement [TLTL-5].

1870 A.D.

- *Twenty Thousand Leagues Under the Sea*, written by science fiction author Jules Verne, is first published in France [REAL].

1873 A.D.

- *Twenty Thousand Leagues Under the Sea*, by French science fiction author Jules Verne, is first translated into English [REAL].

Sometime Before 1875 A.D.

- The Hill Valley Historical Society is established. Devoted to preserving the city's history for posterity, the organization is also called the Historical Society of Hill Valley [TLTL-v].

1875 A.D.

- Marty McFly visits the Parker Ranch, along with Jules and Verne Brown, in an effort to stop Wendel Parker—the great-great-grandfather of Marty's girlfriend, Jennifer—from signing over the deed to Thaddeus Tannen. The trio helps Wendel and his wife, Genevieve, raise their barn with the assistance of friends and neighbors, including Hepzibah Tannen, Thaddeus' sister.

				SUFFIX MEDIUM			
NIKE	BTTF-themed TV commercial: Nike	SCRT	2010 Scream Awards: Back to the Future 25th Anniversary Reunion (trailer)	-b	BTF2's Biff Tannen Museum video (extended version)	-s1	Screenplay (draft one)
NTND	Nintendo Back to the Future—The Ride Mini-Game	SIMP	Simulator: The Simpsons Ride			-s2	Screenplay (draft two)
		SLOT	Back to the Future Video Slots	-c	Animated series credit sequence	-s3	Screenplay (draft three)
PIZA	BTTF-themed TV commercial: Pizza Hut	TEST	Screen tests: Crispin Glover, Lea Thompson and Thomas F. Wilson	-d	Film deleted scene	-s4	Screenplay (draft four)
REAL	Real life			-n	Film novelization	-sp	Screenplay (production draft)
RIDE	Simulator: Back to the Future—The Ride	TLTL	Telltale Games' Back to the Future—The Game	-o	Film outtake	-sx	Screenplay (Paradox)
SCRM	2010 Scream Awards: Back to the Future 25th Anniversary Reunion (broadcast)	UNIV	Universal Studios Hollywood promotional video	-v	Video game print materials or commentaries		

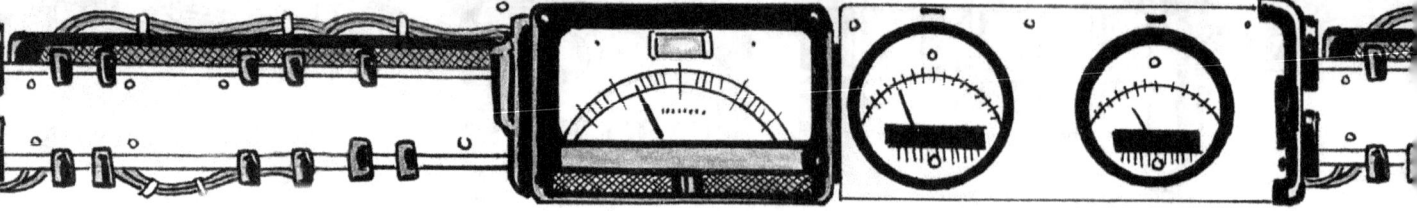

When Marty is injured while attempting to rescue Hepzibah from a collapsing barn wall, the husky woman takes an immediate shine to the young man and drags him to her home, to tend to his injuries. There, Marty meets Thaddeus and, due to Hepizbah's infatuation with him, is pulled into the Tannen gang of outlaws, along with a tall, bald brute named Ox McPhips.

While Jules and Verne work for the Parkers as ranch hands, Marty goes undercover in the Tannen gang, hoping to prevent Thaddeus from acquiring the Parker place. Marty becomes involved with a stage coach robbery and a bank heist, but sees no sign of Tannen making a move on Wendel's property.

Marty's time spent with the Tannens cements Hepzibah's romantic feelings for him, and she decides they should wed, giving Marty little say in the matter. Thaddeus and Ox prepare a special honeymoon surprise, in the form of Wendel Parker's ranch. Tannen and McPhips tie Genevieve to railroad tracks, in the path of the impending 3:15 locomotive to Cheyenne, and force Wendel to sign over the deed to his land in order to save her life.

Marty arrives, and though unable to rescue Genevieve, offers Wendel his pen—a joke pen filled with disappearing ink, purchased in 1991 at the Hill Valley Humor Hut—to sign the deed. Tannen leaves with his prize, kicking Marty out of the gang for meddling in his affairs. Ox then admits he's always loved Hepzibah, and she returns his attraction.

Marty and the Brown boys rescue the Parkers and return to 1991. Meanwhile, Hepzibah and Ox vow to walk the straight and narrow together. In the spirit of this decision—and as retaliation for Tannen's treatment of Marty—Hepzibah turns her brother over to the authorities. He is arrested for his crimes, but not before burying the signed deed on his property, where his great-great-great-grandnephew, Biff Tannen, will discover it 116 years later [BFAN-16].

1876 A.D.

- Wealthy entrepreneur Beauregard B. Tannen, a former Confederate general, arrives in Hill Valley, where he begins constructing the Palace Saloon and Hotel [TLTL-5].

Tuesday, June 13, 1876 A.D.

- Edna Strickland arrives from 1931 in a time-traveling DeLorean she stole from Marty McFly. Assuming the name "Mary Pickford," Edna settles into the rustic Hill Valley, falling in love with the simple life and even meeting her late grandfather, Marshal James Strickland, whom she'd greatly admired in the future [TLTL-5].

Tuesday, June 13, to Monday, July 17, 1876 A.D.

- Edna Strickland finds her idyllic view of Hill Valley challenged by Beauregard Tannen's decision to open the Palace Saloon and Hotel. An arsonist in her own era, Edna decides to set fire to the saloon [TLTL-5].

Monday, July 17, 1876 A.D.

- While torching Tannen's saloon, Edna accidentally lights all of Hill Valley ablaze, burning down the very paradise she sought to preserve [TLTL-5].

Monday, July 17, 1876 A.D.—2:00 AM

- Emmett Brown and Marty McFly travel back in time in an effort to stop Edna from burning down the Palace Saloon and prevent Hill Valley's destruction. Doc tries to reason with Edna, having been married to her in a parallel future, but she refuses to back down from what she sees as her moral obligation. Events reach a fevered pitch when Beauregard Tannen arrives, aiming a scattergun at the duo. It's a tense standoff, with Edna's torch hovering dangerously close to a pile of kerosene-soaked hay. Doc

CODE	STORY						
ARGN	BTTF-themed TV commercial: Arrigoni	**BTF1**	Film: Back to the Future	**CITY**	BTTF-themed music video: Owl City, "Deer in the Headlights"	**HUEY**	BTTF-themed music video: Huey Lewis and the News, "The Power of Love"
BFAN	Back to the Future: The Animated Series	**BTF2**	Film: Back to the Future Part II	**DCTV**	BTTF-themed TV commercial: DirecTV	**LIMO**	BTTF-themed music video: The Limousines, "The Future"
BFCG	Back to the Future: The Card Game	**BTF3**	Film: Back to the Future Part III	**ERTH**	The Earth Day Special		
BFCL	Back to the Future comic book (limited series)	**BUDL**	BTTF-themed TV commercial: Bud Light	**GALE**	Interviews and commentaries: Bob Gale and/or Robert Zemeckis	**MCDN**	BTTF-themed TV commercial: McDonald's
BFCM	Back to the Future comic book (monthly series)	**CHEK**	BTTF-themed music video: O'Neal McKnight, "Check Your Coat"			**MITS**	BTTF-themed TV commercial: Mitsubishi Lancer
BFHM	BTTF-themed McDonald's Happy Meal boxes	**CHIC**	Photographs hanging in Doc Brown's Chicken restaurant at Universal Studios	**GARB**	BTTF-themed TV commercials: Garbarino	**MSFT**	BTTF-themed TV commercial: Microsoft
BTFA	Back to the Future Annual (Marvel Comics)			**GETV**	BTTF-themed TV commercial: GE		

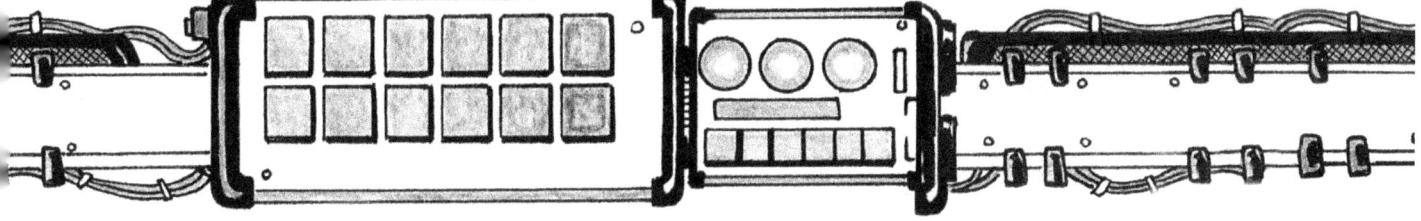

keeps Tannen distracted while Marty sneaks behind the scenes to incapacitate both Beauregard and Edna.

Edna flees once more, ducking inside the stolen DeLorean and racing across the uneven terrain, with Doc and Marty giving chase in their DeLorean. Using Doc's Flux Synchronization Modules, Marty pulls off a harrowing stunt, climbing aboard Edna's speeding vehicle and attaching the modules to the car's diagnostic lights. Once the modules are in place, Doc synchs up to Edna's wayward vehicle and tows it back to 1931 [TLTL-5].

Sometime Between 1876 and 1885 A.D.

• Hill Valley's Palace Saloon and Hotel becomes a regular hangout for a number of grizzled locals, including Jeb, Levi, Zeke, Toothless, Eyepatch and Moustache. Serving the old-timers are bartender Chester and his assistant, Joey [BTF3-sx, BTF3-sp, BTF3-n].

Sometime in or After 1876 A.D.

• Delores Miskin, an ancestor of Marty McFly, has her image painted and adorned at Beauregard Tannen's Palace Saloon and Hotel [TLTL-5].

> *NOTE: The book* **Hill Valley Historical Society, 1865-1990** *would later dub Miskin "the face that inspired a thousand barroom brawls" [TLTL-v].*

Friday, November 12, 1880 A.D.

• The novel *Ben-Hur: A Tale of the Christ* is published by Harper & Brothers. The book, authored by Lew Wallace, tells the story of Judah Ben-Hur, a Jewish prince sold into slavery who vows revenge against the one-time friend who put him there [REAL].

> *NOTE: In BFAN-5, Marty McFly and the Browns encountered Judah Ben-Hur in 36 A.D., leading Marty to conclude they'd met the historic figure on whose life the novel was based. This would imply that in the BTTF mythos, unlike in reality, Ben-Hur was not a fictional character.*

1881 A.D.

• Seamus and Maggie McFly move from Ballybowhill, a village in County Dublin, Ireland, to the United States, in search of a better life and land of their own [BTF3-n]. Seamus' brother, Martin, travels with them. The trio settles in Virginia City, where a saloon patron provokes Martin into a fight by calling him a coward, and then shoves a Bowie knife into his belly [BTF3-sp].

• Mourning Martin's loss, Maggie and Seamus relocate to Hill Valley, California, where they purchase a farm and become respected members of the town. Thereafter, Seamus strives to avoid a fight at all times, even if it means looking cowardly to others [BTF3].

Sunday, August 26, 1883 A.D.

• After stealing the DeLorean in order to turn a profit, crooked television personality Walter Wisdom—known on TV as "Mr. Wisdom"—escapes to 1883, hoping to elude Emmett Brown, Marty McFly and Doc's sons. The group, pursuing Wisdom aboard the *Jules Verne Train*, attaches a tether to the DeLorean, but the car thief severs the connection and watches gleefully as the locomotive barrels for the active volcano Krakatoa. Wisdom then returns to 1992, leaving them for dead. Only by donning Doc's Full-Body Oven Mits do the Browns survive the deadly lava [BFAN-15].

1884 A.D.

• A newspaper editor prints an unfavorable story about Wild West outlaw Buford "Mad Dog" Tannen. Unhappy with the article, Tannen shoots the man. Following the murder, other editors opt not to document Tannen's exploits [BTF3].

> *NOTE: In an early-draft script titled* **Paradox**, *Buford was known as "Black Biff" Tannen.*

NIKE	*BTTF*-themed TV commercial: Nike	**SCRT**	2010 Scream Awards: *Back to the Future*	**SUFFIX**	**MEDIUM**	**-s1**	Screenplay (draft one)
NTND	Nintendo *Back to the Future—The Ride* Mini-Game		25th Anniversary Reunion (trailer)	**-b**	*BTF2's* Biff Tannen Museum video (extended version)	**-s2**	Screenplay (draft two)
		SIMP	Simulator: *The Simpsons Ride*			**-s3**	Screenplay (draft three)
PIZA	*BTTF*-themed TV commercial: Pizza Hut	**SLOT**	*Back to the Future* Video Slots	**-c**	Animated series credit sequence	**-s4**	Screenplay (draft four)
REAL	Real life	**TEST**	Screen tests: Crispin Glover, Lea Thompson and Thomas F. Wilson	**-d**	Film deleted scene	**-sp**	Screenplay (production draft)
RIDE	Simulator: *Back to the Future—The Ride*			**-n**	Film novelization	**-sx**	Screenplay (*Paradox*)
SCRM	2010 Scream Awards: *Back to the Future* 25th Anniversary Reunion (broadcast)	**TLTL**	Telltale Games' *Back to the Future—The Game*	**-o**	Film outtake		
		UNIV	Universal Studios Hollywood promotional video	**-v**	Video game print materials or commentaries		

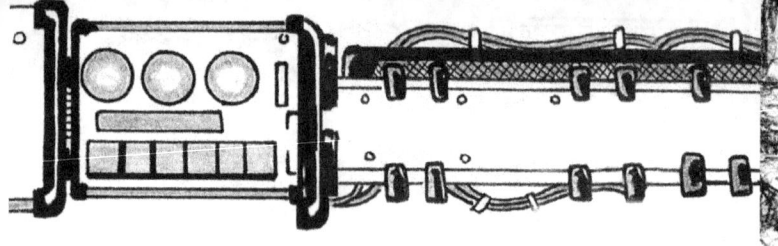

CHAPTER IV:
1885 A.D.

FRONTIER DAYS:
DOC ARRIVES IN OLD
WEST HILL VALLEY

Sometime Before 1885 A.D.

- Clara Clayton marries her first husband [BTF3-s1].

- Clara Clayton's beloved uncle, "Jumpin'" Jehoshaphat, makes a name for himself as a carnival stunt man [BFAN-21].

Sometime in or Before 1885 A.D.

- Numerous businesses open in and around the newly constructed Courthouse Square, including Apaline's; an assay office; a bath house and barber stand; D. Merchant, Doctor; Fabrics, Buttons, Notions; a fortune teller booth; Gen'l Mercantile, containing a Cha's Fees dealer and a post office; Hill Valley Hook & Ladder; the *Hill Valley Telegraph* newspaper; Honest Joe Statler Fine Horses; the Livery & Feed Stable; M. Fennigot Millinery; a marshal's office; a meat market; Mrs. M.W. Keen, Dress Maker; Nicks Cantina—The Road to Ruin; the Palace Saloon and Hotel; a sign-making shop; T.L. Livingston, Cabinet Maker; an undertaking firm owned by Mr. Phipps; Wells Fargo & Co.; and W. J. Chang, Chinese Laundry [BTF3].

    NOTE: View the map on page 183 to see where each business was located.

- After suffering several "unfortunate events" while living in the Eastern United States [BTF3-n], including becoming a widow in Silver City [BTF3-s1], Clara Clayton decides to move back west. She accepts a teaching position in the frontier town of Hill Valley, California, and arranges to travel there via locomotive, intending to build a new life for herself [BTF3-n].

NOTE: It's unclear in which Silver City this occurred, as there are several within the United States. The husband's name is unknown; Clara apparently began using her maiden name, Clayton, once more upon his death.

• Amazed at the frontier town's railroad and other advanced technology, undertaker Mr. Phipps falls in love with Hill Valley and finds it amusing whenever foreigners are awed by amenities he takes for granted, such as the town's barber shop. The mortician forms a dislike of outlaw Buford "Mad Dog" Buford and hopes Marshall James Strickland will someday bring him to justice—but privately realizes that Tannen, as a murderer, enables him to stay in business [BTFA].

NIKE	*BTTF*-themed TV commercial: Nike	**SCRT**	2010 Scream Awards: *Back to the Future* 25th Anniversary Reunion (trailer)	**SUFFIX**	**MEDIUM**			**-s1**	Screenplay (draft one)
NTND	Nintendo *Back to the Future—The Ride* Mini-Game			**-b**	*BTF2's* Biff Tannen Museum video (extended version)			**-s2**	Screenplay (draft two)
		SIMP	Simulator: *The Simpsons Ride*					**-s3**	Screenplay (draft three)
PIZA	*BTTF*-themed TV commercial: Pizza Hut	**SLOT**	*Back to the Future* Video Slots	**-c**	Animated series credit sequence			**-s4**	Screenplay (draft four)
REAL	Real life	**TEST**	Screen tests: Crispin Glover, Lea Thompson and Thomas F. Wilson	**-d**	Film deleted scene			**-sp**	Screenplay (production draft)
RIDE	Simulator: *Back to the Future—The Ride*			**-n**	Film novelization			**-sx**	Screenplay (*Paradox*)
SCRM	2010 Scream Awards: *Back to the Future* 25th Anniversary Reunion (broadcast)	**TLTL**	Telltale Games' *Back to the Future—The Game*	**-o**	Film outtake				
		UNIV	Universal Studios Hollywood promotional video	**-v**	Video game print materials or commentaries				

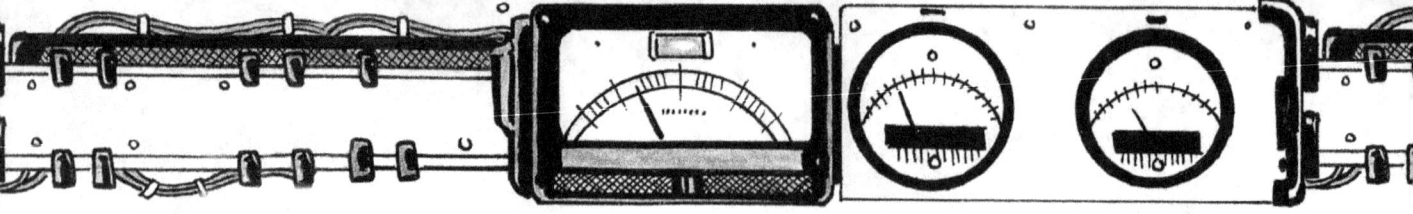

- A farmer named Dingus Peabody settles in Hill Valley. Grizzled and missing several teeth, Dingus develops a fondness for pine trees that will later be shared by his descendant, Otis Peabody [BTF3-sp].

    NOTE: Two characters named Dingus Peabody and Farmer Peabody appeared in different drafts of BTF3's screenplay. It is thus likely they were intended to be the same character.

- An outlaw named Stinky Lomax is apprehended in Haysville and sentenced to hang. Hill Valley's marshal, James Strickland, decides to attend the execution [BTF3].

    NOTE: Strickland's attendance at the hanging may indicate an adversarial relationship between the marshal and Lomax.

- A grizzled old-timer named Levi, a frequent patron of Hill Valley's Palace Saloon and Hotel, discovers his son wearing "fancy" clothing after the youth returns from a trip to the east [BTF3-n, BTF3-o]. Disgusted by his son's behavior, the oldster sets fire to the lad [BTF3-n].

- The Lazy J Riders become famous for raising livestock at the Lazy J Ranch, one of the Hill Valley area's most profitable ranches. Photographs of the group are documented in the archives of the Hill Valley Historical Society. A dispute between the Lazy J Riders and Buford Tannen results in many ranchers dying during a shootout. At the inquest that follows, Tannen is acquitted since no witnesses are willing to testify against him. Some attribute this to his purchasing a new set of Colt pistols and boasting that he "wanted to try them out" [BTF3].

- M.R. Gale is named the editor of the *Hill Valley Telegraph* [BTF3].

    NOTE: Gale was named after Bob Gale, a cowriter of the BTTF film trilogy.

- Author Samuel Clemens (a.k.a. "Mark Twain") visits Hill Valley and tells a number of tall tales to the patrons of the Palace Saloon and Hotel. The bartender, Chester, later compares Twain's stories to Emmett Brown's claim of being from the future [BTF3-sp, BTF3-n].

- A train conductor known as "Fearless Frank" Fargo successfully manages to achieve a speed of 70 miles per hour using a steam-powered locomotive, out past Verde Junction [BTF3].

Thursday, January 1, 1885 A.D.—12:00 AM

- The citizens of Hill Valley decide to hire a new blacksmith and a school teacher [BFCG].

- Emmett Brown is transported to the Old West after his flying DeLorean is struck by lightning in 1955. Soon after arriving in that era, he accepts the blacksmith job [BFCG].

    NOTE: In the unused film draft titled Paradox, *Doc was originally stranded in July 1888.*

Sometime After January 1, 1885 A.D.

- Emmett Brown moves into the former Livery & Feed Stable and opens a blacksmith shop containing three horses, called Archimedes, Galileo and Newton. Archimedes, his favorite of the three, becomes Doc's trusted riding steed [BTF3-n].

- For protection in the Old West, Emmett Brown builds a four-barrel shotgun loaded with double-aught buck, nails, broken glass and shiny new dimes, making the weapon exceedingly deadly. He dubs it the Terminator [BTF3-sx, BTF3-sp], and boasts that it can "shoot the fleas off a dog's back at 500 yards" [BTF3].

    NOTE: Doc apparently named the weapon after James Cameron's 1984 science fiction film The Terminator, *starring Arnold Schwarzenegger and Linda Hamilton.*

- The U.S. government issues a Wanted poster for an outlaw known as the Deadwood Kid [BTF3].

April 1885 A.D.

- William Sean McFly is born to Irish immigrants Seamus and Maggie McFly, becoming the first McFly born in America [BTF3-n].

Sometime Between January and September 1885 A.D.

- Blacksmith Emmett Brown shoes a horse for Buford "Mad Dog" Tannen. Afterwards, the horse throws that shoe—and Mad Dog—costing the outlaw a bottle of Kentucky Red Eye whiskey. Furious, Tannen shoots the horse and blames Doc for the damages. [BTF3].

Wednesday, June 10, 1885 A.D.

- Clara Clayton, from 1991, returns to her Old West roots, passing through Hill Valley to purchase groceries for supper. Whilst there, she finds herself amidst a standoff between two gunslingers in the streets: one, an old-timer with a black eye, the other Buford "Mad Dog" Tannen. The old-timer draws iron, just as Emmett Brown arrives in his DeLorean, running him over. Buford abandons the gunfight and scoops Clara in his arms, trying to steal a kiss, but Clara pulls the brute's ten-gallon hat over his head, stomps on his boot, climbs into the car and receives a kiss from her husband. The Browns then blast away to go retrieve their children for a family dinner [BFAN-c].

  NOTE: This event, depicted in the opening credits of the animated series' first season, featured Clara Clayton visiting Hill Valley before the Clara of 1885 moved there in September.

Saturday, July 4, 1885 A.D.

- During Hill Valley's Independence Day festivities, Emmett Brown imbibes whiskey—and promptly passes out. The bartender, Chester, decides that Doc cannot handle liquor [BTF3].

Tuesday, September 1, 1885 A.D.

- Still stranded in the Old West, Emmett Brown writes a farewell letter to Marty McFly—who is himself stuck in 1955—and provides detailed instructions about where he will hide the DeLorean so that his 1955 counterpart can retrieve and repair it, allowing the teen to return to 1985. Doc sends the letter via Western Union, instructing the agency to hold the letter until November 12, 1955, at the precise moment after Marty will have seen the lightning-struck DeLorean vanish. The mail-carrier service follows this strange request to the letter (so to speak) [BTF3].

Wednesday, September 2, 1885 A.D.—8:00 AM

- Marty McFly disembarks in 1885, in search of Emmett Brown—who, according to a tombstone that Marty had discovered in 1955, will be murdered by Buford Tannen on September 7. Upon arrival, the youth encounters stampeding Pohatchee Indians, who fire weapons at the DeLorean, severing the vehicle's fuel line. Marty hides the car in a cave until it can be repaired, but is chased from the hiding place by a bear. Stumbling down a hill, Marty smacks his head and falls unconscious, awakening hours later on the farm of his ancestors, Seamus and Maggie McFly and their infant son (Marty's great-grandfather), William Sean McFly. Marty assumes the alias of "Clint Eastwood" [BTF3].

  NOTE: In an unused screenplay draft titled Paradox, *Marty traveled to April 11, 1888, at 7:00 AM.*

LOVE AT FIRST SIGHT:
WHEN EMMETT MET CLARA

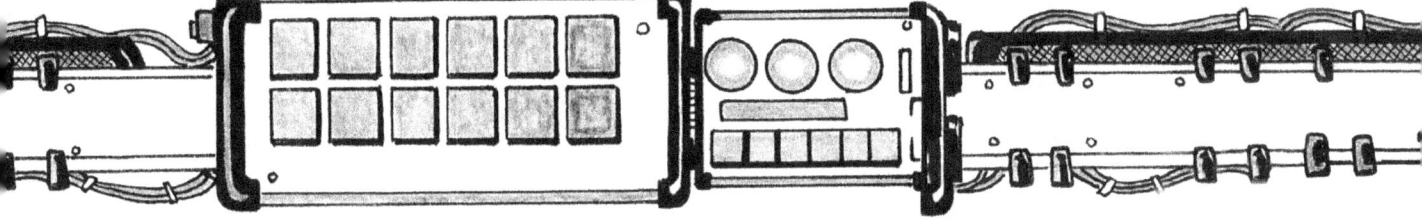

Thursday, September 3, 1885 A.D.

- Marty walks to Hill Valley, which in this era is a budding frontier settlement with a brand-new Clock Tower under construction. He finds his way to the Palace Saloon and Hotel, where he runs afoul of Buford Tannen and his three cronies, Ceegar, Stubble and Buck. When Marty makes the mistake of calling the outlaw by his infamous moniker, "Mad Dog," Tannen becomes furious and his gang chases the teen out of the saloon, roping him up with the intention of hanging him from the tower [BTF3].

- At the Palace Saloon, Chester the bartender witnesses this crime about to be committed. With Marshal James Strickland out of town to attend the hanging of Stinky Lomax, Chester instructs his employee, Joey, to notify the blacksmith [BTF3-n].

- Near death, Marty is saved by a bullet from a modified rifle—known as the Terminator—wielded by Emmett Brown [BTF3-n]. The precise shot severs the rope, dropping Marty to the ground. Tannen threatens Doc, claiming the blacksmith owes him for a thrown shoe on his horse and the bottle of Kentucky Red Eye whiskey he spilled as a result. The total sum, Mad Dog says, came to eighty dollars—the same amount Marty had seen on Doc's gravestone. Doc chases off the outlaws and reunites with his young friend.

   At the blacksmith shop, Marty tells Doc about his impending murder. When Marty asks who the enigmatic "Clara" (named on the scientist's gravestone) is, Brown has no clue, but rejects the notion that he could ever become romantically involved with someone in the past, as that could jeopardize the very fabric of the space-time continuum. At this moment, a man named Hubert—Hill Valley's mayor—arrives, reminding Emmett that he'd volunteered to pick up the new schoolteacher when she arrives via train the next day. Her name: Miss Clara Clayton.

   Fearful of entering into a relationship with Clara, and of his own imminent demise, Doc tells Marty that Clayton will need to find another ride since the two of them must restore the DeLorean and go back to the future. Marty, however, recalls his turbulent reentry into the Old West, and that the DeLorean is out of gas—a major setback, Doc says, as there won't be a gas station in Hill Valley until sometime in the next century [BTF3].

- In an effort to avoid his fate, Doc asks Dingus Peabody—a local farmer with a penchant for pine tree breeding—to pick up Clara for him. Dingus readily agrees, but soon forgets to follow through on his promise [BTF3-sp].

- Doc and Marty begin a series of experiments in the hope of getting the DeLorean up to 88 miles per hour, thereby sending them back to their own era. At sunset, they try pulling the car behind a team of horses, but are unable to reach even 30 miles per hour. They return to Doc's stable after midnight, preparing for another day of experimentation [BTF3-n].

Friday, September 4, 1885 A.D.—5:11 PM

- Clara Clayton's train pulls into the Hill Valley train station [BFCG]. With no one to pick her up at the station, Clara rents a horse-drawn buckboard and rides to town [BTF3].

- In one possible timeline, Clara Clayton arrives safely at the town of Hill Valley, bypassing Shonash Ravine without incident [BFCG].

- In another reality, Clara finds herself in grave danger when a snake spooks her horses. Out of control, the steeds race for Shonash Ravine. Tragically, Clayton is thrown off the edge of the cliff and into the ravine, dying on impact [BTF3, BFCG].

   NOTE: A century later, Marty McFly and his high school classmates would recall the legend of Clayton Ravine, renamed in the schoolteacher's memory.

Friday, September 4, 1885 A.D.—After 5:11 PM

- After spending the morning using his blacksmith tools to repair the damaged DeLorean, Doc pours the bartender's strongest whiskey into the gas tank as a substitute for gasoline—a move that detonates the fuel-injection manifold. Running out of options (and time), the scientist considers that they may be able to *push* the DeLorean up to 88 miles per hour in order to go back to the future.

   Together, Doc and Marty approach a conductor at the Hill Valley Railroad Station and ask some nonchalant

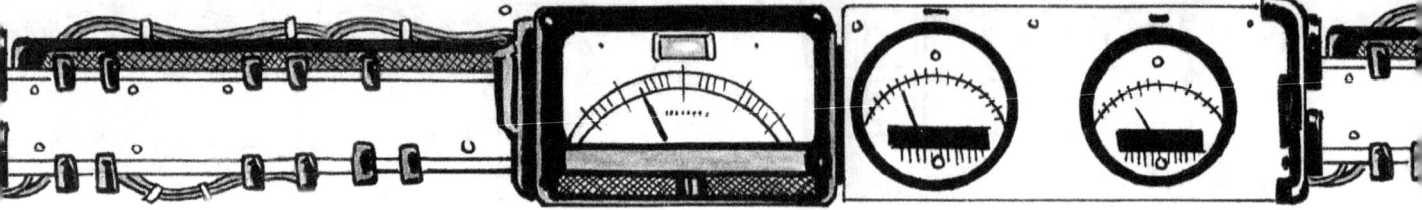

questions about his train, Locomotive No. 131. They discover that the next locomotive will pass through Hill Valley on Monday morning, September 7—the day on which Doc is fated to be murdered by Buford Tannen. As the duo prepares to hijack the train and escape to 1985, they spot a young woman on a runaway buckboard, headed for Shonash Ravine. Doc performs a daring rescue, saving her life, and discovers that the woman is Clara Clayton.

Doc falls instantly in love with her—and Clara does likewise. The scientist collects her thrown luggage, and he and Marty escort her to her new home at the schoolhouse. Doc grows hopelessly infatuated with the woman, as he and Clara realize they have a mutual passion for science. When Marty recalls that the gulch was called Clayton Ravine in his own era, Doc realizes that Clara was meant to die, and that by intervening he has seriously altered the timeline. Marty suggests the consequences couldn't be that dire, but Doc now understands that the ability to time-travel is too dangerous—and too painful [BTF3].

Saturday, September 5, 1885 A.D.

• While cementing details for their trip back to 1985, Emmett Brown and Marty McFly are interrupted when Clara Clayton visits Doc's blacksmith shop. She says her telescope was damaged in the buckboard incident, and asks if he'd be able to fix it. The scientist quickly agrees, volunteering to forgo attending that night's Hill Valley Festival. Clara doesn't want him to miss the celebration however—and, in fact, hopes to see him there. Doc assures her he will be [BTF3].

Saturday, September 5, 1885 A.D.—8:00 to 8:01 PM

• Courthouse Square's Clock Tower counts its very first minute, to much public fanfare [BTF3].

Saturday, September 5, 1885 A.D.—8:09 PM

• In one possible timeline, festivities at the Clock Dedication celebration are halted when Buford "Mad Dog" Tannen shoots Emmett Brown in the back. Brown dies three days later and is laid to rest on September 8 by his beloved Clara Clayton [BTF3, BFCG].

• In another reality, as the townspeople celebrate the christening of the brand-new Clock Tower at the Hill Valley Festival, the festivities are interrupted when Buford Tannen crashes the party and confronts Doc regarding the eighty dollars he feels owed. Mad Dog makes unwanted advances on Clara but Doc defends her honor, and is saved an early meeting with Tannen's hidden pistol thanks to Marty's quick thinking with a thrown pie plate.

Outraged, Tannen challenges the youth to a confrontation in the streets at 8:00 Monday morning [BTF3]. Salesman Elmer H. Johnson, manning a kiosk selling Colt Peacemaker revolvers, offers Marty a free firearm for the impending duel, hoping for bragging rights if Marty somehow wins [BTF3-sp]. While Marty considers the possibility that he will die in two days, Doc Brown escorts Clara home, where they watch the stars and discuss their mutual love of Jules Verne. The two share a kiss, their romance blossoming [BTF3].

Sunday, September 6, 1885 A.D.

• Hill Valley's citizens hail Marty McFly as a hero for standing up to Buford Tannen and agreeing to the showdown. At first, Marty lets the praise go to his head, but Emmett Brown points out the photo that Marty brought with him from 1955, of a tombstone with Doc's name on it. The scientist's name is now gone, but the tombstone and date remain. It's possible, he says, that while his life has been spared, it may now be Marty who will die on September 7.

Despite Marty's fear of dying, he pridefully refuses

CODE	STORY						
ARGN	BTTF-themed TV commercial: Arrigoni	BTF1	Film: Back to the Future	CITY	BTTF-themed music video: Owl City, "Deer in the Headlights"	HUEY	BTTF-themed music video: Huey Lewis and the News, "The Power of Love"
BFAN	Back to the Future: The Animated Series	BTF2	Film: Back to the Future Part II	DCTV	BTTF-themed TV commercial: DirecTV	LIMO	BTTF-themed music video: The Limousines, "The Future"
BFCG	Back to the Future: The Card Game	BTF3	Film: Back to the Future Part III	ERTH	The Earth Day Special		
BFCL	Back to the Future comic book (limited series)	BUDL	BTTF-themed TV commercial: Bud Light	GALE	Interviews and commentaries: Bob Gale and/or Robert Zemeckis	MCDN	BTTF-themed TV commercial: McDonald's
BFCM	Back to the Future comic book (monthly series)	CHEK	BTTF-themed music video: O'Neal McKnight, "Check Your Coat"	GARB	BTTF-themed TV commercials: Garbarino	MITS	BTTF-themed TV commercial: Mitsubishi Lancer
BFHM	BTTF-themed McDonald's Happy Meal boxes	CHIC	Photographs hanging in Doc Brown's Chicken restaurant at Universal Studios	GETV	BTTF-themed TV commercial: GE	MSFT	BTTF-themed TV commercial: Microsoft
BTFA	Back to the Future Annual (Marvel Comics)						

to back down from the shootout. Doc tries to reason with his friend, letting slip that Marty's temper will lead to an accident in his future that will have far-reaching effects. Marty presses the matter, but Doc decides he has said too much already, and instead encourages Marty to follow his heart—just as he must do.

That night, as the duo place the DeLorean on the railroad tracks in preparation for the next day's train heist, Doc admits he's in love with Clara and wants to stay in 1885 with her. Marty protests that it could still be Doc's name on the tombstone, but the scientist no longer cares, wishing only to be with Clara. But in the end, Marty convinces him to do the *logical* thing. Doc concedes, vowing to dismantle the DeLorean once they return home. Time travel, he says, has brought him nothing but heartache.

Marty sleeps while Doc visits Clara. Although determined to leave, Doc professes his love for her, revealing the truth about who he is. Clara, however, angrily slaps him, believing he is manipulating her feelings by exploiting her interest in Jules Verne. A distraught Brown enters the Palace Saloon, prepared to drink his woes away. There, a traveling barbed wire salesman attempts to cheer Brown up, encouraging him that there are other women to pursue, but Doc is certain he'll never find anyone as special as Clara [BTF3].

Monday, September 7, 1885 A.D.

• Marty McFly awakens at their railroad-side camp to discover that Doc is gone. Frantic, he rides to Hill Valley to find his friend, aware that hijacking the soon-to-depart train is their only chance of pushing the DeLorean up to 88 miles per hour, returning to the future and avoiding the duel with Mad Dog Tannen. Marty finds Doc holed up in the Palace Saloon, where the wild-eyed inventor has been nursing a broken heart following his emotional break-up with Clara.

Marty implores Doc to leave the Old West behind and return with him to 1985. Doc steels himself to

continue with their course of action, toasting his barroom companions with a shot of whiskey. Unfortunately, Doc's tolerance for alcohol is remarkably low, and he immediately passes out [BTF3].

• While Marty, Chester the bartender, and an employee named Joey mix up some "wake-up juice" to bring Doc back to his senses, Buford Tannen and his gang ride toward Hill Valley for the scheduled shootout, but are intercepted by James Strickland. The marshal and his young son train shotguns on the outlaws, warning Tannen to turn back. Buford shoots Strickland's weapon out of his hand and threatens to gun him down in front of his son unless he moves out of the way.

Fearing for his son's life, Strickland orders a retreat. But the cowardly Tannen shoots the marshal in the back anyway, mortally wounding him. Tannen and his gang ride on to Hill Valley as the law-enforcement officer dies in his son's arms. His last charge to the boy is to remember one word: discipline. The youth vows to remember that word, and to pass it on to future Strickland generations [BTF3-d, TLTL].

> *NOTE: This child's name was not revealed in the film, but James' grandchildren (Robert, Gerald and Edna) had a father named Roger, according to Telltale Games' video game. This would strongly indicate that was the boy's name, since the marshal was not shown to have any other children.*

Monday, September 7, 1885 A.D.—Approximately 8:00 AM

• Buford Tannen arrives at the Palace Saloon, ready to kill Marty. Marty struggles to wake up Doc, intending to slip out the back unnoticed by the outlaws. Tannen calls Marty's manhood into question, raising the teenager's ire, and those within the saloon goad the boy into a fight. Marty is faced with the familiar temptation to give into his anger and do something foolish, but instead ignores

CLINT EASTWOOD OFFERS BUFORD TANNEN A FISTFUL OF DOLLARS

CODE	STORY							
ARGN	BTTF-themed TV commercial: Arrigoni	BTF1	Film: *Back to the Future*	CITY	BTTF-themed music video: Owl City, "Deer in the Headlights"	HUEY	BTTF-themed music video: Huey Lewis and the News, "The Power of Love"
BFAN	*Back to the Future: The Animated Series*	BTF2	Film: *Back to the Future Part II*	DCTV	BTTF-themed TV commercial: DirecTV	LIMO	BTTF-themed music video: The Limousines, "The Future"
BFCG	*Back to the Future: The Card Game*	BTF3	Film: *Back to the Future Part III*	ERTH	*The Earth Day Special*		
BFCL	*Back to the Future* comic book (limited series)	BUDL	BTTF-themed TV commercial: Bud Light	GALE	Interviews and commentaries: Bob Gale and/or Robert Zemeckis	MCDN	BTTF-themed TV commercial: McDonald's
BFCM	*Back to the Future* comic book (monthly series)	CHEK	BTTF-themed music video: O'Neal McKnight, "Check Your Coat"	GARB	BTTF-themed TV commercials: Garbarino	MITS	BTTF-themed TV commercial: Mitsubishi Lancer
BFHM	BTTF-themed McDonald's Happy Meal boxes	CHIC	Photographs hanging in Doc Brown's Chicken restaurant at Universal Studios	GETV	BTTF-themed TV commercial: GE	MSFT	BTTF-themed TV commercial: Microsoft
BTFA	*Back to the Future Annual* (Marvel Comics)						

Tannen's taunts, no longer caring what names others call him. At that moment, Doc awakens, and the two sneak out the back.

Tannen's gang spots them, however, and a shootout ensues. Doc is captured in the scuffle and held hostage as Tannen insists Marty face him like a man. Marty obliges, and Tannen shoots him in a quick draw. Onlookers are stunned by the youth's tragic end—and are doubly surprised to discover he was wearing a 19th-century "bulletproof vest" fashioned from a furnace door—a trick learned from Clint Eastwood's *A Fistful of Dollars*. Marty removes the slab of metal and bashes Tannen in the face, knocking the villain face-first into an A. Jones Manure Hauling cart, and leaving him easy pickings for arriving deputies [BTF3].

- A young child named D.W. Griffith asks Marty where he learned such a trick, and he tells the boy that he saw it in a movie. Amazed, young Griffith gains inspiration to one day become a filmmaker [BTF3-n].
  NOTE: David Llewelyn Wark "D. W." Griffith, born in 1875, was a pioneering film director of the early 20th century.

Monday, September 7, 1885 A.D.—8:16 AM

- In one possible timeline, Mad Dog Tannen succeeds in killing Emmett Brown, after which Marshal Strickland's deputy arrests the outlaw for the crime [BFCG].

- In another reality, Tannen is arrested for the robbery of the Pine City Stage and the murder of Marshal James Strickland [BFCG, TLTL-1].

- Emmett Brown and Marty McFly rush to meet the train and begin their journey back to the future. Meanwhile, a brokenhearted Clara Clayton boards a train herself, intending to leave Hill Valley behind. Inside, she overhears a salesman discussing Doc Brown's lamenting for her and decides to return to him. She leaves the train and races back to Doc's blacksmith shop, but finds it empty. Upon

NIKE	BTTF-themed TV commercial: Nike	SCRT	2010 Scream Awards: *Back to the Future* 25th Anniversary Reunion (trailer)	**SUFFIX**	**MEDIUM**	
NTND	Nintendo *Back to the Future—The Ride* Mini-Game	SIMP	Simulator: *The Simpsons Ride*	-b	*BTF2*'s Biff Tannen Museum video (extended version)	-s1 Screenplay (draft one)
PIZA	BTTF-themed TV commercial: Pizza Hut	SLOT	*Back to the Future* Video Slots	-c	Animated series credit sequence	-s2 Screenplay (draft two)
REAL	Real life	TEST	Screen tests: Crispin Glover, Lea Thompson and Thomas F. Wilson	-d	Film deleted scene	-s3 Screenplay (draft three)
RIDE	Simulator: *Back to the Future—The Ride*	TLTL	Telltale Games' *Back to the Future—The Game*	-n	Film novelization	-s4 Screenplay (draft four)
SCRM	2010 Scream Awards: *Back to the Future* 25th Anniversary Reunion (broadcast)	UNIV	Universal Studios Hollywood promotional video	-o	Film outtake	-sp Screenplay (production draft)
				-v	Video game print materials or commentaries	-sx Screenplay (*Paradox*)

seeing a miniature layout of the train heist, containing a futuristic vehicle marked "time machine," Clara realizes Emmett was telling the truth about his temporal origins, and rides horseback to intercept the train.

Doc and Marty successfully—and peaceably— "borrow" the locomotive and get it in place to push the DeLorean up to 88 miles per hour. Marty mans the train's controls, while Doc uses special fuel to make the

CODE	STORY							
ARGN	BTTF-themed TV commercial: Arrigoni	BTF1	Film: *Back to the Future*	CITY	BTTF-themed music video: Owl City, "Deer in the Headlights"	HUEY	BTTF-themed music video: Huey Lewis and the News, "The Power of Love"
BFAN	*Back to the Future: The Animated Series*	BTF2	Film: *Back to the Future Part II*				
BFCG	*Back to the Future: The Card Game*	BTF3	Film: *Back to the Future Part III*	DCTV	BTTF-themed TV commercial: DirecTV	LIMO	BTTF-themed music video: The Limousines, "The Future"
BFCL	*Back to the Future comic book (limited series)*	BUDL	BTTF-themed TV commercial: Bud Light	ERTH	*The Earth Day Special*		
		CHEK	BTTF-themed music video: O'Neal McKnight, "Check Your Coat"	GALE	Interviews and commentaries: Bob Gale and/or Robert Zemeckis	MCDN	BTTF-themed TV commercial: McDonald's
BFCM	*Back to the Future comic book (monthly series)*					MITS	BTTF-themed TV commercial: Mitsubishi Lancer
BFHM	BTTF-themed McDonald's Happy Meal boxes	CHIC	Photographs hanging in Doc Brown's Chicken restaurant at Universal Studios	GARB	BTTF-themed TV commercials: Garbarino		
BTFA	*Back to the Future Annual (Marvel Comics)*			GETV	BTTF-themed TV commercial: GE	MSFT	BTTF-themed TV commercial: Microsoft

on board. The scientist urges her to climb out and travel with him to the future, but as the engine overheats and explodes from the released energy, Clara is thrown from the train and nearly dies, spared from death only by Doc rescuing her with Marty's hoverboard. The teen watches helplessly as Doc rides away from the train with Clara in his arms. Finally, the DeLorean reaches 88 miles per hour and vanishes over Shonash Ravine, leaving the couple behind in the Old West [BTF3].

Tuesday, September 8, 1885 A.D.—2:00 PM

- In one possible timeline, Hill Valley holds a funeral for schoolteacher Clara Clayton, who—with no one to save her when her horses were spooked by a snake—plummeted into the Shonash Ravine [BFCG].

- In another reality, Hill Valley holds a funeral for Emmett Brown, shot three days prior by Buford Tannen at the christening of the new Clock Tower [BFCG].

Tuesday, September 15, 1885 A.D.—2:00 PM

- Hill Valley celebrates the wedding of Emmett Brown and Clara Clayton [BFCG].
    *NOTE: The ninth episode of the **BTTF** animated series cited their wedding date as December 15 of an unspecified year. The card game, however, placed their nuptials on September 15, 1885.*

Tuesday, December 1, 1885 A.D.—12:00 PM

- The Hill Valley Town Council renames Shonash Ravine "Clayton Ravine" in one timeline, following the tragic death of Clara Clayton [BFCG].

- In another reality, the council renames it "Eastwood Ravine," following the train wreck thought to have taken the life of Clint Eastwood (Marty McFly's alias in this era) [BFCG].

train's fire especially hot. With the train in place and its speed rising on cue, Doc climbs along the iron to reach the DeLorean—only to find that Clara has stowed away

"PEE WEE" MCFLY PITCHES A WINNING GAME FOR THE BEANEATERS

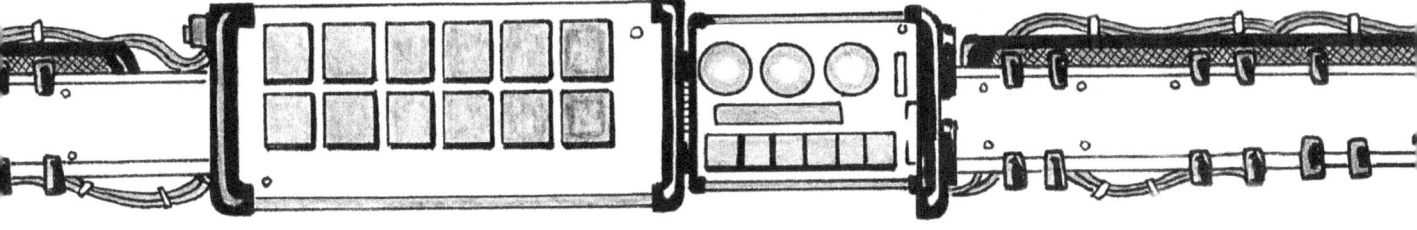

CHAPTER V:
1886 A.D. TO 1930 A.D.

Sometime After 1885 A.D.

- Seamus McFly teaches his son, William, that there is no sense in getting riled up about things over which one has no control—advice that Willie takes to heart [TLTL-5].

- Seamus and Maggie McFly have a second son [BTF3].
    NOTE: In an aged photograph seen briefly in BTF3, William, his wife and their three children posed behind a seated Seamus and Maggie. To their left stood another man; since he appeared younger than William but was too old to be his son, it seems likely that this individual was Willie's brother. His name remains unknown.

- Doc builds a flying, time-traveling train modeled after the engine car of a late 19th-century locomotive, which he names the *Jules Verne Train*, after his sons Jules and Verne, as well as author Jules Verne. The front of the locomotive resembles Captain Nemo's submarine *Nautilus*, featured in Verne's novels *Twenty Thousand Leagues Under the Sea* and *The Mysterious Island* [BTF3].

1886 A.D.

- Construction of the Shonash Ravine Bridge is scheduled to be completed during the summer of this year [BTF3].

1886 or 1887 A.D.

- Jules Eratosthenes Brown is born to Emmett and Clara Brown [BTF3].

Sometime in or Before 1888 A.D.

- While living in the Old West with Clara, Emmett Brown invents a contraption called the Auto-Infant Cleanser, to automatically bathe their infant son, Jules. He also builds steam-powered snowshoes. The shoes are not entirely

effective, however, as the steam sometimes condenses, causing an ice storm around a wearer's ankles [BFAN-21].

1888 A.D.

- Windjammer Diefendorfer, a kindly old veterinarian, helps a number of animals in need. These include Benny, a wild bald eagle, whom he gives a toupée; Buck, a wild beaver, whom he fits with braces; Dave, a wild horned deer, from whose horns he removes several hats; Ellie-Mae, a fearful wild bear; and Robert, a wild rattlesnake, whom he sometimes bathes [BFAN-21].

- "Jumpin'" Jehoshaphat, a beloved uncle of Clara Clayton, makes a name for himself working at county fairs, jumping from hot-air balloons into buckets of water [BFAN-21].
    NOTE: "Jumpin' Jehoshaphat" was a common expostulation of Jon Pertwee's incarnation as the Doctor on BBC's Doctor Who.

Monday, October 29, 1888 A.D.

- Vernon "Verne" Newton Brown is born to Emmett and Clara Brown. On the day of his birth, an older Verne travels back from the year 1992 with Marty McFly, hoping to convince his parents to name him something else, and thereby spare him the future taunting of school bullies. While Marty hides the DeLorean, Verne visits his parents' cabin. His older brother Jules—still a baby at this time—takes to him, and the Browns welcome Verne into their home.
    Clara is expecting Verne's imminent birth, but she and Doc are still uncertain what to name the child. If the baby is female, they have decided to name her "Florence," after Florence Nightingale. Regarding male names, Clara is partial to "Jehoshaphat," named after her uncle, carnival stunt man "Jumpin'" Jehoshaphat, while Doc prefers "Galileo," after Italian physicist and astronomer Galileo Galilei. Verne offers his own suggestions, including

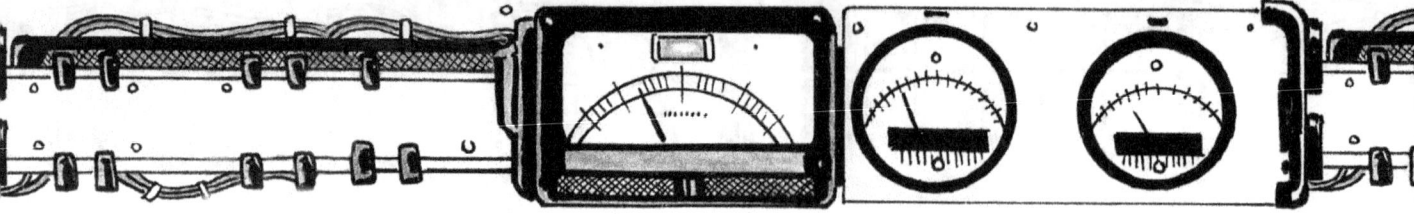

"James Bond," but to no avail. When the couple enters a heated argument over the name, Doc leaves to cool off in the late autumn snow.

While he's away, Clara goes into labor, and it falls to Verne to race into town for a doctor to assist in his own birth. Verne trudges through the thick snow, finding his father along the way. Doc's excitement at the news inadvertently triggers a snowslide. The two are caught in the avalanche, which usurps a neighboring cabin: the home of Windjammer "Windy" Diefendorfer, the town's diminutive physician and veterinarian.

With the doctor in tow, Doc and Verne race back to Clara's bedside, where Diefendorfer delivers the baby. Impressed by the doctor's skill—if not his silly name—Verne begins to understand that the name does not make the man. Clara announces that she plans to name their new son Verne, after the brave boy who helped them during their time of need. As Verne and Marty travel back to their own era, Verne is finally at peace with his chosen name [BFAN-21].

> *NOTE: The sixth episode of the animated series suggested that Verne was born in 1889, but episode 21 established his birth as occurring in October 1888.*

1889 A.D.

• The Eiffel Tower is erected in Paris, France, as the entrance arch to the 1889 Exposition Universelle, or World's Fair [REAL]. Emmett and Clara Brown later vacation at this historic landmark [BFAN-21]

Late 1880s to Early 1990s A.D.

• A dedicated scholar from a young age, Jules Brown often seeks to increase his knowledge, finding complex science and mathematics more fun than the video games and childhood diversions enjoyed by his brother Verne. At age two, Jules draws a DNA molecule on his Etch A Sketch toy. His intelligence intimidates Verne, who

is far less into studying [BFAN-1].

> *NOTE: As seen in BTF3, Jules and Brown relocated to the 20th century when the boys were already elementary-school age. As such, it seems extremely improbable that the boys could have had an Etch A Sketch or video games while living in the Old West. Time travel may have been a factor in their acquisition of such items.*

1891 A.D.

• The Hill Valley Police Station is established [TLTL-1].

1892 A.D.

• The Hill Valley Hotel is established. This small, one-floor hotel features a wooden porch and a pair of swinging doors at its entrance. During a trip back to that era, Emmett Brown notices several oddities about the building, including an upside-down clock hanging on its porch [BFHM].

• An infant named Rebecca Anne dies at the age of five months and is buried at the Boot Hill Cemetery, near the entrance of the abandoned Delgado Mine [BTF3].

> *NOTE: Rebecca Anne's surname was not included on her gravestone.*

1895 A.D.

• Emmett Brown, still living in the Old West with Clara, visits the Hill Valley Patent Office to obtain a patent for his latest invention: a steam-powered locomotive, capable of space and time travel. He is laughed out of the office [BFAN-25].

Wednesday, February 6, 1895 A.D.

• Future baseball player George Herman "Babe" Ruth Jr. is born in Baltimore, Maryland [REAL]. Emmett Brown

CODE	STORY
ARGN	BTTF-themed TV commercial: Arrigoni
BFAN	Back to the Future: The Animated Series
BFCG	Back to the Future: The Card Game
BFCL	Back to the Future comic book (limited series)
BFCM	Back to the Future comic book (monthly series)
BFHM	BTTF-themed McDonald's Happy Meal boxes
BTFA	Back to the Future Annual (Marvel Comics)

BTF1	Film: Back to the Future
BTF2	Film: Back to the Future Part II
BTF3	Film: Back to the Future Part III
BUDL	BTTF-themed TV commercial: Bud Light
CHEK	BTTF-themed music video: O'Neal McKnight, "Check Your Coat"
CHIC	Photographs hanging in Doc Brown's Chicken restaurant at Universal Studios

CITY	BTTF-themed music video: Owl City, "Deer in the Headlights"
DCTV	BTTF-themed TV commercial: DirecTV
ERTH	The Earth Day Special
GALE	Interviews and commentaries: Bob Gale and/or Robert Zemeckis
GARB	BTTF-themed TV commercials: Garbarino
GETV	BTTF-themed TV commercial: GE

HUEY	BTTF-themed music video: Huey Lewis and the News, "The Power of Love"
LIMO	BTTF-themed music video: The Limousines, "The Future"
MCDN	BTTF-themed TV commercial: McDonald's
MITS	BTTF-themed TV commercial: Mitsubishi Lancer
MSFT	BTTF-themed TV commercial: Microsoft

will later credit him as being "the greatest baseball player who ever lived," though erroneously citing his birth date as February 7 [BFAN-1].

Wednesday, September 1, 1897 A.D.

• Marty McFly arrives in Emmett Brown's DeLorean, accompanied by Jules and Verne Brown, to assist Boston Beaneaters pitcher Pee Wee McFly—Marty's fifth cousin, thrice removed—in winning the most important baseball game of his life. The time-travelers arrive one day before a humiliating defeat that will cause Pee Wee to retire from baseball. Marty hopes to convince his predecessor to remain in the game and salvage the McFly family name.

During the game between the Beaneaters and the Baltimore Orioles, Marty excitedly calls out to his cousin, distracting Pee Wee as a line drive beans him in the head. The pitcher is knocked out cold, leaving the Beaneaters in danger of losing the game, and thereby throwing history off-course. Marty, who bears a striking resemblance to his cousin, disguises himself as Pee Wee and—equipped with an experimental exo-skeleton enabling its user to become a perfect baseball player—takes the diamond. With the help of bionic modifications created by Doc Brown, Marty wins the game and Pee Wee is hailed a hero.

Once the real Pee Wee recovers, he is upset to learn that the Beaneaters have won the game. Marty soon discovers that in the original timeline, his cousin threw the game to appease local criminal Diamond Jim Tannen. Now that Pee Wee has won, he has earned Diamond Jim's retribution [BFAN-8].

> *NOTE: In reality, the Boston Beaneaters played the Chicago Colts on that date, beating them seven to four. The team won the National League Pennant that year, but lost the Temple Cup series to the Orioles.*

Thursday, September 2, 1897 A.D.

• In one possible timeline, Pee Wee McFly retires from baseball after striking out during a crucial third playoff game that costs his team the National League Pennant [BFAN-8].

• After Marty McFly changes history by posing as Pee Wee McFly and helping the Beaneaters defeat the Orioles, the real Pee Wee leaves town for fear of retribution from Diamond Jim Tannen. Determined to defend the McFly family name, Marty poses as Pee Wee once more and uses the bionic exo-skeleton to assist him in winning the big game. As the Beaneaters' score stacks up, however, an outraged Diamond Jim rushes the field and attacks Marty. The exo-skeleton breaks during the scuffle, and he loses his edge. With a malfunctioning suit, Marty plays worse than before and is in danger of losing the game.

Pee Wee, meanwhile, heads to the docks, seeking passage out of town, where he spots a group of neighborhood youths playing baseball, pretending to be the Beaneaters. He realizes these children idolize him, and is disheartened when a dockhand informs the children that Pee Wee is, in fact, a cheat and a coward owned by Diamond Jim Tannen. Upon seeing the children's faith falter, Pee Wee determines to win back his good name. He tells the kids that he doesn't work for Tannen anymore, and races back to the diamond to win the game.

Just as Marty is about to lose to the Orioles, Pee Wee arrives and plays the best game of his life. Diamond Jim is arrested for his earlier altercation, and discovers that his girlfriend, Vera Muldoon, is actually a police officer who has been collecting evidence against him to cripple his organization. Pee Wee McFly goes on to be named the hero of the 1897 Championship Series [BFAN-8].

NIKE	*BTTF*-themed TV commercial: Nike	**SCRT**	2010 Scream Awards: *Back to the Future*	**SUFFIX**	**MEDIUM**	**-s1**	Screenplay (draft one)
NTND	Nintendo *Back to the Future—The Ride*		25th Anniversary Reunion (trailer)	**-b**	*BTF2's* Biff Tannen Museum video	**-s2**	Screenplay (draft two)
	Mini-Game	**SIMP**	Simulator: *The Simpsons Ride*		(extended version)	**-s3**	Screenplay (draft three)
PIZA	*BTTF*-themed TV commercial: Pizza Hut	**SLOT**	*Back to the Future* Video Slots	**-c**	Animated series credit sequence	**-s4**	Screenplay (draft four)
REAL	Real life	**TEST**	Screen tests: Crispin Glover, Lea Thompson	**-d**	Film deleted scene	**-sp**	Screenplay (production draft)
RIDE	Simulator: *Back to the Future—The Ride*		and Thomas F. Wilson	**-n**	Film novelization	**-sx**	Screenplay (*Paradox*)
SCRM	2010 Scream Awards: *Back to the Future*	**TLTL**	Telltale Games' *Back to the Future—The Game*	**-o**	Film outtake		
	25th Anniversary Reunion (broadcast)	**UNIV**	Universal Studios Hollywood promotional video	**-v**	Video game print materials or commentaries		

Back in Time: The Unauthorized Back to the Future Chronology

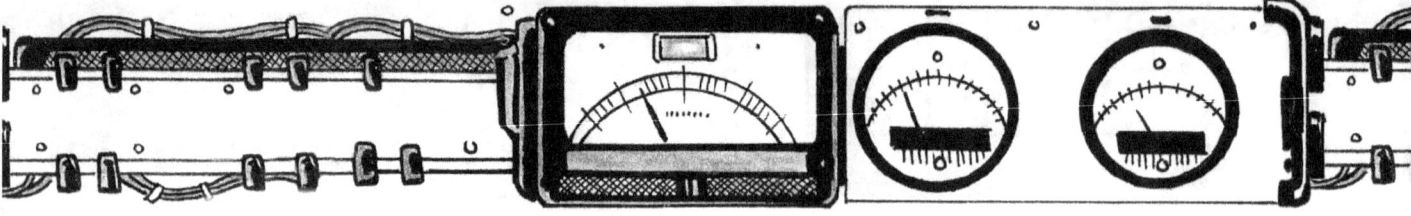

Circa Late 19th or Early 20th Century A.D.

- Frankie Needles, an ancestor of Douglas Needles, is born [TLTL-2].

    NOTE: Frankie was of driving age in 1931, placing his birth years prior.

1900 A.D.

- Arriving from the year 1990, Emmett Brown makes many trips across the globe to Asia, Africa and Europe, to study how the world was before man began to pollute it. His journey finally lands him in Los Angeles, California, and he is astounded to find it a small town surrounded by beautiful snow-capped mountains and bright blue sky. It is a Los Angeles free from smog and contamination, and the sight inspires Brown to return to his own time to inform others of what humanity has done to its planet and discuss ways of reversing the damage [ERTH].

Sometime Before 1902 A.D.

- William Sean McFly gets married while still in his teen years [BTF3].

    NOTE: William was an infant in 1885, as seen in BTF3. His son Arthur, according to BTF1's novelization, was born in 1902. That would indicate Willie was married and a father by age 17.

1902 A.D.

- Arthur "Artie" McFly is born [BTF1-n] to William Sean McFly and his wife [BTF3].

Early 1900s A.D.

- William Sean McFly and his wife have two additional children—both daughters [BTF3].

    NOTE: Arthur's two sisters were seen in a family

photo of William McFly's family in Back to the Future III. *The girls' names are unknown.*

Thursday, December 17, 1903 A.D.

- Orville and Wilbur Wright make their historic first successful powered airplane flight near Kitty Hawk, North Carolina [REAL]. Time-traveler Emmett Brown witnesses the momentous occasion during a tour across time, visiting key dates of significance and his own personal heroes [RIDE].

Sometime in or Before 1904 A.D.

- Sideshow barker P.T. Tannen and his assistant, Clyde, debut P.T. Tannen's Villains Through History in Wax at the 1904 St. Louis World Exposition. The museum exhibit contains wax likenesses of infamous historical persons, including Attila the Hun, Ivan the Terrible and Bob the Nasty (P.T.'s uncle, Bob Tannen). Unable to draw in visitors, P.T. starts paying passersby a nickel apiece to attend [BFAN-25].

Wednesday, June 29, 1904 A.D.

- Frustrated by the high prices and vomit-inducing rides of a 20th-century amusement park, Emmett and Clara Brown take the DeLorean back to simpler times, to visit the 1904 St. Louis World Exposition. There, they enjoy old-fashioned lemonade, the innocent Ferris Wheel and reasonable fees, and record themselves singing "Meet Me in St. Louis, Louis" on an old-style recording device.

    The Browns' romantic getaway is interrupted, however, when their sons, Jules and Verne, arrive in the time train with Marty McFly in tow. Marty explains that in an effort to get a free haircut for a date, he'd taken advantage of Doc's experimental Hair-O-Matic. The results were catastrophic, as Marty's hair now continually takes on outrageous hairstyles, each more ridiculous than the last.

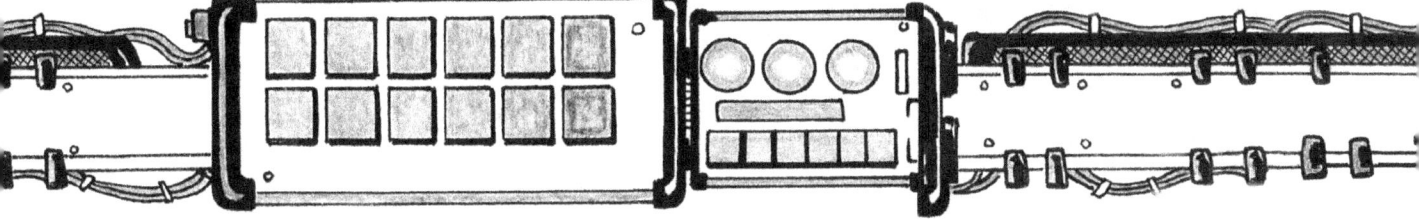

While in 1904, Marty runs afoul of P.T. Tannen, who operates a failing Villains Through History in Wax exhibit featuring horrible figures from the past. Tannen and his carnival barker, Clyde, see Marty and his freakishly changing hair as their ticket to success. They kidnap McFly and put him on display, charging folks a nickel to behold the horror of his perpetually bad hair day. The Browns form a complicated rescue plan to free Marty and, with Tannen still chasing his golden goose, the time travelers return to the future [BFAN-25].

1905 A.D.

• The Hill Valley Mercantile Deliveries company, William McFly's future employer, is established [TLTL-5].

• In a timeline in which Hill Valley is destroyed in its infancy by Edna Strickland, the Haysville Mercantile Deliveries firm is established twenty-five miles away [TLTL-5].

Circa Early 1900s A.D.

• William McFly obtains employment with Hill Valley Mercantile Deliveries [BTF3].
   NOTE: The identity of Willie's wife is unknown.

Wednesday, April 18, 1906 A.D.—5:12 AM

• Nearly two miles off the California coast, a massive earthquake erupts along the San Andreas fault, hitting San Francisco, and causing one of the worst natural disasters in United States history. An estimated three thousand people die in the earthquake and subsequent fires, in what is dubbed the greatest loss of life in California's history [REAL].

Sometime After Wednesday, April 18, 1906 A.D.

• Following the San Francisco earthquake, the Hill Valley Courthouse becomes a shelter for refugees. Many displaced San Franciscans remain in Hill Valley, forming a large portion of the town's population [TLTL-3].

1908 A.D.

• Erhardt von Braun travels to America against his father's wishes, unable to speak English and with only two dollars to his name [TLTL-5].

Circa Late 1900s or Early 1910s A.D.

• Edna Strickland is born to Roger and Irene Strickland, and grows up with an older brother, Robert, and a younger brother, Gerald. The family is widely considered Hill Valley's "first family during the gaslight era" [TLTL-v].
   NOTE: Emmett Brown (age 17 in 1931, placing his birth in 1914) noted that Edna was a few years older than him.

• As a child, Gerald Strickland enjoys wearing his mother's clothing, and is even photographed in one of her outfits [TLTL-1].

1910 A.D.

• Otis Peabody is born. Sam Baines is also born that year [BTF1-n].

Sometime Before 1914

• Erhardt Brown and Sarah Lathrop are married [TLTL-1].

NIKE	BTTF-themed TV commercial: Nike	**SCRT**	2010 Scream Awards: *Back to the Future* 25th Anniversary Reunion (trailer)	**SUFFIX**	**MEDIUM**		**-s1**	Screenplay (draft one)
NTND	Nintendo *Back to the Future—The Ride* Mini-Game	**SIMP**	Simulator: *The Simpsons Ride*	**-b**	BTF2's Biff Tannen Museum video (extended version)		**-s2**	Screenplay (draft two)
		SLOT	*Back to the Future* Video Slots				**-s3**	Screenplay (draft three)
PIZA	BTTF-themed TV commercial: Pizza Hut	**TEST**	Screen tests: Crispin Glover, Lea Thompson and Thomas F. Wilson	**-c**	Animated series credit sequence		**-s4**	Screenplay (draft four)
REAL	Real life			**-d**	Film deleted scene		**-sp**	Screenplay (production draft)
RIDE	Simulator: *Back to the Future—The Ride*	**TLTL**	Telltale Games' *Back to the Future—The Game*	**-n**	Film novelization		**-sx**	Screenplay (*Paradox*)
SCRM	2010 Scream Awards: *Back to the Future* 25th Anniversary Reunion (broadcast)	**UNIV**	Universal Studios Hollywood promotional video	**-o**	Film outtake			
				-v	Video game print materials or commentaries			

A SNAGGED FISHING LINE LEADS YOUNG EMMETT BROWN TO HOLLYWOOD

1914 A.D.

- Emmett Lathrop Brown is born to Erhardt and Sarah Lathrop Brown [TLTL-1].

    NOTE: This was one of two possible birthdates provided for Emmett in various sources, leading to age discrepancies throughout Doc's history. See also 1922. Temporal tampering may be to blame.

Sometime Between July 28, 1914 and November 11, 1918 A.D.

- Erhardt von Braun settles in Hill Valley and, during World War I, changes his family's surname to "Brown" [BTF3].

1915 A.D.

- Stella Baines is born [BTF1-n].

1916 A.D.

- Judge Erhardt Brown accepts a seat on the Hill Valley Criminal Court [TLTL-5].

1918 A.D.

- Sixteen-year-old Arthur McFly enlists in the U.S. Army, despite being underage, and is dispatched to France. When his age is discovered, he is promptly shipped home again before firing even a single shot [BTF1-n].

1920 A.D.

- Czechoslovakian writer Karel Čapek coins the term "robot" in his play *R.U.R. (Rossum's Universal Robots)* [REAL]. Seventy-two years later, Verne Brown will write a paper about this subject [BFCL-1].

Circa 1920s A.D.

- Sometime during this decade, Emmett Brown journeys back from the 1990s to meet one of his idols, inventor Thomas Alva Edison, who autographs a giant-sized light bulb for him [BFAN-11, RIDE].

1922 A.D.

- Emmett Lathrop Brown is born to Erhardt and Sarah Lathrop Brown [BFAN-11, BTF3-s1].

    NOTE: This was one of two possible birthdates provided for Emmett in various sources, leading to age discrepancies throughout Doc's history. See also 1914. Temporal tampering may be to blame.

1925 A.D.

- Eleven-year-old Emmett Brown discovers the writings of Jules Verne. After reading *Twenty Thousand Leagues Under the Sea*, the boy has an epiphany, knowing with certainty that he must devote his life to science [BTF3].

    NOTE: This entry's dating is based on the birth year given for Doc in Telltale Games' video games.

Sometime in or Before 1926 A.D.

- A child prodigy, Emmett Brown learns several languages, the elements of the periodic table, numerous constellations of the Northern Hemisphere and a large chunk of the encyclopedia while still quite young [BFAN-11].

- The stunt-heavy film *Aaaargh! My Leg!*, from Hollywood producer D.W. Tannen, is released [BFAN-11].

    NOTE: Given that the first feature-length motion picture with synchronized dialogue sequences was **The Jazz Singer,** *in 1927,* **Aaaargh! My Leg!** *was likely a silent film.*

1926 A.D.

- Twelve-year-old Emmett Brown spends weeks preparing an expedition into the Delgado Mine, adjacent to Boothill Cemetery, after indulging in Jules Verne's novel *Journey to the Center of the Earth*. Despite his enthusiasm, the imaginative child does not make it very far [BTF3].

    NOTE: This entry's dating is based on the birth year given for Doc in Telltale Games' video games.

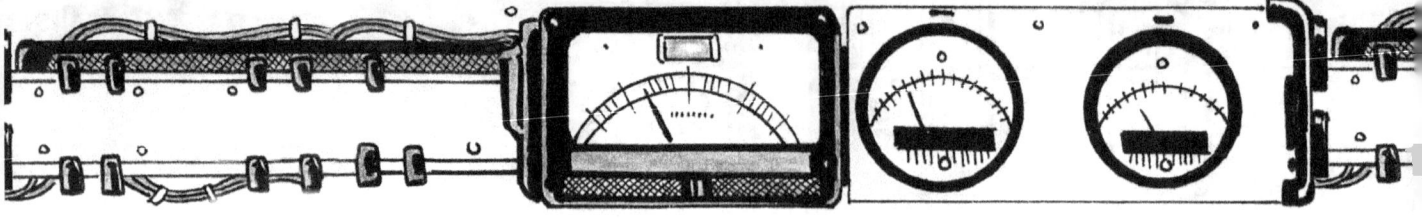

August 1926 A.D.

- Four-year-old Emmett Brown spends time living in Milwaukee, Wisconsin, under the care of his oddball Uncle Oliver [BFAN-11].

    NOTE: *The dating for this and the following entries is based on the birthdate given for Emmett in the animated series.*

Thursday, August 5, 1926 A.D.

- Four-year old Emmett Brown's Uncle Oliver promises to take the child fishing, but instead cancels their plans while attempting to earn the world record for flagpole-sitting. Disappointed, Emmett wanders off by himself and falls into a stream. This event leaves him traumatized and afraid of fishing throughout his adult life [BFAN-11].

- Jules and Verne Brown travel back to this date, along with Marty McFly, to prevent the fishing accident that will leave Doc emotionally scarred. They take young Emmett fishing in the stream, and the accident never occurs. However, events take an unexpected turn when Emmett rears back to cast his fishing line, snagging his hook on a low-flying stunt plane performing aerial tricks nearby for Roris von Hinklehofen's Flying Circus. Emmett is whisked away, the pilot unaware that he has picked up a passenger. The child manages to hold on, and the amazing sight is caught on film by the circus' resident cameraman. Emmett is dubbed "Daredevil Brown," and a Hollywood career is born [BFAN-11].

Sometime After August 5, 1926 A.D.

- Uncle Oliver, seeing his nephew's penchant for surviving dangerous situations, cashes in on the boy's success by naming himself as Emmett's manager. Together, the two set off for Hollywood to make motion pictures. The child star takes the country by storm.

    Daredevil Brown, a newspaper comic strip featuring Emmett's fictional exploits, begins publication, while numerous products bearing his name also debut, including soda, nuts, soup and more. Recording label ELB Records releases the song "Doin' the Daredevil Brown," and the *Hollywood Gazette* newspaper publishes an article about the stunt actor's adventures. Eventually, Emmett's fame catches the attention of director D.W. Tannen, who is filming his latest sensationalist epic, *Raging Death Doom*, at the time. D.W. hires Daredevil Brown to go over the edge of a waterfall in a barrel for a key scene in that film.

    Marty and the Brown brothers enjoy living in the lap of luxury offered by young Emmett's success, but realize the boy might not survive this stunt—which would result in a grave paradox. At the main event, Marty dons a costume and the name "Courageous Clyde," and performs a tightrope walk while Jules swaps out Emmett for Verne in a Daredevil Brown disguise. The plan: to have Verne go over in the barrel but activate a handheld Flux Capacitor, enabling him to time-jump out of harm's way.

    The stunt goes as planned, with Oliver believing that a stand-in dummy will be used in Emmett's place. Upon learning that Tannen intends to have the boy remain inside the barrel, however, Oliver is appalled that the director would jeopardize a child's life for profit, and realizes his own mistakes in exploiting his young nephew. Unaware that Emmett is no longer in the barrel, Uncle Oliver dives into the waterfall to rescue him, and is himself saved by Marty.

    The barrel plummets over the edge, reaching 88 miles per hour and vanishing in a brilliant light show. The crowd is amazed, doubly so when little Emmett races out of the stands, unharmed. Uncle Oliver embraces the boy and, when an impressed D.W. offers another contract to make Daredevil Brown more famous than Harry Houdini, Oliver tears up the document, concerned only for his nephew's safety. Leaving Hollywood behind, Oliver and Emmett return to Milwaukee and begin a longstanding tradition of fishing together [BFAN-11].

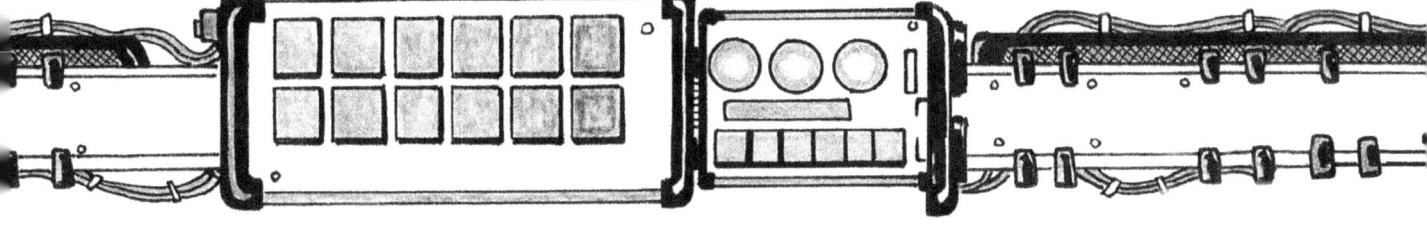

Sometime in or Before 1927 A.D.

- The book *Lurid Crime Stories* is published [BFCM-1].
  NOTE: The book's title was seemingly printed on the back cover, rather than the front (a common error in animation).

- Numerous criminals scrawl their name on a cell wall while incarcerated at a jail on Chicago's South Side, including Ernie Caesar, Capone, Frank Nitti and S.J. [BFCM-1].

- The U.S. government issues Wanted posters for criminals named Robert "Robbin" Zemeckis, "Big Bob" Gale and Nelson "Fatty" Dewey [BFCM-1].
  NOTE: Zemeckis and Gale were named after **Back to the Future**'s *co-creators, while Dewey was the writer of Harvey Comics'* **BTTF** *comic books.*

Sometime Before Tuesday, January 18, 1927 A.D.

- Don "Spacey" Tracy campaigns for election as the city dog catcher of Chicago, Illinois [BFCM-1].

Tuesday, January 18, 1927 A.D.

- Emmett Brown and Marty McFly visit Chicago, Illinois, to find a distillery to brew a juniper berry medicine to cure Doc's dog, Einstein, of a condition known as "cat-aracts." Marty foolishly asks a beat cop where he can find the nearest gin joint, landing himself in jail. Doc tries to post Marty's bail with coins minted in 1985, and ends up joining his friend behind bars.

  In their cell, the two time travelers meet Mugsy Tannen and his oversized enforcer, "Battleship" Potempkin. Mugsy confuses Marty with "Bathtub Jim" McFly, a brewmaster working for their crime boss, Arnie "Eggs" Benedict. Mugsy prepares to pound Marty, but Doc hastily intervenes, claiming Marty is Jim's distant cousin, "Zipper" McFly [BFCM-1].
  NOTE: The actual battleship's name was spelled "Potemkin," sans the second "p."

Wednesday, January 19, 1927 A.D.

- After an overnight stay in the city jail, Mugsy Tannen introduces Marty and Doc to Arnie "Eggs" Benedict. The gangster boss invites the duo back to his speakeasy, and the time travelers accept, posing as "Zipper" McFly and his brewmaster, "Doc" Brown. Benedict admits he doesn't usually take to outsiders, but considers them family since Zipper's "cousin," Jim "Bathtub" McFly, is on his payroll. He offers Marty and Doc a place in his gang, with the proviso that they provide protection against a new mob moving in on Benedict's territory. They accept, and Mugsy ushers them downstairs to see Jim and the distillery.

  While Doc investigates the still to make sure it can produce the juniper berry cure for Einstein's "cat-aracts," Marty learns about his distant relative. Though a member of Benedict's gang, Jim McFly has a wife and baby, and thus longs to pursue a normal—legal—life as a pharmacist. His fear of Benedict, however, keeps him from standing up for himself and putting aside the criminal lifestyle.

  Jim, Marty and Doc join Benedict and Mugsy in the speakeasy for drinks. Doc, unable to hold his liquor, passes out at the worst possible time. A gunman wielding a Tommy gun kicks down the gin joint's door, delivering a message from a rival boss by spraying the place with lead. No one is injured, but the speakeasy is destroyed. Benedict tells Marty that this is exactly why he needs Zipper's protection. Meanwhile, the brush with death is enough to convince Jim that he must leave this dangerous life behind. He pleads to be released from his employment, but Mugsy says he's in for life.

  Later that night, Jim finds Marty and Doc (now recovered) at their hotel room. He asks Zipper to talk to Benedict on his behalf, to help him leave the brewery business. Jim then helps Doc adjust the distillery to

NIKE	BTTF-themed TV commercial: Nike	**SCRT**	2010 Scream Awards: Back to the Future	**SUFFIX**	**MEDIUM**	**-s1**	Screenplay (draft one)
NTND	Nintendo Back to the Future—The Ride Mini-Game		25th Anniversary Reunion (trailer)	**-b**	BTF2's Biff Tannen Museum video (extended version)	**-s2**	Screenplay (draft two)
		SIMP	Simulator: The Simpsons Ride			**-s3**	Screenplay (draft three)
PIZA	BTTF-themed TV commercial: Pizza Hut	**SLOT**	Back to the Future Video Slots	**-c**	Animated series credit sequence	**-s4**	Screenplay (draft four)
REAL	Real life	**TEST**	Screen tests: Crispin Glover, Lea Thompson	**-d**	Film deleted scene	**-sp**	Screenplay (production draft)
RIDE	Simulator: Back to the Future—The Ride		and Thomas F. Wilson	**-n**	Film novelization	**-sx**	Screenplay (Paradox)
SCRM	2010 Scream Awards: Back to the Future 25th Anniversary Reunion (broadcast)	**TLTL**	Telltale Games' Back to the Future—The Game	**-o**	Film outtake		
		UNIV	Universal Studios Hollywood promotional video	**-v**	Video game print materials or commentaries		

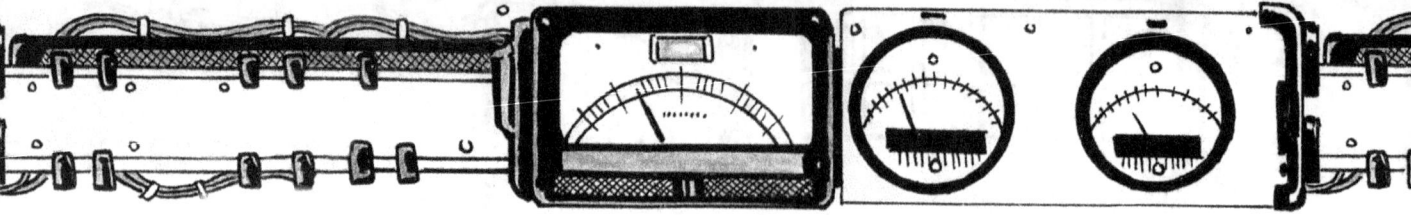

produce the juniper berry cure. Doc is eager to get back to the future, but Benedict, Mugsy and Potempkin storm into the basement.

Mugsy says he has been asking around, but hasn't found anyone who has ever heard of "Zipper" McFly. The gangsters pull their guns on Doc and Jim, but Marty uses his 1991-era keychain—which produces various sound effects—to trick the thugs into believing the police are raiding the speakeasy. Marty continues the audio charade, casting himself as the anti-hero by shooting it out with the cops. He then returns to the brewery "victorious," threatening to return with his entire gang if Benedict denies Jim a chance to live his life in peace. The mobster agrees, and Marty's relative is freed from his employment.

Outside, Jim thanks Marty for his help, musing that he may move his family far away from Chicago—to Hill Valley, California, where he already has family. Finally, with Einstein's cure in hand, Doc and Marty return to 1991 [BFCM-1].

Circa 1920s to Early 1930s A.D.

- As a youth, Emmett Brown often plays sandlot football, earning the nickname "The Streak" due to his ability to outrun opponents [TLTL-1]. During his teen years, he spends much of his time at pool halls [BFCM-4]. He spends several summers on the farm of his maternal uncle, Abraham Lathrop [BTF3-sx], and works on the ranch of a local businessman named Statler [BTF3-sp]. Learning how to ride, shoot and rope instills in him a desire to be a cowboy [BTF3-sx, BTF3-sp]. He also watches numerous Saturday matinees of Western films, starring such actors as Roy Rogers and Tim Holt [BTF3-n].

- Emmett Brown attends Hill Valley High School, where he is twice voted most likely to violate the laws of Newtonian physics [BFAN-12]. Emmett is also educated at a boy's school. Since author Jules Verne had been sketchy in his novels when creating female characters, Emmett comes to idealize women, and gains little experience interacting with them as a teenager [TLTL-4].

Sometime Before 1930 A.D.

- William McFly and his wife have at least four grandchildren: two boys and two girls [BTF3].

1930 A.D.

- Marty McFly's future social-studies teacher, Mister Arky, is born [BTF1-s1, BTF1-s2, BTF1-n].

Sometime in or After 1930 A.D.

- The Hill Valley Historical Society publishes *A History of Hill Valley: 1850-1930*, a hardbound book containing an early 20th-century photograph of William McFly and his family [BTF3].

Before 1931 A.D.

- Sarah Lathrop (Emmett Brown's mother), begins compiling a hardbound book titled *Von Braun Family Album*, containing many photographs of the Von Brauns, the ancestors of her husband, Erhardt Brown [TLTL-4].

Sometime in or Before 1931 A.D.

- Numerous businesses open in and around Courthouse Square, including the Bank of Italy; Eastern Auto Stores; the Essex Theater; Hill Billiards; the Hill Valley Apartments; Hill Valley Stationers; Lamont's House of Ermine; the Law Offices of Gale, Zemeckis, & Fine; the Majestic Arms Inn; O'Malley & Sons Barber Shop; the Sisters of Mercy Soup Kitchen; the Town Theater and Valley Bakery [TLTL-1 to TLTL-5]. Statler DeSoto also operates, though not in Courthouse Square [TLTL-4].

NOTE: View the map on page 183 to see where each business was located.

CODE	STORY						
ARGN	BTTF-themed TV commercial: Arrigoni	BTF1	Film: *Back to the Future*	CITY	BTTF-themed music video: Owl City, "Deer in the Headlights"	HUEY	BTTF-themed music video: Huey Lewis and the News, "The Power of Love"
BFAN	*Back to the Future: The Animated Series*	BTF2	Film: *Back to the Future Part II*	DCTV	BTTF-themed TV commercial: DirecTV	LIMO	BTTF-themed music video: The Limousines, "The Future"
BFCG	*Back to the Future: The Card Game*	BTF3	Film: *Back to the Future Part III*	ERTH	*The Earth Day Special*		
BFCL	*Back to the Future* comic book (limited series)	BUDL	BTTF-themed TV commercial: Bud Light	GALE	Interviews and commentaries: Bob Gale and/or Robert Zemeckis	MCDN	BTTF-themed TV commercial: McDonald's
BFCM	*Back to the Future* comic book (monthly series)	CHEK	BTTF-themed music video: O'Neal McKnight, "Check Your Coat"			MITS	BTTF-themed TV commercial: Mitsubishi Lancer
BFHM	BTTF-themed McDonald's Happy Meal boxes	CHIC	Photographs hanging in Doc Brown's Chicken restaurant at Universal Studios	GARB	BTTF-themed TV commercials: Garbarino		
BTFA	*Back to the Future Annual* (Marvel Comics)			GETV	BTTF-themed TV commercial: GE	MSFT	BTTF-themed TV commercial: Microsoft

- Cartoonist Zane Williams, despite his hope of becoming a professional cartoonist for *The New Yorker*, instead ends up a mobster and bartender working for Irving "Kid" Tannen, alongside bouncer Matches and enforcer "Cue Ball" Donnely. A skilled pianist performing at Kid's speakeasy, Cue Ball secretly wishes to leave the criminal life behind and perform at Carnegie Hall [TLTL-2].

  > *NOTE: Zane's first name paid homage to actor Billy Zane, who portrayed Match in the first two films. His surname, Williams, was revealed in supplemental materials included with the packaging to the Telltale Games video game.*

- Jack "Gentleman Jack" Thomas, a heavyset man with greased black hair and a handlebar mustache, is elected mayor of Hill Valley, earning a reputation as the "Good Time Mayor" [TLTL-1] for his tendency to violate Prohibition law by hanging out in Irving "Kid" Tannen's speakeasy [TLTL-2].

- The Stay Sober Society (S.S.S.) begins encouraging abstinence from alcohol, in an effort to "turn hopeless drunken bums into former hopeless drunken bums." Its slogan: "Listen to your mothers—stay sober!" Among its founding members is Edna Strickland. The group meets at the Sisters of Mercy Soup Kitchen, until gangster Irving "Kid" Tannen purchases that facility and revokes their access [TLTL-1].

- A motion picture called *Shark* is produced, starring Cooper Jackson and Claire Stephens. Its tagline: "You will never bathe in the ocean again." The Essex Theater begins showing this movie [TLTL-1].

  > *NOTE: This film paid homage to the tagline of Stephen Spielberg's* Jaws, *"You'll never go in the water again!" Upon seeing a poster for this movie, Marty McFly commented that the shark looked real—an homage to his statement, in* BTF2, *that the shark in* Jaws 19 *looked fake.*

- As a teen, Emmett Brown invents a type of self-cleaning windows [TLTL-v].

- Emmett Brown sees the film *The Public Enemy*, starring James Cagney, about a thug's rise up through the American criminal underworld during the Prohibition era [TLTL-4].

- Ernest Philpott, a middle-aged citizen of Hill Valley, begins dating a woman named Eunice. A mean drunk, Ernie sometimes accuses other men of showing Eunice inappropriate attention whenever he drinks at the El Kid speakeasy [TLTL-2]. An entrepreneurial scientist, Ernie is hired to coordinate the 1931 Hill Valley Exposition [TLTL-4], where he decides to market a healthy snack-food called Professor Fringle's Algae-Cakes [TLTL-5].

- Emmett Brown creates a number of so-called Personal Tunneling Devices [TLTL-v].

- Sylvia Miskin performs in the play *The Parlormaid's Predicament*, the plot of which involves a woman pretending to be a man's lover and the mother of his illegitimate child, in order to break up his relationship with another woman [TLTL-4].

- Emmett Brown invents the Oscillator Gigathruster, a component of the Static Accumulator, which generates a static charge enabling cars to fly [TLTL-v].

- Judge Erhardt Brown begins working on a court case of Moloney v. Tannen. His son, Emmett Brown, is assigned to handle the case's paperwork [TLTL-v].

  > *NOTE: Presumably, the case involved Irving "Kid" Tannen, given Emmett's role in having him imprisoned.*

- Prohibition-era chanteuse Sylvia Miskin works as a nightclub singer in her hometown of Manitoba, Canada, where she is known as "the Songbird of the Sierras," "the

TRIXIE TROTTER MAKES HER DEBUT AS EL KID'S NEW CHANTEUSE

Nightingale of the North," "the Floozy of the Foothills" and the "Winsome Wench of Winnpieg" [TLTL-2]. In addition, Sylvia poses for a set of "artistic" nude postcards, which she quickly regrets [TLTL-4], including one advertising Calgary, with her breasts obscured by a moose's antlers [TLTL-v]. Moving to Hill Valley,

California, Sylvia claims to be from Seattle, Washington, and changes her name to "Trixie Trotter," hoping to keep her past (and even her name) a secret [TLTL-2].

• Edna Strickland publishes a pamphlet titled "Lost Fortnight," to be handed out at her street-corner Salvation

Station, warning others about the evils of alcohol. This handout tells the true-life story of Johnny, who "woke up in a pile of his own sick, completely unable to remember the previous two weeks of his life" [TLTL-2].

- As a young man working for his father as a clerk at the Hill Valley Courthouse, Emmett Brown obtains several legal textbooks containing rules and guidelines governing citizens' behavior, including a volume simply titled *Law*, as well as a multi-volume set of *Law Journals* [TLTL-1, TLTL-5].

- Gangster Irving "Kid" Tannen murders a number of individuals and boasts about it by having his bartender, Zane Williams, illustrate a caricature of each person for the Wall of Honor at his speakeasy, El Kid. The deceased include men called Buck, Checkerboard Charlie, D, Happy-Feet Henderson, Louie and The Shrew [TLTL-2, TLTL-v].

- Emmett Brown conceives of an apian (bee)-powered aircraft, and considers demonstrating the vehicle (powered by bees) at the 1931 Hill Valley Exposition [TLTL-v].

- Edna Strickland begins writing an etiquette column titled "Ask Edna" for the *Hill Valley Herald*, which serves as a pro-temperance soapbox for the conservative journalist to condemn liquor, organized crime and debauchery [TLTL-1].

- A manufacturer called Atlas introduces a line of unbreakable and soundproof glass, which it later showcases as part of a proposed modular living space for future families, along with a Future Furnishings display, at the 1931 Hill Valley Exposition [TLTL-5].

- An academic article is published titled "Brainwaves and You," discussing theta-band transmissions and other topics. Emmett Brown will later use the article as reference material while devising his Mental Alignment Meter [TLTL-5].

- Canadian chanteuse Sylvia "Trixie Trotter" Miskin begins performing at the El Kid speakeasy in Hill Valley, California, and becomes the girlfriend of mobster club owner Irving "Kid" Tannen. Accompanied by "Cue Ball" Donnely on piano, Sylvia entertains bar patrons by singing such tunes as "I Don't Care," "My Melancholy Baby," "Rage," "Ain't We Got Fun?" and "Whisper in My Ear (The Secret Song)" [TLTL-2].

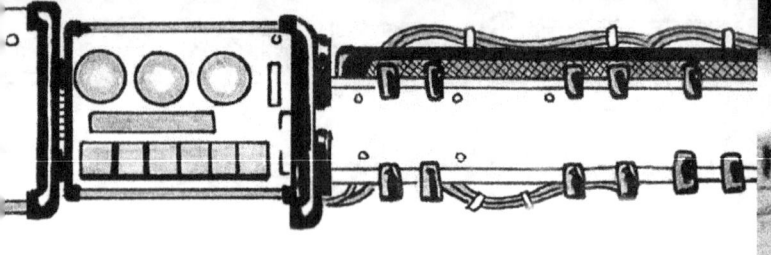

CHAPTER VI:

1931

Sometime Before June 1931 A.D.

• Judge Erhardt Brown hires a butler named Hampton to work for his family [TLTL-1].

• Emmett Brown invents a rocket-powered drill and applies for a patent for the device [TLTL-1].

• Arthur McFly, the bookkeeper for Irving "Kid" Tannen's gang, provides Sylvia "Trixie Trotter" Miskin—a sultry songstress and Kid's main squeeze—with an education, teaching her about accounting. During her apprenticeship, Trixie discovers that Tannen has been committing tax evasion. Trixie decides to turn the evidence over to authorities as leverage to get out from under Tannen's thumb [TLTL-2].

June 1931 A.D.

• Emmett Brown visits 1931 to prepare a special high-school graduation gift for his friend Marty McFly. While in this era, he assumes the alias of a drifter named "Carl Sagan" and intends to indulge in nostalgia, procure some first-edition books for Clara's birthday and solve an "historical mystery or two." But during Doc's sightseeing trip, self-appointed crusader Edna Strickland torches Irving "Kid" Tannen's speakeasy, and Doc, a stranger in town, is arrested for the crime. With Emmett trapped in 1931, the DeLorean's auto-pilot engages, returning the vehicle to 1986 with a message and instructions for Marty to come rescue him [TLTL-1, TLTL-5].

Saturday, June 13, 1931 A.D.—4:00 AM

• Marty McFly and Doc's dog, Einstein, arrive in 1931, finding themselves in the midst of a high-speed shootout between gangster Irving "Kid" Tannen's rum-runners and police officer Danny Parker. The DeLorean comes under fire from a hail of bullets from both directions, and the

MARTY IS CAUGHT IN A SHOOTOUT BETWEEN OFFICER PARKER AND KID TANNEN

distraction enables the criminals to elude pursuit. Officer Parker, mistaking the DeLorean for another outlaw, shoots at the futuristic car, but Marty evades the cop and stashes the time machine behind a sign advertising the upcoming Hill Valley Exposition. Once the coast is clear, Marty and Einstein walk the two miles back to Hill Valley's city limits [TLTL-1].

Saturday, June 13, 1931 A.D.—6:15 AM

- Marty McFly and Einstein finally reach Hill Valley. While Marty takes in the sights, he is accosted by Edna Strickland, a young writer for the *Hill Valley Herald* and a staunch supporter of law and discipline. Edna is composing an editorial piece about the recent destruction of Irving "Kid" Tannen's speakeasy and the suspected arsonist, Carl Sagan, and questions Marty (traveling under the names Harry Callahan, Michael Corleone and Sonny Crockett) about what he knows. Einstein reacts foully to Edna, ending the impromptu interview. Freed from the reporter's questioning, Marty seeks out Doc at the local police station.

Marty hails Emmett through his cell window. Doc is excited to see the teen, but fails to recognize the

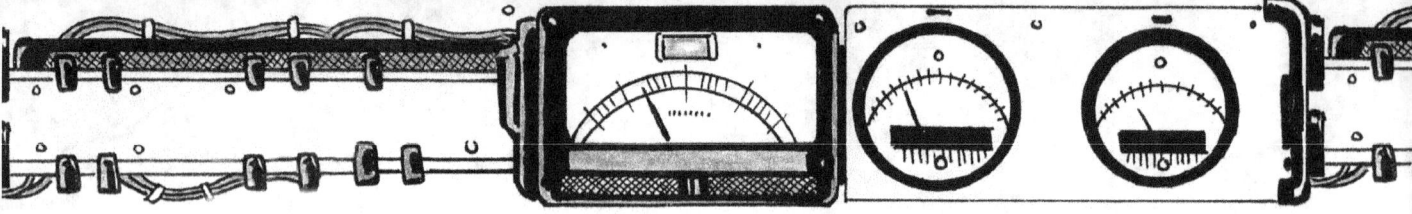

seriousness of his predicament until Marty shows him the June 15, 1931, edition of the *Hill Valley Telegraph,* announcing Doc's death. According to the paper, Doc (Sagan) will be gunned down the next day on the steps of the Hill Valley Courthouse, in retaliation for burning down the speakeasy.

The two friends brainstorm about how to break Doc out of jail without causing irreparable harm to the space-time continuum. Doc suggests they recruit his 17-year-old self since, in this era, young Emmett is a fledgling scientist who recently invented a rocket-powered drill, for which he applied for a patent. Doc encourages Marty to find the teenaged Emmett, convince him to finish his invention and use the drill to free Doc from his cell. To that end, Doc provides him with the phone number to the Brown estate, suggesting that Marty visit the Sisters of Mercy Soup Kitchen next door to begin his quest.

At the soup kitchen, Marty witnesses a confrontation between his own grandfather, Arthur McFly, and Kid Tannen, for whom Artie works as a bookkeeper. Kid has been keeping Artie holed up alone in an apartment, to prevent an overzealous district attorney intent on crumbling Tannen's empire from issuing the accountant a subpoena. Arthur had ignored this restriction, however, leaving his hiding spot to enjoy a free meal at the soup kitchen. Tannen orders Arthur to return to the safehouse before the D.A. can find him.

Marty uses the soup kitchen's phone to call the Brown estate, but the family's butler, Hampton, tells him that Emmett—who works as a clerk at the Hill Valley Courthouse—is not home. Marty runs into Emmett outside as the anxious young clerk is delivering paperwork for his father, Judge Erhardt Brown. When Emmett says he's too busy to talk to him, Marty reveals that he knows the teen is constructing a rocket drill in his laboratory. Emmett reacts in fear, his love of science a carefully guarded secret from his practical, no-nonsense father.

Emmett hurries away, mumbling to himself regarding a scientific riddle he's been unable to unravel. Marty surreptitiously tapes the ramblings and takes them to the imprisoned Doc, who decodes the puzzle and gives Marty the answer to help earn Emmett's confidence. Marty then returns to young Emmett and introduces himself as a representative of the patent office, on official business in Hill Valley to observe his rocket-powered drill before awarding a patent.

The young scientist is thrilled, until Marty tells him he must have a fully functioning prototype that very night. Emmett insists it can't be done in so short a time, especially since he lacks the main ingredient for the drill's fuel: 190 proof grain alcohol, virtually impossible to obtain in this era of Prohibition. What's more, he must also fulfill his obligations to the Courthouse before he'd be able to begin such an endeavor. Marty offers to help Emmett serve his papers and acquire the alcohol, if the young scientist will agree to complete the experiment that night. To Marty's surprise, Arthur McFly's name is on the subpoena list.

Marty and Emmett deduce that the Sisters of Mercy Soup Kitchen is, in fact, a front for Kid Tannen's rum-running operation. At the counter, serving as cook, is "Cue Ball" Donnely, a member of Kid's gang who oversees the barrels of soup served to the community, as well as "special" soup served exclusively to Tannen's customers. Marty realizes those "special" barrels contain hooch, and cooks up a scheme to confuse Cue Ball into giving him one. Just as the plan is about to succeed, Edna Strickland arrives to pick up an order of cabbage soup for a charity function. Cue Ball hands her a barrel and Edna leaves, unaware that she has received a barrel containing alcohol. Marty chases after her, hoping to convince her to give him the barrel.

Marty discusses charities with Edna and discovers that she is distraught. The Stay Sober Society previously met in the Sisters of Mercy Soup Kitchen's cellar, she explains, but ever since Kid Tannen assumed management, no one is allowed down there but his mob—which she suspects is because the cellar houses Tannen's bootlegging operation.

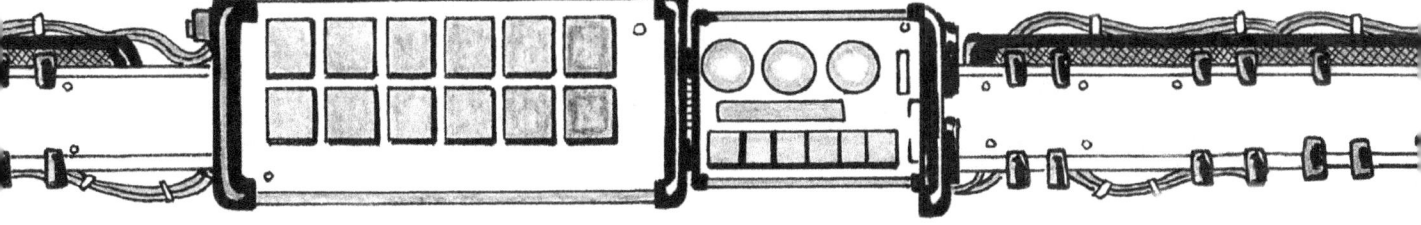

Marty offers to let her conduct that evening's meeting at the Brown residence. Edna is overjoyed by his generosity, but Emmett is dubious, fearing that so many visitors in his home will interrupt his father's rest. But when Marty threatens to award the drill patent to Brown's competitor—a fellow scientist named "Dr. McCoy"—Emmett relents. With the drill fuel taken care of, the two prepare to subpoena Arthur, though they have no idea where the bookkeeper is hiding [TLTL-1].

> *NOTE: The name "Dr. McCoy" was an in-joke reference to Dr. Leonard "Bones" McCoy, from the American science fiction TV series* **Star Trek.** *In the episode "The City on the Edge of Forever," McCoy inadvertently changed history in the 1930s after meeting Edith Keeler (whose first name was similar to Edna's) at a soup kitchen. This would not be the first time (or last, depending on one's fourth-dimensional placement) that Marty would riff on* **Star Trek** *to intimidate someone into doing his bidding (see also 1955).*

- Kid Tannen sits outside the O'Malley & Sons barbershop, his goon Matches giving him a shoeshine. Dissatisfied with his work, Tannen dismisses Matches and mistakes Marty for an employee, ordering him to shine his shoes instead. Marty obliges, gently prodding the man about the location of Arthur's safehouse. Tannen grows suspicious and refuses to provide the information. Noticing that Kid is using Arthur's hat as a peanut bowl, Marty steals the cap and runs off. The youth ditches Tannen and Matches in a foot pursuit around Courthouse Square, then hands the cap to Einstein, harnessing Einie's canine sense of smell to locate Artie.

    However, Marty's and Emmett's attempts to get Arthur to leave the safehouse and join them on the street—where they can then surprise him with the legal papers—fail, as Artie refuses to leave without a specific order from Kid Tannen. Therefore, as Kid exits the barbershop, Marty provokes him into a fight, leading

Kid and Matches on another chase. This time, Marty climbs atop the Courthouse Square gazebo and uses his 1980s-era Sony Walkman to tape the gangster's demands that he "get down from there."

With Einstein distracting the thugs, Marty descends from the gazebo, sneaks back to the safehouse and uses Kid's recorded voice to trick Arthur into leaving the apartment. As the accountant unwittingly walks into their trap, Emmett serves him the subpoena, which sends Arthur into a panic, fearing that Kid will murder him if he turns in evidence against him. Caught between Tannen's retaliation and getting into trouble with the law, Artie turns himself over to the court's protection [TLTL-1].

Saturday, June 13, 1931 A.D.—4:00 PM

- Marty and Emmett escort Arthur McFly to the Hill Valley Courthouse and prepare to host Edna Strickland, the Stay Sober Society and their barrel of hooch at the Brown residence [TLTL-1].

Saturday, June 13, 1931 A.D.—4:45 PM

- A slightly older Marty McFly arrives from seven hours in the future, to save Arthur McFly from a deadly run-in with Kid Tannen, and thereby prevent himself from vanishing from existence [TLTL-2].

Saturday, June 13, 1931 A.D.—4:55 PM

- Ten minutes later, Marty rushes to Courthouse Square to intercept Arthur before he can be abducted by Kid's goons. Artie is inside, turning evidence of Tannen's operation over to the district attorney. As Marty rushes toward the steps, Edna Strickland interrupts, seeking public opinions regarding the fate of accused speakeasy arsonist Carl Sagan. With time running out, Marty evades her questioning, but is prevented from entering the Courthouse when he spots his hours-younger self conversing with the teenage Emmett Brown.

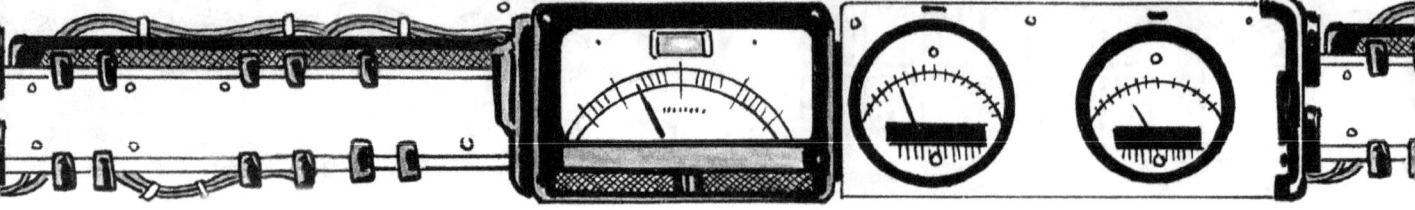

Marty ducks behind a tree, lest his past self sees him, but is not fast enough to dodge the notice of faithful dog Einstein. Einie, thinking his human friend is playing a game, brings a stick to the hiding Marty, ready to play catch. This earns the attention of the *other* Marty, who comes closer to Einstein in order to investigate what has captivated the canine. Fearing that running into his other self could create another paradox, Marty quickly tosses the stick to distract Einie—and aims right for Edna Strickland.

In his haste to fetch the branch, Einstein accosts the woman, causing the other Marty to work harder to bring the hound to heel. The hiding Marty uses that opportunity to race for the Courthouse steps, but is interrupted by Emmett, who believes him to be the Marty with whom he'd just been speaking. With Tannen's men closing in on the Courthouse, Marty has just enough time to distract Emmett and duck into a hiding spot. Finally, the other Marty returns, and he and Emmett set off to finish their rocket-drill experiment. With the coast clear, the second Marty meets Arthur coming out of the Courthouse—but they are approached by Kid's thugs. Marty tries to buy his grandfather time to escape, but is clubbed on the back of the head by a blackjack. Momentarily dazed, Marty quickly comes to and realizes that Arthur's been grabbed.

Following clues, Marty tracks his grandfather around the back of the Sisters of Mercy Soup Kitchen, the legal front for Kid Tannen's rum-running operation. He sees the criminals ushering Arthur through the back door, then sneaks inside and finds his granddad tied to a chair, being interrogated by Kid's cronies. Through clever thinking and misdirection, Marty gets Artie out of the basement, preventing the gangsters from murdering the man—and thus ensuring his father's and his own future existences [TLTL-2].

Saturday, June 13, 1931 A.D.—Between 4:55 and 11:25 P.M.

• Sometime after dark, as Emmett and Marty are about to convert the alcohol into rocket fuel, the duo are interrupted by Judge Erhardt Brown. The surly German is angry to find an unannounced party congregating on his front lawn. He demands an explanation, but since the procedure to create the fuel has already commenced, halting the conversion would ruin the mixture. Therefore, Marty carries on the process while Emmett enters a shouting match with his father in the next room.

During the argument, Emmett admits his scientific pursuits to his father, defending his dreams to the pragmatic older man. Marty struggles to finish the complicated process, aided by hidden code words sprinkled throughout Emmett's tantrum against the judge. Once the fuel's creation is completed and the rocket-powered drill is ready to go, Emmett ends the argument with his father. The young scientist feels vindicated—but is heartbroken moments later when Marty confesses that he is not really with the patent office and is, in fact, here to take the machine for his own use.

With the drill in hand, Marty hurries to the police station to free Doc from jail. The untested contraption explodes, however, under the stress of operation. At that moment, Edna Strickland happens by on her bicycle, looking to get a quote from the police regarding the speakeasy arsonist story. She tells Marty that Carl Sagan has been moved to another facility—which Marty confirms upon witnessing a paddy wagon passing by on the street. What's more, the future newspaper's headline changes, reporting the vehicle's interception and Doc's assassination. As Edna heads inside to pursue her story, Marty removes the rockets from the decimated drill, rigs them to the journalist's bicycle and takes off after his friend.

On his rocket-powered bike, Marty quickly catches up to the paddy wagon and prepares to sneak Doc out the back. To his surprise, Kid Tannen himself is driving

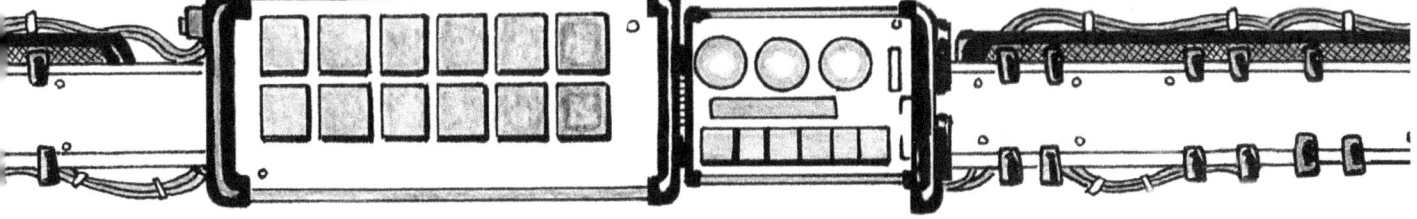

the vehicle. Marty frees the elder scientist from Tannen's clutches, but not before the gangster discovers the plot. A struggle erupts in the speeding vehicle, causing Kid to ram the paddy wagon into the back of a D. Jones Manure Hauling truck. Marty and Doc get away and return to the hidden DeLorean, intent on going back to the future [TLTL-1].

Saturday, June 13, 1931 A.D.—11:25 PM

• In one possible timeline, Kid Tannen's gang murders Arthur McFly and dumps his broken body on the County Courthouse steps, in retaliation for the accountant turning evidence of Kid's rum-running operation over to the police [TLTL-2].

> **NOTE: This paradoxical event was initially caused by Marty's time-traveling, though he later saved Artie's life and repaired the space-time continuum.**

Saturday, June 13, 1931 A.D.—11:30 PM

• As Emmett Brown and Marty McFly prepare to return to 1986, the friends realize something is terribly wrong, when Marty begins vanishing from the timestream [TLTL-1].

Saturday, June 13, 1931 A.D.—11:31 PM

• Doc notices that the future newspaper has changed, now reporting that Arthur was beaten to death. As a result, he realizes, George McFly will never be born; the timeline is thus catching up to Marty, erasing him from existence. Doc punches in new coordinates to go back earlier in the day, in order to intervene and save Arthur's life—but before they can make the trip, Officer Danny Parker happens on the scene, holding Brown at gunpoint. Marty hides before being spotted, and Doc distracts the well-meaning beat cop long enough for the youth to grab the keys, jump into the DeLorean

and blast back to the past, before Parker's stunned eyes [TLTL-2].

> **NOTE: See Saturday, June 13, 1931—4:00 PM.**

• With Arthur in tow, Marty returns to the DeLorean and drives back to the spot at which he previously vanished. He passes his prior self on the road, heading back to 4:45 PM, then swings by and picks up Doc Brown—again, before Danny Parker's stunned eyes. But before they can return to their own era, they must first do something to keep Arthur safe and prevent further meddling with the timestream. They convince Artie to lay low, but not to leave Hill Valley since he has yet to meet Marty's grandmother, Sylvia. Arthur happily agrees, believing them to be government agents working to topple Tannen's empire. With that loose end tied up, Marty and Doc return to 1986 [TLTL-2].

Sunday, June 14, 1931 A.D.

• In one possible timeline, Kid Tannen's gangsters gun down Emmett Brown (still disguised as Carl Sagan) on the Hill Valley Courthouse steps, in revenge for the speakeasy arson [TLTL-1].

• In another potential reality, Marty discovers that by helping Emmett serve Arthur a subpoena and rescue Carl Sagan from Kid's gang, he has again altered history. This time, the front page of the June 15 *Hill Valley Telegraph* edition now reads, "Local Accountant Beaten: Left for Dead." This would create a paradox, erasing both George and Marty McFly from existence. As Marty begins to fade from history, Doc theorizes that Arthur was murdered by Kid Tannen's mob shortly after giving his deposition [TLTL-2].

Monday, June 15, 1931 A.D.

• In one possible timeline, the *Hill Valley Telegraph*'s front page reads "Speakeasy Arsonist Slain," after

Back in Time: The Unauthorized Back to the Future Chronology

Kid Tannen's gang murders Emmett Brown on the steps of the Hill Valley Courthouse, in retaliation for the speakeasy fire. Ironically, the article's author, Edna Strickland, is the crime's actual perpetrator [TLTL-1].

Sometime Between June 15 and August 25, 1931 A.D.

- After seeing the futuristic DeLorean vanish out of sight, Danny Parker's life goes downhill. Doc's and Marty's intrusion into the timestream wrecks Parker's

CODE	STORY						
ARGN	BTTF-themed TV commercial: Arrigoni	BTF1	Film: *Back to the Future*	CITY	BTTF-themed music video: Owl City, "Deer in the Headlights"	HUEY	BTTF-themed music video: Huey Lewis and the News, "The Power of Love"
BFAN	*Back to the Future: The Animated Series*	BTF2	Film: *Back to the Future Part II*			LIMO	BTTF-themed music video:
BFCG	*Back to the Future: The Card Game*	BTF3	Film: *Back to the Future Part III*	DCTV	BTTF-themed TV commercial: DirecTV		The Limousines, "The Future"
BFCL	*Back to the Future* comic book (limited series)	BUDL	BTTF-themed TV commercial: Bud Light	ERTH	*The Earth Day Special*	MCDN	BTTF-themed TV commercial: McDonald's
BFCM	*Back to the Future* comic book (monthly series)	CHEK	BTTF-themed music video: O'Neal McKnight, "Check Your Coat"	GALE	Interviews and commentaries: Bob Gale and/or Robert Zemeckis	MITS	BTTF-themed TV commercial: Mitsubishi Lancer
BFHM	BTTF-themed McDonald's Happy Meal boxes	CHIC	Photographs hanging in Doc Brown's	GARB	BTTF-themed TV commercials: Garbarino	MSFT	BTTF-themed TV commercial: Microsoft
BTFA	*Back to the Future Annual* (Marvel Comics)		Chicken restaurant at Universal Studios	GETV	BTTF-themed TV commercial: GE		

DOC INTRODUCES HILL VALLEY—AND HIS FATHER—TO HIS FIRST FLYING CAR

Tuesday, August 25, 1931 A.D.

- After years of dodging prosecution, Irving "Kid" Tannen is finally apprehended and sentenced to San Quentin State Prison [TLTL-2].

- Upon discovering that their previous interruption in 1931 resulted in an alternate 1986 in which Kid Tannen was never arrested and the Tannen mob grew powerful and unchecked, Emmett Brown and Marty McFly return to 1931—on the very night that Kid was originally betrayed by his girlfriend, Sylvia "Trixie Trotter" Miskin, and arrested by Officer Danny Parker—to unravel the mystery surrounding the parallel future. To avoid running into his past self or being re-apprehended by local law enforcement (who would recognize him as suspected speakeasy arsonist Carl Sagan), Doc holes up at the Majestic Arms Inn.

  Marty dons a disguise to infiltrate Tannen's new speakeasy, El Kid, and discover what went wrong with the timeline. While investigating, he reunites with 17-year-old Emmett Brown, newly invigorated thanks to Marty's prodding to stand up to his father regarding his love for science. Emmett, along with Einstein—stranded in 1931 since Marty's last visit—is working on a prototype for a flying car in Courthouse Square. After some tweaks, the radio-controlled car becomes airborne, with Einstein as its stand-in pilot. Unfortunately the bugs have not been entirely worked out, and the young inventor loses control of the car, dumping Einstein unceremoniously on the Courthouse rooftop.

  Marty rushes to the Majestic Arms Inn to seek aid from the older, wiser Doc Brown, who instructs him to keep young Emmett distracted long enough for future Doc to retrieve the hidden DeLorean, fly up to the roof and rescue the dog. Marty finds Edna Strickland in Courthouse Square, staunchly defending Prohibition policies, and convinces her to pester Emmett for a headline regarding his failed project, as well as his having stranded a dog on the roof. As the older scientist quietly

investigations into the Tannen mob, and Danny is demoted and deemed unstable upon relaying his story to his superiors. Subsequently, he takes to drinking, loses his girlfriend, Betty Lapinski—Jennifer Parker's future grandmother—and undergoes a short stint of psychiatric therapy [TLTL-2].

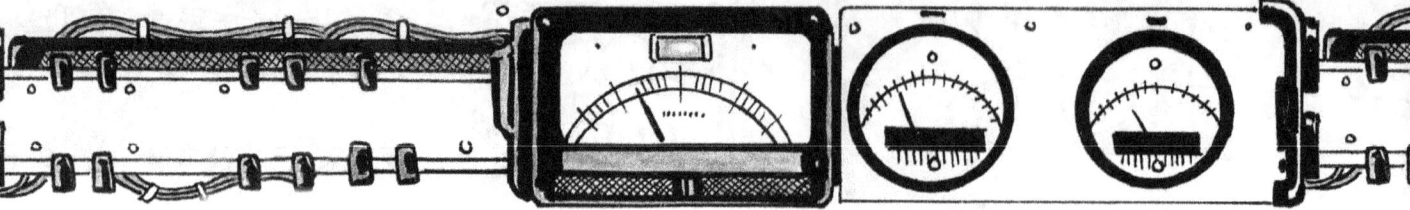

rescues Einstein, Edna and Emmett bicker—which soon turns to playful banter.

Marty enters the Sisters of Mercy Soup Kitchen via the back entrance and discovers El Kid, Irving "Kid" Tannen's illegal gin joint. Seated at the bar is Officer Danny Parker, who, instead of arresting Tannen, is getting properly sauced. Marty earns the man's confidence, learning that Parker's life has fallen apart, following his encounter with the mysterious DeLorean back in June. Now a cop on the take, he willingly looks the other way while Kid carries out his dirty dealings. Marty urges Parker to turn his life around and do something about Kid's Hill Valley operation.

Also at El Kid is lounge singer Sylvia "Trixie Trotter" Miskin, Kid's moll. The gangster keeps her on a short leash, though she has been secretly plotting with her friend Arthur McFly to run away from mob life. Trixie has uncovered information detailing Kid's tax-evasion schemes and had planned to turn in the evidence to the authorities in an effort to escape Kid's control. Marty urges her to carry through with that plan by offering her findings to the police, but she will only share the information with the one man she trusts: Artie McFly.

Marty and Doc locate Arthur as he sneaks into town to watch the film *Frankenstein* on the big screen, and convince him to privately meet with Trixie outside of El Kid. Tannen interrupts the rendezvous, however, threatening to kill Artie for answering the subpoena that got them into trouble in the first place. Trixie pleads for Arthur's life, promising her undying loyalty to Tannen if he spares her friend. Trixie, therefore, refuses to turn in the evidence against Kid, saying she plans to burn it after that night's performance.

Marty orchestrates a charade to deceive Trixie into thinking Tannen has reneged on their deal and murdered Arthur anyway. Heartbroken and outraged, she turns her evidence over to Officer Parker, who closes the speakeasy, making several arrests. Kid, however, slips out the back after learning that the speakeasy arsonist is lurking outside. Fearing for Doc's life, Marty rushes outside to save his friend.

With help from Einstein's powerful nose, Marty follows Tannen to a disguised garage door in the alley behind the soup kitchen. There, he discovers that Kid has captured Edna Strickland after finding the Prohibition crusader laying sticks of dynamite around his speakeasy. As Parker engages Tannen in a shootout, Marty mocks the mobster as a distraction for Edna to slip out of harm's way, then uses one of Kid's own hooch barrels to spark an explosion.

Still, the criminal escapes to the rooftop, where young Emmett attempts to repair the damage done to his experimental rocket car during that evening's failed test. Tannen takes the young scientist hostage, but Marty intervenes, trapping Kid inside the hover vehicle. Doc remotely pilots the rocket car, crashing Tannen to the street below, where authorities then nab him. Officer Parker is redeemed, and an excited Trixie learns that Arthur is alive and well. The two share a passionate kiss, long-held feelings finally bubbling to the surface. Edna approaches young Emmett, meanwhile, crediting his science expertise for bringing Hill Valley's most notorious criminal to justice. To celebrate, the two decide to go on a date and see *Frankenstein*—the same film that historically cemented Doc's decision to pursue a career in science [TLTL-2].

> **NOTE: First Arthur, and then Emmett and Edna, would have had to wait some time to see** Frankenstein, **as it was not released until November 21, 1931—almost three months in the future.**

Tuesday, August 25, 1931 A.D.—11:17 PM

- Thinking their troubles are finally over, Marty and Doc pile into the DeLorean with Einstein and head back to the future. As the vehicle achieves a speed of 88 miles per hour, however, Doc suddenly vanishes [TLTL-2].

CODE	STORY		
ARGN	BTTF-themed TV commercial: Arrigoni	**BTF1**	Film: *Back to the Future*
BFAN	*Back to the Future: The Animated Series*	**BTF2**	Film: *Back to the Future Part II*
BFCG	*Back to the Future: The Card Game*	**BTF3**	Film: *Back to the Future Part III*
BFCL	*Back to the Future* comic book (limited series)	**BUDL**	BTTF-themed TV commercial: Bud Light
BFCM	*Back to the Future* comic book (monthly series)	**CHEK**	BTTF-themed music video: O'Neal McKnight, "Check Your Coat"
BFHM	BTTF-themed McDonald's Happy Meal boxes	**CHIC**	Photographs hanging in Doc Brown's
BTFA	*Back to the Future Annual* (Marvel Comics)		Chicken restaurant at Universal Studios

CITY	BTTF-themed music video: Owl City, "Deer in the Headlights"	**HUEY**	BTTF-themed music video: Huey Lewis and the News, "The Power of Love"
DCTV	BTTF-themed TV commercial: DirecTV	**LIMO**	BTTF-themed music video: The Limousines, "The Future"
ERTH	*The Earth Day Special*		
GALE	Interviews and commentaries: Bob Gale and/or Robert Zemeckis	**MCDN**	BTTF-themed TV commercial: McDonald's
GARB	BTTF-themed TV commercials: Garbarino	**MITS**	BTTF-themed TV commercial: Mitsubishi Lancer
GETV	BTTF-themed TV commercial: GE	**MSFT**	BTTF-themed TV commercial: Microsoft

Sometime Between Tuesday, August 25 and Monday, October 12, 1931 A.D.

- In one timeline, Edna Strickland offers a gift to her beau, Emmett Brown: a pristine white suit once worn by her grandfather, Marshal James Strickland. It is one of Edna's prized possessions, and she comments that Emmett looks quite fetching wearing it [TLTL-4].

- For his part in Irving "Kid" Tannen's arrest, Officer Danny Parker is promoted to detective [TLTL-5].

- "Cue Ball" Donnely avoids prison time by testifying against Kid—as he sees it, "exhibiting an admirable sense of self-preservation." Cue Ball later obtains employment as a truck driver at the 1931 Hill Valley Exposition, working for Arthur McFly. The former mobster tries to make an honest living in this position, though he can't resist stealing a case of Professor Fringle's Algae-Cakes from the Expo—which summarily turn his teeth green [TLTL-4]. Cue Ball provides security at the expo, removing unruly or non-paying visitors, and soon realizes that he enjoys being on the right side of the law for a change [TLTL-5].

- Lamont's House of Ermine, a furrier located in Hill Valley hit hard by the Great Depression, closes its business [TLTL-1]. The company donates its furs for use at a dinosaur diorama at the 1931 Hill Valley Exposition [TLTL-4].

- A speakeasy in Georgetown is destroyed by an arsonist, and journalist Edna Strickland blames Emmett Brown (disguised in that era as drifter Carl Sagan) of committing the crime, given Doc's prior arrest for torching Irving "Kid" Tannen's Hill Valley speakeasy. Unbeknownst to the police, Edna herself is responsible for both blazes, as well as a third in Colfax [TLTL-2].

- Doc and Edna see the film *The Virtuous Husband* on their first date, thereby launching Citizen Brown's dystopian timeline [TLTL-3].

- As a follow-up to the failure of his Rocket Car, Emmett Brown conceives another flying vehicle known as the Airborne Personal Transport Device, powered by super-ionized static electricity [TLTL-4].

- Emmett Brown also invents a Canine Retrieval Apparatus to rescue dogs from great heights, as a result of Einstein becoming trapped atop Hill Valley's Clock Tower [TLTL-v].

Monday, October 12 to Thursday, October 15, 1931 A.D.

- Emmett Brown enters his experimental rocket-powered drill into the first annual Hill Valley Science Exposition. A colossal failure, it nonetheless succeeds in making young Emmett more determined than ever to pursue his love of science [TLTL-4].

- As Emmett Brown's romantic courtship with Edna Strickland blossoms, the crusader's strict principles guide his budding scientific mind in non-scientific directions [TLTL-2].

Monday, October 12, 1931 A.D.—Before 8:00 PM

- In an effort to prevent a dystopian 1986 Hill Valley (created by Emmett Brown's tyrannical alternate-future self and wife Edna Strickland), Marty McFly and the reformed First Citizen Brown travel back to August 1931 to stop young Emmett from becoming involved with Edna. However, the DeLorean's malfunctioning time circuits instead bring them two months ahead, to *October* 1931.
  By now, young Emmett is already madly in love with Edna, making Marty's task of breaking them up

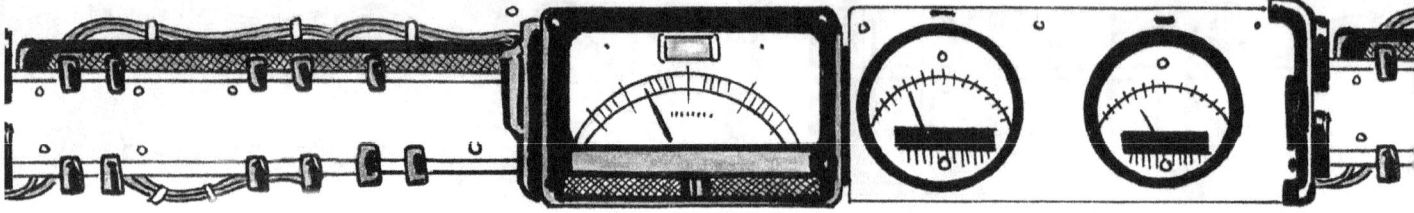

all the more difficult. By convincing young Emmett to see *Frankenstein* at the movies, as he did in the original timeline, Marty and Citizen Brown hope to restore history.

Marty catches up with young Emmett, but the teenager no longer has any desire to build rocket cars or other fanciful scientific experiments. Instead, thanks to Edna's influence, he has invented the Mental Alignment Meter, a device that detects degenerate minds, making it easier for authorities to single out miscreants from healthy society. What's more, he's tested it out on numerous citizens, including a man named Needleman (whom the device branded a "hooligan"). Emmett shows no interest in seeing *Frankenstein* or continuing his work on the rocket—his mind is only on earning Edna's approval.

Marty fails to convince Emmett to break up with Edna. Therefore, Citizen Brown encourages Marty to instead focus on Edna, whom Marty finds at the science exposition being held at Hill Valley High School. Marty tells her that her new boyfriend is not as faithful or virtuous as she believes him to be, but Edna thinks he's speaking in jest, refusing to buy into such allegations. Citizen Brown, once more posing as "Carl Sagan," engages Edna in conversation to keep her distracted while Marty devises a scheme to break up the couple. The elder Brown asks not to be told the plan's details, however; although he realizes breaking up with Edna is necessary for the good of Hill Valley, he still has feelings for her and greatly regrets the heartache his younger self will face.

Marty runs into Trixie Trotter. Thanks to Arthur McFly, Trixie has been getting her life together since Kid Tannen's arrest. Arthur, as manager and accountant of the Hill Valley Science Expo, has hired her to be the fair's spokeswoman—Techne, Muse of Progress—a role that Trixie takes very seriously. Marty explains that he's trying to break up Emmett and Edna in order to save his friend. Trixie understands, but though she's never liked Edna, she refuses to pretend she's having an affair with

Emmett, as she has vowed to put that kind of reputation behind her.

Disgruntled, Marty conspires to goad Edna into getting Trixie fired due to her checkered past, in order to create strife between the two women and win Trixie's aid. His manipulative plan succeeds, and Arthur finds himself forced to fire his sweetheart when he discovers that she's not an American citizen (she's from Canada, known in burlesque circles as the "Winsome Wench of Winnipeg"). This drives a wedge between Artie and Trixie, but the angry singer is now willing to help break up Edna's relationship. To that end, she tasks Marty with acquiring certain props so she can re-enact a scene from *The Parlormaid's Predicament*, a theater show in which she once performed.

Marty stops by Emmett's garage lab and again tries to convince him to end his affair with Edna. When that doesn't work, he takes to more drastic measures, tampering with Emmett's Mental Alignment Meter. The device is designed to discern, by a simple stimulus-response analysis, degenerates from those contributing to society; Edna's goal is to subject every Hill Valley citizen to the experiment, in order to catalogue them for future control. Since Emmett has taken the test and been declared a model citizen, Marty sabotages the readout to label Emmett a degenerate criminal on par with Kid Tannen. Unbeknownst to Marty, however, Emmett intends to propose to Edna at the expo.

Marty rushes back to the school, armed with everything he needs to accomplish his mission of turning Edna against Emmett. But when he catches up with Citizen Brown, the elder exhibits suspicious behavior, as though having second thoughts about their scheme. Nonetheless, Citizen Brown continues experimenting with the faulty time circuits. After three trips back into time, he determines that the circuits' chromium elements have become unstable. He must replace them with titanium, he says, but that won't be possible until the Kroll process (a pyrometallurgical industrial method for producing metallic titanium, invented by William J.

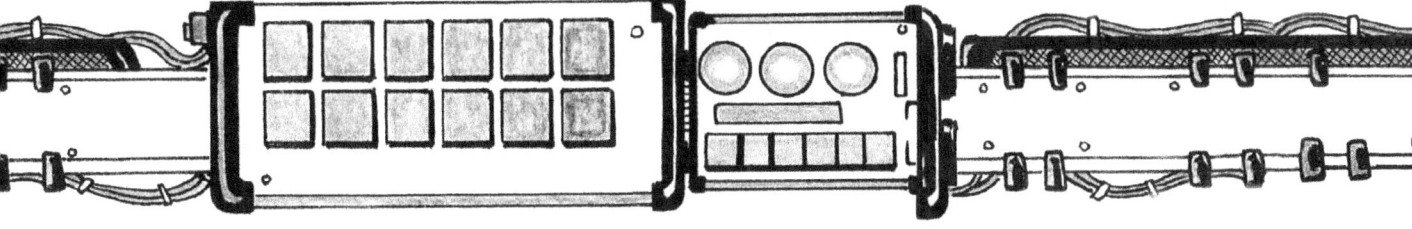

Kroll) is perfected in another nine years.

The First Citizen admits he's reluctant to carry out their plan. Marty tells Brown of the wonderful life he'll lead with Clara and his sons, but Brown is more concerned with sparing Edna from living out her life as the old "cat lady" whom Marty knew from his timeline. Brown hopes to work out a third option, in which he and Edna can remain married, but not turn Hill Valley into a police state. When Marty refuses to entertain the notion, adamant that his friend is meant to be with Clara, Brown leaves in anger.

Moments later, younger Emmett arrives with his Mental Alignment Meter, telling Marty that he plans to propose. In preparation, he has worn a suit once belonging to her grandfather, Marshal James Strickland, which she cherishes. With a heavy heart, Marty enacts his plot, sabotaging one of Emmett's inventions to cause the suit to become ruined by acid. Next, Trixie approaches, claiming she and Emmett have produced a love child named Emmett Jr. Edna is outraged, and when Emmett claims he's the noble man she believed him to be, Edna puts his doctored card into the Mental Alignment Meter, which deems him a degenerate criminal. Her faith shattered, she dumps him and leaves in tears [TLTL-4].

Monday, October 12, 1931 A.D.—8:00 PM

- As the Opening Ceremonies of the first annual Hill Valley Science Expo are about to commence, young Emmett Brown ascends to the ledge of the Courthouse Clock Tower, reflecting on his miserable life. Marty McFly climbs up to join him, hoping to convince him to watch *Frankenstein* and not give up his scientific dreams of inventing. Emmett, however, is heartbroken, his zeal for life lost.

   Marty tries a different tactic: ridiculing his friend, belittling his scientific aspirations and calling him a failure. Emmett defends himself and his love of science, rediscovering his passion in the process, and ready to return to his own experiments, rather than Edna's. In

fact, he realizes a new angle for his rocket car, utilizing static electricity. His excitement is interrupted, however, when he falls from the tower and is snared by a rope used to lift statues into place. Marty frantically saves his life and helps him to the ground, and the two youths, their friendship mended, race to perform Emmett's latest science experiment.

Meanwhile, on the outskirts of Hill Valley, Edna Strickland walks alone at night, brokenhearted and dejected as well. Citizen Brown pulls alongside her in the DeLorean, offering a ride. She accepts, and he assures her that her future can still be bright. Recognizing a common enemy, they conspire to destroy Marty's plans for young Emmett Brown [TLTL-4].

Monday, October 12, 1931 A.D.—After 8:00 PM

- After Sylvia "Trixie Trotter" Miskin is revealed to be Canadian and fired from the Hill Valley Science Expo, Arthur McFly exploits a loophole in the rules and proposes marriage, finally professing his love for her. If they are married, she can be granted a work permit despite her Canadian citizenship. The two elope to Reno, Nevada [TLTL-5].

   NOTE: According to the fifth episode of the Telltale Games video game, Arthur and Sylvia were originally married sometime in 1936, but after Marty's interference with his own past, the two lovebirds escalated their romance quicker than expected. It's unknown whether this affected son George's birthdate.

Tuesday, October 13, 1931 A.D.

- Marty McFly awakens in Emmett Brown's garage. Emmett has slipped out early, hoping to avoid his father, Erhardt Brown, who sternly disapproves of his scientific pursuits. Following the previous night's breakthrough, Emmett has been developing a flying car—powered by static electricity, and dubbed the Electrokinetic

Back in Time: The Unauthorized Back to the Future Chronology

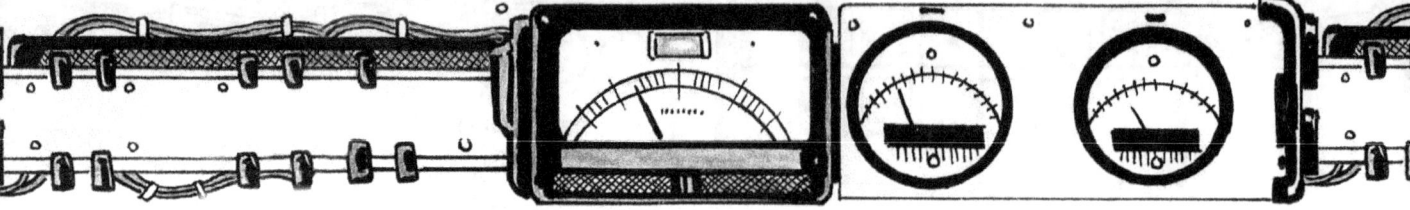

Levitator—to enter into the Hill Valley Science Expo. He phones Marty from the high school, where the event is being held, and asks him to retrieve the static accumulator that he spent all night building.

Marty brings the device to the school, where he encounters Citizen Brown. The elder Brown was supposed to be repairing the DeLorean so he and Marty could prevent Emmett's younger self from marrying Edna and restore their future, but he is no longer willing to carry out their mission. Brown still loves Edna, and believes that it was his science, not her values, that caused their problems. If he can convince his younger self to give up science, Brown reasons, then they could still get married and avoid the bleak future Marty witnessed.

Marty runs into problems at the Science Expo, for the jilted Edna has vowed vengeance against Emmett—and Citizen Brown has now befriended the young crusader, claiming Marty's real name is "Yakov Smirnoff," and that he is a Communist subversive trying to turn Emmett against her. Having published articles against vice and corruption in Hill Valley, Edna holds sway with the police department, and it falls to Detective Danny Parker to arrest Marty and shut down Emmett's project. However, Parker confides in Marty that he doesn't believe Edna, and thinks she's not in her right mind following her recent breakup. If Marty could dig up dirt on Edna that would soil her reputation with the law, the cop adds, Parker could then refuse to carry out her wishes.

Impersonating Doc's "Carl Sagan" voice, Marty calls Edna and learns her darkest secret: *She* was the speakeasy arsonist. Via clever subterfuge, he records her confession and presents it to Parker, but Edna flees the scene before being apprehended.

Marty searches for young Emmett, whose demonstration timeslot fast approaches. Citizen Brown has kidnapped his younger self, however, and—posing as oceanographer Jacques Douteux, from the Oceanic

Institute—is hiding him in the Bathysphere on display at the Enlightenment Under the Sea exhibit. Marty pressures the imposter into exposing his deeds, but the First Citizen gets away while Marty is freeing his friend.

Emmett rushes back to his own booth, but as he is about to activate the Electrokinetic Levitator, his outraged father, Judge Erhardt Brown, enters the auditorium, demanding that his son abandon the demonstration. Emmett and the judge get into a screaming match, with Marty mediating in an effort to bridge the gap between father and son. Finally, the two Browns realize how alike they are, and Erhardt accepts his son's scientific pursuits, promising to stand by his side. Emboldened by his father's confidence, Emmett activates the levitating car and, for one glorious moment, it works. Emmett is vindicated, and Judge Brown looks on in pride as his son actually flies.

Moments later, Marty spots Citizen Brown and Edna arguing outside. As he runs outside, Emmett crashes the flying car behind him. Edna pushes past Brown and steals the DeLorean, driving at high speeds to avoid arrest. She whips the car around the parking lot, barreling straight for Marty. Brown pushes the youth out of the way, and is struck by the time machine as Edna vanishes into the past. Marty comes to his friend's side, but Citizen Brown fades from existence, his reality erased.

Emmett emerges from the school, covered in ash. Though his experiment was a failure, he is more inspired than ever. When he asks Marty about his true identity, the time traveler gives him a torn page from a 1986 newspaper announcing Brown's receiving of Hill Valley's key to the city. Marty urges him not to read the article until the day he eventually receives the key, assuring him that it will explain everything. Emmett agrees to the odd request, bidding his mysterious friend farewell.

A DeLorean suddenly arrives, out of which steps Doc Brown, dressed and acting like his original self.

After receiving the key to the city in 1986, Doc explains, he went back in time to retrieve Marty. Before they can return to the future, however, they must first stop Edna from doing irreparable harm to the space-time continuum.

William McFly—Arthur's father and Marty's great-grandfather—arrives on the scene, angrily looking for his son, who has impulsively married Trixie Trotter, of whom William does not approve. Marty panics, wondering what effect this amorous act will have on his existence. Soon thereafter, Detective Danny Parker returns from chasing Edna, saying she vanished in the same car from the future he encountered months prior.

To Doc's and Marty's shock, Parker suddenly disappears—quickly followed by the rest of Hill Valley, leaving the time travelers standing in an empty countryside. William McFly happens by again, this time on an errand for the Haysville Mercantile Delivery service. They question the friendly older man about Hill Valley's whereabouts, but William claims there hasn't been a town by that name since before he was born. He encourages them to seek out "Scary Mary" Pickford, an old-timer who lives by herself in the middle of nowhere. Mary collects newspapers, he says, and purportedly knows everything about local history.

Marty and Doc find Scary Mary, who turns out to be a much older (and apparently deranged) Edna Strickland. Since taking the DeLorean into the past, she has been stranded here alone, psychologically scarred by the time-jump and some past incident causing her immense guilt.

Marty and Doc patiently break through her confusion and discern what transpired: After fleeing from Detective Parker, she traveled back to sometime before 1876, meeting her grandfather, Marshal James Strickland. Edna lived in the early days of Hill Valley for a time, enjoying its more innocent lifestyle—that is, until Beauregard B. Tannen moved into town and broke ground on a new bar called the Palace Saloon and Hotel. Fearful that the introduction of alcohol would lead to Hill Valley's damnation, she took it upon herself to resume her arsonist ways. On July 17, 1876, Edna set fire to the saloon—but the conflagration quickly spread, consuming all of Hill Valley.

Destroying the town she sought to protect has broken Edna, who now is prone to fits of rage. As she raises a shotgun at Doc and Marty, William McFly intervenes, enabling the duo to escape back to 1876 to prevent Hill Valley's destruction.

After securing Edna in 1876, Doc and Marty return her and the stolen DeLorean to 1931, where Danny Parker arrests her for arson. With the timeline restored, her anomalous DeLorean is absorbed back into the timestream, erased from existence. One loose end remains: Arthur McFly's marriage to Trixie Trotter, rather than to Marty's grandmother, Sylvia McFly. To Marty's surprise, however, it turns out that "Trixie Trotter" is only a stage name—for Sylvia Miskin, his actual grandmother.

Artie's father, William McFly, finally accepts his new daughter-in-law, giving the happy couple his blessing. With history more or less restored, Marty and Doc make their way back to the future [TLTL-5].

"OLD MAN" PEABODY HAS A CRAZY IDEA ABOUT BREEDING PINE TREES

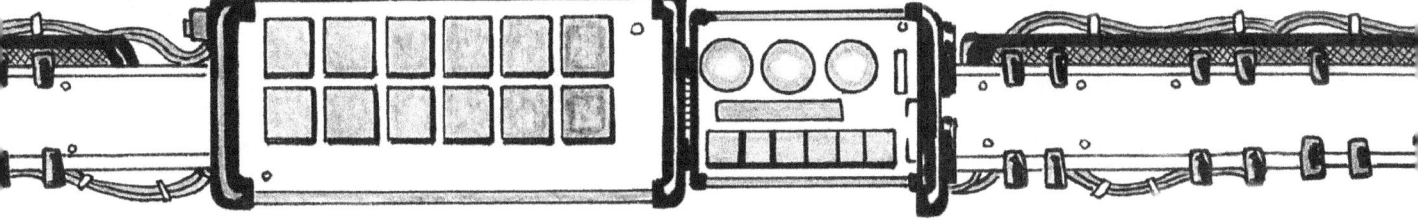

CHAPTER VII:
1932 A.D. TO 1954 A.D.

Sometime After 1931 A.D.

- After seeing his son Emmett demonstrate a flying car at the 1931 Hill Valley Exposition, Judge Erhardt Brown grows fiercely proud of his accomplishments and thereafter supports his scientific pursuits—even going so far as to set up the Erhardt Brown Scholarship for Young Scientists [TLTL-5].

- Betty Lapinski and Daniel Parker marry and have a son, Daniel Jr.— the future father of Jennifer Parker [TLTL-3].

Early 1930s A.D.

- Emmett Brown invents an Automated Flapjack Maker, capable of cooking more than 300 pancakes per hour on a rotating griddle. The device fails to catch on since it produces sawdust pancakes [RIDE].

- Daphne, a future beatnik and a frequent attendee of Emmett Brown's parties in the 1950s, is born [BTF1-s4].

Circa 1930s A.D.

- A book titled *Modern Discipline* is published, outlining how to maintain strict order [BTF1-s3].
  > *NOTE: Gerald Strickland later used this book as the basis of his policies while serving as the principal of Hill Valley High School.*

1932 A.D.

- Emmett Brown enters the Hill Valley Junior Science Fair with his latest invention: a working video tape recorder with full 14-day programming capability. Unfortunately, since television has not yet been invented, the device is useless [BFAN-13].
  > *NOTE: Hill Valley produced the first of three Hill Valley Science Expos in 1931, with the third occurring in 1933. That would place the second event in 1932; as such, the Junior Science Fair may have been the second annual Hill Valley Science Expo. As an aside, televisions were introduced in the 1920s in the real world.*

February 1932 A.D.

- The building housing Irving "Kid" Tannen's former speakeasy (burnt to the ground by Edna Strickland in June 1931) is restored [TLTL-1].

1933 A.D.

- Mayor Jack Thomas holds the third annual Hill Valley Science Expo. A strain of influenza virus breaks out from an exhibit, infecting the concession stand and halting the program. No future such festivals are held [TLTL-4].

Sometime Before Friday, April 7, 1933 A.D.

- The Bob Brothers All-Star International Circus arrives in Hill Valley. Acts include clowns, a human cannonball, aerialists, a bearded lady, acrobats, seals, elephants, lions, tigers and bears, as well as a band that plays off-key. The circus' owners, Robert and Bob Brothers, arrange with local farmer "Old Mac" Tannen to set up operations on his property, located outside of town [BFAN-18].

Friday, April 7, 1933 A.D.

- Verne Brown, his friend Chris and Marty McFly travel from 1992 back to 1933 to enjoy the Bob Brothers All-Star International Circus, long defunct by their era. The acts are lackluster, however; the only excitement occurs when Marty volunteers to take the place of the injured human cannonball. Safely jettisoned from the cannon, Marty lands the DeLorean hard, damaging the carburetor and grounding them in 1933.

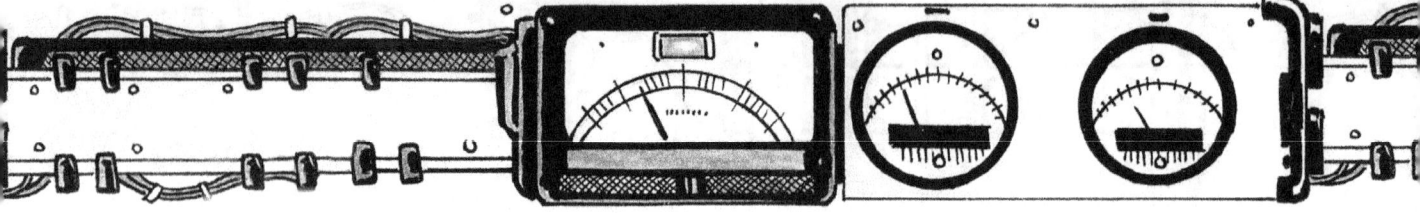

- While Marty makes repairs, Verne and Chris wander around the circus and overhear Tannen strong-arming the Bob Brothers for a larger cut of their profits. The eavesdropping children inadvertently damage the property. Enraged, Old Mac threatens to take over the circus unless he receives even more money by the following night [BFAN-18].

Saturday, April 8, 1933 A.D.

- To work off the damages incurred, Verne and Chris agree to work for the Bob Brothers' circus while Marty repairs the DeLorean. The two youths perform menial labor throughout the day, until realizing a way to increase business for the circus, thereby allowing the owners to pay Tannen. In a radical promotional campaign, Verne and Chris litter Hill Valley's streets with free passes to that night's performance, anticipating great profits made from concession sales.

  The plan succeeds: Attendance that night is record-breaking, though ill-timed, as the trapeze artists quit for more legitimate day-jobs, leaving the Bob Brothers without their star attractions. The brothers fear ruination, but Verne and Chris again intercede, volunteering to perform the high-wire act themselves. Using special Booster Belts designed by Emmett Brown to make it possible to wax his car's roof without using a ladder, the youths perform a death-defying show, enabling the Bob Brothers to make enough money to save their business.

  To his surprise, Verne discovers that his friend Chris is actually female—her full name is Christine—and feels betrayed, having assumed her to be a boy. As Marty finishes work on the DeLorean, the three return to 1992, the youths' friendship strained by the revelation [BFAN-18].

Friday, March 26, 1937 A.D.

- Biff Howard Tannen is born to a woman impregnated by gangster Irving "Kid" Tannen [BTF2-b, BFCG, TLTL-3].

NOTE: The identity of Biff's mother (and whether she was married to Kid) is unknown.

1938 A.D.

- Farmers Otis and Elsie Peabody are married [BTF1-n].
  NOTE: In the original screenplay draft for BTF2, Elsie was named "Maybelle."

- Lorraine Baines is born to Sam and Stella Baines [BTF1-n].

Sometime in or After 1938 A.D.

- Cliff Tannen is born to a woman impregnated by gangster Irving "Kid" Tannen [TLTL-2].
  NOTE: It's unclear whether Cliff (who was never mentioned in the films) existed in the original timeline. Kid was in prison for years, but may have had conjugal visits.

Monday, August 18, 1938 A.D.

- George Douglas McFly is born to Arthur and Sylvia McFly [BTF1-n].
  NOTE: The novelization of BTF1 placed George's birth on August 18, 1938. In the unfilmed Paradox script, his birthdate was listed as April 1, 1936. Since that would have made him 19 during the events of the first film, the 1936 date was likely a simple typo. George's middle initial was given as M in early drafts of BTF1's screenplay, and as F in BTF2's first-draft script, but his gravestone in the second film revealed his middle name to be Douglas.

Sometime in or After 1939 A.D.

- Riff Tannen is born to a woman impregnated by gangster Irving "Kid" Tannen [TLTL-2].

CODE	STORY						
ARGN	BTTF-themed TV commercial: Arrigoni	**BTF1**	Film: *Back to the Future*	**CITY**	BTTF-themed music video: Owl City, "Deer in the Headlights"	**HUEY**	BTTF-themed music video: Huey Lewis and the News, "The Power of Love"
BFAN	*Back to the Future: The Animated Series*	**BTF2**	Film: *Back to the Future Part II*	**DCTV**	BTTF-themed TV commercial: DirecTV	**LIMO**	BTTF-themed music video: The Limousines, "The Future"
BFCG	*Back to the Future: The Card Game*	**BTF3**	Film: *Back to the Future Part III*	**ERTH**	*The Earth Day Special*	**MCDN**	BTTF-themed TV commercial: McDonald's
BFCL	*Back to the Future* comic book (limited series)	**BUDL**	BTTF-themed TV commercial: Bud Light	**GALE**	Interviews and commentaries: Bob Gale and/or Robert Zemeckis	**MITS**	BTTF-themed TV commercial: Mitsubishi Lancer
BFCM	*Back to the Future* comic book (monthly series)	**CHEK**	BTTF-themed music video: O'Neal McKnight, "Check Your Coat"	**GARB**	BTTF-themed TV commercials: Garbarino	**MSFT**	BTTF-themed TV commercial: Microsoft
BFHM	BTTF-themed McDonald's Happy Meal boxes	**CHIC**	Photographs hanging in Doc Brown's Chicken restaurant at Universal Studios	**GETV**	BTTF-themed TV commercial: GE		
BTFA	*Back to the Future Annual* (Marvel Comics)						

NOTE: It's unclear whether Riff (who was never mentioned in the films) existed in the original timeline. Kid was in prison for years, but may have had conjugal visits.

Late 1930s to Early 1940s A.D.

- Arthur and Sylvia McFly have a son named John [TEST].
  NOTE: Test footage created prior to **Back to the Future***'s filming included a scene in which Marty mentioned his uncle John. Since all of Lorraine's siblings' names are known, it's likely he was George's brother. If so, it is unknown who was older. It's also possible that Uncle John was a great-uncle on either side of the family, or merely a close family friend of the McFlys, and not actually a son of Artie and Sylvia.*

- Otis and Elsie Peabody plant a pair of pine trees at the entrance to their farm in Hill Valley. Otis hopes one day to be able to breed the saplings [BTF1].
  NOTE: This event was undated in the film, but the trees' apparent age in 1955 would make a planting in the late 1930s or mid-1940s likely.

Early 1940s A.D.

- Emmett Brown wins a jitterbug dance competition when the judges misconstrue a series of clumsy accidents as a new dance step. His contestant number is 99, and he earns the nickname "Twinkle Digits" [BFAN-17].

1941 A.D.

- Martha Peabody is born to farmers Otis and Elsie Peabody [BTF1-n].

1943 A.D.

- Milton Baines is born to Sam and Stella Baines [BTF1-n].

1944 A.D.

- Sherman Peabody is born to farmers Otis and Elsie Peabody [BTF1-n].

Mid-1940s A.D.

- Emmett Brown works as a private contractor for the U.S. Defense Department during World War II, aiding in military efforts against Nazi Germany. At the time, Doc lives in a small apartment above a gas station located at 1191 South Kelsey [BFAN-17]. During this era, the scientist works on the Manhattan Project, a U.S.-led research and development program, resulting in the creation of the world's first atomic bomb [GALE].

- Comedian Jerry ("Odie") Cologne travels with the United Service Organizations (USO) to help raise U.S. troop morale during the war, along with emcee Bobby Dawson and singing group The Anderson Sisters [BFAN-17].
  NOTE: Odie Cologne (a play on the phrase "eau de cologne") was a cartoon skunk on the 1960 animated series, **King Leonardo and his Short Subjects.**

Wednesday, September 27, 1944 A.D.

- Hoping to steal the blueprints for his father's old Fance-O-Dance Memorizing Shoes, and thus dance better in his waltz class, Verne Brown journeys to 1944, with Marty McFly along for the ride on the promise of food. Under cover of darkness, the duo sneaks into Doc's apartment at 1191 South Kelsey.

  Since Emmett is not home, Verne and Marty break into his apartment, and Verne locates the Fance-O-Dance blueprints without a hitch. As the two make their escape, however, a soldier claiming to be the town's blackout warden—and bearing a strong resemblance to Marty's former principal, Gerald Strickland—confronts them. They evade the warden, watching helplessly as the

NIKE	*BTTF*-themed TV commercial: Nike	SCRT	2010 Scream Awards: *Back to the Future*	SUFFIX	MEDIUM		-s1	Screenplay (draft one)
NTND	Nintendo *Back to the Future—The Ride*		25th Anniversary Reunion (trailer)	-b	*BTF2's* Biff Tannen Museum video		-s2	Screenplay (draft two)
	Mini-Game	SIMP	Simulator: *The Simpsons Ride*		(extended version)		-s3	Screenplay (draft three)
PIZA	*BTTF*-themed TV commercial: Pizza Hut	SLOT	*Back to the Future* Video Slots	-c	Animated series credit sequence		-s4	Screenplay (draft four)
REAL	Real life	TEST	Screen tests: Crispin Glover, Lea Thompson	-d	Film deleted scene		-sp	Screenplay (production draft)
RIDE	Simulator: *Back to the Future—The Ride*		and Thomas F. Wilson	-n	Film novelization		-sx	Screenplay (*Paradox*)
SCRM	2010 Scream Awards: *Back to the Future*	TLTL	Telltale Games' *Back to the Future—The Game*	-o	Film outtake			
	25th Anniversary Reunion (broadcast)	UNIV	Universal Studios Hollywood promotional video	-v	Video game print materials or commentaries			

Back in Time: The Unauthorized Back to the Future Chronology

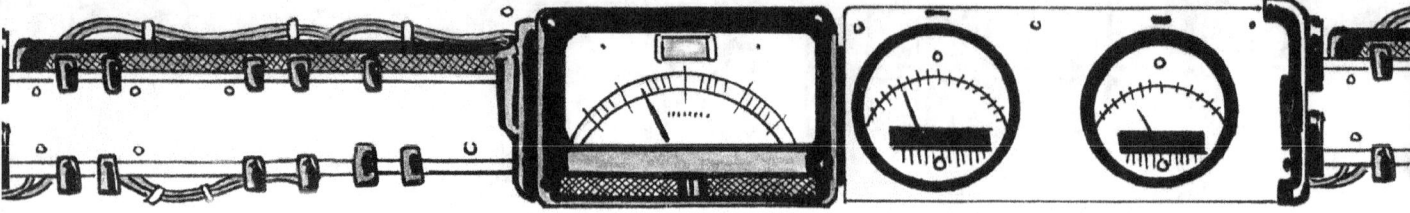

soldier discovers the DeLorean. Mistaking the vehicle for a German super-weapon, the warden summons other soldiers to commandeer the time machine.

Verne and Marty spend the night in the Victory Garden outside the County Courthouse, until being awakened by a beautiful woman named Rosie and her younger sister, Dorothy (Verne's future dance instructor, unbeknownst to him). The girls befriend the strangers, but their conversation is interrupted by Sergeant Frank Tannen—who knows a lot of German for a supposed Allied officer. When Tannen makes unwanted advances on Rosie, Marty defends her honor. Humiliated and angry, Tannen chases the boys through Hill Valley.

NOTE: It was strongly implied that Tannen may have been a German spy.

• Marty and Verne become separated while attempting to hide. Verne finds his way into a movie theater, while Marty enters a food line, prepared to do anything to get a meal—even joining the military. The recruiter shaves Marty's head and sends him off to a local boot camp, where he discovers that Frank Tannen is his commanding officer.

When Verne learns of Marty's patriotic predicament—and that the military plans to dismantle the DeLorean, stranding the time travelers in 1944—the child crafts a hasty plan to free Marty. The Army, branding the teen a German spy, searches for him throughout Hill Valley, but the time-travelers lose themselves in the crowd at a war bonds rally hosted by Bobby "Doodles" Dawson.

As the Anderson Sisters take the stage to provide music for a jitterbug contest, Tannen closes in on Verne and Marty. Verne asks Dorothy to enter the contest with him, to which she gladly agrees. Meanwhile, a cross-dressing Marty poses as the fourth Anderson Sister—with disastrous results. Verne and Dorothy thwart Tannen with their jive moves, winning the trophy in the process. Verne lets her keep the trophy as he retrieves Marty, and the two outwit guards watching over the DeLorean.

Firing up the Flux Capacitor, they travel back to the future [BFAN-17].

1945 A.D.

• A fire caused by discarded oily rags claims a gas station and the adjoining loft apartment in which Emmett Brown lives, at 1191 South Kelsey. No causalities are reported, though many of Doc's inventions, including a batch of blueprints stored in a dresser, are destroyed [BFAN-17].

1949 A.D.

• Sally Baines is born to Sam and Stella Baines [BTF1-n]. *NOTE: Early* **BTF2** *screenplay drafts placed Sally's birthdate in 1948.*

• Emmett Brown begins developing the Photo-Electric Chemical Power Converter, a device designed to efficiently convert radiation into electrical energy [BTF1-s1].

Circa 1950s A.D.

• A beatnik poet named Bartholomew attends several parties hosted at Emmett Brown's mansion, where he sits quietly in a zen position, offering such nuggets of wisdom as "Hydrogen is like life: It's a gas." Other beatniks in attendance hang on Bartholomew's every word, including Daphne, an attractive young woman who wears heavy avant-garde makeup and claims to be from the ninth system of the Andromeda Galaxy [BTF1-s4].

1950 A.D.

• Twelve-year-old George McFly watches helplessly as a bully punches out his friend Billy Stockhausen. George is filled with righteous fury, knowing that with a single punch, he could level the bully—but he fearfully retracts at the last minute, and his opponent sneers in derision.

CODE	STORY						
ARGN	BTTF-themed TV commercial: Arrigoni	BTF1	Film: *Back to the Future*	CITY	*BTTF*-themed music video: Owl City, "Deer in the Headlights"	HUEY	*BTTF*-themed music video: Huey Lewis and the News, "The Power of Love"
BFAN	*Back to the Future: The Animated Series*	BTF2	Film: *Back to the Future Part II*	DCTV	*BTTF*-themed TV commercial: DirecTV	LIMO	*BTTF*-themed music video: The Limousines, "The Future"
BFCG	*Back to the Future: The Card Game*	BTF3	Film: *Back to the Future Part III*	ERTH	*The Earth Day Special*		
BFCL	*Back to the Future* comic book (limited series)	BUDL	*BTTF*-themed TV commercial: Bud Light	GALE	Interviews and commentaries: Bob Gale and/or Robert Zemeckis	MCDN	*BTTF*-themed TV commercial: McDonald's
BFCM	*Back to the Future* comic book (monthly series)	CHEK	*BTTF*-themed music video: O'Neal McKnight, "Check Your Coat"	GARB	*BTTF*-themed TV commercials: Garbarino	MITS	*BTTF*-themed TV commercial: Mitsubishi Lancer
BFHM	*BTTF*-themed McDonald's Happy Meal boxes	CHIC	Photographs hanging in Doc Brown's Chicken restaurant at Universal Studios	GETV	*BTTF*-themed TV commercial: GE	MSFT	*BTTF*-themed TV commercial: Microsoft
BTFA	*Back to the Future Annual* (Marvel Comics)						

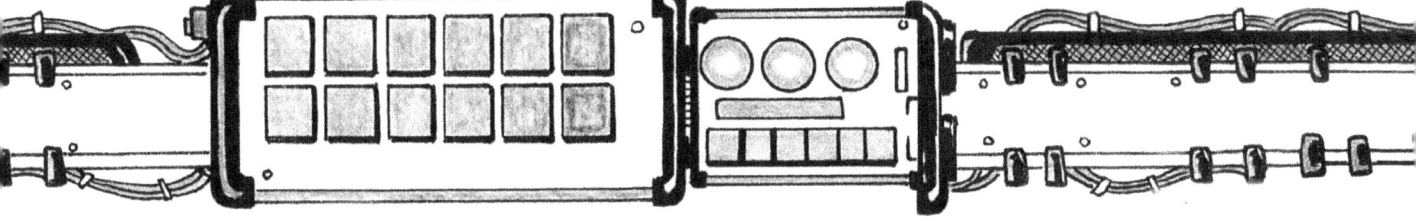

This sets a pattern in young George's life of letting people walk all over him [BTF1-n].

1951 A.D.

• Toby Baines is born to Sam and Stella Baines [BTF1-n].
> *NOTE: The original draft of the* **BTF2** *screenplay indicated that Toby would be 18 in 1968 and thus eligible for the military draft, thereby placing his birthdate at 1950. The novelization, however, moved the year to 1951.*

• Emmett Brown travels from 1990 A.D., on a mission to explore the long-term effects of global pollution and discover a means of reversing the damage. While his journey for answers takes him across the timeline, he makes a layover to deposit his dog Einstein until such a time as he can safely return to retrieve him [ERTH].

Sometime in or Before 1952 A.D.

• Emmett Brown develops the Projecto-Recollector, a helmet-mounted device enabling a wearer to project thoughts onto a nearby screen [BFAN-24].

• Teamster Abraham Jones opens a Hill Valley business called Abraham Jones, Junk Dealer [BFT1-s2].

1952 A.D.

• Mister Arky, a social-studies teacher at Hill Valley High School, tries to instill a sense of optimism into his students [BTF1-s1, BTF1-s2, BTF1-n].
> *NOTE: By 1985, Arky would become paranoid and pessimistic. By* **BTF1***'s third-draft screenplay, he was replaced by a woman called Mrs. Woods. Neither character appeared in the final version of the movie.*

• In one possible timeline, Marty McFly visits an aboveground atomic bomb testing site in Atkins, Nevada, hoping to harness a bomb blast's nuclear energy to power Doc's time machine and thereby return to his own era. Marty brings the device, attached to a refrigerator, out to the desert site, strapped to the back of a truck. He survives the explosion by climbing into the fridge while the vehicle barrels toward ground zero. As the bomb detonates, Marty is propelled back to the future [BTF1-s1].
> *NOTE: The test-site sequence was cut from the final version of* **BTF1** *(the setting of which was changed to 1955) due to producer Steven Spielberg's fear that children emulating Marty might climb into refrigerators and become trapped. Storyboards were included as a Blu-ray extra. The first two script drafts set the base in the fictional Nevada city of Atkins, while the third moved it to New Mexico. This unused ending was revisited in the Spielberg-directed film* **Indiana Jones and the Kingdom of the Crystal Skull***.*

• While visiting 1952 in one possible timeline, Marty McFly tries to change history and attain fame by performing the rockabilly song "Blue Suede Shoes" for an agent at the Midwest Talent Agency, but the man decides it's not commercial enough and throws Marty out of his office. Reginald Washington, a visiting band manager, likes what he hears and asks Marty to play it again for a New York record executive. This meeting never comes to pass, however, since Marty returns to his own era beforehand [BTF1-s1].

• Charles, a colleague of Emmett Brown, urges him to invest in the fledgling Xerox Corp. Convinced that the company has no future—since few would know how to pronounce its name (Doc mispronounces it as "X-rox")—Brown turns down the offer, missing out on a profitable investment opportunity [BTF1-s1].
> *NOTE: This individual was likely Xerox co-founder Charles Peter McColough.*

NIKE	BTTF-themed TV commercial: Nike	**SCRT**	2010 Scream Awards: *Back to the Future* 25th Anniversary Reunion (trailer)	**SUFFIX MEDIUM**		**-s1**	Screenplay (draft one)
NTND	Nintendo *Back to the Future—The Ride* Mini-Game			**-b**	*BTF2's* Biff Tannen Museum video (extended version)	**-s2**	Screenplay (draft two)
		SIMP	Simulator: *The Simpsons Ride*			**-s3**	Screenplay (draft three)
PIZA	BTTF-themed TV commercial: Pizza Hut	**SLOT**	*Back to the Future* Video Slots	**-c**	Animated series credit sequence	**-s4**	Screenplay (draft four)
REAL	Real life	**TEST**	Screen tests: Crispin Glover, Lea Thompson and Thomas F. Wilson	**-d**	Film deleted scene	**-sp**	Screenplay (production draft)
RIDE	Simulator: *Back to the Future—The Ride*			**-n**	Film novelization	**-sx**	Screenplay (*Paradox*)
SCRM	2010 Scream Awards: *Back to the Future* 25th Anniversary Reunion (broadcast)	**TLTL**	Telltale Games' *Back to the Future—The Game*	**-o**	Film outtake		
		UNIV	Universal Studios Hollywood promotional video	**-v**	Video game print materials or commentaries		

MEGA BRAINMAN,
DOC BROWN'S
SHORT-LIVED
SUPERHERO ALTER-EGO

• Emmett Brown purchases the Cusimano Brothers Gearworks Factory from a man named Fredman, for $1.85 million, and launches Emmett Brown Enterprises so he can follow his dream of inventing a Photo-Electric Chemical Power Converter that could efficiently convert radiation into electrical energy [BTF1-s2]. The company eventually evolves into Dr. E. Brown Enterprises, offering atomic engineering and technical guidance, as well as clock and refrigerator repair services [BTF1-s3].

Shortly Before Friday, February 15, 1952 A.D.

• At the local Hoggly Woggly supermarket, Emmett Brown wrestles over the final potato with another man, who turns out to be a manager for the Small Town Professional Wrasslin association. Upon seeing Brown's strength, he proposes that the scientist take up wrestling as a career. Caught up in the moment, Emmett agrees [BFAN-24].

Friday, February 15, 1952 A.D.

• The front page of the *Hill Valley Chronicle*'s morning edition advertises a Small-Town Professional Wrasslin match between Emmett "Brainbuster" Brown and Mad Maximus. Emmett, however, backs down from the fight, preferring to continue his scientific pursuits.

Jules and Verne Brown, along with Marty McFly, arrive from the year 1992, where bullies have goaded Verne into proving himself a "Mega Muscleman." By intervening in his father's short-lived career as small-town professional wrestler "Brainbuster" Brown, Verne believes he can help Emmett earn a strongman reputation, thereby winning Verne popularity among his peers. Marty and the boys head to the fight, but Brainbuster is a no-show. Marty, therefore, puts on the costume and takes Emmett's place in the fight until the Brown brothers can collect their future father to finish the match.

While Marty gets pummeled, Jules and Verne visit young Emmett at the scientist's apartment, and attempt to convince him to go through with his proposed match against Mad Maximus. Verne shows him a Mega Muscleman comic, hoping to inspire in Emmett the nobler aspects of donning an outlandish costume and fighting muscled opponents. Under pressure, Emmett agrees, and the boys strap him to a pair of booster boots—footwear invented by Emmett himself, four decades in the future.

At the arena, Marty hands the costume to Emmett, who takes the ring as Brainbuster Brown. A backstage fluke causes a microphone to drop from the ceiling and smack Brown on the head, however, and he suffers a mental breakdown, believing himself to be Mega Brainman, Hill Valley's superheroic protector. Still wearing his booster boots, Emmett leaves the wrestling match and speeds about town, attempting many heroic deeds—which all turn out to be misunderstandings that he inadvertently makes worse.

Doc's friends try to convince him of his true identity, but he is so entrenched in his comic book delusion that, upon coming across a dilapidated, TNT-rigged building scheduled for demolition, he believes it his duty to save anyone trapped within. The building is empty, however, and Emmett is caught in the blast. Miraculously, he suffers only minor scratches, but debris falls on his head, clearing his mind. Coming to his senses, he finally fights Mad Maximus in the ring—and is summarily trounced [BFAN-24].

1954 A.D.

• Joey Baines is born to Sam and Stella Baines [BTF1-n].

• Emmett Brown invents a motor engine that runs on salt water, and promptly sells the concept to Standard Oil for five million dollars. The engine is never mass-produced, however, as the company buries the idea to keep it from threatening the oil industry [BTF1-s4].

• After reading Dale Carnegie's *How to Win Friends and Influence People*, the overly shy George McFly, age 16, begins trying out the book's advice to generally creepy results. This causes others to see him as even more of a weirdo than before—including his own parents. When George tells Biff Tannen that he's "sincerely interested" in learning about him, in the hope of disarming Biff's bullying, George instead receives a hero sandwich to the face [BTF1-n].

A RED-LETTER DAY IN SCIENTIFIC HISTORY: DOC INVENTS TIME TRAVEL

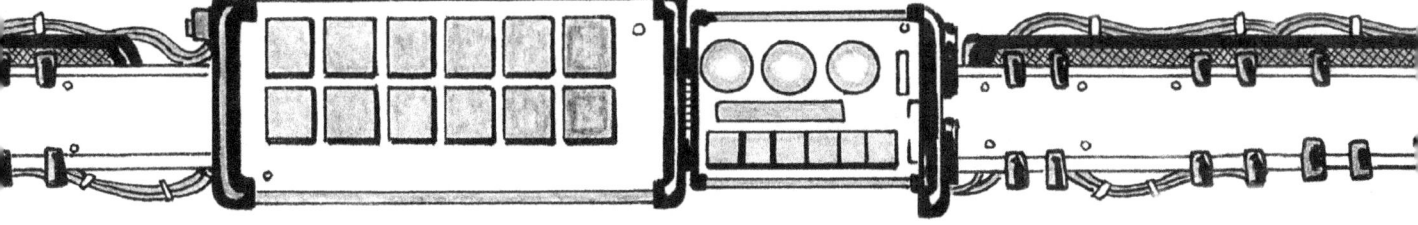

CHAPTER VIII:

1955 A.D.

Sometime in or Before 1955 A.D.

• Numerous businesses open in and around Courthouse Square, including Ask Mr. Foster; Bank of America; the Blue Bird Motel; Broadway Florist; Elite Barber Shop; Gaynor's Hideaway; Hal's Bike Shop; Hill Valley Stationers; Holt's Diner; J. D. Armstrong Realty; the Lawrence Building; Lou's Cafe; Orson and Tillich, Attorneys at Law (known as Jacobson & Field, Attorneys at Law in one possible timeline); Roy's Records; Ruth's Frock Shop; Sherwin-Williams; Statler Motors Studebaker; Texaco; a U.S. Army Recruitment Office; Western Auto Stores; and Zales Jewelers [BTF1, BTF2].

> *NOTE: View the map on page 183 to see where each business was located.*

• Al's Tattoo & Art Studio relocates from Courthouse Square to Burbank. Its windows are painted over, with the messages "Out of Business" and "Al Has Moved—So Long, Hill Valley" scrawled on the glass, as well as a "For Sale" sign from Harry Kaven Realtor [BTF1].

• Biff Tannen's gang—Match, Joey ("Skinhead") and 3-D—begin frequently beating up a classmate named Lester, who is too scrawny to fight back [BTF2-n]. Meanwhile, nerdy George McFly becomes the target of frequent tormenting from a redheaded classmate named Mark Dixon [BTF1-n], as well as from Biff and his cronies [BTF1].

• Frank "Red" Thomas is elected mayor of Hill Valley, using the campaign slogans "Progress Is His Middle Name" and "Honesty, Decency, Integrity" [BTF1].

• Cigarette manufacturer Sir Randolph films a television commercial in which a surgeon promotes the Sir Randolph brand, claiming its tobacco flavor soothes his nerves and improves his circulation after a long day spent performing lung operations [BTF1-d].

> *NOTE: This fake commercial, starring John*

McCook, was produced for **BTF1** *but was cut before the film's release, though it did appear in the novelization. The deleted scene was announced as being included on the movie's initial DVD release, but was later removed. Fans discovered the file on the disc, however, and made it available online.*

• A red-haired teenager in Hill Valley known as Red—a high school classmate of George McFly and Lorraine Baines—begins dating a young woman [BTF1-s3].

> *NOTE: This youth would later grow up to be the homeless man seen in the first two* **Back to the Future** *films. The young woman's name is unknown.*

• Sherman Peabody begins reading science fiction-based comic books, such as *Tales from Space*, and becomes convinced of the existence of extraterrestrial life [BTF1-n].

• Issue #29 of French magazine *Oh LàLà* is published, featuring photographs of attractive women clad in lingerie [BTF2].

• Martha Peabody discovers that the family of her schoolmate, Peggy Ann McVey, owns a television, which makes her quite jealous. Martha's old-fashioned father, Otis Peabody, refuses to buy one, however [BTF1-n].

• Marvin Berry, a cousin of Chuck Berry, forms a band called Marvin Berry and the Starlighters, which includes Berry on guitar and lead vocals, Reginald on drums, and other musicians on piano, saxophone and bass fiddle [BTF1], including a member named Bob Jordan [BTF1-n].

> *NOTE: In* **BTF1**'s *first-draft script, the band was called Lester Moon and the Midnighters, and Reginald was known as Sax. The second draft listed them as Marvin Berry and the Starlighters.*

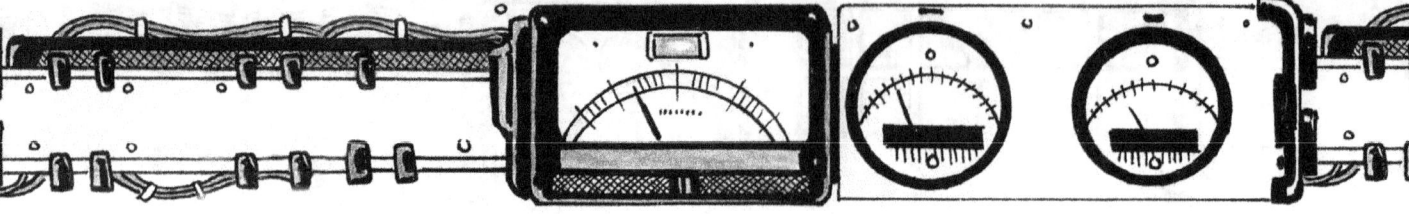

By the third draft, this had changed to Marvin Moon and the Midnighters, which was changed back to Starlighters by the time of filming.

- George McFly, an avid science fiction fan, spends much of his youth alone, watching *The Honeymooners* and *Science Fiction Theater*, and also reading such sci-fi magazines as *Amazing Stories*, *Fantastic Story Magazine* and *Astounding Science Fiction* [BTF1], as well as the works of Isaac Asimov [TLTL-5].

- Hill Valley's Essex Theater begins showing *The Atomic Kid* [BTF1], a 1954 black-and-white science fiction comedy starring Mickey Rooney and Robert Strauss, involving a uranium prospector accidentally exposed to radiation following an atomic bomb test [REAL].
  > *NOTE: The first film's originally scripted ending involved Marty visiting an atomic bomb testing site in 1952 and surviving a detonation at ground zero by climbing into a refrigerator—in essence, becoming an "atomic kid."*

- Emmett Brown invents the Brain-wave Analyzer, enabling a wearer to telepathically hear others' thoughts, and consisting of a mass of vacuum tubes, rheostats, gauges, wiring and antennae [BTF1-n].

- Emmett Brown begins raising a puppy that he names Copernicus, after Renaissance scientist Nicholas Copernicus [BTF1-n, BTF3].

- Emmett Brown invents the Deep-Thinking Mind-Reading Helmet, which harnesses electromagnetic impulses created by synaptic responses from the cerebrum and the cerebellum, transmitting mind waves into the helmet's interpreting circuitry, thereby translating the impulses into written language [RIDE]. Doc also creates a similarly named device, the Deep-Thought Mind-Reading Helmet, to hear the unspoken thoughts of others [BFAN-1].

1955 A.D.

- Biff Tannen graduates from Hill Valley High in the Class of '55 [RIDE], but is asked to repeat his senior year so that the football team can benefit from his athletic prowess [BTF2-b].
  > *NOTE: Biff's claim, in the museum footage, that he was asked to repeat his senior year may have been propaganda intended to cover up his having failed twelfth grade.*

- Ron Woodward, a student at Hill Valley High School, begins running for senior class president, under the platform "The Right Man for the Job" [BTF1].

- The firm of Hansen, Misetich & Gaynor oversees the construction of Hill Valley's Lyon Estates housing development, promoted as being "the home of tomorrow... today." A pair of stone lion statues flanks the development's entrance [BTF1].

- The Pohatchee Drive-in Theater begins showing *Abbott and Costello Meet the Mummy*, *Ma and Pa Kettle at Waikiki*, *Revenge of the Creature*, *Tarantula* and *Francis in the Navy* [BTF3], while the Essex Theater features *Cattle Queen of Montana* [BTF1].

- Emmett Brown works at Hill Valley University, and begins dating Jill Wooster, the daughter of the college's dean. Dean Wooster and his colleagues, Cooper and Mintz, pressure Brown into taking part in one of three projects: developing the Edsel automobile, creating a chemical-warfare compound (to be called Agent Brown in his honor) or helping to build the new Xerox company (which Doc's friend Charles had urged him to invest in three years prior). When Doc declines, the dean puts an end to his relationship with Jill [BTF3-s1].

- As a young child, future prison inmate Joey Baines is happiest sitting in his playpen. His parents, Sam and

CODE	STORY				
ARGN	BTTF-themed TV commercial: Arrigoni	**BTF1**	Film: *Back to the Future*	**CITY**	BTTF-themed music video: Owl City, "Deer in the Headlights"
BFAN	*Back to the Future: The Animated Series*	**BTF2**	Film: *Back to the Future Part II*	**DCTV**	BTTF-themed TV commercial: DirecTV
BFCG	*Back to the Future: The Card Game*	**BTF3**	Film: *Back to the Future Part III*	**ERTH**	*The Earth Day Special*
BFCL	*Back to the Future* comic book (limited series)	**BUDL**	BTTF-themed TV commercial: Bud Light	**GALE**	Interviews and commentaries: Bob Gale and/or Robert Zemeckis
BFCM	*Back to the Future* comic book (monthly series)	**CHEK**	BTTF-themed music video: O'Neal McKnight, "Check Your Coat"		
BFHM	BTTF-themed McDonald's Happy Meal boxes	**CHIC**	Photographs hanging in Doc Brown's	**GARB**	BTTF-themed TV commercials: Garbarino
BTFA	*Back to the Future Annual* (Marvel Comics)		Chicken restaurant at Universal Studios	**GETV**	BTTF-themed TV commercial: GE

HUEY	BTTF-themed music video: Huey Lewis and the News, "The Power of Love"		
LIMO	BTTF-themed music video: The Limousines, "The Future"		
MCDN	BTTF-themed TV commercial: McDonald's		
MITS	BTTF-themed TV commercial: Mitsubishi Lancer		
MSFT	BTTF-themed TV commercial: Microsoft		

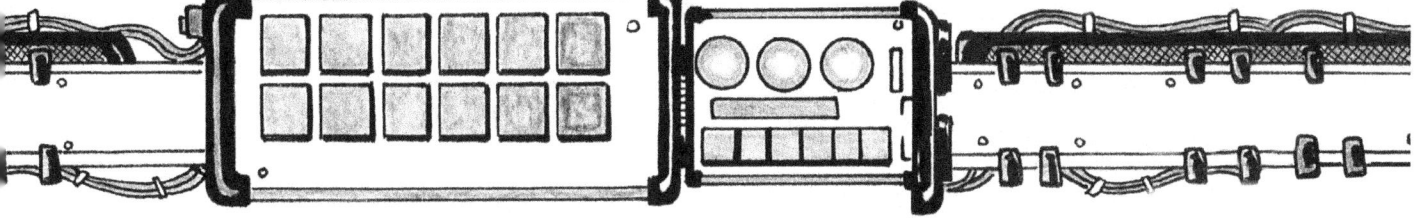

Stella Baines, let him spend most of his time within its confines—a preview of his later lifelong incarceration [BTF1].

- The song "The Ballad of Davy Crockett" is recorded by three different artists: Bill Hayes, Fess Parker and Tennessee Ernie Ford [REAL]. Roy's Records sells recordings of this song that year in Hill Valley, and many children, including Milton Baines, ride the Crockett craze by wearing coonskin caps [BTF1].

- Emmett Brown decides that the Brooklyn Dodgers are his favorite Major League Baseball team [BTF1-n].

Sometime Before November 1955 A.D.

- Emmett Brown befriends Charlie, the night watchman at Hill Valley City Hall. The two bond over their mutual love for the "Old West" and Hill Valley history. Charlie often bends the rules, allowing Doc to spend time afterhours in the City Archives, provided that the scientist shares his historical discoveries with the man [BTF3-n].

Saturday, November 5, 1955 A.D.—Shortly After 6:15 AM

- Marty McFly arrives in 1955 following a car chase with Libyan nationalists in 1985 that caused him to travel back in time in Emmett Brown's DeLorean. Disorientated, he careens into the barn of Otis Peabody's Twin Pines Ranch. Mistaking Marty and the DeLorean for an extraterrestrial and its spaceship, "Old Man" Peabody opens fire. Marty speeds away from the farm, accidentally obliterating one of the farmer's young pine trees [BTF1-n].
    NOTE: The time was briefly visible on the DeLorean's chronometer, though it is curious that Doc would have specified a different arrival time, given that he had intended to leave 1985 at around 1:35 AM. In the first film's fourth-draft

screenplay, Marty's time-traveling adventures began on March 19, 1955.

- Panic-stricken, Marty McFly drives along a barren road devoid of familiar landmarks, unaware he has traveled back in time. He discovers a billboard advertising Lyon Estates' Home of Tomorrow—the same subdivision where he will live thirty years in the future. But with the DeLorean's lone plutonium charge expended, he is unable to return to his own era [BTF1].

- In one timeline, Marty discovers his own house, now just a prototype used to market Lyon Estates, and parks in his future driveway, listening to a 1955 broadcast on the car's radio. He hides down in the seat when a police cruiser passes by, then uses his future key to unlock the garage. Stashing the DeLorean in the garage, Marty begins the two-mile hike to Hill Valley [BTF1-n].
    NOTE: That Marty was able to open the garage would indicate that the lock was never changed throughout the next three decades, from prototype through multiple owners.

Saturday, November 5, 1955 A.D.—Shortly Before 8:30 AM

- In another reality, Marty hides the vehicle behind a Lyon Estates billboard and walks into town. He reaches Hill Valley proper, stunned at the sight of the pristine Courthouse Square. A discarded newspaper confirms the impossible: The year is 1955. Disorientated, he wanders into Lou's Café, run by Lou Caruthers, and peruses the telephone directory, searching for Doc's phone number. No one answers when he calls, so Marty orders a coffee and sits at the counter to collect his senses

    While there, Marty meets Goldie Wilson, an African-American youth working as a busboy. Goldie longs to do more than bus tables, and Marty's comment that he'll one day be Hill Valley's mayor inspires him to enter politics. [BTF1].

NIKE	*BTTF*-themed TV commercial: Nike	**SCRT**	2010 Scream Awards: *Back to the Future*	**SUFFIX**	**MEDIUM**	
NTND	Nintendo *Back to the Future—The Ride* Mini-Game		25th Anniversary Reunion (trailer)	**-b**	*BTF2's* Biff Tannen Museum video (extended version)	**-s1** Screenplay (draft one)
		SIMP	Simulator: *The Simpsons Ride*			**-s2** Screenplay (draft two)
PIZA	*BTTF*-themed TV commercial: Pizza Hut	**SLOT**	*Back to the Future* Video Slots	**-c**	Animated series credit sequence	**-s3** Screenplay (draft three)
REAL	Real life	**TEST**	Screen tests: Crispin Glover, Lea Thompson	**-d**	Film deleted scene	**-s4** Screenplay (draft four)
RIDE	Simulator: *Back to the Future—The Ride*		and Thomas F. Wilson	**-n**	Film novelization	**-sp** Screenplay (production draft)
SCRM	2010 Scream Awards: *Back to the Future*	**TLTL**	Telltale Games' *Back to the Future—The Game*	**-o**	Film outtake	**-sx** Screenplay (*Paradox*)
	25th Anniversary Reunion (broadcast)	**UNIV**	Universal Studios Hollywood promotional video	**-v**	Video game print materials or commentaries	

• When a teenaged Biff Tannen enters the café, Marty realizes he's been sitting next to George McFly, his own father, now a young man. Marty watches a scene all too familiar, as Tannen bullies George into doing his homework. George concedes to Biff's wishes, and Tannen and his three cronies (Match, 3-D and Skinhead) leave the eatery. George leaves as a distracted Marty tries to make sense of it all, and Marty follows him [BTF1].

CODE	STORY
ARGN	BTTF-themed TV commercial: Arrigoni
BFAN	*Back to the Future: The Animated Series*
BFCG	*Back to the Future: The Card Game*
BFCL	*Back to the Future* comic book (limited series)
BFCM	*Back to the Future* comic book (monthly series)
BFHM	*BTTF*-themed McDonald's Happy Meal boxes
BTFA	*Back to the Future Annual* (Marvel Comics)

BTF1	Film: *Back to the Future*
BTF2	Film: *Back to the Future Part II*
BTF3	Film: *Back to the Future Part III*
BUDL	*BTTF*-themed TV commercial: Bud Light
CHEK	*BTTF*-themed music video: O'Neal McKnight, "Check Your Coat"
CHIC	Photographs hanging in Doc Brown's Chicken restaurant at Universal Studios

CITY	*BTTF*-themed music video: Owl City, "Deer in the Headlights"
DCTV	*BTTF*-themed TV commercial: DirecTV
ERTH	*The Earth Day Special*
GALE	Interviews and commentaries: Bob Gale and/or Robert Zemeckis
GARB	*BTTF*-themed TV commercials: Garbarino
GETV	*BTTF*-themed TV commercial: GE

HUEY	*BTTF*-themed music video: Huey Lewis and the News, "The Power of Love"
LIMO	*BTTF*-themed music video: The Limousines, "The Future"
MCDN	*BTTF*-themed TV commercial: McDonald's
MITS	*BTTF*-themed TV commercial: Mitsubishi Lancer
MSFT	*BTTF*-themed TV commercial: Microsoft

GEORGE KNOCKS OUT BIFF TANNEN WITH ONE PUNCH, WINNING LORRAINE BAINES' LOVE

Saturday, November 5, 1955 A.D.—Midday

• In one possible timeline, George McFly climbs a tree and uses a pair of binoculars to watch a beautiful young woman named Lorraine Baines undressing in her bedroom. George loses his hold and slips out of the tree, landing in the middle of the street, where he is hit by a car driven by Loraine's father, Sam Baines. Sam brings the injured youth into his home, where George and Lorraine fall in love. She agrees to accompany him to the Enchantment Under the Sea dance, and a lifelong romance begins [BTF1].

• In an altered timeline, Marty McFly pushes George McFly out of the way of Sam Baines' oncoming car, and is instead hit by the vehicle himself. George recovers and flees the scene in fear, leaving Marty unconscious on the road. Sam rushes to Marty's aid, carrying the youth (instead of George) into his home.

   Marty later awakens inside the Baines home, to the sight of his mother, Lorraine Baines, thirty years younger. To his horror, his future mother flirts with him, calling him Calvin Klein (the name stamped on his designer underwear). Marty resists her advances, but agrees to dine with her family (his future grandparents, aunt and uncles). When Lorraine suggests that he spend the night with them while recovering from the accident, Marty makes a hasty retreat, determined to avoid his mother's incestuous interest, and to locate Doc Brown and get back to the future [BTF1].

Saturday, November 5, 1955 A.D.—4:20 PM

• In one possible timeline, Emmett Brown stands on a porcelain toilet and hangs a wall clock in his bathroom without incident, thus never conceiving of the Flux Capacitor or inventing time travel [BFCG].

• In another reality, Emmett Brown slips on the porcelain toilet while hanging the clock and bumps his head. He receives a "revelation" during the injury, enabling him to conceive of a device called a Flux Capacitor, which he believes will make time travel possible [BFCG].

   NOTE: In BTF1's original screenplay, this occurred on March 19, 1955.

				SUFFIX	MEDIUM		
NIKE	BTTF-themed TV commercial: Nike	**SCRT**	2010 Scream Awards: Back to the Future 25th Anniversary Reunion (trailer)			**-s1**	Screenplay (draft one)
NTND	Nintendo Back to the Future—The Ride Mini-Game	**SIMP**	Simulator: The Simpsons Ride	**-b**	BTF2's Biff Tannen Museum video (extended version)	**-s2**	Screenplay (draft two)
PIZA	BTTF-themed TV commercial: Pizza Hut	**SLOT**	Back to the Future Video Slots	**-c**	Animated series credit sequence	**-s3**	Screenplay (draft three)
REAL	Real life	**TEST**	Screen tests: Crispin Glover, Lea Thompson and Thomas F. Wilson	**-d**	Film deleted scene	**-s4**	Screenplay (draft four)
RIDE	Simulator: Back to the Future—The Ride			**-n**	Film novelization	**-sp**	Screenplay (production draft)
SCRM	2010 Scream Awards: Back to the Future 25th Anniversary Reunion (broadcast)	**TLTL**	Telltale Games' Back to the Future—The Game	**-o**	Film outtake	**-sx**	Screenplay (Paradox)
		UNIV	Universal Studios Hollywood promotional video	**-v**	Video game print materials or commentaries		

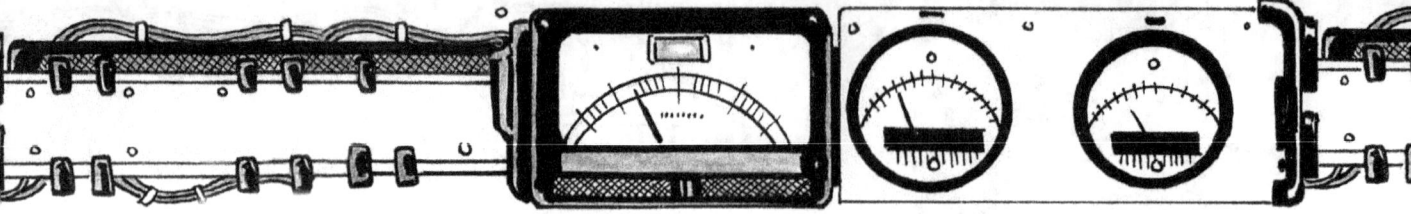

Saturday, November 5, 1955 A.D.—After 4:20 PM

• In one possible timeline, Marty McFly visits 1640 Riverside Drive to find Emmett Brown and seek his help in getting back to his own era. The scientist doesn't believe him, however, even when he recounts Doc's accident that resulted in his inventing the Flux Capacitor. Frustrated, Marty leaves the inventor's house and kills some time until midnight, intending to sneak the DeLorean to Brown's home. In the meantime, he stops at the Essex Theatre to watch *The Atomic Kid*, starring Mickey Rooney. After the movie, he returns to the DeLorean, still parked in his future home, and gets some sleep for the next several hours, waking up around midnight [BTF1-n].

• In another reality, Marty's recount of how Doc invented time travel succeeds in convincing the scientist that Marty is from the future. The two drive to the Lyon Estates highway billboard where Marty stashed the DeLorean. Upon seeing proof that he will finally invent something that works, Doc feels overjoyed and vindicated. The two sneak the car back to Brown's garage, where Marty shows him videotape documentation of the time machine's 1985 maiden voyage.

• In viewing the tape, Doc learns that without plutonium, the vehicle will never receive the 1.21 jigowatts of electricity necessary to return to the future. Distraught, he tells Marty that the youth is stuck in 1955. Marty protests, but Doc insists that only a bolt of lightning has the required power, and that no one can predict when lightning will strike. Marty shows him a "Save the Clock Tower" campaign flyer from 1985, describing the exact date and time on which the tower will be struck by lightning—and it's only one week away.

> *NOTE: "Jigowatts," an incorrect spelling of "gigawatts," is how the term appeared in the various* **Back to the Future** *screenplays. As such, that spelling is used in this book.*

• Invigorated by the possibilities, Doc vows to get Marty back to the future, but strongly urges him to stay out of sight in the meantime, lest he inadvertently alter his own future. Marty awkwardly reveals, however, that he's already bumped into his parents. A quick look at a photograph of Marty's siblings confirms Doc's fears—Marty's older brother, David, is already beginning to vanish from the picture. Like a ripple effect, the teen's interaction with his parents has altered time, and he, too, will soon cease to exist as well [BTF1].

> *NOTE: In* **BTF1***'s fourth-draft screenplay, Marty arrives at Doc's house to find a swinging party in progress. An eclectic mix of high-society types, beatniks and beautiful women congregate in Doc's house, with Marvin and the Moonlighters providing live music.*

Sunday, November 6, 1955 A.D.—12:00 AM

• In the timeline in which Doc Brown didn't believe Marty's story, the teen drives the DeLorean down the deserted Hill Valley streets under cover of darkness, to Doc's garage. Since the scientist hides his key in the same place in 1955 that he will in 1985, Marty is able to park the DeLorean inside and wake up the inventor. At first, Brown is outraged at the intrusion, but upon seeing the working DeLorean, he is overcome with pride and excitement, knowing that he has finally invented something that works [BTF1-n].

• After viewing the DeLorean for the first time, Brown calls his stock broker, Murray, and tells him to heavily invest in stainless steel, under the mistaken assumption that all automobiles will be made from this material in the future [BTF1-s4].

Monday, November 7, 1955 A.D.

• Emmett Brown and Marty McFly infiltrate Hill Valley High School at the start of the school morning, hoping to introduce Marty's would-be parents, George McFly

CODE	STORY					
ARGN	BTTF-themed TV commercial: Arrigoni	BTF1	Film: *Back to the Future*	CITY	BTTF-themed music video: Owl City, "Deer in the Headlights"	HUEY	BTTF-themed music video: Huey Lewis and the News, "The Power of Love"

CODE	STORY
ARGN	BTTF-themed TV commercial: Arrigoni
BFAN	*Back to the Future: The Animated Series*
BFCG	*Back to the Future: The Card Game*
BFCL	*Back to the Future* comic book (limited series)
BFCM	*Back to the Future* comic book (monthly series)
BFHM	BTTF-themed McDonald's Happy Meal boxes
BTFA	*Back to the Future Annual* (Marvel Comics)

BTF1	Film: *Back to the Future*
BTF2	Film: *Back to the Future Part II*
BTF3	Film: *Back to the Future Part III*
BUDL	BTTF-themed TV commercial: Bud Light
CHEK	BTTF-themed music video: O'Neal McKnight, "Check Your Coat"
CHIC	Photographs hanging in Doc Brown's Chicken restaurant at Universal Studios

CITY	BTTF-themed music video: Owl City, "Deer in the Headlights"
DCTV	BTTF-themed TV commercial: DirecTV
ERTH	*The Earth Day Special*
GALE	Interviews and commentaries: Bob Gale and/or Robert Zemeckis
GARB	BTTF-themed TV commercials: Garbarino
GETV	BTTF-themed TV commercial: GE

HUEY	BTTF-themed music video: Huey Lewis and the News, "The Power of Love"
LIMO	BTTF-themed music video: The Limousines, "The Future"
MCDN	BTTF-themed TV commercial: McDonald's
MITS	BTTF-themed TV commercial: Mitsubishi Lancer
MSFT	BTTF-themed TV commercial: Microsoft

and Lorraine Baines, and restore the damaged space-time continuum. But when Marty presents George to Lorraine, the dreamy-eyed young woman ignores him, having eyes only for Marty. Doc suggests setting them up for a date, and Marty remembers that the Enchantment Under the Sea Dance—the occasion during which his parents historically shared their first kiss—will take place the following Saturday.

Marty repeatedly tries to convince George to ask Lorraine out, but George fears rejection and is dead-set against putting his heart on the line, especially since local bully Biff Tannen is also pursuing Lorraine's "affection." Through his talks with George, Marty learns that his father is a science fiction fan and an aspiring writer—though he's too fearful to let anyone read his work. Marty begins to understand that he and his father are not so unalike, and forms a plan, based on George's sci-fi interests, to get his parents back on the path to love [BTF1].

• Marty McFly follows George home, where he witnesses first-hand the source of many of George's insecurities: his father (Marty's grandfather), Arthur McFly, who is washing the family car in the driveway. George announces that he wants to go to college in order to become a better writer—perhaps even a journalist—but Arthur quickly shoots down his son's dreams, citing numerous obstacles he would face, and encouraging him not to risk failure. Defeated, George concedes his father's advice [BTF1-n].

• The *Hill Valley Telegraph* runs a front-page story titled "Local Farmer Claims 'Space Zombie' Wrecked His Barn," reporting that Otis Peabody is under observation at the county asylum following claims of an extraterrestrial encounter on his farm [BTF1-n].

• Inspired by George's love of science fiction, as well as the article about Otis Peabody, Marty stages an elaborate ruse utilizing 1980s-era technology, such as a radiation

suit, a Sony Walkman containing a Van Halen cassette tape, and an electric hairdryer. Posing as "Darth Vader from the planet Vulcan," he demands that George ask Lorraine to the Enchantment Under the Sea Dance, or else suffer a melted brain. Terrified, George readily agrees [BTF1, BTF1-n].

> **NOTE: In a deleted scene from BTF1, as well as in the film's novelization, Marty's ruse also included Vader's extraterrestrial leader the Supreme Klingon, and his spaceship, the Battlestar Galactica.**

• Marty uses chloroform to knock out George after issuing his commands. Since the dosage is too high, George oversleeps for most of the next day, missing school [BTF1-d].

Tuesday, November 8, 1955 A.D. — Afternoon

• George McFly awakens with a new purpose in life: to ask Lorraine Baines on a date. Looking for advice, he seeks out Marty, who coaches him on how to treat women and offers several pickup lines. Emboldened with newfound confidence, George enters Lou's Café and approaches Lorraine—but his amorous proposal is cut short by the untimely intervention of Biff Tannen and his gang.

Biff orders George to leave the diner, but Marty steps in and stands up to the brute, sparking a fight that spills out onto the Courthouse Square. Marty leads Biff on a chase around the courtyard—Marty on a skateboard made from a passing child's scooter, Biff's gang in his Ford—increasing Lorraine's infatuation and leading her further away from George. Using a combination of street smarts and boarding skills, Marty outmaneuvers Biff, causing the bully and his friends to plow into a D. Jones Manure Hauling truck's rear end, and dumping fresh refuse all over the thugs. As witnesses crowd around Marty, George sulks away unnoticed, while lovestruck Lorraine vows to find out where "Calvin Klein" lives [BTF1].

MARTY PERFORMS FOR HIS
LIFE AT THE ENCHANTMENT
UNDER THE SEA DANCE

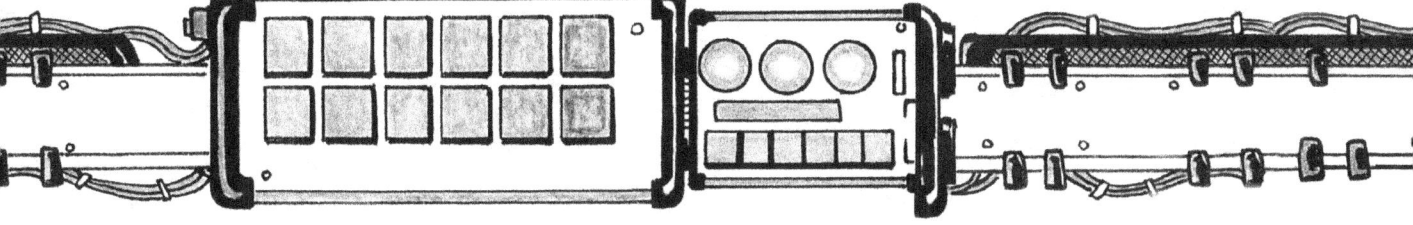

• Lorraine convinces her friend Babs to give her a ride in Babs' sister's car so they can follow Marty and find out where he lives. As they approach the vehicle, George marshals the courage to walk up to Lorraine and formally asks her to the dance. Her mind still on the enigmatic Calvin Klein, she blows him off, leaving him humiliated. She and Babs then trail Marty to Doc's garage [BTF1-n].

• Marty McFly finds Doc watching the 1985 video tape chronicling the DeLorean's maiden voyage. Knowing what's coming on the tape, Marty tries to warn him that he'll be killed by Libyan nationalists, but the scientist refuses to hear it, fearing that such foreknowledge could have dire consequences for the space-time continuum.

Changing the subject, Doc shows the teen a nearly scale model of Courthouse Square, explaining his plan to harness the lightning that will strike the Clock Tower on Saturday, and channel that energy into the Flux Capacitor. Lorraine Baines arrives, asking for Calvin. To Marty's surprise, she asks him to accompany her to the Enchantment Under the Sea Dance. Dumbstruck by the invitation and its incestuous implications, Marty tries to convince her to go with George McFly instead. Lorraine admits she finds George attractive, but says it's Marty's bravery that has won her over. Unable to dissuade her, Marty reluctantly agrees to go [BTF1].

• While bathing himself to clean off the manure, Biff Tannen is surprised when future versions of Doc and Marty inexplicably crawl in through his bathroom window and hurry out the door—impossibly stepping into a bowling alley, due to a bend in space-time caused by Verne Brown in 1992 [BFCL-3].

   NOTE: It's unknown whether Biff later remembered this event once Doc set history right.

Wednesday, November 9, 1955 A.D.

• Despite having accepted Lorraine's invitation to the Enchantment Under the Sea Dance, Marty devises a plot to help George win her affections. The plan: At approximately 9:00 PM that Saturday, Marty will pretend to take advantage of Loraine at the dance, giving George the opportunity to swoop in, "fight" Marty for her honor and prove his bravery to the young woman. George is nervous about the plan's success probability, but Marty gives him a quick lesson in self-confidence [BTF1].

Saturday, November 12, 1955 A.D.—6:00 AM

• Just before dawn, another Emmett Brown and Marty McFly arrive outside Hill Valley from an alternate 1985, in which Biff Tannen is wealthy, powerful and married to Lorraine, and has corrupted the town into a haven of lawlessness. The time-traveling duo has tracked an elderly Biff Tannen back to this date, after old Biff stole the DeLorean in 2015 in order to give his 1955 self a copy of *Grays Sports Almanac.* This second Marty's mission is to intercept the almanac and prevent young Biff from using it to bet on upcoming racing events and thereby bring about that dark future. Doc warns Marty to be careful and inconspicuous, and to avoid his slightly younger self, still working to make Lorraine fall in love with George. Emmett parks the DeLorean behind the Lyon Estates housing development sign, intending to wait there with the time machine so no one else can steal it [BTF2].

   NOTE: In the original script draft of BTF2, old Biff brought the almanac to September 20, 1967, rather than to the first film's events in 1955. That original storyline differed greatly from what appeared onscreen, beginning with the almanac itself. Originally, Marty retrieved the book within minutes of arriving, but was mistaken by authorities for a draft dodger and was put in jail. On his side were Goldie "Mohammad" Wilson, a young attorney (and Hill Valley's future mayor), and Vietnam War protestor Lorraine McFly. Believing Marty to be suffering for the cause, Lorraine spent her last five hundred dollars to bail him out of jail—money that she and husband George had originally used to pay for a second honeymoon, during which Marty was conceived. Once again, Marty placed his own existence in jeopardy, and the remainder of this script version involved Marty and Doc making multiple attempts to reimburse Lorraine for the money. Finally, during an anti-war rally, Marty made a stirring speech about the dangers of sacrificing family for politics and money, which moved the crowd to take up a donation for Lorraine and George, thereby securing Marty's conception.

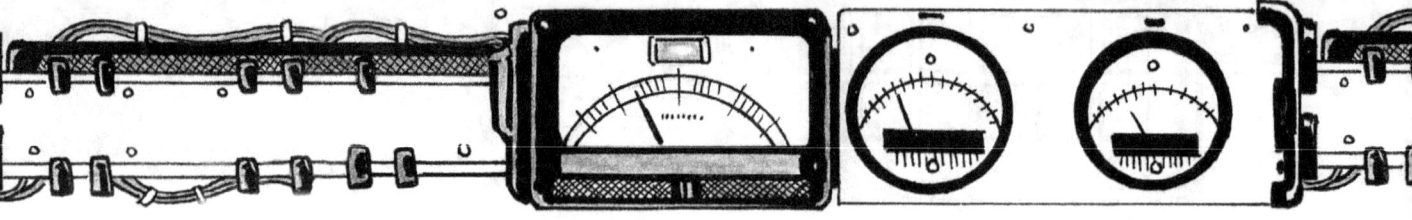

Saturday, November 12, 1955 A.D.—Midday

• Later that morning, the second Marty tracks down Biff to 1809 Mason Street, where the bully lives with his grandmother, Gertrude Tannen. Biff leaves for Courthouse Square to pick up his newly detailed, manure-free 1946 Ford convertible, and Marty discreetly follows. While Tannen haggles over price with a mechanic named Terry, Marty slips into the back seat and covers himself in a tarp [BTF2].

> *NOTE: BTF2's novelization cited Biff's address as 2311 Mason Street, and his car as a 1940 model. Onscreen, however, he lived at house 1809 and drove a 1946 vehicle.*

• Meanwhile, Lorraine Baines and Babs emerge from Ruth's Frock Shop with a dress that Lorraine plans to wear to the Enchantment Under the Sea Dance. Biff makes aggressive advances on Lorraine, but she spurns them, insisting she'd never marry him, even if he had a million dollars. Tannen vows he'll one day change her outlook, then is approached by his older self, posing as a distant relative. Old Biff drives Tannen home in the Ford, giving him *Grays Sports Almanac* and explaining its significance. At first, the burly teen doesn't believe the stranger, but when the book accurately predicts the radio-reported outcome of that day's UCLA-Washington football game, young Biff becomes intrigued.

As the two Biffs leave the garage, the older Tannen shoves the almanac in the teen's pocket and instructs him to keep the book safe and hidden—and, above all else, to kill a crazy scientist and his teenage friend if they ever come asking about it. Overhearing the exchange, Marty tries to follow Biff into the house so he can steal the almanac, but the garage door is locked, trapping him within. He radios Doc via walkie-talkie, but the scientist says it's too dangerous to take the DeLorean out in the daylight, and promises to devise a way to rescue Marty [BTF2].

Saturday, November 12, 1955 A.D.—6:38 PM

• That night, as young Biff Tannen prepares to attend the Enchantment Under the Sea Dance [BFCG], the Biff from 2015 returns to his own era [BTF2].

• With the *Grays Sports Almanac* in his back pocket, young Biff drives to Hill Valley High School, unaware that Marty is stowing away in the back seat. En route, Tannen passes by Doc Brown, traveling incognito with newly purchased 1950s-era clothing and a new bicycle. Doc arrives at Biff's garage, but Marty is no longer there. The youth discreetly radios Doc from Tannen's car to report that they are on the way to the dance. His plan: to snatch the almanac as soon as Biff is distracted.

The older Doc inadvertently stumbles upon his 1955 self as the latter is setting up the Courthouse Square experiment to send the first Marty back to 1985. Doc has a small conversation with himself, even assisting his younger counterpart in his preparations, and then hurries off to avoid damaging the timeline [BTF2].

Saturday, November 12, 1955 A.D.—Between 6:38 and 8:45 PM

• While the 1955 Emmett makes final adjustments to his experiment to send Marty back to 1985, the two friends reflect on the past week and the implications of all they've been through. While Doc is excited at what the future holds for him, Marty recalls that in 1985, the scientist will be murdered by vengeful terrorists moments before Marty travels back to the past. Once again, Marty tries to warn him, but Doc refuses to hear it, preferring to discover the future through the natural progression of time. Nonetheless, Marty visits Lou's Café and writes a note to his friend, hoping to persuade him to prepare for that fateful night [BTF1]. While Doc bribes a policeman to ignore the cables he has wired up to the Clock Tower, Marty sneaks the note into the scientist's coat [BTF1, BTF1-d].

CODE	STORY						
ARGN	BTTF-themed TV commercial: Arrigoni	BTF1	Film: *Back to the Future*	CITY	BTTF-themed music video: Owl City, "Deer in the Headlights"	HUEY	BTTF-themed music video: Huey Lewis and the News, "The Power of Love"
BFAN	*Back to the Future: The Animated Series*	BTF2	Film: *Back to the Future Part II*	DCTV	BTTF-themed TV commercial: DirecTV	LIMO	BTTF-themed music video: The Limousines, "The Future"
BFCG	*Back to the Future: The Card Game*	BTF3	Film: *Back to the Future Part III*	ERTH	*The Earth Day Special*		
BFCL	*Back to the Future* comic book (limited series)	BUDL	BTTF-themed TV commercial: Bud Light	GALE	Interviews and commentaries: Bob Gale and/or Robert Zemeckis	MCDN	BTTF-themed TV commercial: McDonald's
BFCM	*Back to the Future* comic book (monthly series)	CHEK	BTTF-themed music video: O'Neal McKnight, "Check Your Coat"			MITS	BTTF-themed TV commercial: Mitsubishi Lancer
BFHM	BTTF-themed McDonald's Happy Meal boxes			GARB	BTTF-themed TV commercials: Garbarino		
BTFA	*Back to the Future Annual* (Marvel Comics)	CHIC	Photographs hanging in Doc Brown's Chicken restaurant at Universal Studios	GETV	BTTF-themed TV commercial: GE	MSFT	BTTF-themed TV commercial: Microsoft

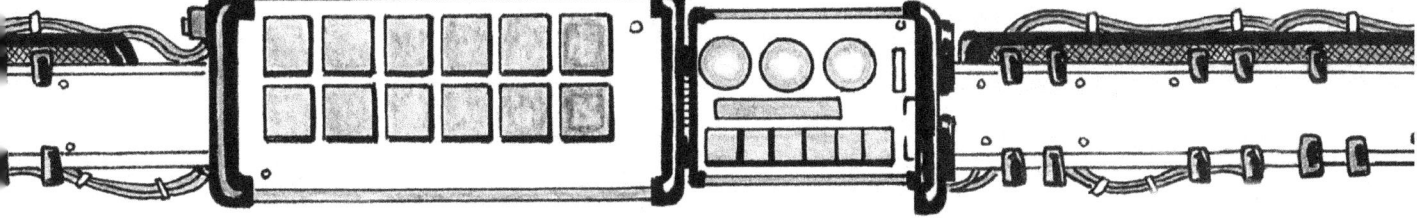

NOTE: Doc's bribery was implied in the film's theatrical release without specifically being shown—he pulled out a wallet, but the audience saw no monetary exchange. A deleted scene, however, zeroed in on a twenty-dollar bill in the scientist's wallet, thereby removing any ambiguity.

Saturday, November 12, 1955 A.D.—8:45 PM

• A second Marty McFly, attempting to prevent a gritty parallel 1985, follows Biff Tannen into the school gym, keeping an eye on the *Grays Sports Almanac*. Biff joins Match, Skinhead and 3-D by the punch bowl—which they spike—as the goons look through *Oh LàLà*, a racy French magazine featuring scantily clad lingerie models. Principal Gerald Strickland becomes suspicious of the young ne'er-do-wells' activity by the punch bowl, so Tannen and his friends head outside.

Biff instructs his gang to find "Calvin Klein" so he can settle the score over the manure incident. As Biff's cronies head out in search of Marty, Biff casually thumbs through *Oh LàLà*, the almanac resting in his back pocket. With Biff distracted, Marty sneaks up behind him and reaches for the almanac, but jumps back into hiding when Strickland confronts Tannen about his troublemaking and confiscates the book. Scolding Tannen for being a slacker, the principal returns to his office with the almanac. Marty follows, careful not to be seen as the *other* Marty arrives in Doc Brown's Packard with Lorraine [BTF2].

• As Marty tries to grab the almanac, Doc rides the bicycle to the Lyon Estates billboard to retrieve the DeLorean. However, he discovers a raving Otis Peabody and a police officer searching the area for extraterrestrials. Peabody is convinced that the "space alien" he claims killed one of his pines is still on the loose, and has drafted the cop's help in tracking the creature down. To throw them off the scent, Doc tells them he also saw a flying saucer, heading in the opposite direction. Peabody and the policemen rush to capture the mutating space monster, giving Doc the opportunity to reload the DeLorean's Mr. Fusion in preparation for his rendezvous with Marty [BTF2-n].

Saturday, November 12, 1955 A.D.—9:00 PM

• At Hill Valley High School's Enchantment Under the Sea Dance, George McFly enjoys the rock-n-roll music of Marvin Berry and the Starlighters while awaiting his cue. Marty, meanwhile, prepares to "force" himself on Lorraine, giving George the opportunity to intervene, defend Lorraine's honor and win her heart. Sitting in a parked car with his own immodestly dressed mother, however, he finds himself hesitant to go through with the act.

To his horror, Marty discovers that his young mom is no stranger to smoking, drinking or parking in cars with boys. Lorraine impulsively kisses Marty, but pulls away, feeling as though she's just kissed her brother. The door suddenly opens, but rather than George, he finds Biff standing there. Drunk and angry, Biff sends his cronies to rough up Marty while he makes his move on Lorraine [BTF1].

• George suffers from nervous stomach cramps while awaiting his big moment, making repeated visits to the men's room. His third return interrupts Mark Dixon (George's frequent tormentor) and other teens enjoying a smoking break. Dixon drops his joint, fearing he's been busted, and is furious when he realizes it was just McFly. In retaliation, he waits for George to enter a stall, then blocks it and leaves. George pleads to be let out, but Dixon says he and his friends will take ten-minute shifts for the remainder of the night, holding the door closed, to make George miss the dance. This continues for nearly twenty minutes, before Principal Strickland breaks up the shenanigans and calls McFly a slacker. The frazzled youth runs to the parking lot, late for his date with destiny [BTF1-n].

NIKE	*BTTF*-themed TV commercial: Nike	**SCRT**	2010 Scream Awards: *Back to the Future*	**SUFFIX**	**MEDIUM**	**-s1**	Screenplay (draft one)

NIKE — *BTTF*-themed TV commercial: Nike
NTND — Nintendo *Back to the Future—The Ride* Mini-Game
PIZA — *BTTF*-themed TV commercial: Pizza Hut
REAL — Real life
RIDE — Simulator: *Back to the Future—The Ride*
SCRM — 2010 Scream Awards: *Back to the Future* 25th Anniversary Reunion (broadcast)

SCRT — 2010 Scream Awards: *Back to the Future* 25th Anniversary Reunion (trailer)
SIMP — Simulator: *The Simpsons Ride*
SLOT — *Back to the Future* Video Slots
TEST — Screen tests: Crispin Glover, Lea Thompson and Thomas F. Wilson
TLTL — Telltale Games' *Back to the Future—The Game*
UNIV — Universal Studios Hollywood promotional video

SUFFIX MEDIUM
-b — *BTF2*'s Biff Tannen Museum video (extended version)
-c — Animated series credit sequence
-d — Film deleted scene
-n — Film novelization
-o — Film outtake
-v — Video game print materials or commentaries

-s1 — Screenplay (draft one)
-s2 — Screenplay (draft two)
-s3 — Screenplay (draft three)
-s4 — Screenplay (draft four)
-sp — Screenplay (production draft)
-sx — Screenplay (*Paradox*)

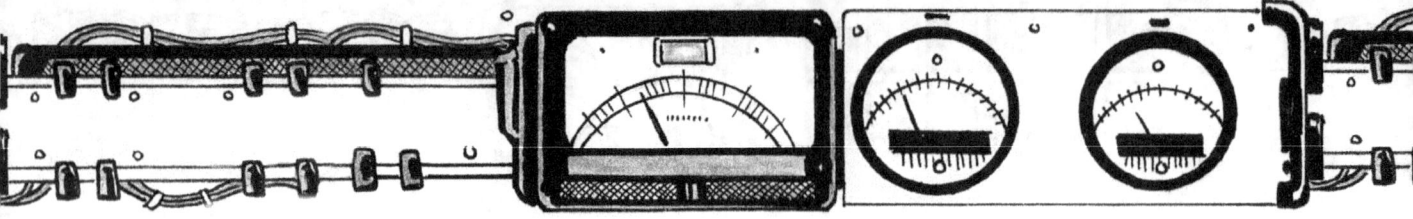

Saturday, November 12, 1955 A.D.—9:05 PM

• George sees a struggle in Marty's car and steadies himself to carry out Marty's plan—but to his horror, he finds Biff in the car with Lorraine, not Marty. Lorraine begs George to save her, while Tannen warns him to step away. Despite his fear, George confronts the thug, telling him to leave her alone. Biff steps out of the car and attacks George, enabling the young man to conquer his fear and slug him hard in the face, knocking Tannen out cold with a single punch. George turns his attention to Lorraine and gently helps her to her feet. Astonished, Lorraine truly sees George for the first time [BTF1].

• In an alternate timeline, George, fearing confrontation, avoids the parking-lot fight with Biff [BFCG].

Saturday, November 12, 1955 A.D.—9:00 to 9:05 PM

• The Marty attempting to prevent future Biff from criminalizing Hill Valley sneaks into Strickland's office and secures the *Grays Sports Almanac*—or so he thinks. In fact, he has only nabbed the dust jacket, wrapped around Biff's copy of *Oh LàLà*. Distraught, he reports his failure to Doc via walkie-talkie. The scientist urges him to find the book, or else the future will be bleak.

   Marty hears George standing up to Biff in the parking lot and realizes his opportunity is at hand. He hurries outside in time to see George knock Biff unconscious. As George helps Lorraine to her feet and back to the dance, Marty rushes to Tannen's side, finding the actual almanac tucked inside his coat pocket. Biff comes to, but Marty knocks him out again, stealing the book and racing off [BTF2]. A nearby student named Lester mistakenly assumes Marty is stealing his wallet [BTF2-n].

• Meanwhile, Biff's gang locks the first Marty in the trunk of Marvin Berry's car. The band, enjoying a smoke break, chase off the hooligans and pry Marty free, but at the cost of lead guitarist Berry slicing his hand open with a screwdriver. Marty rushes to find his father, but

although George has saved the day, Marty's 1985 photo is still fading. For history to be righted, Marty realizes, George and Lorraine must kiss on the dance floor. With Berry's hand out of commission, however, all hope seems lost—until Marty volunteers to take his place onstage [BTF1].

Saturday, November 12, 1955 A.D.—9:18 to 9:55 PM

• As Marty performs with the Starlighters, he slowly begins fading from existence. On the dance floor, George has trouble working up the courage to kiss Lorraine, particularly when Mark Dixon rudely cuts in. Just as Marty is about to vanish completely, George finally makes his move. He pushes Dixon out of the way and kisses Lorraine, restoring Marty's full form and repairing the damaged space-time continuum. With the crisis averted, Marty indulges himself in one last show-stopping number, playing a Van Halen-esque rendition of "Johnny B. Goode" that is far ahead of its time. The rollicking tune is so catchy that it prompts Marvin to phone his cousin, Chuck Berry, so he can listen to it over a backstage phone [BTF1].

• The other Marty, attempting to retrieve the *Grays Sports Almanac* from Biff Tannen, runs into complications when Biff's gang finds him and chases him into the gym. The thugs spot the first Marty onstage playing "Johnny B. Goode," and wait in the wings for him to finish his song, so that they can pounce on him. This would prevent Marty from making it back to 1985 in the first place, thereby causing a paradox. The second Marty's only chance is to intervene on his younger self's behalf. Climbing backstage scaffolding, the second Marty drops sandbags on Biff's gang, knocking them out as the song ends, and saving the onstage version from harm [BTF2].

• At the Lyon Estates billboard, Doc prepares to lift off in the newly refueled DeLorean [BTF2]. Otis Peabody drives by, sees the vehicle becoming airborne, hops out of his truck and opens fire with a shotgun. While

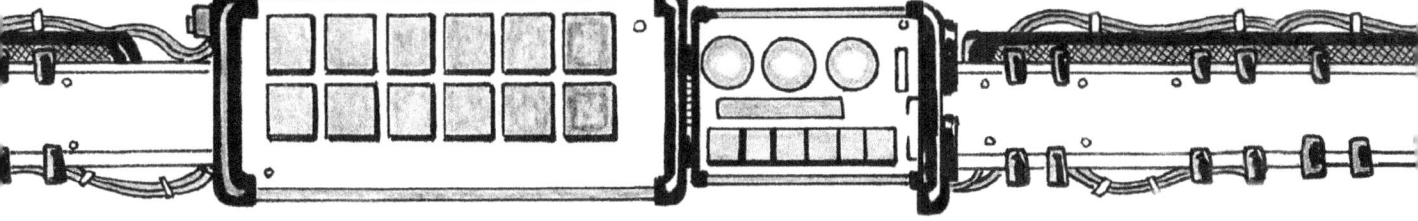

maneuvering around the blasts, Doc hits the sign, then zooms over the pine breeder's head and flies off toward the high school [BTF2-n], unaware that the car is trailing pennants [BTF2].

- After finishing his guitar solo, Marty bids farewell to his parents, confident that they can now forge a happy relationship together. As he leaves, Lorraine reflects on how much she likes the name "Marty" [BTF1].

- The newly bolstered George confides in Lorraine that he is determined to go to college, regardless of what his father, Arthur McFly, might say [BTF1-n].

- In one timeline, sans Marty's intervention, George McFly and Lorraine Baines go to the Enchantment Under the Sea Dance together and kiss for the first time on the dance floor, leading to a lasting but dull marriage [BFCG, BTF1]. In another turn of events, Marty botches up the timeline, causing George and Lorraine not to make a love connection, get married or have children [BFCG].

- The second Marty McFly races outside with the *Grays Sports Almanac*, preparing to meet Doc and the DeLorean on the roof. While he stops to enjoy the sight of his future parents cuddling, Biff Tannen shows up and challenges him to a fight. Marty is about to walk away, but Biff calls him a "chicken." His pride called into question, Marty turns to face the bully, just as the first Marty hastily exits through the door, which slams the older Marty in the face, dazing him.

  As the first Marty hurries off, unaware of what he's done, Biff sees that the second Marty has the almanac in his possession. The thug kicks the older Marty in the gut and retrieves the book, making his getaway before Marty can catch up with him. Empty-handed, Marty climbs to the roof and informs Doc that Biff got away with the almanac. Together, the duo enter the flying DeLorean and follow Biff's Ford [BTF2].

Saturday, November 12, 1955 A.D.—9:55 to 9:58 PM

- Changing out of his 1955 attire, the first Marty McFly arrives at Courthouse Square with only moments to spare before lightning will strike the Clock Tower. As he and Doc exchange a heartfelt goodbye, the scientist discovers a note that Marty had written and slipped into his coat, detailing the events surrounding Doc's future death, in the hope that he will take precautions to avoid that fate. Outraged that Marty would further jeopardize the space-time continuum, Doc tears up the letter. Marty tries to warn him outright, but is interrupted when Doc's carefully constructed configuration of wires is torn down by a tree felled by the lightning storm. With only minutes to reach the DeLorean's starting point and attain a speed of 88 miles per hour at exactly 10:04, Marty rushes off without warning his friend, trusting Doc to fix the equipment [BTF1].

- Out on the highway, older Doc lowers the flying DeLorean so the second Marty can slip outside and use the hoverboard (procured in 2015) to retrieve the *Grays Sports Almanac* from Biff. Marty discreetly hovers close to Tannen's car as Doc pulls away to avoid being noticed [BTF2].

- Marty tries unsuccessfully to steal the almanac from Biff's front seat, culminating in a high-speed struggle through the Deacon's Hill Tunnel [BTF2-n], and nearly costing Marty his life. At last, Marty grabs the book and starts hoverboarding toward the tunnel entrance, Biff's faster vehicle bearing down on him. As Doc sweeps in at the entrance, Marty grabs the pennants trailing from the DeLorean and ascends to safety.

  Tannen loses control of his car and crashes into a D. Jones Manure Hauling truck for the second time that week. Doc and Marty bring the sports almanac to the Lyon Estates billboard as the lightning storm worsens. Marty burns the book to ash, restoring the original timeline and saving his father's life—but before Doc

NIKE	*BTTF*-themed TV commercial: Nike	**SCRT**	2010 Scream Awards: *Back to the Future*	**SUFFIX**	**MEDIUM**	**-s1**	Screenplay (draft one)
NTND	Nintendo *Back to the Future—The Ride*		25th Anniversary Reunion (trailer)	**-b**	*BTF2*'s Biff Tannen Museum video	**-s2**	Screenplay (draft two)
	Mini-Game	**SIMP**	Simulator: *The Simpsons Ride*		(extended version)	**-s3**	Screenplay (draft three)
PIZA	*BTTF*-themed TV commercial: Pizza Hut	**SLOT**	*Back to the Future* Video Slots	**-c**	Animated series credit sequence	**-s4**	Screenplay (draft four)
REAL	Real life	**TEST**	Screen tests: Crispin Glover, Lea Thompson	**-d**	Film deleted scene	**-sp**	Screenplay (production draft)
RIDE	Simulator: *Back to the Future—The Ride*		and Thomas F. Wilson	**-n**	Film novelization	**-sx**	Screenplay (*Paradox*)
SCRM	2010 Scream Awards: *Back to the Future*	**TLTL**	Telltale Games' *Back to the Future—The Game*	**-o**	Film outtake		
	25th Anniversary Reunion (broadcast)	**UNIV**	Universal Studios Hollywood promotional video	**-v**	Video game print materials or commentaries		

DOC SENDS MARTY BACK...
TO THE FUTURE!

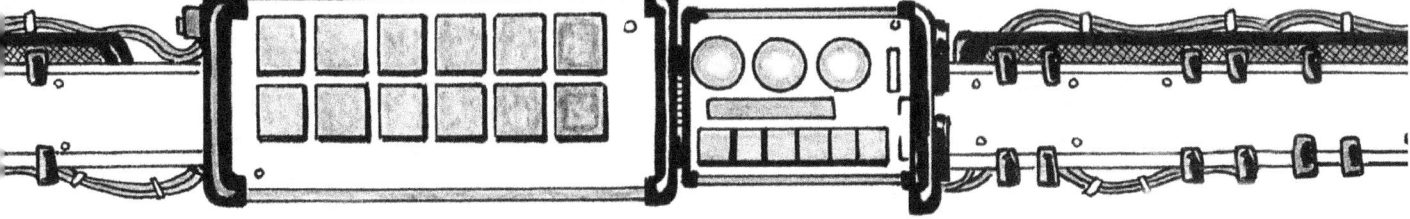

can swing back around to pick him up, the DeLorean is struck by a random lightning bolt. The time machine vanishes in a flash, leaving behind twin trails of fire. As the first drops of rain fall, Marty stands in shock, having apparently just witnessed his friend being vaporized [BTF2].

Saturday, November 12, 1955 A.D.— 10:00 to 10:04 PM

• Back in town, the first Marty races the DeLorean to his predetermined starting line, while 1955 Doc struggles at the Clock Tower to repair the connection to the cables that will channel the lightning into the Flux Capacitor. Upset that he failed to warn Doc of his grim future, the teen resets the time coordinates so the vehicle will arrive in 1985 before he actually left, enabling him to intervene in Doc's assassination. At the last second, Doc manages to reestablish the lightning-catching cables, just as Marty crosses the finish line [BTF1].

Saturday, November 12, 1955 A.D.—10:04 PM

• Lightning strikes the Clock Tower, destroying the clock and channeling 1.21 jigowatts into the Flux Capacitor, thereby sending Marty and the DeLorean back to 1985 [BTF1].

> **NOTE: In the fourth draft of BTF1's screenplay, the Clock Tower was struck at 10:02:11 PM on March 26, 1955.**

• As soon as Marty vanishes, Doc suddenly realizes he forgot to tell Marty to sign up for DirectTV HD after returning to 1985 [DCTV].

> **NOTE: This strange aside originated in a DirecTV commercial from 2007, in which Christopher Lloyd reprised his role as Doc Brown. DirecTV HD did not yet exist in 1985, however, so even if Doc had remembered to tell Marty, it would have been in vain.**

• Just as one Marty is sent back to the future, the second Marty remains at the Lyon Estates billboard, gaping in horror as the 1985 Doc has been struck by lightning and vanished. Unbeknownst to either Marty or Doc,

the flying DeLorean being struck by lightning causes a "temporal duplicate" to be created and instantly transported seventy years into the future, to the year 2025 [TLTL-1].

Saturday, November 12, 1955 A.D.—After 10:04 PM

• Suddenly, a mysterious car pulls up. The driver, a Western Union courier, has a letter for Marty, to be delivered at this exact location and time. Western Union, he explains, has had the letter for seventy years, two months and twelve days. Dumbfounded, Marty opens the letter, dated September 1, 1885, and learns that Doc survived the lightning strike and became stranded in the Old West. Marty vows to go back to 1885 and rescue his friend, but to do that, he'll need help. Therefore, he rushes back to Hill Valley to find the one man who can save the older Emmett Brown—namely, the Emmett of 1955 [BTF2].

> **NOTE: In the original screenplay draft for BTF2, Marty and Doc successfully returned to the corrected 1985 without the above complications. In that version, the film's climax was set in 1967. Throughout the course of the film, Marty learned to let go of his greed—most literally when, during a tense scene, the overweight DeLorean needed to shed a few pounds in order to reach 88 miles per hour. After stripping the car of all unnecessary parts, including the gullwing doors, Marty at last had to release the Grays Sports Almanac. As soon as the book dropped into the cavern below, the DeLorean blasted to 1985. Otis Peabody later stumbled upon the scrap metal at the bottom of the ravine; he also discovered the almanac, but burned it, mistaking it for trash. When Doc and Marty returned to 1985, they learned that Otis had collected the strange technology from the discarded DeLorean parts, believing them to be alien artifacts, and displayed them in a Hill Valley museum. In that draft, Peabody had achieved a measure of success from his find—recompense of a sort for the repeated traumas visited on him by the time-travelers.**

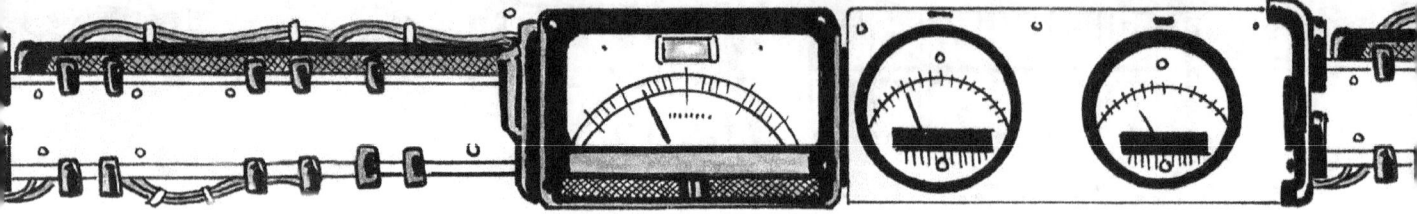

- Moments after successfully sending Marty back to the future, the 1955 Doc is floored when, inexplicably, a *second* Marty rounds a corner, wearing a leather jacket, and pleads for help. Overwhelmed, Doc simply passes out in the street [BTF2]. McFly then drives the unconscious scientist back to his estate [BTF3].

Sunday, November 13, 1955 A.D.—7:01 AM

- Upon awakening in his home, Doc assumes the second Marty was just a hallucination. He begins recording his memories of the evening for posterity, panicking when he discovers the youth in his living room. Initially skeptical of Marty's story, he realizes it's true when Marty shows him the letter Doc's older self wrote in 1885. According to the letter, the elder Brown lived a peaceful life as a blacksmith starting in 1885, safely stowing the DeLorean in the Delgado Mine, across from Boot Hill Cemetery, so that Marty would be able to return to his own era.

  Future Doc's letter includes explicit instructions for his 1955 counterpart to repair the damaged vehicle, and orders Marty to destroy the car after going back to the future, as their struggles with Biff Tannen have proven time travel to be far too dangerous. He asks that Marty not attempt to retrieve him from 1885, as he is happy in his new life [BTF3].

Sunday, November 13, 1955 A.D.—2:00 to 5:00 PM

- The Hill Valley Women's Club holds a bake sale at the Community Center on Forest Road [BTF2].

Monday, November 14, 1955 A.D.

- Utilizing dynamite, Doc creates an opening into the Delgado Mine, and fondly recounts to Marty his boyhood attempts at exploring this mine after being inspired by the works of Jules Verne. Inside, they find a walled-up portion of the cave, marked with Doc's initials, ELB. Removing the wall with a crowbar, the duo discovers the DeLorean, stored there since 1885 [BTF3-n].

  ***NOTE: Doc's clever use of initials was directly lifted from a trick employed by Arne Saknussemm, a character in Jules Verne's 1864 novel,* A Journey to the Center of the Earth.**

- Doc tows the vehicle out of the cave that night, while Marty makes a grisly discovery in nearby Boot Hill Cemetery: Emmett Brown's grave, dated September 7, 1885. According to the gravestone, erected by a mysterious woman named "Clara," Doc was shot in the back by Buford "Mad Dog" Tannen over a matter of eighty dollars [BTF3].

  Doc convinces Charlie, the night watchman of the City Archives, to let him and Marty into the basement of Hill Valley City Hall [BTF3-n]. There, the two friends uncover further details about the murder. Despite the letter's urging, Marty decides that as soon as the 1955 Doc completes repairs on the DeLorean, he will travel back to 1885 and save his friend from assassination [BTF3].

  NOTE: In the unfilmed script draft titled* Paradox, *Doc's death date was listed as Friday, April 13, 1888.

Wednesday, November 16, 1955 A.D.—9:55 AM

- After repairing the damaged DeLorean, Doc and Marty drive to the Pohatchee Drive-In Theatre since it offers a long patch of unobstructed land, both now and in 1885. Doc provides Marty with "authentic" 1955 Western wear for his rescue mission, and the two friends say goodbyes once more [BTF3].

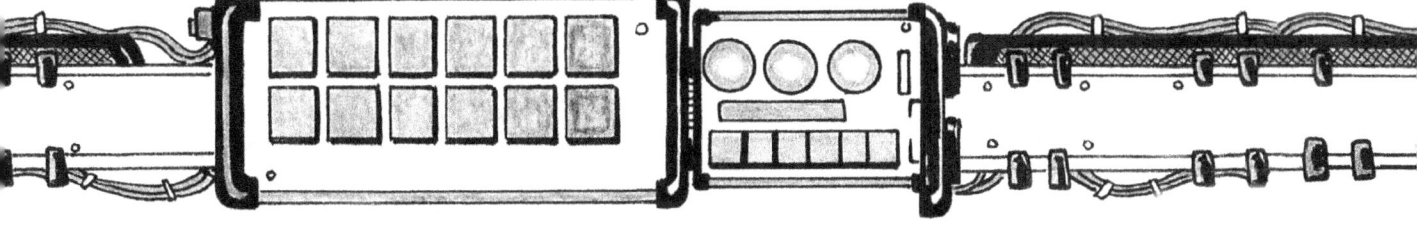

Wednesday, November 16, 1955 A.D.—10:00 AM

- Marty McFly drives the DeLorean straight at a wall containing a painting of the Pohatchee Indian tribe. Moments before impact, the DeLorean attains a speed of 88 miles per hour and travels back to September 2, 1885—where he encounters the actual tribe in the painting's place [BTF3].

Wednesday, November 16, 1955 A.D.—10:04 PM

- A research team from the Institute of Future Technology travels back from 1991 to conduct time-travel experiments with an experimental Eight-Passenger DeLorean Time-Travel Vehicle. Biff Tannen stows away in the vehicle, returning with the team to 1991 without their knowledge. Eventually, the IFT personnel apprehend Biff and send him back to 1955 [RIDE].

December 31, 1955 A.D.

- An episode of *The Honeymooners* titled "The Man From Space" airs for the first time on television [REAL].

  > *NOTE: In the first film, Lorraine Baines' family watched this episode while Marty McFly ate dinner at their home. This occurred, however, in November 1955, almost two months before "The Man From Space" aired on TV in the real world.*

Sometime After 1955 A.D.

- Riverside Drive is renamed John F. Kennedy Drive [BTF1].

Sometime Between 1955 and 1985 A.D.

- Red, a former classmate of George McFly and Lorraine Baines, becomes a homeless drunk, sleeping on an outdoor bench in Courthouse Square and ranting about "crazy drunk drivers" [BTF1].

  > *NOTE: Some Web sites have misidentified Red the bum as being the 1980s version of Frank "Red" Thomas, Hill Valley's mayor in 1955. However, a campaign-van photo of Thomas featured set decorator Hal Gausman, while the vagrant was played by George "Buck" Flower. Since BTF1's third-draft screenplay featured Red as a young man in the 1950s, he could not have been an adult politician at the time. Moreover, the bum would be far too young in 1985 to have been the mayor's visible age 30 years prior—by the 1980s, Thomas would have been a very old man.*

CHAPTER IX:
1956 A.D TO 1984 A.D.

1956 A.D.

• Ellen Baines is born to Sam and Stella Baines [BTF2-s1].
> *NOTE: Ellen was first named in BTF2's original screenplay draft, making her the only of Lorraine's siblings to be born after Marty McFly's adventures in 1955. Stella was visibly pregnant with Ellen in BTF1.*

• Biff Tannen graduates from Hill Valley High a second time, after being asked by the football team to repeat his senior year [BTF2-b].
> *NOTE: Biff's claim, in the museum footage, that he was asked to repeat his senior year may have been propaganda intended to cover up his having failed twelfth grade.*

1958 A.D.

• George McFly and Lorraine Baines are married [BFCG].

• Chuck Berry records the popular rock-n-roll song "Johnny B. Goode" [REAL], three years after his cousin, Marvin Berry, had called him up to hear Marty McFly performing the song at Hill Valley High School's Enchantment Under the Sea Dance in 1955 [BTF1].
> *NOTE: This would seem to indicate that in the altered timeline resulting from Marty's trip to 1955, Berry stole the song as his own (even though it was already his to begin with). Luckily for him, Marty was no longer around to sue him.*

Late 1950s A.D.

• While attending the American College of Technological Science & Difficult Math, both Emmett Brown and his roommate (and friendly rival inventor) Walter Wisdom enter the Inter-Collegiate Science Invent-Off. Hoping to capitalize on the hula-hoop craze, Brown invents the Perpetual Motion Hula Hoop. Realizing how lucrative such an invention could be, Wisdom betrays his friend, steals the device and claims it as his own design. Wisdom wins first place in the contest, signs a business deal with Clunko Toys for mass reproduction of the new and improved hula hoop, and parlays his victory into a television science show. As a result, Doc and Wisdom do not speak to one another for the next thirty years [BFAN-15].
> *NOTE: Given the styles of clothing and hair, as well as the "hula hoop fad" taking place at the time, Doc's college flashback sequences very likely took place in the late 1950s. The hula-hoop craze was at its zenith in 1958—but since that was three years after the first film, it seems unlikely that Doc would have attended college at the time. On the other hand, Wisdom recognized the Flux Capacitor and mentioned that Doc had talked about it in college, jibing with BTF1's timeline. As such, it's possible that Doc, in an effort to further his education before building the time machine, enrolled in classes after meeting Marty in 1955.*

Wednesday, March 26, 1958 A.D.—2:22 PM

• In one possible timeline, Biff Tannen turns 21 and celebrates his birthday by visiting the race track, where he loses all of his money [BFCG].

• In an alternate timeline, Biff Tannen visits that same racetrack equipped with a 21st-century copy of *Grays Sports Almanac*. By betting on the winners as outlined in the book, he becomes a millionaire overnight, resulting in a reality in which Biff becomes a powerful criminal kingpin and turns Hill Valley into a hellish city of sin. This begins a long winning streak that earns Biff the nickname "The Luckiest Man on Earth" [BTF2-b, BFCG].
> *NOTE: Onscreen, Emmett Brown unofficially dubbed this series of events as "Timeline A."*

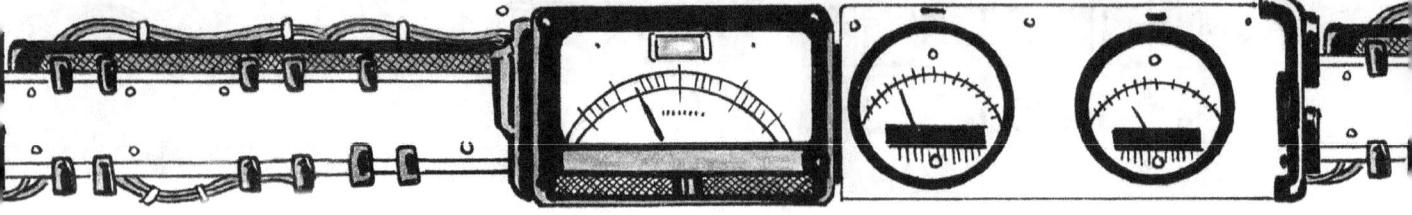

According to **Back to the Future: The Official Book of the Complete Movie Trilogy**, *BTF2's crew christened this reality as "Biffhorrific" while the movie was being produced. Other monikers for this alternate Hill Valley included "Hell Valley" (scrawled on the city's greeting sign), "Biff City" (mentioned in the movie's first-draft screenplay) and "Tannen Valley" (seen in the second-draft script).*

1960 A.D.

• Uranda, a future fashion model and terrorist, is born [BTF1-n].

Circa 1960s A.D.

• Ellen Baines becomes fascinated by science fiction, particularly the TV series *Lost in Space* [BTF2-s1].

• Emmett Brown develops a fondness for the type of college education offered during this decade, leading him, years later, to consider sending his sons, Jules and Verne, back to the 1960s to pursue their higher education [TLTL-1].
> *NOTE: Why Doc would wish to thus limit his sons' education is unclear.*

1961 A.D.

• As a result of experimental testing gone awry, Emmett Brown accidentally breaks every window in the Greater Hill Valley Medfield Basin [BFAN-3].
> *NOTE: The nature of this experimentation is unknown.*

Wednesday, August 1, 1962 A.D.

• Emmett Brown's family mansion, located at 1640 Riverside Drive, burns to the ground. Emmett, the estate's lone occupant at the time, lives thereafter in the house's surviving garage [BTF1].
> *NOTE: For years, fans have speculated that Doc may have burnt the house down himself in order to raise money for his experiments. Telltale Games referenced this popular theory by having Doc accused of burning down Irving "Kid" Tannen's speakeasy.*

Tuesday, November 5, 1963 A.D.—3:21 PM

• David McFly is born to Lorraine and George McFly [BTF1-n, BFCG].
> *NOTE: The first draft of BTF2's screenplay stated that Dave was five years old in 1967, placing his birthdate in 1962. The novelization, however, specified that he was born in 1963.*

Saturday, November 23, 1963 A.D.—8:22 PM

• In one possible timeline, Lorraine Baines finally agrees to a dinner-and-movie date with millionaire Biff Tannen, following years of pestering on Biff's part [BFCG].
> *NOTE: This was only one day after the assassination of U.S. President John F. Kennedy, so Lorraine, like many Americans, may have been emotionally upset at the time, and thus vulnerable to Biff's attentions, stemming from a desire not to be alone. The card game placed their relationship several years before Marty's birth in 1968, as well as before George's 1973 murder in BTF2, making it unlikely that this took place in the Biffhorrific timeline. In fact, it's unclear whether Lorraine ever married George in this version of history.*

1964 A.D.

• The Dixie Cups record their hit song "Chapel of Love" [REAL].

CODE	STORY						
ARGN	BTTF-themed TV commercial: Arrigoni	**BTF1**	Film: *Back to the Future*	**CITY**	BTTF-themed music video: Owl City, "Deer in the Headlights"	**HUEY**	BTTF-themed music video: Huey Lewis and the News, "The Power of Love"
BFAN	*Back to the Future: The Animated Series*	**BTF2**	Film: *Back to the Future Part II*	**DCTV**	BTTF-themed TV commercial: DirecTV	**LIMO**	BTTF-themed music video: The Limousines, "The Future"
BFCG	*Back to the Future: The Card Game*	**BTF3**	Film: *Back to the Future Part III*	**ERTH**	*The Earth Day Special*	**MCDN**	BTTF-themed TV commercial: McDonald's
BFCL	*Back to the Future* comic book (limited series)	**BUDL**	BTTF-themed TV commercial: Bud Light	**GALE**	Interviews and commentaries: Bob Gale and/or Robert Zemeckis	**MITS**	BTTF-themed TV commercial: Mitsubishi Lancer
BFCM	*Back to the Future* comic book (monthly series)	**CHEK**	BTTF-themed music video: O'Neal McKnight, "Check Your Coat"	**GARB**	BTTF-themed TV commercials: Garbarino	**MSFT**	BTTF-themed TV commercial: Microsoft
BFHM	BTTF-themed McDonald's Happy Meal boxes	**CHIC**	Photographs hanging in Doc Brown's Chicken restaurant at Universal Studios	**GETV**	BTTF-themed TV commercial: GE		
BTFA	*Back to the Future Annual* (Marvel Comics)						

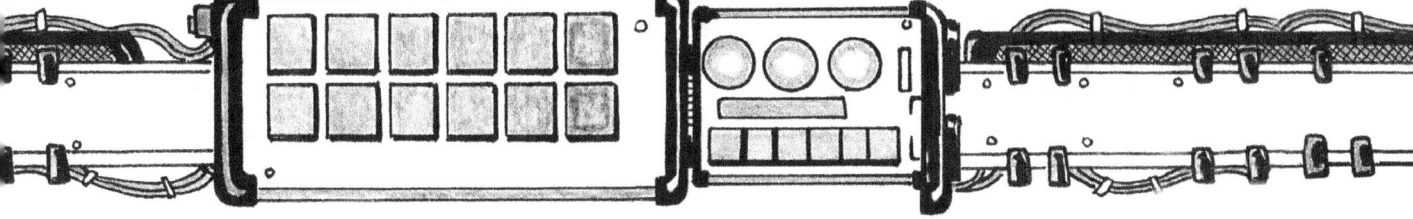

• In an alternate version of 1964, the United States comprises 87 states by 1964, including Cuba. In this timeline, the escapades of scientist Dr. Feldstein in the Bermuda Triangle—a portion of the western North Atlantic Ocean in which numerous surface vessels and aircraft have vanished under mysterious circumstances—result in the U.S. government banning time-travel experiments [BTF1-s1].

> *NOTE: The nature of Feldstein's exploits in the Triangle is unknown.*

• *A Fistful of Dollars*, a so-called "Spaghetti Western" starring Clint Eastwood, debuts in theaters, launching a trilogy of films starring Eastwood's character, The Man With No Name [REAL].

Friday, February 7, 1964 A.D.

• British pop sensation The Beatles make their first United States appearance, touching down at John F. Kennedy International Airport, in Queens, New York [REAL]. The band appears at a press conference shortly thereafter, where a time-traveling Emmett Brown stands in the front row, taking pictures for his own collection. After one snapshot, Doc nods in approval and utters, "Let it be" [RIDE].

> *NOTE: Let It Be was the final studio album released by The Beatles, in May 1970. It's possible that Doc, in remarking "Let it be" six years prior, inspired the band to use that title.*

Saturday, July 10, 1965 A.D.—10:01 AM

• In one timeline, George McFly accepts a menial office job rather than pursuing his dreams of publishing a science fiction novel. His boss is Biff Tannen, a bully who has been terrorizing George since their high school days [BFCG].

• In another reality, following the time-traveling intervention of his future son Marty, George McFly publishes his first short story—involving time travel—in the pages of *Amazing Tales* magazine [BFCG].

1966 A.D.

• Linda McFly is born to George and Lorraine McFly [BTF1-n].

> *NOTE: The original draft of BTF2's screenplay indicated that Linda was two and half years old in 1967, implying a birthdate of 1964 or '65. The novelization, however, established her birth as occurring in 1966.*

• In Citizen Brown's timeline, Hill Valley is granted a special regional exemption from California state legislation. Using a tax and property loophole, the town consolidates itself into a gated community, with special allowances for business and residential zoning. As a result, Hill Valley becomes a state unto itself, fully self-sufficient, self-monitored and self-governed [TLTL-3].

• In a timeline in which George McFly becomes a middleweight boxing champion, he bests a competitor named Liston in a match at Madison Square Garden [BTF1-s1].

> *NOTE: Charles L. "Sonny" Liston became the World Heavyweight Champion in 1962, after knocking out Floyd Patterson during the first round of the match.*

Sometime Before 1967 A.D.

• Goldie Wilson changes his name to Muhammad Goldie Wilson, puts himself through law school and begins serving as a public defender, facing derision from many of Hill Valley's white citizens [BTF2-s1].

> *NOTE: Such a name change may indicate that Wilson converted to Islam in the 1960s, though*

NIKE	*BTTF*-themed TV commercial: Nike	SCRT	2010 Scream Awards: *Back to the Future*	SUFFIX	MEDIUM	-s1	Screenplay (draft one)
NTND	Nintendo *Back to the Future—The Ride*		25th Anniversary Reunion (trailer)	-b	*BTF2's* Biff Tannen Museum video	-s2	Screenplay (draft two)
	Mini-Game	SIMP	Simulator: *The Simpsons Ride*		(extended version)	-s3	Screenplay (draft three)
PIZA	*BTTF*-themed TV commercial: Pizza Hut	SLOT	*Back to the Future* Video Slots	-c	Animated series credit sequence	-s4	Screenplay (draft four)
REAL	Real life	TEST	Screen tests: Crispin Glover, Lea Thompson	-d	Film deleted scene	-sp	Screenplay (production draft)
RIDE	Simulator: *Back to the Future—The Ride*		and Thomas F. Wilson	-n	Film novelization	-sx	Screenplay (*Paradox*)
SCRM	2010 Scream Awards: *Back to the Future*	TLTL	Telltale Games' *Back to the Future—The Game*	-o	Film outtake		
	25th Anniversary Reunion (broadcast)	UNIV	Universal Studios Hollywood promotional video	-v	Video game print materials or commentaries		

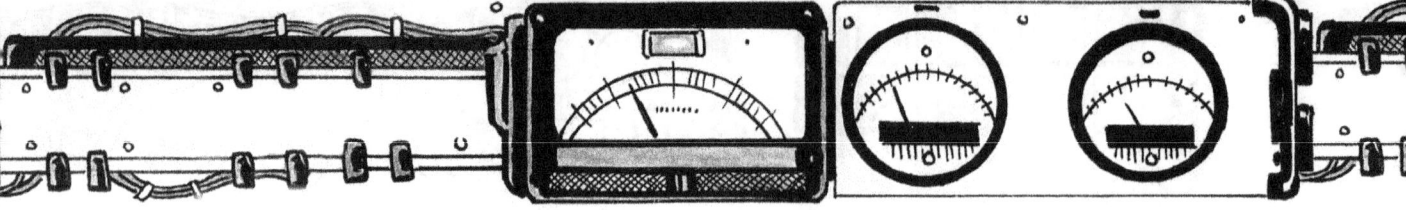

since he would likely have altered his **entire name** in such a scenario, this might not be the case.

1967 A.D.

• Comet Kahooey passes over Hill Valley, resulting in reports of late-running buses, spooky lights and weird noises. Emmett Brown constructs a jalopy spacecraft known as the Flying Observatory, in order to reach the upper levels of Earth's atmosphere and get a closer look. In so doing, he unwittingly creates a powerful electromagnetic field. Biff Tannen, age thirty, mistakes Doc's craft for an extraterrestrial vessel. This experience terrifies him, leaving him deeply paranoid about aliens. In a panic, Tannen summons the National Guard to apprehend the scientist.

Jules and Verne Brown, after learning about these events in the future, travel back to 1967 with Marty McFly to witness Biff's UFO sighting first-hand. Marty (using the alias "Michael J. Fox") and the Brown brothers stow away aboard Doc's ship.

While trying to help Doc keep the ship airborne, Marty accidentally spills corrosive acid on the controls, causing the vessel to crash. The four leave the site unscathed, parting on good terms. To ensure that Biff's unfounded alien fears do not put their father in jeopardy in the future, the boys and Marty pose as aliens in the DeLorean and threaten Biff into swearing his silence. Satisfied, the time travelers return to the future to check on the older Doc [BFAN-23].

> *NOTE: Marty's alias in this episode was an in-joke reference to actor Michael J. Fox, who portrayed Marty McFly in all three* **Back to the Future** *films. Oddly, despite their shared adventures just twelve years prior, Doc did not remember his young friend. In fairness, though, he was quite focused on piloting the spacecraft at the time.*

• Emmett Brown owns a dog called Newton, named after scientist Sir Isaac Newton [BTF2-s1].

• Biff Tannen writes an autobiography titled *Aliens Who I Have Known & Loved*, describing what he believes to have been a visit from extraterrestrials (though the "aliens" were actually Marty McFly and Jules and Verne Brown in disguise). He also opens a roadside stand called Biff's Alien Souvenirs, where he sells the book, along with bumper stickers and a beverage known as Jupiter Juice. This venture ultimately proves to be a failure [BFAN-23].

> *NOTE: In keeping with Biff's usual motif, the book's title was grammatically incorrect.*

• Sally Baines, age 19, watches the film *To Sir, With Love*, starring Sidney Poitier, with her friends Jeanne and Mary Ann [BTF2-s1, BTF2-s2].

• As Toby Baines approaches U.S. military draft age, his sister Lorraine, concerned that he might be sent to fight in the Vietnam War, takes an active stance against the government-imposed draft. Toby wants to join the conflict, hoping to "kick some Commie butt," but his mother, Stella Baines, prefers that he attend college. (Toby's poor academic grades, however, make that unlikely.) Toby's father, Sam Baines, strongly supports the war, accusing Hippie protestors of ruining the United States, and is proud of his son's interest in military service [BTF2-s1].

• A Hill Valley beat cop called Officer Reese decides he dislikes the Hippie movement since he can't tell the men from the women [BTF2-s1].

• Lorraine Baines donates her time to a Vietnam War protest rally organized by Janis Steinberg. Among the featured guests are musical group Blue Nirvana and speakers Jo Potosi, Guru Ahm Dali Raj and Muhammad Goldie Wilson [BTF2-s1].

CODE	STORY						
ARGN	BTTF-themed TV commercial: Arrigoni	**BTF1**	Film: *Back to the Future*	**CITY**	BTTF-themed music video: Owl City, "Deer in the Headlights"	**HUEY**	BTTF-themed music video: Huey Lewis and the News, "The Power of Love"
BFAN	*Back to the Future: The Animated Series*	**BTF2**	Film: *Back to the Future Part II*	**DCTV**	BTTF-themed TV commercial: DirecTV	**LIMO**	BTTF-themed music video: The Limousines, "The Future"
BFCG	*Back to the Future: The Card Game*	**BTF3**	Film: *Back to the Future Part III*	**ERTH**	*The Earth Day Special*		
BFCL	*Back to the Future* comic book (limited series)	**BUDL**	BTTF-themed TV commercial: Bud Light	**GALE**	Interviews and commentaries: Bob Gale and/or Robert Zemeckis	**MCDN**	BTTF-themed TV commercial: McDonald's
BFCM	*Back to the Future* comic book (monthly series)	**CHEK**	BTTF-themed music video: O'Neal McKnight, "Check Your Coat"			**MITS**	BTTF-themed TV commercial: Mitsubishi Lancer
BFHM	BTTF-themed McDonald's Happy Meal boxes	**CHIC**	Photographs hanging in Doc Brown's	**GARB**	BTTF-themed TV commercials: Garbarino		
BTFA	*Back to the Future Annual* (Marvel Comics)		Chicken restaurant at Universal Studios	**GETV**	BTTF-themed TV commercial: GE	**MSFT**	BTTF-themed TV commercial: Microsoft

- Biff Tannen, meanwhile, staunchly supports U.S. involvement in the war. At the time, he lives in an apartment at 2920 Pearl Street—a small tract house with an attached garage and a picket fence—which he shares with his pet German Shepherd, Chopper. Biff drives a 1965 Ranchero with bumper stickers proudly proclaiming "America: Love It or Leave It" [BTF2-s1].

- Lorraine McFly's aunt, Doris, spends some time in a hospital, cared for by her husband, Mickey [BTF2-s1].

Wednesday, January 18, 1967 A.D.

- After a successful three-year run in Italy, Sergio Leone's spaghetti western *A Fistful of Dollars* debuts to American audiences, starring Clint Eastwood as The Man With No Name [REAL].

Wednesday, September 20, 1967 A.D.

- After twelve years of suffering mental duress following his encounter with a "space man," Hill Valley pine breeder Otis Peabody is released from a sanitarium in the care of his wife, Elsie. Otis returns to his farm on the advice of his psychiatrist, to prove to himself that flying saucers do not exist. Upon arriving, however, he sees the DeLorean flying overhead and suffers a relapse, then is re-admitted to the asylum—along with Elsie, who this time sees the "spacecraft" as well [BTF2-s1].

Sometime After September 20, 1967 A.D.

- After being released from a sanitarium for a second time, Otis Peabody discovers the discarded door of the DeLorean time machine that put him in the asylum in the first place. Finally able to prove the experience occurred, he earns renown as a UFO expert and writes a book on the subject, titled *Trash Dumps of the Gods* [BTF2-s1].

Sometime Before June 1968 A.D.

- Erhardt Brown, the father of Emmett Brown, dies [TLTL-3].
    > *NOTE: According to Doc, Erhardt died prior to Marty McFly's birth.*

Thursday, June 20, 1968 A.D.

- Martin Seamus McFly is born to George and Lorraine McFly [BTF2-s1, TLTL-3].
    > *NOTE: The first-draft script for **BTF2** cited Marty's middle name as Hopkins, after the Mark Hopkins Hotel in San Francisco, California, where he was conceived. Subsequent sources established his middle name as Seamus, after his Irish ancestor featured in **BTF3.***

Tuesday, October 29, 1968 A.D.

- Jennifer Jane Parker is born [BTF2-s1].

Friday, August 15 to Sunday, August 17, 1969 A.D.

- The Woodstock Music & Art Fair is held at Max Yasgur's dairy farm in Bethel, New York [REAL]. Emmett Brown deems this event the "biggest concert of all time" [BFAN-12]
    > *NOTE: It's unclear if Doc actually attended the event himself.*

Late 1960s or Early 1970s A.D.

- Ricky Strickland, a relative of Edna and Gerald Strickland, is born [TLTL-v].
    > *NOTE: This character, created for the Telltale Games video game, was not utilized in the final game. However, an illustration of Ricky appeared in supplemental materials included with the game's packaging, with no additional*

NIKE	*BTTF*-themed TV commercial: Nike	**SCRT**	2010 Scream Awards: *Back to the Future*	**SUFFIX**	**MEDIUM**	
NTND	Nintendo *Back to the Future—The Ride* Mini-Game		25th Anniversary Reunion (trailer)	**-b**	*BTF2's* Biff Tannen Museum video (extended version)	**-s1** Screenplay (draft one)
PIZA	*BTTF*-themed TV commercial: Pizza Hut	**SIMP**	Simulator: *The Simpsons Ride*			**-s2** Screenplay (draft two)
REAL	Real life	**SLOT**	*Back to the Future* Video Slots	**-c**	Animated series credit sequence	**-s3** Screenplay (draft three)
RIDE	Simulator: *Back to the Future—The Ride*	**TEST**	Screen tests: Crispin Glover, Lea Thompson and Thomas F. Wilson	**-d**	Film deleted scene	**-s4** Screenplay (draft four)
SCRM	2010 Scream Awards: *Back to the Future* 25th Anniversary Reunion (broadcast)	**TLTL**	Telltale Games' *Back to the Future—The Game*	**-n**	Film novelization	**-sp** Screenplay (production draft)
		UNIV	Universal Studios Hollywood promotional video	**-o**	Film outtake	**-sx** Screenplay (*Paradox*)
				-v	Video game print materials or commentaries	

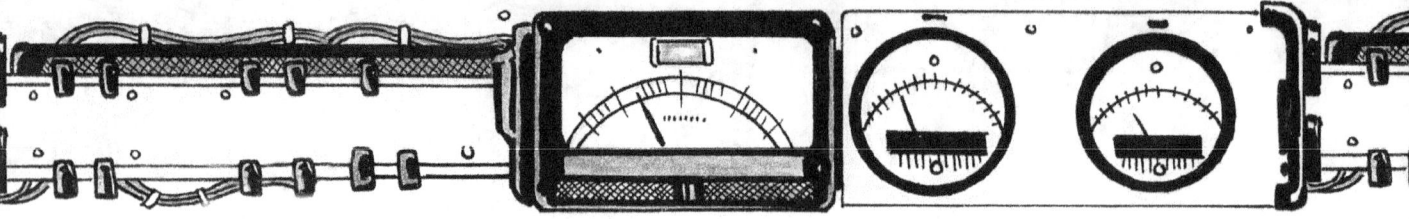

information provided. His exact age is unknown, but he appeared to be a teenager in 1986.

- Biff Tannen's daughter, Tiffany "Tiff" Tannen, is born [BFAN-16].

   NOTE: Tiff's exact age is unknown, but she appeared to be a teenager in 1986. Her mother's identity is also unknown.

Friday, March 6, 1970 A.D.

- The Beatles release "Let It Be" as a single off their album of the same name [REAL], six years after Emmett Brown uttered the phrase to the band at their first press conference in the United States [RIDE]

1971 A.D.

- In the Citizen Brown timeline, Edna Brown convinces her husband, First Citizen Emmett Brown, to tear down the Town Theatre, on the grounds that films do nothing more than promote bad behavior. Despite his fond memories of watching movies there as a youth, Emmett obediently carries out Edna's command [TLTL-4].

Sometime Before 1973 A.D.

- Biff Tannen endures two failed marriages in the Biffhorrific reality, remaining attracted to Lorraine Baines all the while [BTF2-b, BFCG].

February 1973 A.D.

- Hill Valley Community Hospital is built under a great deal of controversy. The City Council claims that it cannot afford to build the hospital, and that one is not necessary at this location. However, the council actually hopes to sell off the land and construct a nuclear power plant at the site instead. When no one offers to purchase the land for the desired amount, the council begrudgingly builds the medical facility after all [BTF2-s1].

NOTE: This event was described in the first draft of BTF2's screenplay, in which Lorraine McFly, in 2015, held a press conference to dedicate the hospital's new George F. McFly Memorial Wing. In this timeline, George had passed away in 2013 and bequeathed his entire fortune to the hospital, as a token of thanks for saving his life in 1973. This sentimental anecdote helped to set up that draft's suspense—originally, Marty McFly's obsession over the Grays Sports Almanac resulted in an elderly Biff Tannen passing off the book to his younger self in 1967. This gave thirty-year-old Biff the means to purchase the land on which the hospital would have been built, and to launch his BiffCo empire—a domino effect leading to George's death. Also of note, George's middle initial was given as "F" in that draft, though in the finished film, his middle name was revealed to be "Douglas." What's more, he was still alive in 2015.

Tuesday, February 27 to Saturday, May 5, 1973 A.D.

- Following their failure to impeach tribal president Richard Wilson for abuse of power, Oglala Lakota and members of the American Indian Movement occupy the South Dakota town of Wounded Knee in protest. The standoff lasts for seventy-one days [REAL].

Thursday, March 15, 1973 A.D.

- The *Hill Valley Telegraph* publishes a front-page story bearing the headline "Indians Continue Wounded Knee Occupation: South Dakota Standoff in 16th Day" [BTF2].

Thursday, March 15, 1973 A.D.—9:35 PM

- In one possible timeline, Hill Valley science fiction author George McFly receives an award from a local newspaper [BFCG].

CODE	STORY						
ARGN	BTTF-themed TV commercial: Arrigoni	**BTF1**	Film: *Back to the Future*	**CITY**	BTTF-themed music video: Owl City, "Deer in the Headlights"	**HUEY**	BTTF-themed music video: Huey Lewis and the News, "The Power of Love"
BFAN	*Back to the Future: The Animated Series*	**BTF2**	Film: *Back to the Future Part II*	**DCTV**	BTTF-themed TV commercial: DirecTV	**LIMO**	BTTF-themed music video: The Limousines, "The Future"
BFCG	*Back to the Future: The Card Game*	**BTF3**	Film: *Back to the Future Part III*	**ERTH**	*The Earth Day Special*		
BFCL	*Back to the Future* comic book (limited series)	**BUDL**	BTTF-themed TV commercial: Bud Light	**GALE**	Interviews and commentaries: Bob Gale and/or Robert Zemeckis	**MCDN**	BTTF-themed TV commercial: McDonald's
BFCM	*Back to the Future* comic book (monthly series)	**CHEK**	BTTF-themed music video: O'Neal McKnight, "Check Your Coat"			**MITS**	BTTF-themed TV commercial: Mitsubishi Lancer
BFHM	BTTF-themed McDonald's Happy Meal boxes	**CHIC**	Photographs hanging in Doc Brown's Chicken restaurant at Universal Studios	**GARB**	BTTF-themed TV commercials: Garbarino	**MSFT**	BTTF-themed TV commercial: Microsoft
BTFA	*Back to the Future Annual* (Marvel Comics)			**GETV**	BTTF-themed TV commercial: GE		

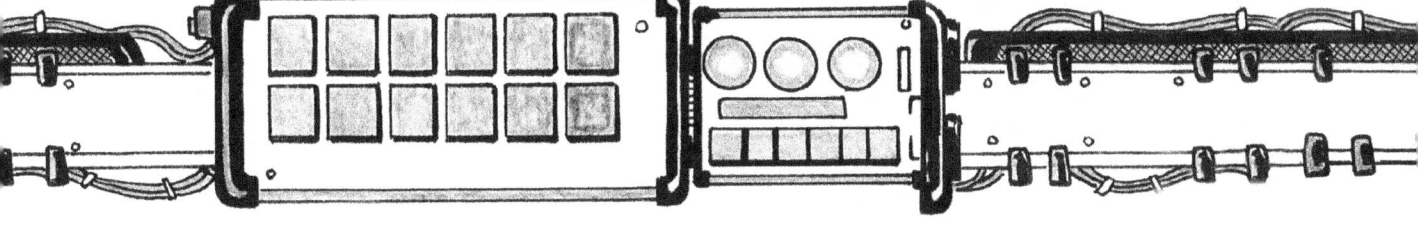

In another reality, George is murdered during an apparent holdup on his way to receive a book award [BTF2-n]. Police find no witnesses to the murder, and he is laid to rest in Oak Park Cemetery, survived by his wife, Lorraine, and his children, David, Linda and Martin. The killer, high school rival Biff Tannen, is never identified since Tannen, in this reality, is rich, powerful and influential over the police [BFCG, BFT2].

In a third potential timeline, George McFly is involved in a serious car accident during a severe thunderstorm. County General Hospital, though five miles from the crash site, is deemed inaccessible due to the Groby Road Bridge being washed out in the rain. Therefore, George is taken to nearby Hill Valley Community Hospital, which saves his life [BTF2-s1].

Sometime After April 30, 1973 A.D.

Hill Valley Telegraph, March 1—April 30, 1973, a hardbound collection of all *Telegraph* newspapers produced during this two-month period, is published [BTF2].

Friday, December 7, 1973 A.D.—3:00 PM

In one possible reality, Biff Tannen marries the widowed Lorraine Baines-McFly—his third marriage—following the death (at Biff's hands) of George McFly [BTF2-b, BFCG].

In another timeline, Lorraine and George McFly celebrate their fifteenth wedding anniversary [BFCG].

Sometime in or Before 1975 A.D.

Otis Peabody, renowned UFO expert and author of the book *Trash Dumps of the Gods*, begins offering lectures on alien spaceships, using the discarded door of Emmett Brown's time-traveling DeLorean (which he found in 1967) as evidence of alien life [BTF2-s1].

April 30, 1975 A.D.

The Cold War conflict known as the Vietnam War comes to an end when Saigon, South Vietnam's capital city, is captured by the National Liberation Front and the People's Army of Vietnam, in an event later dubbed the Fall of Saigon [REAL]. In the Biffhorrific timeline, the war continues beyond this date, until at least November 1985 [BTF2].

1976 A.D.

Eight-year-old Marty McFly sets fire to his parents' living room rug, claiming it was an accident. After traveling back to the year 1955 and meeting his parents, Marty's older self asks that they "take it easy on him" when this event occurs [BTF1].

In the Citizen Brown timeline, Martin McFly, age eight, sets fire to his family's living room rug—so that he can demonstrate for his parents a fire retardant that he made with his chemistry set [TLTL-3].

As part of a town-wide initiative to restore downtown Hill Valley in the Citizen Brown timeline, the damaged Clock Tower is dismantled and a new clock is installed as the window to First Citizen Emmett Brown's new mayoral office [TLTL-3].

1979 A.D.

In the Biffhorrific timeline, millionaire Biff Tannen—who, as the founder of the BiffCo empire, has turned Hill Valley into an industrial center, including power plants and toxic waste-disposal facilities—successfully lobbies to legalize gambling within the city. Biff also begins converting the Hill Valley Courthouse and ruined Clock Tower into a multi-storied hotel-casino known as Biff Tannen's Pleasure Paradise Casino & Hotel [BTF2-b].
NOTE: An unfilmed screenplay draft, titled

NIKE	*BTTF*-themed TV commercial: Nike	**SCRT**	2010 Scream Awards: *Back to the Future* 25th Anniversary Reunion (trailer)	**SUFFIX**	**MEDIUM**	
NTND	Nintendo *Back to the Future—The Ride* Mini-Game	**SIMP**	Simulator: *The Simpsons Ride*	**-b**	*BTF2*'s Biff Tannen Museum video (extended version)	**-s1** Screenplay (draft one)
PIZA	*BTTF*-themed TV commercial: Pizza Hut	**SLOT**	*Back to the Future* Video Slots	**-c**	Animated series credit sequence	**-s2** Screenplay (draft two)
REAL	Real life	**TEST**	Screen tests: Crispin Glover, Lea Thompson and Thomas F. Wilson	**-d**	Film deleted scene	**-s3** Screenplay (draft three)
RIDE	Simulator: *Back to the Future—The Ride*	**TLTL**	Telltale Games' *Back to the Future—The Game*	**-n**	Film novelization	**-s4** Screenplay (draft four)
SCRM	2010 Scream Awards: *Back to the Future* 25th Anniversary Reunion (broadcast)	**UNIV**	Universal Studios Hollywood promotional video	**-o**	Film outtake	**-sp** Screenplay (production draft)
				-v	Video game print materials or commentaries	**-sx** Screenplay (*Paradox*)

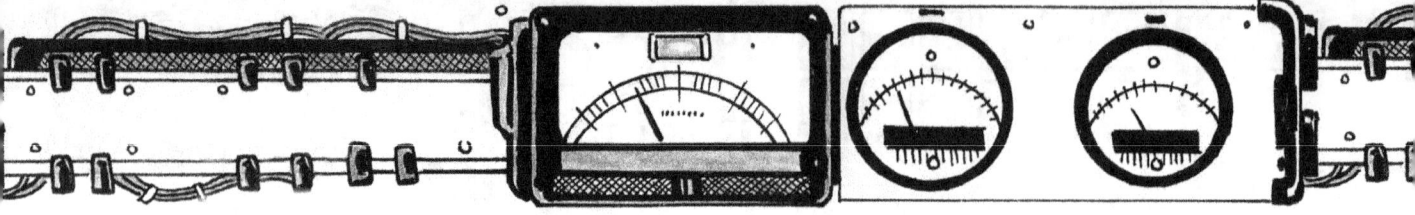

Paradox, *indicated that Biff's legalization of gambling in Hill Valley occurred by 1969. Onscreen, however, this was moved up to 1979.*

• Hill Valley High School burns down in the Biffhorrific timeline [BTF2-b].

Circa Late 1970s or Early 1980s A.D.

• Biff Tannen's son, Biff Tannen Jr., is born [BFAN-16]. *NOTE: Biff Jr.'s exact age is unknown, but he appeared to be a young teenager in 1992. His mother's identity is also unknown.*

Circa 1980 A.D.

• Emmett Brown entertains the notion that all mammals speak a common language, but this research proves fruitless. Other failed schemes include mining gold by superheating the Earth's surface, as well as determining everyone's predetermined age by studying the composition of their fingernails. He also publishes a paper claiming a baby's sex can be ascertained prior to conception. Most of his ideas receive little notice, so he continues working privately, hoping to create something that will earn his peers' acclaim [BTF1-n].

1980 A.D.

• Twelve-year-old Marty McFly has an accident while attempting to skateboard down the steps of the Hill Valley Courthouse. This incident leaves him with a scar on his left knee [TLTL-2].

Sunday, August 24, 1980 A.D.—9:53 AM

• In one possible reality, Biff Tannen opens an automotive detailing business and has matchbooks containing his company's logo printed up for promotional purposes [BFCG].

• In the Biffhorrific timeline, the former Hill Valley Courthouse officially reopens as Biff Tannen's Pleasure Paradise Casino & Hotel [BFCG].

Circa 1981 or 1982 A.D.

• Emmett Brown first meets Marty McFly when the youth is 13 or 14 years old. Having heard Doc described as a dangerous crackpot and a lunatic, and curious why people would say such things, Marty sneaks into Brown's laboratory and is fascinated by the equipment contained within. Finding him in the lab, Doc is delighted to learn that Marty accepts him and thinks him cool. Since both are the black sheep in their respective environments, a friendship forms. Doc offers Marty a part-time job helping with experiments, tending to his lab, sweeping out his garage and watching Emmett's dog, Einstein [GALE]. He, in turn, pays Marty fifty dollars per week, providing him with free beer and access to his vintage record collection [BTF1-s4].

Early 1980s A.D.

• A computer game called *Game Grid* is released, which Hollywood adapts as a theatrical film. Marty McFly deems the movie version superior [TLTL-3].

• Tiffany Tannen, the daughter of Biff Tannen [TLTL-1, BFCG], begins wearing punk-rock fashion, her hair dyed several colors [TLTL-v]. A teen hoodlum, she often steals cars' hubcaps [TLTL-1]. Meanwhile, Tiff's obese and unkempt younger brother, Biff Jr., takes to bullying smaller children to deal with his frequent unhappiness [BFAN-16].

Sometime in or Before 1982 A.D.

• Emmett Brown obtains a simian pet called Shemp [BTF1-s1, BTF1-s2]. *NOTE: Shemp—named after Samuel Horwitz*

CODE	STORY						
ARGN	*BTTF*-themed TV commercial: Arrigoni	**BTF1**	Film: *Back to the Future*	**CITY**	*BTTF*-themed music video: Owl City, "Deer in the Headlights"	**HUEY**	*BTTF*-themed music video: Huey Lewis and the News, "The Power of Love"
BFAN	*Back to the Future: The Animated Series*	**BTF2**	Film: *Back to the Future Part II*			**LIMO**	*BTTF*-themed music video:
BFCG	*Back to the Future: The Card Game*	**BTF3**	Film: *Back to the Future Part III*	**DCTV**	*BTTF*-themed TV commercial: DirecTV		The Limousines, "The Future"
BFCL	*Back to the Future* comic book (limited series)	**BUDL**	*BTTF*-themed TV commercial: Bud Light	**ERTH**	*The Earth Day Special*	**MCDN**	*BTTF*-themed TV commercial: McDonald's
BFCM	*Back to the Future* comic book (monthly series)	**CHEK**	*BTTF*-themed music video:	**GALE**	Interviews and commentaries: Bob Gale and/or Robert Zemeckis	**MITS**	*BTTF*-themed TV commercial:
BFHM	*BTTF*-themed McDonald's Happy Meal boxes		O'Neal McKnight, "Check Your Coat"				Mitsubishi Lancer
BTFA	*Back to the Future Annual* (Marvel Comics)	**CHIC**	Photographs hanging in Doc Brown's Chicken restaurant at Universal Studios	**GARB**	*BTTF*-themed TV commercials: Garbarino	**MSFT**	*BTTF*-themed TV commercial: Microsoft
				GETV	*BTTF*-themed TV commercial: GE		

"Shemp" Howard, a member of The Three Stooges comedy team—appeared in BTF1's early-draft screenplays. In draft one, he was a Capuchin (or "organ-grinder monkey"), while draft two changed his species to chimpanzee. Onscreen, Doc had a dog named Einstein.

1982 A.D.

• George McFly works hard at his office job to earn a promotion, but company executive Mister Callahan instead promotes a worker named Jenkins, which George chalks up to Jenkins playing golf with the man [BTF1-s2].

Sometime in or Before 1983 A.D.

• Goldie Wilson is elected mayor of Hill Valley, vowing to "clean up" the town [BTF1, BTF2].

> *NOTE: Wilson's mayorship was established in **BTF1**. An issue of the **Hill Valley Telegraph**, seen in **BTF2**, indicated that he already held that position by 1983.*

1983 A.D.

• Fifteen-year-old Marty McFly attempts to sneak out of his parents' home late one night to rendezvous with friends. The sound of his skateboard on asphalt gives him away, however, and his mother, Lorraine McFly, arrives in her car to drag him back home [BTF1-n].

Wednesday, March 23, 1983 A.D.

• Emmett Brown travels back from January 13, 2011, to two years before the DeLorean's maiden voyage [GARB].

> *NOTE: The purpose of this trip is unknown.*

Wednesday, March 23, 1983 A.D.—12:45 PM

• Later that day, Doc returns to January 13, 2011 [GARB].

Monday, May 23, 1983 A.D.—1:01 PM

• In the Biffhorrific timeline, the *Hill Valley Telegraph* publishes a front-page news story with the headline "Emmett Brown Committed: Crackpot Inventor Declared Legally Insane." In the article, Doc is pictured being escorted away in a straightjacket. A smaller article reports that President Richard Nixon seeks a fifth term in office, vowing to end the Vietnam War by 1985. In local news, BiffCo Enterprises announces plans to build a new Dioxin plant [BTF2, BFCG].

> *NOTE: The novelization of **BTF2** placed this event in July of that year, while onscreen, it occurred on May 23.*

• With the Biffhorrific timeline eliminated, the *Hill Valley Telegraph* instead reports "Emmett Brown Commended: Local Inventor Receives Civic Award." A shorter article relays President Ronald Regan's decision to seek a second term, with no Republican challengers expected. In local news, Mayor Goldie Wilson vetoes a zoning bill [BTF2, BFCG].

> *NOTE: The novelization of **BTF2** placed this event in July of that year, while onscreen, it occurred on May 23.*

1984 A.D.

• Linda McFly, the older sister of Marty McFly, graduates from Hill Valley High School. That year, she purchases a sweatshirt proclaiming herself as a member of the Class of 1984 [BTF1].

NIKE	*BTTF*-themed TV commercial: Nike	**SCRT**	2010 Scream Awards: *Back to the Future*	**SUFFIX**	**MEDIUM**	**-s1**	Screenplay (draft one)
NTND	Nintendo *Back to the Future—The Ride*		25th Anniversary Reunion (trailer)	**-b**	*BTF2's* Biff Tannen Museum video	**-s2**	Screenplay (draft two)
	Mini-Game	**SIMP**	Simulator: *The Simpsons Ride*		(extended version)	**-s3**	Screenplay (draft three)
PIZA	*BTTF*-themed TV commercial: Pizza Hut	**SLOT**	*Back to the Future* Video Slots	**-c**	Animated series credit sequence	**-s4**	Screenplay (draft four)
REAL	Real life	**TEST**	Screen tests: Crispin Glover, Lea Thompson	**-d**	Film deleted scene	**-sp**	Screenplay (production draft)
RIDE	Simulator: *Back to the Future—The Ride*		and Thomas F. Wilson	**-n**	Film novelization	**-sx**	Screenplay (*Paradox*)
SCRM	2010 Scream Awards: *Back to the Future*	**TLTL**	Telltale Games' *Back to the Future—The Game*	**-o**	Film outtake		
	25th Anniversary Reunion (broadcast)	**UNIV**	Universal Studios Hollywood promotional video	**-v**	Video game print materials or commentaries		

DOC LEARNS NEVER TO STEAL PLUTONIUM FROM LIBYAN NATIONALISTS

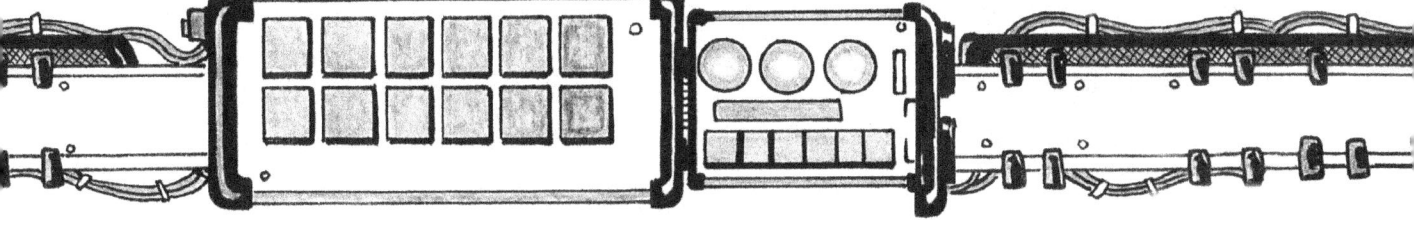

Mid-1980s A.D.

• Marty McFly forms a rock-and-roll band called The Pinheads, featuring Marty on guitar and lead vocals [BTF1], as well as other musicians, including his friend Nick [BTF1-s2]. A typical teen, Marty naïvely dreams of becoming a world-famous rock star [BTF1].

• Marty McFly begins dating a beautiful classmate named Jennifer Jane Parker [BTF1], the daughter of shoe salesman Daniel Parker Jr. [TLTL-3], and the granddaughter of Daniel Parker Sr. and Betty Lapinski [TLTL-2], as well as Parker BTQ Ranch proprietor Peter Parker [BFAN-16].

> *NOTE: In the Telltale Games video game, Jennifer's paternal grandfather was named Daniel Parker, but in the animated series, he was called Peter Parker. This discrepancy has not been reconciled. A third grandfather, Norman, was mentioned in BTF2's first-draft screenplay; presumably, Norman was Jen's maternal grandmother. No mention has been made of Jen's mother, though at least one grandmother was still alive in 1985, as indicated in BTF1.*

• Marty and Jen often visit Clayton Ravine so the two can make out in private [BTF3-s1]. A typical teenager, Marty listens to the music of Eddie Van Halen, as well as Huey Lewis and the News [BTF1]; frequently hangs out at the Del-Wood Plaza Complex [BTF3-s1]; and enjoys such films and TV shows as *Weird Science*, *Frankenstein* and *Miami Vice* [TLTL-1]. Jen, meanwhile, is a fan of music group Walk DMC [BFAN-14].

• Marty's other classmates include Crump, Donaldson, Fredman, Jackson, Jenkins, Lomax, Newton, Stevenson, Weeze, Willis and Winch [BTF1-s1, BTF1-s2, BTF1-s3], as well as Nick, a member of The Pinheads [BTF1-s2], and rivals Douglas J. Needles [BTF2] and Leech [TLTL-3].

• Among Marty's instructors at Hill Valley High School are Mister Arky, an embittered, pessimistic social-studies teacher paranoid about the looming threat of nuclear destruction [BTF1-s1, BTF1-s2, BTF1-n]; Mister Turkle, whose ill-informed advice to play a Barry Manilow tune causes Marty's band, The Pinheads, to flub an audition for the Springtime in Paris Dance [BTF1-s2]; and Mrs. Woods, who has little patience with Marty's tendency to violate school rules by playing his Walkman in class [BTF1-s3].

• In the Biffhorrific timeline, Biff Tannen purchases a personal yacht called the *Monkey Business*, on which he often entertains beautiful women [BTF2-b]. In this reality, Biff Tannen Jr. is elected governor of California, thanks to the influence of his powerful and corrupt father [BTF2-s2].

> *NOTE: Given that Biff Jr. would have been a young child in 1985 (he was a teen in the animated series, set in 1991 to 1992), it's unclear how he could have been California's governor, even with his wealthy father's backing.*

Sometime Before 1985 A.D.

• In a timeline in which George McFly is confident and successful, George writes a science fiction novel called *A Match Made in Space*, based on what he believes to have been a real-life extraterrestrial encounter in 1955 (the alien, "Darth Vader from the planet Vulcan," was actually his future son, Marty). The book involves a young couple falling in love thanks to alien interference [BTF1].

> *NOTE: Marty's references to Vulcan and Darth Vader indicate that he was well aware of both the Star Trek and Star Wars franchises. However, the fact that George used these terms in his novel without being condemned for ripping off Gene Roddenberry and George Lucas may mean that Marty's adventures in the past somehow prevented those two series from existing.*

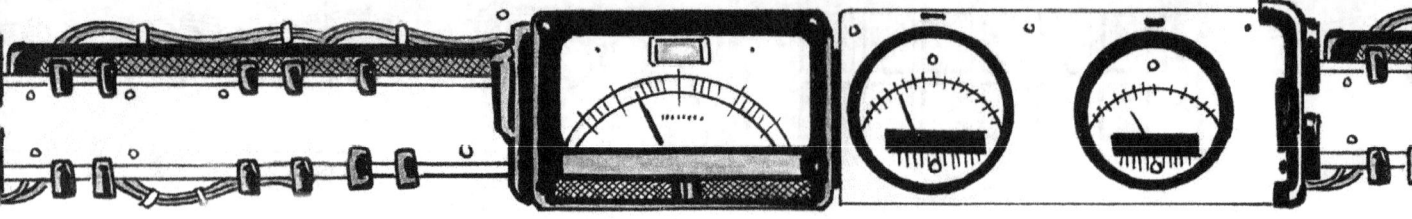

- Piano tuner Warren Lester and his two young daughters move into Marty McFly's neighborhood [BTF2-s1].

- Loraine Baines' brother, Joey Baines, is arrested and sent to prison [BTF1].
  > **NOTE: The nature of Joey's crime is unknown.**

- In a timeline altered due to Marty McFly's intervention, Cleveland, Ohio, becomes a beautiful, clean and modern city dubbed the City of the Future, with streamlined skyscrapers and flying cars [BTF1-s1].

- Uranda, an ex-fashion model from Damascus, Syria, joins a group of Libyan nationalists. Resenting that the terrorist organization is not perceived as ruthless enough, she often shoots people to disprove that misperception [BTF1-n].

Sometime in or Before 1985 A.D.

- An office of the U.S. Department of Social Services is added to the Hill Valley Courthouse. In addition, numerous businesses open in and around Courthouse Square, including Abram's Brokerage Corp.; Allstate Insurance; the Assembly of Christ church; Cupid's; Elmo's Ribs; Goodwill Industries; Hog Heaven; Loans on Anything of Value; Lou's Aerobic Fitness Center; Statler Toyota; and The Third Eye [BTF1].
  > **NOTE: View the map on page 183 to see where each business was located.**

- In the Biffhorrific timeline, the Hill Valley Courthouse is converted into Biff's Pleasure Palace, Biff Tannen's Pleasure Paradise and the Biff Tannen Museum. In addition, numerous businesses open in and around the Square, including Bad Rap Bail Bonds; Bangkok Sauna & Asian Massage; Biff Springs; Bondage; Dee Dee's Delight; French Fantasies; Hard X Core; Hell Hole XXX; the Hill Valley Theater of Live Sex Acts; Naughty and Naked; Naughty XXX; a pawn shop; Peep Show; Peeparama; Pig Mart; Sin; Tanya Exotic Sex Goddess; Time to Shoot; the Toxic Waste Reclamation Plant; Video All Nude Hardcore Movies; War Zone; and the Wrecking Yard [BTF2].
  > **NOTE: View the map on page 183 to see where each business was located.**

- Emmett Brown invents the Write-o-Matic, consisting of a pen and a wire-attached suction cup [BTF1-s1].

- Marty McFly develops a deep-seated fear of being called a "chicken." This frequently gets him into trouble, as it compels him to accept any challenges, no matter how ill-advised, whenever he feels his manhood has been questioned [BTF2, BTF3].

- While working at the University of California, Berkeley, Emmett Brown undertakes a project known as Temporal Dynamics Model 580, involving capacitor discharge, in an effort to develop a working time machine [TLTL-1].

- Marty McFly obtains a copy of *Reference Quarterly* (*RQ*), a magazine for library professionals [BTF1, TLTL-1].

- Hill Valley's Essex Theater begins showing *Orgy American Style* [BTF1], a 1973 X-rated film directed by Carlos Tobalina, and starring Sharon Kelly [REAL].
  > **NOTE: This film's title satirized Love, American Style, *a comedy anthology TV series that aired on ABC from 1969 to 1974. The cast included actor George "Buck" Flower, who portrayed Red the bum in the first two* Back to the Future *films.*

- George McFly decides to invite his co-worker Martha to a family barbecue in 1985. However, his wife, Lorraine, nixes the idea [TEST].

- In the Biffhorrific timeline, Biff Tannen becomes romantically linked to a number of starlets, including TV and theater actors Jayne Mansfield and Marilyn Monroe [BTF2-b].

CODE	STORY						
ARGN	BTTF-themed TV commercial: Arrigoni	**BTF1**	Film: *Back to the Future*	**CITY**	BTTF-themed music video: Owl City, "Deer in the Headlights"	**HUEY**	BTTF-themed music video: Huey Lewis and the News, "The Power of Love"
BFAN	*Back to the Future: The Animated Series*	**BTF2**	Film: *Back to the Future Part II*	**DCTV**	BTTF-themed TV commercial: DirecTV	**LIMO**	BTTF-themed music video: The Limousines, "The Future"
BFCG	*Back to the Future: The Card Game*	**BTF3**	Film: *Back to the Future Part III*	**ERTH**	*The Earth Day Special*		
BFCL	*Back to the Future* comic book (limited series)	**BUDL**	BTTF-themed TV commercial: Bud Light	**GALE**	Interviews and commentaries: Bob Gale and/or Robert Zemeckis	**MCDN**	BTTF-themed TV commercial: McDonald's
BFCM	*Back to the Future* comic book (monthly series)	**CHEK**	BTTF-themed music video: O'Neal McKnight, "Check Your Coat"	**GARB**	BTTF-themed TV commercials: Garbarino	**MITS**	BTTF-themed TV commercial: Mitsubishi Lancer
BFHM	*BTTF-themed McDonald's Happy Meal boxes*	**CHIC**	Photographs hanging in Doc Brown's Chicken restaurant at Universal Studios	**GETV**	BTTF-themed TV commercial: GE	**MSFT**	BTTF-themed TV commercial: Microsoft
BTFA	*Back to the Future Annual* (Marvel Comics)						

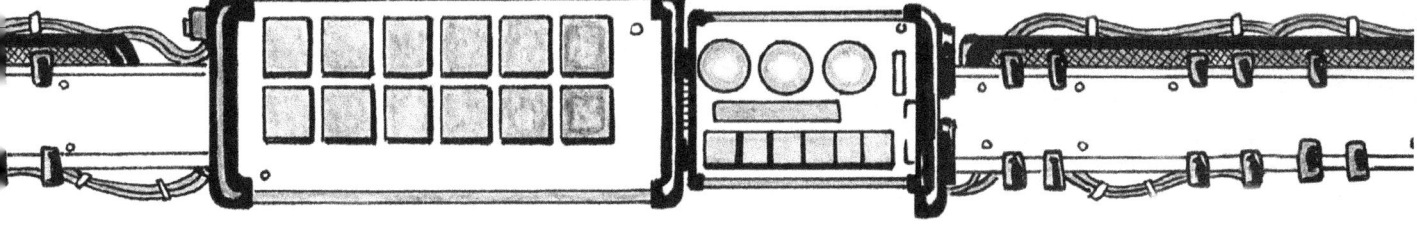

- In one possible timeline, Marty McFly's high school acquaintances, Winch and Lomax, lure Marty into a "once-in-a-lifetime" deal, promising it will earn him "major cash-ola." Roped into participating, Marty cancels a planned trip with Jennifer, but the plan goes sour, and Marty almost ends up in jail as a result [BTF2-s1].

- Emmett Brown invents the Hydraulic Scrapbook, an electronic scrapbook for preserving personal and family-history memorabilia, such as photographs and news clippings, with pneumatic cylinders to automatically turn the pages [BTF1-s1].

- A potbellied and unpleasant man named Howard becomes a neighbor of George and Lorraine McFly [BTF1-s4, BTF1-d, BTF1-n]. Howard, realizing George's meek nature, frequently takes advantage of his neighbor, speaking to him only when he needs something or is looking for someone to berate [BTF1-n].

- In one possible timeline, Emmett Brown invents a flying vehicle known as an Aero-Mobile [BTF1-s1].

- Marty McFly purchases a pin labeled "Art in Revolution," which he displays on his denim jacket [BTF1].

- Emmett Brown purchases an Axis alarm-clock, featuring a silver figure of a man dangling from its minute hand, as well as numerous other clocks, intending to set them all to chime simultaneously [BTF1].

- In a timeline in which George McFly is confident and successful, Biff Tannen opens Biff's Automotive Detailing, with the McFlys among his chief clients [BTF1]. The company's motto: "To make your car spiffy in a jiffy, just call Biff-y!" [TLTL-v].

- Emmett Brown gets a new pet dog, which he names Einstein ("Einie"), after scientist Albert Einstein [BTF1]. Einie's grandfather was a bloodhound, making Einie part bloodhound and, thus, an expert tracker [BTF2-s1].

    NOTE: Onscreen, Einstein did not appear to be part-bloodhound, despite BTF2's first-draft screenplay indicating that to be the case.

- George McFly, in an effort to raise his family's low morale, suggests that he, Lorraine and Marty try out for a game show, such as *The Price Is Right*. Marty, however, recommends *Family Feud*, since that would enable the entire family, including his uncle John, to take part [TEST].

    NOTE: Test footage created prior to Back to the Future's filming included a scene in which Marty mentioned his uncle John. Since all of Lorraine's siblings' names are known, and do not include a John, it's likely that he was George's brother. It's unknown which sibling was older. (It's also possible that "Uncle John" was merely a close family friend of the McFlys, and not actually related.)

- Twelve wooden crates filled with cocaine wash ashore near Boca Raton, Florida. U.S. drug-enforcement agents find no identification marks on the containers [BTF1].

- Huey Lewis and the News record their hit song "Back in Time" [REAL, BTF1].

- BiffCo Enterprises, founded by Biff Tannen in the Biffhorrific timeline, comprises a number of businesses, including the San Andreas Nuclear Power Plant, Biff's Pleasure Palace, Biff's Realty, the Biff Tannen Museum, Biff Tannen's Pleasure Paradise and BiffCo Toxic Waste Disposal. Hugely successful, BiffCo Enterprises changes the face of Hill Valley in that reality, making its focus on industrialization and debauchery [BTF2-b].

NIKE	*BTTF*-themed TV commercial: Nike	SCRT	2010 Scream Awards: *Back to the Future*	SUFFIX	MEDIUM		-s1	Screenplay (draft one)
NTND	Nintendo *Back to the Future—The Ride* Mini-Game		25th Anniversary Reunion (trailer)	-b	*BTF2's* Biff Tannen Museum video (extended version)		-s2	Screenplay (draft two)
		SIMP	Simulator: *The Simpsons Ride*				-s3	Screenplay (draft three)
PIZA	*BTTF*-themed TV commercial: Pizza Hut	SLOT	*Back to the Future* Video Slots	-c	Animated series credit sequence		-s4	Screenplay (draft four)
REAL	Real life	TEST	Screen tests: Crispin Glover, Lea Thompson and Thomas F. Wilson	-d	Film deleted scene		-sp	Screenplay (production draft)
RIDE	Simulator: *Back to the Future—The Ride*			-n	Film novelization		-sx	Screenplay (*Paradox*)
SCRM	2010 Scream Awards: *Back to the Future* 25th Anniversary Reunion (broadcast)	TLTL	Telltale Games' *Back to the Future—The Game*	-o	Film outtake			
		UNIV	Universal Studios Hollywood promotional video	-v	Video game print materials or commentaries			

A SPEEDING LOCOMOTIVE "DISMANTLES" DOC'S DELOREAN

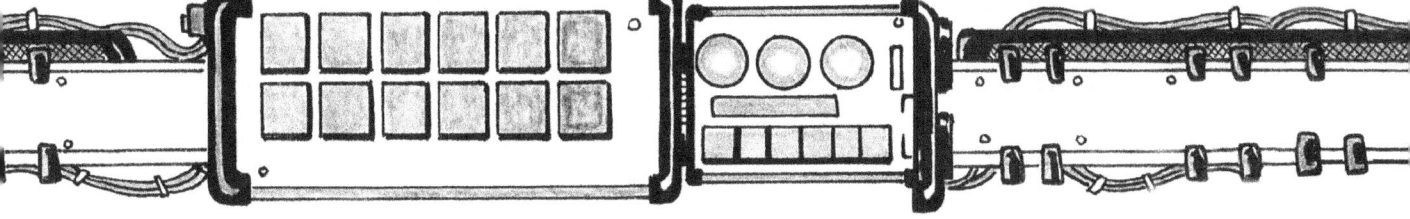

NOTE: One business in Courthouse Square in that timeline (not easily seen onscreen) was Biff Springs, located next to the toxic-waste plant. This would seem to imply BiffCo also owned a beverage company that repurposed contaminated water.

• Hill Valley's mayor, Goldie Wilson, begins campaigning for re-election [BTF1].

Sometime Before October 1985 A.D.

• Joey Baines finds himself up for parole review, but fails to make parole and remains in prison [BTF1].

• In the Biffhorrific timeline, an African-American family of four moves into 2317 Lyon Drive [BTF2].

NOTE: The family was unnamed onscreen, though children Loretta and Harold were identified in BTF2's end credits. The film's novelization identified the father as Lewis, while the movie's first-draft script named the wife Louise. In Marty's reality, in which his family lived there, the house's address was 9303 Lyon Drive.

Shortly Before Friday, October 11, 1985 A.D.

• Marty McFly and his band, The Pinheads, record an audition tape. Marty considers sending it to a record company, but is fearful of rejection. While he deliberates, he lends the tape to his girlfriend Jennifer Parker to give it a listen [BTF1-n].

Circa Friday, October 11, 1985 A.D.

• A Libyan terrorist group steals a case of plutonium from the Pacific Nuclear Research Facility. Their leader, known as "Sam," hires Emmett Brown to use the substance to build them a nuclear bomb [BTF1-n]. The nationalists claim responsibility for the theft, but facility officials publicly deny such rumors, citing a clerical error as being responsible for the missing batch. Doc steals the plutonium for his own experiments, to power his prototype time-traveling DeLorean, and gives the Libyans a fake bomb made out of old pinball machine parts [BTF1].

• Agents Reese and Foley of the Nuclear Regulatory Commission (N.R.C.) are assigned to investigate Emmett Brown's plutonium theft [BTF1-s1].

Saturday, October 19, 1985 A.D.—1:20 to 1:22 AM

• A time-traveling DeLorean pulls up to the Greek Theatre, in Los Angeles, California, as several young people mill about waiting to watch a Loverboy concert. The excited concert-goers crowd around to see the driver—a man in a radiation suit. After the crowd reaches a fever pitch, the mysterious driver adjusts the vehicle's time circuits to take him to October 19, 2010, and then drives away, leaving a twin fire trail behind him as he rockets back to the future [SCRM].

Friday, October 25, 1985 A.D.—8:18 AM

• Seventeen-year-old Marty McFly arrives at the garage home of Emmett Brown, located at 1640 Riverside Drive. Upon discovering that his friend isn't home, Marty helps himself to a huge, experimental amplifier, plugging in his electric guitar and turning the dials up to maximum. One single pluck with the pick shatters the amp, however, propelling Marty backwards and into a shelf. As he recovers, Doc calls via telephone, urging Marty to meet him at the Twin Pines Mall parking lot at 1:15 AM on Saturday [BTF1].

Friday, October 25, 1985 A.D.—8:25 AM

• A cacophony of alarms sounds in Doc's garage, startling Marty. The scientist exclaims that his experiment worked—the clocks are all twenty-five minutes slow—and Marty, suddenly realizing he's late for school, promptly hangs up and hurries to class.

Despite his best efforts, "skitching" rides on the backs of several vehicles, Marty arrives late at Hill Valley High School. His girlfriend, Jennifer Parker, meets him outside and attempts to sneak him in undetected, but they are caught by Principal Gerald Strickland. The bald disciplinarian scolds the two teens, hands them both tardy slips and warns Marty about the dangers of hanging around the ill-reputed Doc Brown. When Marty flippantly responds, Strickland chastises the youth, calling him a "slacker" and saying his family is doomed to failure [BTF1].

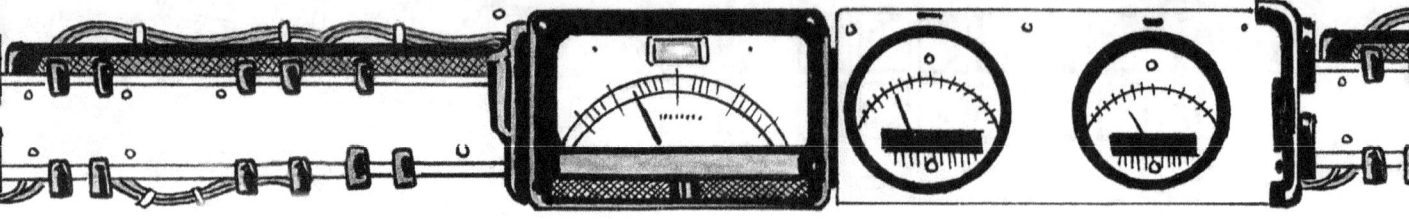

Friday, October 25, 1985 A.D.—Midday

- As his class watches a 1950s educational film about atomic power and the danger it represents, Marty McFly ignores the lesson, listening to his Sony Walkman. Marty is called down to the school office to receive an emergency phone call from Emmett Brown, reminding him to meet him at the mall to assist in his experiment. Strickland chastises him for taking personal calls during school hours. After discovering Marty's Walkman—a violation of school policy—the principal sentences him to after-school detention that day, ruining The Pinheads' plans to audition for an upcoming dance gig [BTF-n].

Friday, October 25, 1985 A.D.— Shortly After 3:00 PM

- A Libyan terrorist known as "Sam" receives a message from his superiors, notifying him that they've been swindled by Emmett Brown, whom Sam had hired to build the group a bomb using stolen plutonium. The nationalist group decrees that the scientist must be killed for his betrayal, and Sam orders another terrorist, Uranda, and an accomplice to trail Doc for the remainder of the day, in preparation for a nighttime strike [BTF1-n].

Friday, October 25, 1985 A.D.—3:42 PM

- Marty arrives at detention to find Principal Strickland supervising the session, which dashes his hopes of ditching detention in order to attend his band's audition. Marty takes his seat with the other punished students, wincing as Strickland collects the "illegal" Walkmans, including Marty's, and crushes them in a table-mounted woodworking vise.

  Marty initiates a scheme to leave detention: Applying a chewed-up wad of bubble gum to a book of matches, he shoots them at the room's smoke detector via rubber band. Then, by harnessing the Sun's rays with a small lens lifted from a carousel projector, Marty remotely lights the matches, setting off the fire alarm.

The sprinklers activate and the students rush out amidst cries of "Fire!" Marty borrows a skateboard from a fellow detainee named Weeze, and coasts down the hall, around Hill Valley's scenic Courthouse Square and to his audition [BTF1-n].

Friday, October 25, 1985 A.D.—3:58 PM

- In one possible timeline, Marty escapes detention and arrives just in time to audition with his band, The Pinheads, for a dance at the local Young Men's Christian Association (YMCA). He barely makes it to his first transition in lead guitar before the judges dismiss the band, refusing them admittance [BTF1-n].

- In another version of events, The Pinheads audition for Hill Valley High's Battle of the Bands competition after school, but are rejected by the judges for being "too darn loud" [BTF1]. A Baldwin-based punk-rock band, French Kiss, beats out The Pinheads for the gig [BTF1-s2].

Friday, October 25, 1985 A.D.—After 3:58 PM

- Dejected, Marty leaves school with Jennifer, stressing that he'll never see his rock-and-roll dreams come true. Jennifer encourages him not to lose faith, returning his audition tape so he can send it to the record company, but Marty changes the subject when he spots a black Toyota SR5, which he wishes they could use for their date. Jen has second thoughts about driving out to a lake together, worried about what Marty's mother would say if she knew. Marty says his prudish mother would never approve, which is why he hasn't told her.

  A representative of the Hill Valley Preservation Society, seeking donations to halt Mayor Goldie Wilson's initiative to repair the Courthouse Clock Tower, interrupts them. Marty offers a quarter and receives a flyer in return, detailing the clock's destruction. Jennifer's father arrives and she leaves with him, but not before scribbling her grandmother's number and a quick "I love you" on the back of the flyer.

CODE	STORY						
ARGN	BTTF-themed TV commercial: Arrigoni	BTF1	Film: Back to the Future	CITY	BTTF-themed music video: Owl City, "Deer in the Headlights"	HUEY	BTTF-themed music video: Huey Lewis and the News, "The Power of Love"
BFAN	Back to the Future: The Animated Series	BTF2	Film: Back to the Future Part II			LIMO	BTTF-themed music video:
BFCG	Back to the Future: The Card Game	BTF3	Film: Back to the Future Part III	DCTV	BTTF-themed TV commercial: DirecTV		The Limousines, "The Future"
BFCL	Back to the Future comic book (limited series)	BUDL	BTTF-themed TV commercial: Bud Light	ERTH	The Earth Day Special	MCDN	BTTF-themed TV commercial: McDonald's
BFCM	Back to the Future comic book (monthly series)	CHEK	BTTF-themed music video: O'Neal McKnight, "Check Your Coat"	GALE	Interviews and commentaries: Bob Gale and/or Robert Zemeckis	MITS	BTTF-themed TV commercial: Mitsubishi Lancer
BFHM	BTTF-themed McDonald's Happy Meal boxes	CHIC	Photographs hanging in Doc Brown's	GARB	BTTF-themed TV commercials: Garbarino	MSFT	BTTF-themed TV commercial: Microsoft
BTFA	Back to the Future Annual (Marvel Comics)		Chicken restaurant at Universal Studios	GETV	BTTF-themed TV commercial: GE		

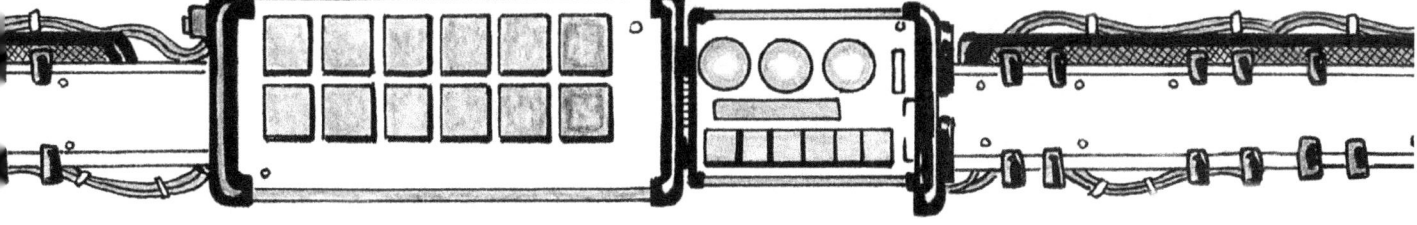

Marty returns to his home in Lyon Estates to discover the family car—which he had planned to use for his lakeside date with Jennifer—has been totaled in an accident. He learns that Biff Tannen, the supervisor of his father, George McFly, had borrowed the car and was then involved in a wreck while drinking, spilling beer all over his coat. Biff bullies George into paying for the cleaning bill, as well as the wrecked car, and to finish up Tannen's reports for work, and George meekly agrees to his demands. After Biff leaves, George apologizes to Marty for letting Biff walk over him, but says he fears confrontation. Marty, however, is more upset about the car and his ruined plans with Jen [BTF1].

• George McFly's neighbor, Howard, pressures him into buying an entire case of peanut brittle, in support of fundraising efforts for his daughter's team, the Cubs. Uncomfortable with confrontation, George agrees to the purchase [BTF1-d, BTF1-s4].

• That night, Marty eats dinner with his parents and older siblings Dave and Linda. The dinner had been intended to welcome home Lorraine's younger brother, Joey, from jail, but Marty's uncle has failed to make parole. Upon hearing of his failure at the Battle of the Bands audition, George tries to convince his son that it's for the best, as the gig would have been a source of stress.

Linda reports that Jennifer called while Marty was lamenting about the wrecked car. Lorraine admits her dislike of any girl who calls a boy, claiming she never called or chased boys as a teenager. Linda fears that she'll never meet a man of her own if she doesn't take the initiative, but Lorraine assures her that love will happen in due time, just as it did for her and George in 1955, with their destiny-sealing kiss at the Enchantment Under the Sea Dance [BTF1].

Saturday, October 26, 1985 A.D.— Shortly After 12:00 AM

• Emmett Brown waits with his dog, Einstein, in the nearly empty parking lot of the Twin Pines Mall while a late-night movie ends at the local theater. As the last cars leave the lot for the night, Doc calls Marty and begins preparing for his time-travel demonstration [BTF1-n].

> *NOTE: In the first film's fourth-draft screenplay, the date of Doc's historic demonstration was October 5, not 26.*

Saturday, October 26, 1985 A.D.—12:28 AM

• Marty McFly is fast asleep when Emmett Brown calls to remind him of their mall meeting at 1:15 AM. Marty promises he'll be there, and Doc asks him to stop at his home to retrieve his video camera [BTF1].

Saturday, October 26, 1985 A.D.—1:00 AM

• Marty arrives at Doc's home, secures the video camera and is startled when all of Brown's clocks simultaneously chime the hour [BTF1-n].

Saturday, October 26, 1985 A.D.—1:00 to 1:16 AM

• In one possible reality, while awaiting Marty's arrival at the Twin Pines Mall parking lot, Emmett Brown conducts a test run of his time-traveling DeLorean. The scientist straps Einstein in and sends him to the year 2012. When the vehicle returns to 1985, it is no longer a DeLorean, but rather a Mitsubishi Lancer, with Einie replaced by a talking robotic dog. Intrigued, Doc takes this new car for a spin [MITS].

> *NOTE: This commercial for the Mitsubishi Lancer, featuring Christopher Lloyd as Doc Brown, does not jibe with the movie's events—not only due to the implausibility of the car and dog*

NIKE	BTTF-themed TV commercial: Nike	**SCRT**	2010 Scream Awards: Back to the Future 25th Anniversary Reunion (trailer)	**SUFFIX MEDIUM**		**-s1**	Screenplay (draft one)

Abbr	Description	Abbr	Description	Suffix	Medium	Suffix	Screenplay
NIKE	BTTF-themed TV commercial: Nike	SCRT	2010 Scream Awards: Back to the Future 25th Anniversary Reunion (trailer)		SUFFIX MEDIUM	-s1	Screenplay (draft one)
NTND	Nintendo Back to the Future—The Ride Mini-Game	SIMP	Simulator: The Simpsons Ride	-b	BTF2's Biff Tannen Museum video (extended version)	-s2	Screenplay (draft two)
PIZA	BTTF-themed TV commercial: Pizza Hut	SLOT	Back to the Future Video Slots			-s3	Screenplay (draft three)
REAL	Real life	TEST	Screen tests: Crispin Glover, Lea Thompson and Thomas F. Wilson	-c	Animated series credit sequence	-s4	Screenplay (draft four)
RIDE	Simulator: Back to the Future—The Ride			-d	Film deleted scene	-sp	Screenplay (production draft)
SCRM	2010 Scream Awards: Back to the Future 25th Anniversary Reunion (broadcast)	TLTL	Telltale Games' Back to the Future—The Game	-n	Film novelization	-sx	Screenplay (Paradox)
		UNIV	Universal Studios Hollywood promotional video	-o	Film outtake		
				-v	Video game print materials or commentaries		

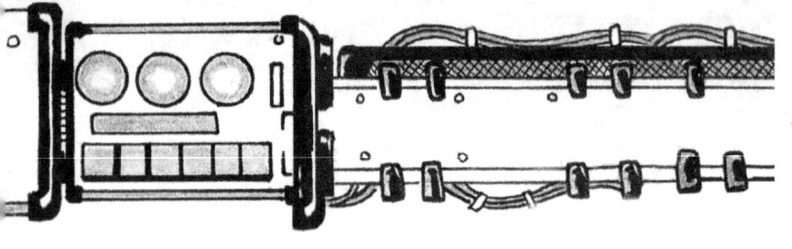

changing shape, but also because in the movie, both were back to their original form when Marty arrived, and no time travel had yet occurred.

Saturday, October 26, 1985 A.D.—1:16 AM

- Arriving one minute later than their scheduled meeting, Marty McFly skateboards to the Twin Pines Mall parking lot, where Einstein awaits his master by a white delivery trucked marked "Dr. E. Brown Enterprises." Marty approaches the friendly canine, looking for Doc, and is startled when the truck's bay opens and a heavily modified DeLorean DMC-12 backs out onto the pavement. Doc Brown exits the steaming sports car, greets his young friend and explains that this is the invention he's waited all his life to build [BTF1].

Saturday, October 26, 1985 A.D.—1:18 AM

- Marty McFly activates Doc's video camera to document Temporal Experiment #1 in the mall's parking lot [BTF1].

Saturday, October 26, 1985 A.D.—1:19 AM

- Doc buckles Einstein into the driver's seat of the modified DeLorean and, via remote control, steers the car across the parking lot. Still filming, Marty stands by in apprehension as Doc releases the brake lock on the remote control, causing the automated DeLorean to barrel toward them at high-speed [BTF1].

Saturday, October 26, 1985 A.D.—1:20 AM

- At the precise moment that the DeLorean achieves 88 miles per hour, the vehicle vanishes in a brilliant display of light, leaving only a pair of fire trails behind. Marty McFly thinks Einstein has been disintegrated, but Doc reveals that his dog has, in fact, become the world's first time traveler. The DeLorean is a time machine, he says,

and Einstein has been sent one minute into the future [BTF1].

Saturday, October 26, 1985 A.D.—1:21 AM

- Doc's stopwatch reaches 1:21. Startled, he pushes Marty out of the way just as the DeLorean—carrying Einstein—reappears from one minute in the past, nearly running

CODE	STORY						
ARGN	BTTF-themed TV commercial: Arrigoni	BTF1	Film: Back to the Future	CITY	BTTF-themed music video: Owl City, "Deer in the Headlights"	HUEY	BTTF-themed music video: Huey Lewis and the News, "The Power of Love"
BFAN	Back to the Future: The Animated Series	BTF2	Film: Back to the Future Part II			LIMO	BTTF-themed music video:
BFCG	Back to the Future: The Card Game	BTF3	Film: Back to the Future Part III	DCTV	BTTF-themed TV commercial: DirecTV		The Limousines, "The Future"
BFCL	Back to the Future comic book (limited series)	BUDL	BTTF-themed TV commercial: Bud Light	ERTH	The Earth Day Special	MCDN	BTTF-themed TV commercial: McDonald's
BFCM	Back to the Future comic book (monthly series)	CHEK	BTTF-themed music video: O'Neal McKnight, "Check Your Coat"	GALE	Interviews and commentaries: Bob Gale and/or Robert Zemeckis	MITS	BTTF-themed TV commercial: Mitsubishi Lancer
BFHM	BTTF-themed McDonald's Happy Meal boxes	CHIC	Photographs hanging in Doc Brown's	GARB	BTTF-themed TV commercials: Garbarino		
BTFA	Back to the Future Annual (Marvel Comics)		Chicken restaurant at Universal Studios	GETV	BTTF-themed TV commercial: GE	MSFT	BTTF-themed TV commercial: Microsoft

THANKS TO NEEDLES,
A FATEFUL ACCIDENT DESTROYS
MARTY'S DREAMS

them over before spinning to a halt, its surface covered in steaming ice [BTF1].

Saturday, October 26, 1985 A.D.—1:22 AM

• Doc determines that Einstein has come through his trip to the future just fine. What's more, his clock reads 1:21— exactly one minute behind Brown's own stopwatch. Marty is stunned, and an enthusiastic Doc sits at the

console of the modified DeLorean to explain how the device works. After punching in a few sample dates, Doc sets the time circuits for November 5, 1955—the date on which he slipped in his bathroom while hanging a clock and experienced a vision of the Flux Capacitor, which makes time travel possible.

Doc reminisces about that fateful day and the thirty-year journey that has led to this moment. His excitement over his scientific breakthrough proves short-lived,

NIKE	BTTF-themed TV commercial: Nike	**SCRT**	2010 Scream Awards: Back to the Future	**SUFFIX**	**MEDIUM**	**-s1**	Screenplay (draft one)
NTND	Nintendo Back to the Future—The Ride		25th Anniversary Reunion (trailer)	**-b**	BTF2's Biff Tannen Museum video	**-s2**	Screenplay (draft two)
	Mini-Game	**SIMP**	Simulator: The Simpsons Ride		(extended version)	**-s3**	Screenplay (draft three)
PIZA	BTTF-themed TV commercial: Pizza Hut	**SLOT**	Back to the Future Video Slots	**-c**	Animated series credit sequence	**-s4**	Screenplay (draft four)
REAL	Real life	**TEST**	Screen tests: Crispin Glover, Lea Thompson	**-d**	Film deleted scene	**-sp**	Screenplay (production draft)
RIDE	Simulator: Back to the Future—The Ride		and Thomas F. Wilson	**-n**	Film novelization	**-sx**	Screenplay (Paradox)
SCRM	2010 Scream Awards: Back to the Future	**TLTL**	Telltale Games' Back to the Future—The Game	**-o**	Film outtake		
	25th Anniversary Reunion (broadcast)	**UNIV**	Universal Studios Hollywood promotional video	**-v**	Video game print materials or commentaries		

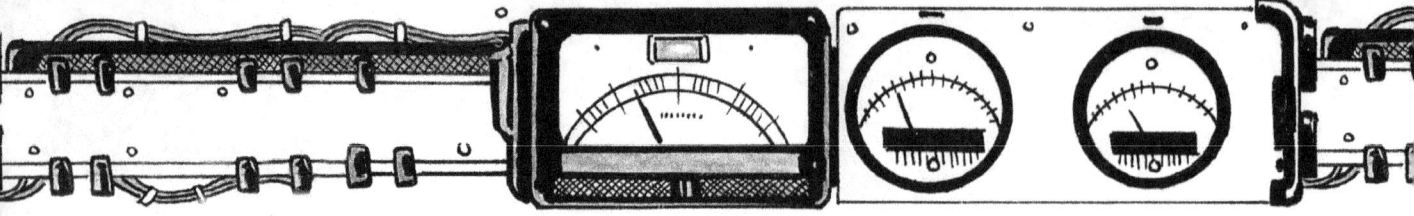

however, when the Libyan terrorists from whom he stole the plutonium return, out for blood [BTF1].

Saturday, October 26, 1985 A.D.—1:24 AM

- A second Marty McFly from slightly in the future, having already traveled into the past and back again, returns from the year 1955, crashing the DeLorean into Courthouse Square's Town Theater. Hoping to save Doc from the Libyans, he has come back ten minutes earlier than he left—but when the car stalls, he has no choice but to run to the shopping center (now called the Lone Pine Mall due to Marty's temporal tampering) on foot. Meanwhile, the terrorists speed by, on their way to murder his friend [BTF1].

Saturday, October 26, 1985 A.D.—1:33 AM

- Emmett Brown attempts to draw the terrorists' fire and allow the first Marty to escape, and is gunned down in the process. The gunmen turn their sights on Marty, but he flees in the DeLorean, inciting a car chase through the mall parking lot [BTF1].

- The second Marty races on foot to the mall, but arrives too late, watching once more as Doc is shot by the Libyan nationalists. To his astonishment, he also witnesses his younger self engaging in a car chase with the terrorists.

Saturday, October 26, 1985 A.D.—1:35 AM

- Desperate to dodge the Libyans' gunfire, the first Marty swerves and speeds ahead, inadvertently reaching 88 miles per hour and activating the Flux Capacitor. With the time circuits still set to November 5, 1955, the DeLorean vanishes, carrying Marty back to the mid-1950s. The Libyans, startled to see their prey disappear, crash into a Fox Photo Lab booth.

  With the terrorists out of commission, the second Marty hurries to the side of his fallen friend, mourning his death once more. However, Doc rises—seemingly

from the dead—and reveals he's been wearing a bulletproof vest. Brown admits that he had taped together Marty's 1955 note warning him of this night, thereby altering the timeline by avoiding his own murder [BTF1]. The two sneak off just as local authorities arrive to apprehend the gunmen [BTF1-n].

- In the pre-dawn morning hours, Doc drives Marty back to his parents' home. Bidding farewell, Doc informs the youth that his next stop will be the year 2015. He promises to look Marty up once he gets there [BTF1].

Saturday, October 26, 1985 A.D.—10:28 AM

- Marty McFly awakens later in the morning with a renewed sense of confidence. Grateful to be home, and inspired by his own morale-boosting speeches to George thirty years prior, Marty decides to send his audition tape to the record company [BTF1-n]. As he enters the kitchen, he is shocked to learn that his temporal meddling has radically altered his own home life. His family is now wealthy and confident, with his siblings in prominent jobs and his father—once a mild-mannered pushover—now an author, with his debut novel, *A Match Made in Space*, about to be released. His parents are healthy and in love, while Biff Tannen is now a meek stooge waxing George's BMW [BTF1].

- To Marty's astonishment, his parents have a uniformed maid in their employ, named Bertha [BTF1-s3, BTF1-s4]. Marty discovers that he also has a new truck: the Toyota SR5 he'd been eyeing before traveling back to the past. Even better, Jennifer arrives, a beautiful sight for sore eyes [BTF1].

Saturday, October 26, 1985 A.D.—10:38 AM

- The happy reunion is interrupted when Emmett Brown's DeLorean crashes through the front yard. The scientist implores Marty and Jen to return with him to the year 2015, where their future children, he says, are in trouble.

CODE	STORY						
ARGN	BTTF-themed TV commercial: Arrigoni	BTF1	Film: *Back to the Future*	CITY	BTTF-themed music video: Owl City, "Deer in the Headlights"	HUEY	BTTF-themed music video: Huey Lewis and the News, "The Power of Love"
BFAN	*Back to the Future: The Animated Series*	BTF2	Film: *Back to the Future Part II*	DCTV	BTTF-themed TV commercial: DirecTV	LIMO	BTTF-themed music video: The Limousines, "The Future"
BFCG	*Back to the Future: The Card Game*	BTF3	Film: *Back to the Future Part III*	ERTH	*The Earth Day Special*		
BFCL	*Back to the Future* comic book (limited series)	BUDL	BTTF-themed TV commercial: Bud Light	GALE	Interviews and commentaries: Bob Gale and/or Robert Zemeckis	MCDN	BTTF-themed TV commercial: McDonald's
BFCM	*Back to the Future* comic book (monthly series)	CHEK	BTTF-themed music video: O'Neal McKnight, "Check Your Coat"			MITS	BTTF-themed TV commercial: Mitsubishi Lancer
BFHM	*BTTF*-themed McDonald's Happy Meal boxes			GARB	BTTF-themed TV commercials: Garbarino		
BTFA	*Back to the Future Annual* (Marvel Comics)	CHIC	Photographs hanging in Doc Brown's Chicken restaurant at Universal Studios	GETV	BTTF-themed TV commercial: GE	MSFT	BTTF-themed TV commercial: Microsoft

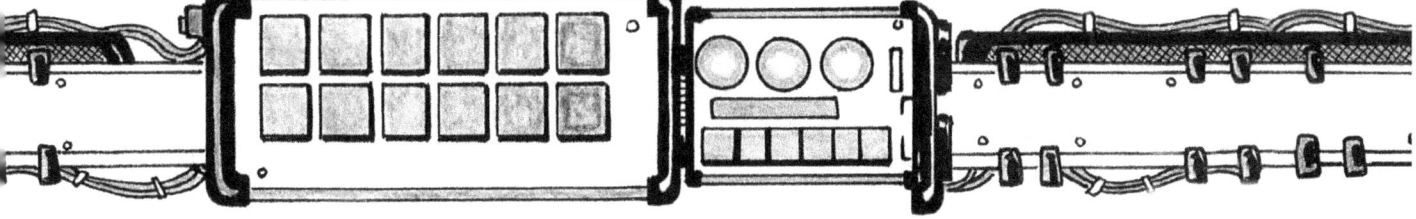

The young couple pile into the time machine and, to their astonishment, the vehicle hovers into the sky and rockets back to the future [BTF1, BTF2].

- As they leave, an excited Biff Tannen exits the McFly home to show Marty the new matchbooks for his auto-detailing shop. In so doing, he bears witness to a DeLorean inexplicably taking flight [BTF1, BTF2].

Saturday, October 26, 1985 A.D.—9:00 PM

- Marty, Doc and Jennifer return from 2015, unaware that the older Biff Tannen, recognizing the flying DeLorean from his past, had overheard talk of its time-traveling capability and used the vehicle to alter time in his favor, thereby creating a dark alternate reality. Marty's first clue that things are now different occurs when he leaves Jennifer—still unconscious from the shock of seeing her future self in 2015—on her front porch, where the windows are now barred. Later, when Marty returns to his home at Lyon Estates, he discovers that another family has been living there for some time. Mistaken for a burglar, Marty is chased out of the house and finds himself in a dilapidated Hill Valley, now a trash-littered den of undesirables [BTF2].

- In this altered reality, the drinking age is 14, industrial smokestacks blot out the nighttime stars [BTF2-n], Hill Valley High School has been burnt down since 1979 and Gerald Strickland is now a paranoid, gun-toting vigilante who trades gunfire with local gangs. At the center of this dark variation on Marty's town is the Courthouse—now converted into Biff Tannen's Pleasure Paradise, a casino hotel and museum chronicling the kingpin's rise to fortune and fame [BTF2].

> *NOTE: The first draft of* **BTF2**'s *screenplay included a subplot involving the construction of a hospital in 1973 that saved George McFly's life following a terrible automobile accident. In that draft, an elderly Biff from 2015 traveled back to 1967, rather than 1955, to hand his younger self the* **Grays Sports Almanac.** *In turn, a newly wealthy Biff Tannen purchased the plot of land that would have housed the hospital, building his Pleasure Paradise on the one-time site of the medical facility. As a result, George died of his injuries and Biff married Lorraine. In that version of the script, Strickland worked as Biff's chief of security.*

- Marty is stunned to see his brother, David McFly, being thrown out of the casino, stumbling drunk. Marty asks Dave what has happened, but his brother is too inebriated to provide a straight answer, saying only that their mother can be found inside [BTF2-d]. Marty approaches the Biff Tannen Museum display outside the lobby, where he views a video detailing Biff's many successes in this reality—including marrying Marty's mother Lorraine.

Floored by this development, Marty causes a scene on the outside steps of the Pleasure Paradise, and is apprehended by Tannen's flunkies—Match, 3-D and Joey ("Skinhead"), Biff's cronies from high school. The enforcers knock Marty out cold and drag him to Biff's penthouse suite to sleep off his blow to the head. Upon awakening, he discovers that Lorraine is now a cosmetically altered buxom beauty whose hard life is etched on her face, and with liquor never far from her reach.

Before Marty can get answers about what created this timeline, Biff—now his step-father—arrives, outraged that Marty is not at the Switzerland boarding school where he's supposed to be. Biff lashes out at the youth, prompting Lorraine to threaten divorce, though she backs down when he says he'll cut her three children off financially, abandoning them to settle their considerable debts and legal scrapes themselves. After the thugs leave, Marty demands to know what happened to his father, and Lorraine sadly says that George has been dead since 1973, buried in Oak Park Cemetery [BTF2].

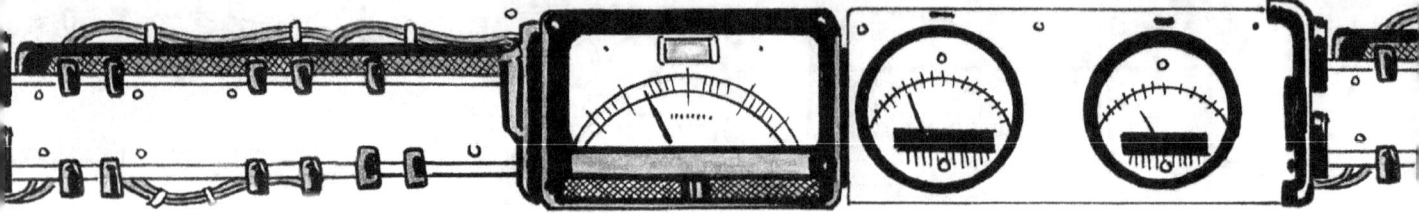

- Distraught, Marty ventures to the graveyard and finds his father's tombstone. Doc arrives and takes Marty back to his garage, which is now a disheveled wreck. Upon discovering the *Grays Sports Almanac* receipt and the handle of future Biff's cane in the DeLorean, they realize that old Biff must have gotten hold of the time machine in 2015 and taken the book back in time to give to his younger self, thereby creating this alternate timeline. A closer inspection of old Hill Valley newspapers reveals that Biff had the almanac in a 1958 photo. Marty realizes this is all his fault, for conceiving the almanac scheme in the first place. Their only hope, Doc says, is to determine the exact date on which old Biff visited himself in the past [BTF2].

    *NOTE: In the initial draft of **BTF2**'s script, Marty pieced together that an event in the past had skewed the timeline and explained it to Doc, but the reverse was true onscreen.*

Sunday, October 27, 1985 A.D.

- Early in the morning, Marty returns to the Pleasure Paradise and confronts his stepfather about the sports almanac. Tannen is surprisingly forthcoming, citing November 12, 1955, as the date in question, when a mysterious visitor claiming to be a distant relation handed him the book. After divulging this information, Biff adds that the old man also told him to buy a gun and kill any "crazy wild-eyed scientist" or "kid" who came asking about it. Tannen opens fire, but Marty escapes to the roof. With Marty cornered, the tycoon gloats that he murdered George McFly using this same firearm. Before he can do the same to Marty, the teen surprises Biff by stepping off the roof. Moments later, the flying DeLorean rises above the roof line, with Marty standing on its hood [BTF2].

Sunday, October 27, 1985 A.D.—2:42 AM

- Doc uses the car's gullwing door to knock Tannen unconscious, and the two time travelers plot a course

for 1955, hoping to rectify the damaged timeline. Doc notes that the time circuits are slightly malfunctioning, promising to fix them at a later date [BTF2].

Sunday, October 27, 1985 A.D.—11:00 AM

- Marty McFly returns from a trip to save Doc from being murdered in 1885, with the DeLorean's tireless rims running along a train track thanks to one of Doc's innovations in that era. Morning commuters waiting at the Eastwood Ravine railroad crossing receive a strange sight when the vehicle rolls along the tracks, driven by a teenager in an Old West costume. Moments later, Marty sees a locomotive barreling down on his location and barely jumps to safety as the car is completely demolished [BTF3].

    NOTE: The third film's novelization placed this event in October 17, 1985, but onscreen, it occurred ten days later. Oddly, neither the train conductor nor any other drivers stopped to find out if anyone was hurt in the collision.

Sunday, October 27, 1985 A.D.— Shortly After 11:00 AM

- In one timeline, Marty McFly takes his Toyota SR5 for a spin and encounters high school rival Douglas J. Needles idling his car at a stoplight. Needles goads Marty into drag-racing by calling him a "chicken." Unable to resist such a challenge, Marty agrees. The traffic light turns green and Marty floors the gas pedal, crashing into the side of a Rolls Royce. The wreck leaves Marty's guitar hand ruined, and his life takes a downward spiral from that day forward, his dreams of a music career destroyed [BTF2].

- In the reality in which the DeLorean is hit by a train, Marty visits Jennifer Parker's home after returning to 1985, and finds her asleep on her front-porch swing. Relieved to see Jen unharmed, he awakens her with a kiss. Initially dismissing her time-traveling as a dream,

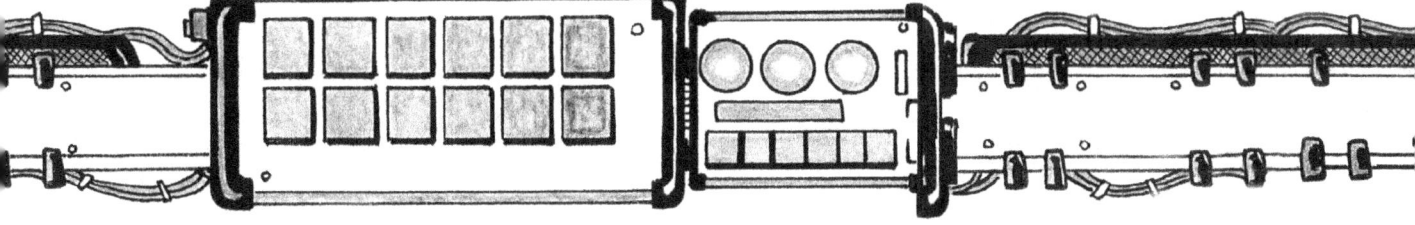

she is stunned when Marty inadvertently references those future events. Revealing the truth, Marty decides to show her the obliterated time machine's remains. En route, however, the two meet Needles at the stoplight, who challenges Marty to a drag race. Despite Needles' taunting, Marty backs out of the race (aware of the future ramifications of doing otherwise), and watches as Needles nearly collides with the Rolls Royce. Jennifer realizes it was this incident that had caused a lasting negative effect on their lives by 2015—and that now, with the accident averted, they have a better chance of being happy [BTF3].

> *NOTE: The* **BTTF** *card game listed the time for this event as 10:55 AM—five minutes before the DeLorean re-entered 1985, which would be impossible. This scene had its origins in the first draft of* **BTF2**, *in which two older teens, Winch and Lomax, urged Marty to be their wheel man during a "once-in-a-lifetime deal" that would supposedly have made them all wealthy. In that original screenplay, Jennifer discovered in 2015 that Marty took the goons up on their offer, landing him in legal trouble, and thus ruining his life. Marty later refused the offer, reclaiming his future. In that draft, all traces of Marty's future—even his kids' existence—were erased. Marty asked Doc if that meant he and Jen were no longer married, to which Doc offered the same advice he provided onscreen in* **BTF3**: *that their future would be whatever they made of it.*

• At the Eastwood Ravine tracks, Marty and Jennifer shuffle through the scrap metal that was once the DeLorean. As Marty comes to grips with never again seeing Doc, a time-traveling locomotive suddenly appears, steam-powered and designed to resemble Captain Nemo's submarine *Nautilus*, from Jules Verne's novels *Twenty Thousand Leagues Under the Sea* and *The Mysterious Island*. Doc and Clara Clayton are aboard,

having come back from 1885 to retrieve Einstein. Doc and Clara have long since married, and now have two young sons, named Jules and Verne in the author's honor. Marty is overjoyed to reunite with his friend, who gives him a framed picture from their stay in the Old West. Jennifer questions Doc about the events of Marty's future changing, and he smiles, assuring her that the future has not yet been written. Marty and Jen embrace, watching as the Brown family power up the time train and travel to new adventures [BTF3].

> *NOTE: Following this final scene of the film trilogy, fans speculated about where the family went. While some have suggested that they visited the Moon—a natural assumption, given Doc's and Clara's affection for Jules Verne—the original screenplay draft for* **BTF2**, *titled* **Paradox**, *offered a possible answer. Before the movies were split in two, a variation of this ending (minus Clara, the boys and the time train) appeared in that script's second half. In that version, Doc announced that having messed up the Fourth Dimension, he now considered it time to set his sights on the Fifth Dimension.*

Sometime After 1985 A.D.

• Emmett Brown drives his time-traveling DeLorean to a club called Charlie's to watch an intimate Huey Lewis and the News concert, where the band performs its hit song, "Power of Love." While Doc enjoys the concert, a young couple enters the vehicle and takes it for a spin [HUEY].

> *NOTE: The events of the film trilogy did not leave a window of time for Doc to have made such a stop in 1985. As such, it's more likely that this occurred at a later date. Since Doc obtained other time-traveling DeLoreans in the Telltale Games video game and the animated series, this would fit established lore. It's unknown whether or not the car-thieving couple was ever brought to justice.*

NIKE	*BTTF*-themed TV commercial: Nike	**SCRT**	2010 Scream Awards: *Back to the Future*	**SUFFIX**	**MEDIUM**	
NTND	Nintendo *Back to the Future—The Ride*		25th Anniversary Reunion (trailer)	**-b**	*BTF2*'s Biff Tannen Museum video	**-s1**	Screenplay (draft one)
	Mini-Game	**SIMP**	Simulator: *The Simpsons Ride*		(extended version)	**-s2**	Screenplay (draft two)
PIZA	*BTTF*-themed TV commercial: Pizza Hut	**SLOT**	*Back to the Future* Video Slots	**-c**	Animated series credit sequence	**-s3**	Screenplay (draft three)
REAL	Real life	**TEST**	Screen tests: Crispin Glover, Lea Thompson	**-d**	Film deleted scene	**-s4**	Screenplay (draft four)
RIDE	Simulator: *Back to the Future—The Ride*		and Thomas F. Wilson	**-n**	Film novelization	**-sp**	Screenplay (production draft)
SCRM	2010 Scream Awards: *Back to the Future*	**TLTL**	Telltale Games' *Back to the Future—The Game*	**-o**	Film outtake	**-sx**	Screenplay (*Paradox*)
	25th Anniversary Reunion (broadcast)	**UNIV**	Universal Studios Hollywood promotional video	**-v**	Video game print materials or commentaries		

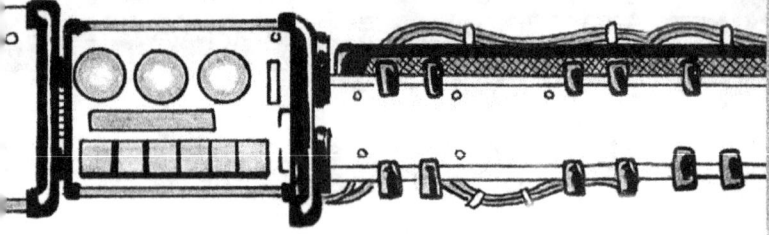

CHAPTER XI:
1986 A.D.

1985 to 1986 A.D.

- George McFly earns local praise as a "cultural treasure" for his science fiction novel *A Match Made in Space*, which ends up a top-ten bestseller [TLTL-v]. A video miniseries based on the novel is also produced [BTF2-s1].

1985 to 2015 A.D.

- The materialism and excesses of the 1980s run rampant to outrageous proportions, resulting in a future in which flying cars, hoverboards and flash-cooked instant meals are commonplace—and at absurdly inflated prices [BTF2].

Sometime in or Before 1986 A.D.

- In the Citizen Brown timeline, Courthouse Square receives a sanitized, uniform facelift, in accordance with Edna Strickland's conservative aesthetic. Numerous businesses open in and around the square, including the All Citizen's Bank; the Citizen Reading Room; The Combformist; E. Brown Industries; the Hill Valley Bureau of Discipline; the Ministry of Tourism; SoupMo; and Stemmles's Staycations [TLTL-3].
    NOTE: View the map on page 183 to see where each business was located.

- In one possible timeline, a law-enforcement agency known as the Time Police is established in Hill Valley [TLTL-v].
    NOTE: This discarded concept for the Telltale Games video game was briefly discussed in the game's commentary track.

- Biff Tannen gives his car the pet name "Sheila" [TLTL-3].

- Statutes 357-K and 476-D are passed in the Citizen Brown timeline, strictly prohibiting Hill Valley's

inhabitants from, respectively, owning a dog and showing public displays of affection—specifically, open-mouth kissing involving tongues. In this reality, Emmett Brown (influenced by his repressed wife, Edna Strickland) mandates that Hill Valley's citizens must all become vegetarians, wear ID badges at all times and adhere to strict dress codes, such as Polo Shirt Thursday and Hawaiian Shirt Friday. Many items and genres are illegalized, including weapons, alcohol, cigarettes, cigars, bubblegum, dogs, Circus Peanuts, science fiction, *Dungeons and Dragons*, skateboards, rock-and-roll music, pinball games, novelty items (such as X-ray

---

THE TANNEN GANG:
TERRORIZING HILL
VALLEY SINCE 1931

specs, joy buzzers and trick gum), pornographic films and magazines, and more, including even mentioning provocative words, such as "hormones." Pornographic movies *Smut Video* and *Stag* are released on VHS, and are summarily deemed illegal. What's more, Hill Valley's walls are coated with Teflon to make them easy to clean, and to cause graffiti paint to quickly streak [TLTL-3].

• In Citizen Brown's dystopian timeline, David McFly leaves Hill Valley to work for a big-city newspaper, losing touch with his family for long stretches of time. His sister Linda also leaves town, in order to live at a women's boardinghouse [TLTL-3].

> *NOTE: Dave's newspaper job was an in-joke reference to actor Marc McClure's casting as Jimmy Olsen in the* **Superman** *films and their spinoff,* **Supergirl.** *Linda's boardinghouse relocation, meanwhile, referred to late actor Wendie Jo Sperber's casting as Amy Cassidy on the television series* **Bosom Buddies.**

• A young Hill Valley couple named Jack and Diane begin dating. Edna Strickland, a spinster who spies on people from her apartment window, publicly taunts the couple

---

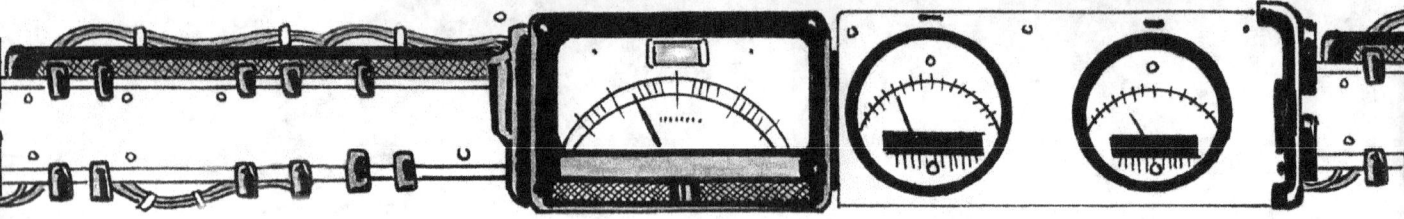

via a bullhorn whenever she sees them hanging out behind a tree [TLTL-1].

> **NOTE: The names Jack and Diane paid homage to John Cougar Mellencamp's 1982 hit song "Jack & Diane," in which the titular couple hid "behind a shady tree."**

• A rock-and-roll album titled *Heavy* is released in the Citizen Brown timeline [TLTL-3].

> **NOTE: This was an in-joke reference to Marty McFly's pet phrase, "heavy."**

• Sportswear manufacturer Adods begins marketing a line of running suits popular with Biff Tannen and his brothers, Cliff and Riff [BTF3].

> **NOTE: This company was named after real-world sportswear firm Adidas.**

• Both Emmett Brown and George McFly become fans of the writings of Isaac Asimov, the author and editor of more than 500 books throughout his lifetime [TLTL-5].

• A punk-rock band called Baby Fist attains popularity. In Citizen Brown's timeline, Jennifer Parker is a fan of the group [TLTL-3].

• Journalist Edna Strickland wins a trio of editorial trophies for her writing in *Cat Lover's Quarterly* magazine, including "Best Litter Columnist" [TLTL-1].

1986 A.D.

• Many of Emmett Brown's home and residence belongings are donated to the Hill Valley Historical Society Archives when the scientist—stranded in 1931—is presumed dead or missing [TLTL-v].

Sometime Between October 1985 and May 1986 A.D.

• With Emmett Brown missing and presumed dead, the city of Hill Valley plans to tear down what's left of the Brown family estate, in order to make room for a parking garage. Marty McFly protests this decision, but no one listens. At the city's behest, George McFly begins working with the bank to foreclose on Doc's garage home [TLTL-1].

Wednesday, May 14, 1986 A.D.

• Marty McFly experiences troubling dreams about the night of Emmett Brown's time-travel experiment at the Twin Pines Mall the year prior. In his dream, Doc's dog, Einstein, never returns from his maiden voyage, creating a paradox. The mall—and Doc himself—begin fading from existence, and before vanishing, the scientist apologizes for having made a terrible mistake. Marty awakens from his nightmare, realizing he's late in meeting his father at Doc's estate sale.

Marty arrives at Doc's garage, and is struck with nostalgia, feeling the loss of his closest friend. While shuffling through decades' worth of accumulated junk, Marty discovers one of Doc's old notebooks tucked inside the model he made of the Hill Valley Courthouse in 1955. Before Marty can lay hands on it, however, Biff Tannen—also perusing the sale—grabs the book, hoping he can make money off "the crackpot's" scratchings and the inventions found therein, including schematics for the Flux Capacitor.

Fearing what could happen should the knowledge of time travel fall into the wrong hands, Marty tries a number of excuses to part Biff from the book, but to no avail. Finally, Marty plugs his guitar into Doc's experimental amplifier, hoping Biff will cut in, determined to show off his skills. As he strikes the first chord, the speaker explodes, hurling Biff backwards. Chuckling, Marty takes the opportunity to grab Doc's notebook [TLTL-1].

CODE	STORY						
ARGN	BTTF-themed TV commercial: Arrigoni	BTF1	Film: *Back to the Future*	CITY	*BTTF*-themed music video: Owl City, "Deer in the Headlights"	HUEY	*BTTF*-themed music video: Huey Lewis and the News, "The Power of Love"
BFAN	*Back to the Future: The Animated Series*	BTF2	Film: *Back to the Future Part II*	DCTV	*BTTF*-themed TV commercial: DirecTV	LIMO	*BTTF*-themed music video: The Limousines, "The Future"
BFCG	*Back to the Future: The Card Game*	BTF3	Film: *Back to the Future Part III*	ERTH	*The Earth Day Special*		
BFCL	*Back to the Future* comic book (limited series)	BUDL	*BTTF*-themed TV commercial: Bud Light	GALE	Interviews and commentaries: Bob Gale and/or Robert Zemeckis	MCDN	*BTTF*-themed TV commercial: McDonald's
BFCM	*Back to the Future* comic book (monthly series)	CHEK	*BTTF*-themed music video: O'Neal McKnight, "Check Your Coat"			MITS	*BTTF*-themed TV commercial: Mitsubishi Lancer
BFHM	*BTTF*-themed McDonald's Happy Meal boxes	CHIC	Photographs hanging in Doc Brown's Chicken restaurant at Universal Studios	GARB	*BTTF*-themed TV commercials: Garbarino		
BTFA	*Back to the Future Annual* (Marvel Comics)			GETV	*BTTF*-themed TV commercial: GE	MSFT	*BTTF*-themed TV commercial: Microsoft

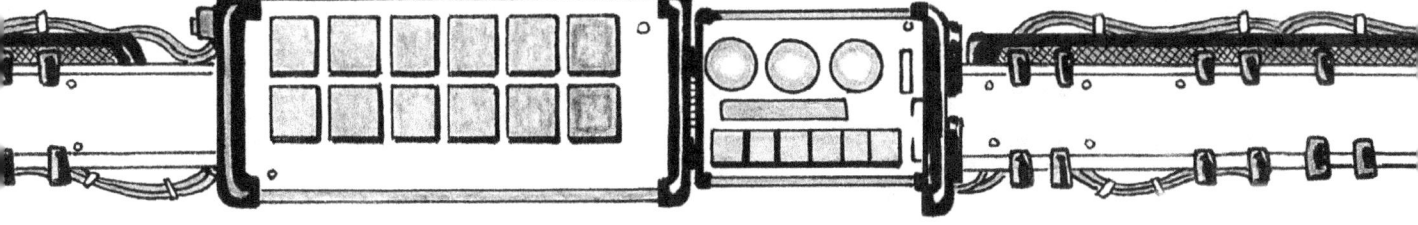

Wednesday, May 14, 1986 A.D.—6:05 to 6:08 PM

• Just then, a DeLorean arrives—a temporal copy of the original, created in 1955 when the vehicle was struck by lightning, which Doc recovered in 2025. Thinking Doc has returned, Marty investigates the vehicle, only to discover that Einstein is its lone occupant. Confused, the youth climbs in and searches for clues, finding only a woman's shoe and a tape recorder.

Pressing "play," Marty hears Doc's voice, informing him that the DeLorean's automatic retrieval feature has been activated—a built-in safety precaution designed to return the DeLorean to these specific fourth-dimensional coordinates in the event that Doc ever fell into trouble and could not return to the time machine in an allotted period of time. As such, Marty cannot be sure in what year Doc became stranded. He activates the time circuits, but the machinery is malfunctioning, making it impossible to determine the DeLorean's last coordinates. Desperate, Marty offers the shoe to Einstein—the only witness to whatever happened to Doc. The dog picks up the footwear's scent and leads Marty across town.

Einstein's nose brings Marty to an apartment building, which elderly Edna Strickland—Gerald Strickland's sister—and her entourage of cats call home. An embittered stickler, Edna wiles away the hours watching people from her window through a pair of binoculars, incessantly hollering for them to behave. She mistakes Marty for a "hooligan," but the teen convinces her to admit him into her home so he can question her about the shoe. Edna recognizes it as the missing half of a pair she's owned for decades, but can't remember the date on which she lost it, except that it fell victim to a scuffle with a dog on the day that Hill Valley's speakeasy burnt down.

Marty presses Edna for the exact date, eyeing her extensive collection of *Hill Valley Telegraph* newspapers. She claims to have every edition since 1871, meticulously organized, but refuses to let Marty near them. In talking to the old woman, however, Marty deduces that the speakeasy once existed on the same site as the current Valley Video—a building rebuilt in February 1932, following a fire. Marty distracts Edna long enough to shuffle through the newspapers, then pieces together the exact date of the fire: June 14, 1931. According to the paper, Doc—under the guise of drifter "Carl Sagan"—was pegged as the speakeasy arsonist, and was murdered by a vigilante mob. Before he can learn anything more, Marty accidentally topples Edna's stacks of collectibles, causing her to angrily chase him from her apartment [TLTL-1].

Wednesday, May 14, 1986 A.D.—7:13 to 7:27 PM

• Having determined Doc's fate, Marty travels back to the year 1931 in the DeLorean with Einstein, hoping to rescue their friend [TLTL-1].

Thursday, May 15, 1986 A.D.—8:30 AM

• In one possible timeline, Marty McFly and Emmett Brown return from 1931, but find that their present has changed dramatically. While Doc visits the bank to stop the sale of his estate, Marty heads home, where his parents are terrified to open their door, claiming their son was run out of town, and insisting that he must be an imposter. Marty eventually convinces them to let him in, and is horrified to find that George McFly is now a paraplegic. Before his father can offer an explanation, Biff Tannen arrives, flanked by his brothers, Cliff and Riff. The three thugs have come to shake down George for protection money, but decide to take their payment out of Marty's hide for returning to Hill Valley after they ran him out of town [TLTL-2].

> *NOTE: It's unclear whether Cliff and Riff (who were never mentioned in the films) existed in the original timeline. Their father, Irving "Kid" Tannen, was in prison for years, but may have had conjugal visits.*

NIKE	*BTTF*-themed TV commercial: Nike	**SCRT**	2010 Scream Awards: *Back to the Future* 25th Anniversary Reunion (trailer)	**SUFFIX**	**MEDIUM**		**-s1**	Screenplay (draft one)
NTND	Nintendo *Back to the Future—The Ride* Mini-Game	**SIMP**	Simulator: *The Simpsons Ride*	**-b**	*BTF2's* Biff Tannen Museum video (extended version)		**-s2**	Screenplay (draft two)
PIZA	*BTTF*-themed TV commercial: Pizza Hut	**SLOT**	*Back to the Future* Video Slots	**-c**	Animated series credit sequence		**-s3**	Screenplay (draft three)
REAL	Real life	**TEST**	Screen tests: Crispin Glover, Lea Thompson and Thomas F. Wilson	**-d**	Film deleted scene		**-s4**	Screenplay (draft four)
RIDE	Simulator: *Back to the Future—The Ride*	**TLTL**	Telltale Games' *Back to the Future—The Game*	**-n**	Film novelization		**-sp**	Screenplay (production draft)
SCRM	2010 Scream Awards: *Back to the Future* 25th Anniversary Reunion (broadcast)	**UNIV**	Universal Studios Hollywood promotional video	**-o**	Film outtake		**-sx**	Screenplay (*Paradox*)
				-v	Video game print materials or commentaries			

- Marty has a brief showdown with the Tannen brothers, whose family has terrorized Hill Valley for fifty years as the much-feared Tannen Gang. As the fifth most dangerous crime family in California, the Tannens are in league with Don J.J. Valenti, the godfather of the Sacramento Mob, who have given them a gold-plated cigarette lighter in the shape of a pistol. In this reality, the Tannens crippled George McFly decades ago in retaliation for his knockout of Biff at the Enchantment Under the Sea Dance.

   As the brothers circle Marty in an attempt to beat him up, he outmaneuvers the trio, tricking them into electrocuting themselves with a bug zapper. He swipes the pistol lighter and prepares to leave as a limousine pulls up, containing an aged Irving "Kid" Tannen—the family patriarch, of whom Marty ran afoul in 1931. Kid pulls a revolver on Marty, but the teen is spared a grisly fate when Doc returns in the DeLorean, smashing into the back of the limo. Marty hurries into the car and the time travelers speed off, returning to 1931 to discern how history went awry [TLTL-2].

Thursday, May 15, 1986 A.D.—2:15 PM

- In the Citizen Brown timeline, Marty McFly returns to 1986 following a harrowing ordeal in Prohibition-era Hill Valley. Because of his intervention in past events, however, Doc inexplicably vanishes before his eyes. Stunned, Marty crashes the DeLorean upon re-entry into the timestream, smashing the car through a billboard outside a gated Hill Valley [TLTL-2, TLTL-3].

- On the billboard is the face of Emmett Brown, but a colder, more conservative version, known in this reality as First Citizen Brown. The sign welcomes visitors to Hill Valley, where "everything is under control."

   Marty spots a young woman nearby, with punk-rock clothing and multi-colored hair, picking up litter. He honks the horn until he gets her attention, and is stunned to discover that she's his girlfriend, Jennifer Parker, but vastly different. This Jennifer is angry and anti-establishment, calling him "Martin" and a "square." Marty discerns that he and this Jennifer do have a romantic past, though it ended badly. He trades her Kid Tannen's flask of booze (obtained in 1931) for a tire iron, to help him climb down from the DeLorean. Once back on the ground, he asks Jennifer for a ride back to town, but she refuses, driving off in an electric golf cart [TLTL-3].

Thursday, May 15, 1986 A.D.—2:32 PM

- The DeLorean jostles loose from the billboard and plummets to the ground, landing in a heap of twisted metal. The time circuits go dark, the car effectively dead [TLTL-3].

Thursday, May 15, 1986—Between 2:32 PM and 5:30 PM

- Marty retrieves Doc's journal from the wreckage, determined to find out what has gone wrong in this timeline. All of Hill Valley, he discovers, is cordoned off behind a high-reaching brick wall. He has landed at the South Gate, but is denied entrance. A voice from a squawk box tells him that all visitors must check in at the North Gate, but Marty is unwilling to walk all the way around the city limits to reach the other side. Using the tire iron, he pries loose one of the hover-converted tires from the DeLorean, and pulls out the car battery—a charged 12-volt Permacell battery from the year 2015. Affixing the battery to the hover-tire's wires does the trick, and Marty rides the levitating tire over the South Gate wall.

   Marty walks the rest of the way to Hill Valley, to discover that his hometown has drastically changed, becoming an Orwellian police state in which everyone drives electric-powered golf carts and lives under the yoke of a strict code of conduct. Dress codes and recycling are ruthlessly enforced, and a wide range of contraband—from alcohol and tobacco to bubblegum and dogs—is strictly prohibited. Any such items are swiftly confiscated and thrown into a decycling bin located outside the new, internationally inspired Hill Valley Courthouse. Demerits are handed out liberally, with cameras mounted on every corner, carefully monitoring citizens' movements. In this new reality, Jennifer Parker's father, Daniel Parker Jr.—a shoe salesman in Marty's timeline—is now a beat cop, taking after his father, Danny Parker Sr.

   What's more, the man behind this vast social reform is Emmett Brown, known in this reality as First Citizen Brown, who now uses his scientific genius to devise new ways of "improving" Hill Valley and making it more

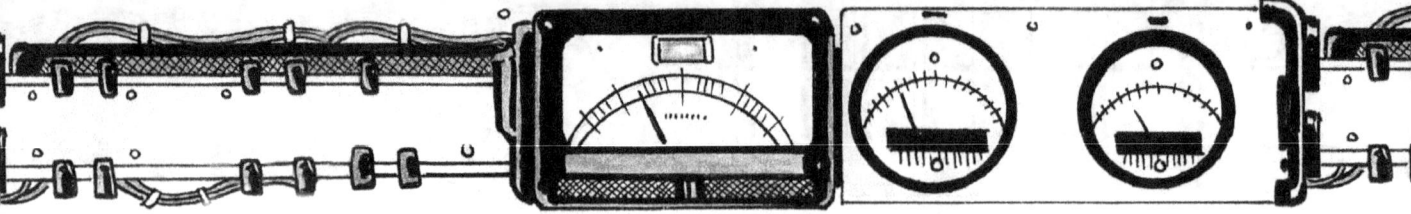

secure. The Courthouse has been rebuilt as the center of local government, with Citizen Brown residing in the private office behind the restored and modernized clock, looking down on citizens below.

Marty tries to visit his friend, but without an appointment, access to the Clock Tower is forbidden. Doc's vehicle pulls up to the courthouse gates, and a very conservative Biff Tannen exits the car. Marty tries to catch up with Brown, but the vehicle enters the courthouse gates without pause.

Marty soon finds Biff in Courthouse Square, manning a booth advertising Hill Valley's new Citizen Plus Program, a voluntary behavior-modification initiative that will eventually become mandatory for every man, woman and child in the town. Speaking with Biff, Marty learns that the former thug is now the prototype model for the program; thanks to a series of hypnotherapy sessions and reconditioning, Tannen has been rendered incapable of breaking rules. Indeed, he becomes violently ill if he even considers doing such things as drinking, fighting, owning dogs or showing public displays of affection. Marty investigates further and discovers that Biff was drafted into the program after his wayward activity became too much for Citizen Edna (Brown's wife, Edna Strickland) and the local authorities. Marty realizes that the only way to reach Doc will be to get into as much trouble as possible and be drafted into the Citizen Plus Program.

To that end, Marty enlists Jennifer Parker's aid. He finds her in an alley behind the Sisters of Mercy Soup Kitchen—now a food stand known as SoupMo—spray-painting graffiti. Marty tries to convince her to help him, but she refuses. In this timeline, Marty is a chess-playing honors student and the president of the Junior Brown Brigade, who participates in the Model United Nations program and listens to smooth jazz—the very antithesis of everything nonconformist Jennifer stands for. Despite his best efforts, Marty cannot get Jen to look beyond his squeaky-clean reputation, and thus fails to convince her to help him contact Citizen Brown.

Marty leaves Jennifer behind, then encounters his mother, Lorraine McFly, who asks him to turn in her time sheet to his father, George. Lorraine has been slacking off in accounting for every moment of her day, and George (a tattletale for the Brown administration) suspects she may be hiding something. Marty questions his mother, hoping to understand this Orwellian world. Lorraine is on clean-up duty, polishing a statue in the town square. Marty discerns that she is not fully on board with all of Hill Valley's strict regulations, and has a hint of mischief in her voice when discussing contraband and kids (like Jennifer) sneaking around the adults' collective backs, breaking the rules. However, when Lorraine looks at the recently reformed Biff Tannen, she tells Marty that maybe it's time she "went with the flow" and signed up for Citizen Plus, as she craves clarity and reconciliation with the city's principles. Marty, however, begs her to hold off making that decision, determined to meet with Citizen Brown and rectify this madness.

Marty arrives at his home to find it under quarantine for a CZ-36 violation—meaning its cleanliness is not up to Hill Valley standards—and a clean-up crew has been summoned to rid the house of dust mites. Marty discovers his father in the garage, closely watching a bank of monitors linked to security cameras placed all over town. George's job, in this timeline, is to collect raw footage to be edited later for use in promotional videos to advertise Hill Valley's harmonious utopia to the rest of the world. In the process, George has also collected a number of dirty secrets and illicit acts caught on tape—including footage of a stray dog roaming the streets. George has left his dreams of writing science fiction stories long behind, since sci-fi has been banned by Hill Valley, and is believed to be subversive propaganda entertaining the notion that there are better worlds or societies than Hill Valley.

Marty returns his mother's time card to George, who inspects it with suspicion. While George seems perfectly content living within the strict confines of Citizen Brown's rule, he knows that Lorraine is struggling, and

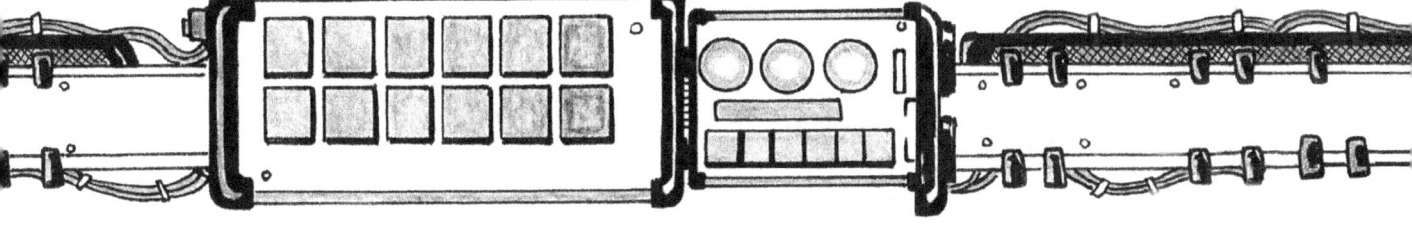

fears that she may be drinking again. Marty questions his father about the current state of Hill Valley, and George confidentially allows him to listen to sound bites from several private conversations he has recorded around town. More than half of the population seems dissatisfied with the Brown administration and speaks ill of Citizen Brown himself. Marty suggests that if the First Citizen were to hear this type of backlash from the people he's sought to protect, he might change. George says that he's sent all of the footage—both good and bad—to the Courthouse, but that he has only received a form memo thanking him for his service. Marty volunteers to take the footage to Citizen Brown directly, to make sure he personally views it, but George refuses, fearing the repercussions.

Marty returns to Courthouse Square to talk to his mother. He attempts to talk to her about her drinking problem, but is constantly interrupted by his father, who is monitoring the entire exchange via a mounted camera, frequently reprimanding his wife through a nearby squawk box. Seeing George and Lorraine fighting, Marty is saddened to see the good marriage they once had falling into ruin. He obscures the camera's vision, allowing him a private moment with his mother. She confides in him that she has slipped into alcoholism in order to handle both her spymaster husband and the fact that Marty's older siblings have left oppressive Hill Valley behind. A lost woman, she seeks solace in a flask hidden among her cleaning supplies, which Marty convinces her to hand over.

Marty decides to earn an audience with Citizen Brown by racking up excessive demerits. To that end, he approaches the Courthouse and its guard, Officer Danny Parker, who confiscates the flask and hands Marty a demerit. However, even when Marty spots Edna Brown and mouths off to her during a brief interrogation, it's still not enough to get him recruited into the Citizen Plus Program.

Next on his tour of rebellion, Marty approaches SoupMo, where he is horrified to find Jennifer inside,

making out with Leech, the soup kitchen's teenage attendant and one of Marty's high school rivals. Marty warns Leech to stay away from her, but in this timeline, Marty is a nerd with little respect from others. Leech sneezes frequently during their confrontation, which he blames on allergies. There's a dog on the loose, he explains, constantly sniffing around SoupMo to steal free liver and peas with soy-cheese hotdog samples—but the pooch only arrives whenever Leech's back is turned.

Marty leaves the soup kitchen and watches from a distance. As soon as Leech is not looking, a muzzled dog hurries into the scene. Leech chases him off, and Marty follows the mutt into an alley out back. Realizing that the dog is Einstein, he frees the pooch from the muzzle and offers him a hotdog sample, earning Einie's trust. Edna Brown arrives, recognizing Einstein as a dog that has repeatedly escaped from the town's kennel. Officer Parker seizes the dog and hands Marty another demerit.

Meanwhile, Marty seeks to prove himself to Jennifer. She still believes that he's a "square," until Marty convinces her otherwise by challenging Leech to an electric guitar battle. Marty easily outmaneuvers the other guitarist, winning Jennifer's admiration once more. When the two hormonal teens move inside SoupMo to indulge in a necking session, Citizen Edna finds them. Outraged, she calls Parker, who hands Marty another demerit and chastises his wayward daughter.

By this time, Marty has racked up more than fifteen thousand demerits in less than twenty-four hours. Finally, Edna Brown personally arrests him, informing him that he's just been recruited into the Citizen Plus Program. Cops in riot gear escort Marty to the Hill Valley Courthouse to meet Citizen Brown.

Once in Brown's presence, Marty tries to convince his old friend that he's living in an alternate timeline as a result of a time-travel experiment gone awry. The First Citizen is reluctant to listen at first, believing Marty to be delusional. But when Marty sees a photograph taken on August 25, 1931, during Kid Tannen's arrest—a picture containing the image of Marty himself—Brown suddenly

remembers working with the youth in 1931 to complete his rocket car, and realizes Marty must be telling the truth. Marty presses Citizen Brown further, informing him of his life in the previous 1986, in which he had a wife, Clara, and two sons, Jules and Verne. Brown is captivated by this story, until Marty suggests that this police state he and Edna have created is making Hill Valley's citizens miserable. Brown refuses to believe such a notion, claiming everyone is perfectly safe and happy, so Marty promises to gather evidence to prove otherwise. Edna, meanwhile, eavesdrops on their discussion [TLTL-3].

Thursday, May 15, 1986 A.D.—5:30 PM

- As George McFly cleans the heads on his VCR surveillance system, Biff Tannen arrives, baseball bat in hand, and knocks George out cold, smashing his surveillance equipment and making off with his video tapes [TLTL-3].

Thursday, May 15, 1986 A.D.—6:00 to 6:30 PM

- Marty McFly hurries to his home in Sector L to procure his father's surveillance tapes as proof that the citizens of Hill Valley are miserable. When he arrives, George lies unconscious on the garage floor, all of his video tapes stolen. Marty helps his father to a chair and investigates the crime scene. He implores George to help him find out who stole the tapes, so that they can right the wrongs of the Brown administration. George refuses, until Marty reminds him of Arthur McFly's brave stand against Kid Tannen a generation prior.

  Emboldened by his father's actions, George decides to help his son. Together, they locate the monitor trained on their own home. By reviewing the footage on the only remaining tape, they discover that the perpetrator was Biff Tannen. Upon closer inspection, Marty sees that Biff's Citizen Plus wristwatch is blinking, and that its digital display reads "X:11." Marty prints a snapshot of the footage and leaves, just as Lorraine shows up and starts another fight with George.

  Marty heads to Courthouse Square and confronts Biff about attacking George and stealing the tapes. Confused, Biff admits to having an hour of missing time in his memory. The last thing he recalls is feeding a squirrel, before Edna Brown conducted a diagnostic

test on his experimental Citizen Plus wristwatch. When Marty performs the same "exercise"—dialing the watch to read "X:11"—Biff enters a mindless trance. In this highly suggestive state, Biff confesses to assaulting George, stealing the tapes and throwing them into the decycling bin. Marty asks Biff to retrieve the tapes. Since Biff's programming has made him obligated to obey any command, he pushes Officer Parker out of the way and dives headfirst into the bin. Parker hurries to tell Citizen Brown what has occurred, and Marty takes the opportunity to follow Biff down the chute.

  Marty uncovers the underground nerve center of Edna Brown's operation, hidden beneath Kid Tannen's former speakeasy. Down here, where all confiscated contraband has been mothballed, Edna monitors everything happening in Hill Valley. She orders Biff to seize Marty, but the teen breaks Biff's brainwashing program by reminding him of the simple pleasures that Tannen once enjoyed before the Citizen Plus Program: hot rods, booze, cigars and pornography. This breaks the spell, but Biff becomes overwhelmed at having his mind tampered with, and passes out.

  First Citizen Brown enters, having witnessed everything. Appalled that Edna has twisted his dream of a happy utopia in order to rob citizens of their free will, he orders his wife to return home. The elderly Brown then breaks down emotionally, regretting his lifetime of wasted scientific potential. Marty, however, shows Brown the journal that Doc kept in the other timeline, containing detailed schematics for the Flux Capacitor. If they can fix the time machine, Marty explains, they can rewrite history, sparing Hill Valley from this dismal fate.

  His vigor renewed, Brown hurries off to begin preparations. Marty stays behind and frees Einstein from his cage, but Biff suddenly awakens, furious at having been manipulated by both Edna and Marty. A scuffle ensues, but Marty outwits him once more and escapes. The teen races to Brown's office at the top of the Clock Tower, to discover that his friend is being carted off for rehabilitation in the Citizen Plus Program. In Doc's place is Edna Brown, hellbent on revenge. Guards seize Marty and carry him away as well [TLTL-3].

Thursday, May 15, 1986 A.D.—After 6:30 PM

- Marty and Doc from slightly in the future, having eliminated the Citizen Brown timeline, return to 1986

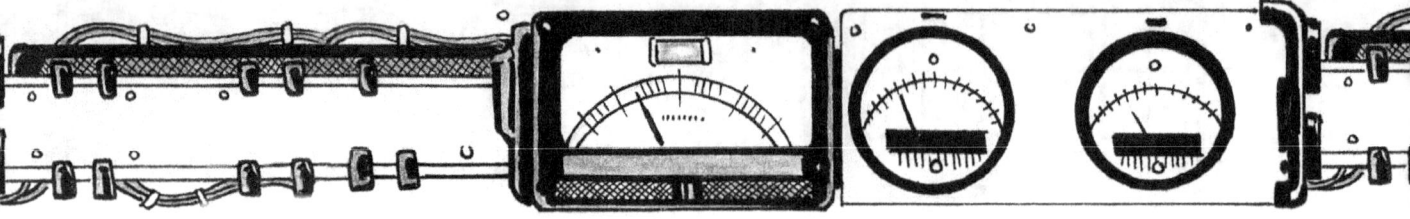

and find everything mostly as they left it. The estate sale at Doc's place is now simply a garage sale, as Emmett and Clara have decided to set up roots in Hill Valley so Doc can oversee his late father's foundation to offer scholarships to young scientists. To both men's shock, Edna Strickland is now Edna Tannen, the wife of Irving "Kid" Tannen—with whom she fell in love while in prison for arson—and the stepmother of Biff Tannen. In this reality, the Tannens are content and on good terms with Doc and the McFlys. Now that the dust has settled, Doc presents Marty with an early high school graduation gift: a chronicle of the Hill Valley McFly clan. Emmett explains that he ended up in 1931 while traveling through the generations cataloging Marty's family for this gift [TLTL-5].

> *NOTE: In this new timeline, Doc's reason for having visited 1931 may not still be valid. In the first episode of the Telltale Games video game, Doc was falsely arrested for the speakeasy arson in 1931, after traveling back to that year to dig up information about Marty's grandmother, Sylvia "Trixie Trotter" Miskin. In the process of rescuing him, Marty altered the past, causing scientist Doc to be erased from history, and making way for dictator Citizen Brown. Marty convinced the First Citizen to return with him to 1931 to repair the temporal damage, but Brown vanished. With Marty stranded in 1931, he gave young Emmett a clue so that, in the future, he would remember Marty and come back for him—which he did. But when this Doc returned to 1931 to retrieve his stranded friend, he had no idea why Marty was there in the first place. What's more, when Doc and Marty returned to 1986, Marty noticed changes that had occurred since the beginning of the game, while Doc did not see that anything had changed. He was thus a parallel Doc, who had apparently never been stranded in 1931 or accused of arson. So, while it stands to reason that, at some point, this Doc still could have gone back to 1931 to learn about Sylvia Miskin, it seems impossible that when he was arrested in 1931, it was because he was investigating Trixie Trotter—since this version of Doc was never arrested.*

- Before they can enjoy their respite from time travel, however, a second DeLorean arrives from the future and an older, panicked Marty McFly emerges, begging them to go with him back to the future to save Marty's great-great-grandkids. This Marty is still married to Jennifer and has twelve children with her. As Marty and Doc sort out this wrinkle, a *third* DeLorean—this one blue—arrives from a parallel future with another older Marty. The two middle-aged Martys recognize each other, as they have been battling across the timestream, erasing each other's pasts. They each implore young Marty to help them and forsake the other. To make matters worse, a *fourth* DeLorean arrives with a grizzled Marty McFly at the wheel—a Marty who has a score to settle with his other two counterparts and seeks to destroy them both. As the three engage in a heated argument, Doc and young Marty climb into their DeLorean, realizing that the future is in shambles and they have much work to do [TLTL-5].

Friday, May 16, 1986 A.D.

- In the Citizen Brown timeline, Marty McFly awakens in a locked room of the Citizen Plus Ward. His guitar and other personal effects have been confiscated and stored in a locked cabinet within his room. Beyond soundproof glass, Marty spots Edna Brown and a guard. By finagling the intercom, he eavesdrops long enough to hear that he's being prepped for his first Citizen Plus treatment, while Citizen Brown is being treated nearby for antisocial behavior. George McFly, meanwhile, makes contact with Marty while monitoring the Citizen Plus Ward, searching for his wife, who has enrolled for treatments.

  Marty discovers that Jennifer is in the room next

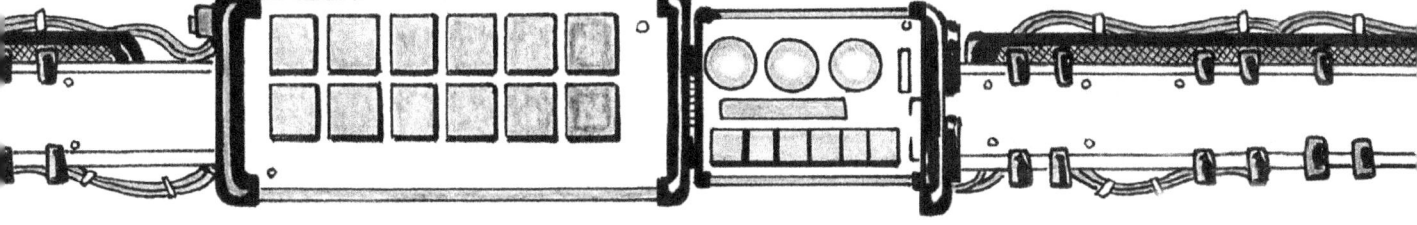

door, and George links the intercom so that his son can communicate with her. To his horror, Jen has already received her first treatment, and has begun conforming to the strict standards of the Brown administration. With help from his father, Marty discovers the combination to the secured locker in his room. He retrieves his guitar and plays a power ballad for Jennifer, hoping to break her spell. Through the power of rock-and-roll, Jen's brainwashing is broken, restoring her to her punk-rock rebel roots. Moments later, a guard enters her room to escort her out of the facility. Jennifer knocks out the guard, steals his uniform and locks him inside her room, then frees Marty and instructs him to don the guard's uniform.

Marty finds Emmett Brown undergoing the Citizen Plus Program. Edna oversees the procedure as Brown's personality is rebuilt from the ground up. Still in disguise, Marty manages to gain access to the control board responsible for Doc's conditioning. He tampers with the equipment, again employing the power of rock-and-roll to evade Edna and her guards while rescuing his friend. The two then escape into Hill Valley.

Edna puts the town on high alert as security forces spill out of the Courthouse in pursuit. Marty and Brown take refuge in the decycling bins, from which Marty spots his mother approaching the Courthouse for her first Citizen Brown treatment. Police interrogate her on the street, but George McFly arrives to stop his wife from going through with the program. George punches out the guards, and he and Lorraine embrace for a passionate kiss before being arrested. Marty considers helping them, but Brown reminds him that if they can restore the DeLorean and the timeline, none of this will have happened.

With the coast clear, Brown instructs Marty to wait for him as he makes his way to Clayton Ravine—where he had the DeLorean wreckage towed—to implement repairs. Once finished with repairs, the First Citizen promises to travel back in time and pick up Marty. Brown races off, but after time passes without Doc's return,

Marty begins to wonder if something has gone wrong. Edna catches up to him, claiming Emmett will never amount to anything without her. Moments later, Brown finally arrives in the DeLorean, explaining that it has taken him six months and his entire family fortune to repair the time machine. Something is still wrong with the vehicle, however, as he had programmed the time circuits to bring him back only seconds after he departed, but he has instead arrived *minutes* later. He shrugs it off as a fluke, and they leave the dystopian Hill Valley—and a raging Edna—in their dust [TLTL-4].

Friday, May 16, 1986 A.D.—3:03 PM

- Marty sets the time circuits for August 26, 1931, and Citizen Brown accelerates the vehicle up to 88 miles per hour. The damage to the time circuits is more extensive than they realize, however, as they instead arrive in October of that year [TLTL-4].

Friday, June 13, 1986 A.D.

- In one possible timeline, Emmett Brown (a famous industrialist in this reality) and wife Edna Strickland decide to end their marriage. The proceedings turn messy as bedlam breaks out at the divorce hearing [TLTL-5].

- In another timeline, Emmett Brown (once again an inventor) receives the key to the city of Hill Valley, as reported by the *Hill Valley Telegraph* [TLTL-5].

  NOTE: This reveal, in the fifth episode of the Telltale Games video game, caused a significant error in internal continuity. During the game's first episode, Marty obtained a newspaper reporting this event in 1986, bearing the date of June 14, 1931. This led Marty to travel back to 1931 to rescue Doc. Over the course of the game, the headline then changed several times, depending on the actions that the two friends had to take in order to repair the timeline—but the

A TALE OF THREE MARTYS— THE BEST OF TIMES OR THE WORST OF TIMES?

effects were always limited to 1931. Starting with this instance, however, the events depicted in the newspaper—still labeled as a 1931 edition—obviously occurred in 1986,

since Doc was shown in the article as an old man receiving the key to the city. Moreover, when Doc did receive the key in 1986, he remembered being given this paper back in 1931, saying this

CODE	STORY						
ARGN	BTTF-themed TV commercial: Arrigoni	BTF1	Film: Back to the Future	CITY	BTTF-themed music video: Owl City, "Deer in the Headlights"	HUEY	BTTF-themed music video: Huey Lewis and the News, "The Power of Love"
BFAN	Back to the Future: The Animated Series	BTF2	Film: Back to the Future Part II				
BFCG	Back to the Future: The Card Game	BTF3	Film: Back to the Future Part III	DCTV	BTTF-themed TV commercial: DirecTV	LIMO	BTTF-themed music video: The Limousines, "The Future"
BFCL	Back to the Future comic book (limited series)	BUDL	BTTF-themed TV commercial: Bud Light	ERTH	The Earth Day Special		
BFCM	Back to the Future comic book (monthly series)	CHEK	BTTF-themed music video: O'Neal McKnight, "Check Your Coat"	GALE	Interviews and commentaries: Bob Gale and/or Robert Zemeckis	MCDN	BTTF-themed TV commercial: McDonald's
BFHM	BTTF-themed McDonald's Happy Meal boxes			GARB	BTTF-themed TV commercials: Garbarino	MITS	BTTF-themed TV commercial: Mitsubishi Lancer
BTFA	Back to the Future Annual (Marvel Comics)	CHIC	Photographs hanging in Doc Brown's Chicken restaurant at Universal Studios	GETV	BTTF-themed TV commercial: GE	MSFT	BTTF-themed TV commercial: Microsoft

prompted him to return to 1931 to rescue Marty. One might speculate that young Emmett received the key to the city, but the date was still June 14, whereas Marty gave this paper to

Emmett in October 1931 with instructions not to read it until he received the city key. It's also possible that Marty simply picked up another newspaper while in the Citizen Brown timeline, but the youth's adventures in that tumultuous reality occurred in May 1986.

One possible solution to this conundrum: Once Marty convinced the First Citizen to return with him to 1931, Brown vanished for six months while repairing the DeLorean, and then journeyed back to May 1986 to retrieve Marty for their journey to 1931. It is thus possible that he may have picked up a newspaper on June 14 and absently left it in the DeLorean prior to returning to May to collect his friend. This would leave only the 1931 dateline incorrect, while allowing the June 14 date to remain intact.

Friday, June 13 to Wednesday, November 5, 1986 A.D.

• In the Citizen Brown timeline, Emmett Brown spends six months repairing the time-traveling DeLorean. The effort costs him his entire family fortune and places him in an unscrupulous situation with Libyan nationalists [TLTL-4].

Saturday, June 14, 1986 A.D.

• The *Hill Valley Telegraph* publishes a news story about the messy divorce hearing of Emmett Brown and Edna Strickland [TLTL-5].

Wednesday, November 5, 1986 A.D.—1:29 AM

• In the Citizen Brown timeline, Emmett Brown at last completes repairs on the time-traveling DeLorean after six months of hard work. He heads back to May 16, 1986, where Marty McFly awaits, and the duo then travel to 1931 to find Edna Strickland [TLTL-4].

NIKE	*BTTF*-themed TV commercial: Nike	SCRT	2010 Scream Awards: *Back to the Future* 25th Anniversary Reunion (trailer)	SUFFIX	**MEDIUM**	
NTND	Nintendo *Back to the Future—The Ride* Mini-Game			-b	*BTF2*'s Biff Tannen Museum video (extended version)	-s1	Screenplay (draft one)
		SIMP	Simulator: *The Simpsons Ride*			-s2	Screenplay (draft two)
PIZA	*BTTF*-themed TV commercial: Pizza Hut	SLOT	*Back to the Future* Video Slots	-c	Animated series credit sequence	-s3	Screenplay (draft three)
REAL	Real life	TEST	Screen tests: Crispin Glover, Lea Thompson and Thomas F. Wilson	-d	Film deleted scene	-s4	Screenplay (draft four)
RIDE	Simulator: *Back to the Future—The Ride*			-n	Film novelization	-sp	Screenplay (production draft)
SCRM	2010 Scream Awards: *Back to the Future* 25th Anniversary Reunion (broadcast)	TLTL	Telltale Games' *Back to the Future—The Game*	-o	Film outtake	-sx	Screenplay (*Paradox*)
		UNIV	Universal Studios Hollywood promotional video	-v	Video game print materials or commentaries		

DINOCITY:
WHERE DINOSAURS
RULE THE VALLEY

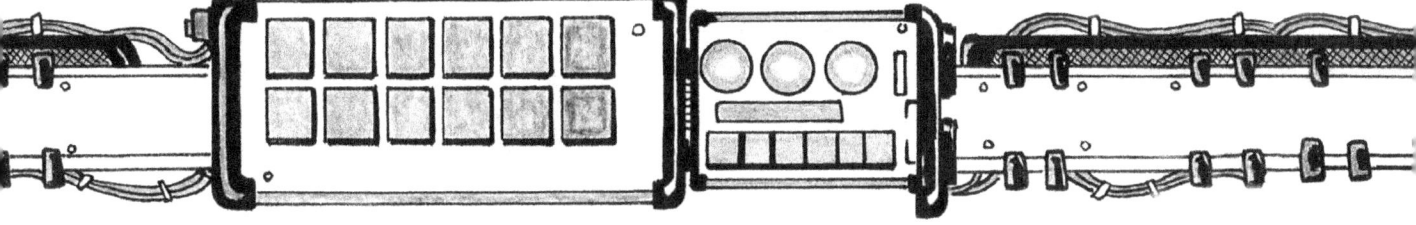

CHAPTER XII:

1987 A.D. TO 1991 A.D.

1988 A.D.

- Universal Studios Florida asks Emmett Brown to assist in documenting its planned theme park. To that end, he jumps two years into the future, to May 1, 1990, and videotapes what he sees [UNIV].

1989 A.D.

- Two fun-loving teenagers steal the DeLorean from the McFlys' home driveway to go on a joyride to the year 2015, where they sample the pizza cuisine of the future [PIZA].

1990 A.D.

- Doc Brown arrives in Los Angeles from the year 2057, where he discovered that the last of the planet's rainforests has been destroyed, to alert an eclectic team of specialists and the media to the imminent danger that Mother Earth faces. With the help of local librarian Mrs. Porter, Doc has uncovered the scientific data he needs to inform the world about the dangers of pollution and the steps they must take to keep from exasperating the situation. He brings a stern warning for humanity to change its ecologically destructive ways before the environment is totally devastated. [ERTH].

- The book *Hill Valley Historical Society, 1865-1990* is published, celebrating the city's 125th anniversary by featuring portraits of numerous distinguished citizens of Hill Valley, including the McFly, Tannen, Strickland and Brown families [TLTL-v].

May 1, 1990 A.D.

- Emmett Brown arrives from 1988 to help Universal Studios Florida document its theme park. Doc walks around the park, recording his interactions with characters and components of numerous attractions,

including *Lassie*; *Ghostbusters'* Stay Puft Marshmallow Man; *Psycho's* Norman Bates; the great-white shark from *Jaws*; Jessica Fletcher from *Murder, She Wrote*; E.T.; King Kong; Fred Flintstone; and more [UNIV].

Sometime in or Before 1991 A.D.

- Law-enforcement official Andy Taylor, a largely mustached man with bushy eyebrows and a southern drawl, becomes the sheriff of California's Hill County [BFAN-16, BFAN-22, BFAN-23], and begins working with a deputy named Barney [BFAN-22].

  NOTE: Sheriff Andy Taylor, portrayed by Andy Griffith, appeared on* The Danny Thomas Show*;* The Andy Griffith Show*;* Gomer Pyle, U.S.M.C.*;* Mayberry R.F.D.*; and* Return to Mayberry*, frequently working alongside Deputy Barney Fife, played by Don Knotts.

- The textbook *Plastic Surgery Made Easy* is published. A copy of the book is made available at Hill Valley's local library, which Marty McFly checks out but fails to return on time [BFCM-3].

- The book *On Robots*, by science fiction author Harlan Ellison, is published [BFCL-1].

  NOTE: No book by this name was written by Ellison in the real world.

- *Positronic Brain Surgery Made Easy*, a book written by science fiction author Isaac Asimov, is published [BFCL-1].

  NOTE: No book by this name was written by Asimov in the real world.

- Time Life publishes a multi-volume series of books titled *Robot*, detailing the robotics industry [BFCL-1].

  NOTE: This book series was fictional, though a direct-market publisher called Time-Life (hyphenated) does exist.

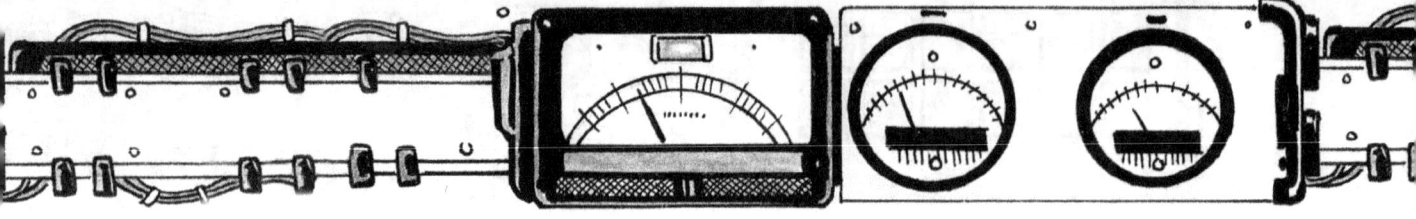

- The book *My Success Secrets* is published [BFCM-3].
  NOTE: The title of this work paid homage to the 1987 film* The Secret of My Success, *starring Michael J. Fox.

- Author Alex Keaton writes the textbook *Keatonsian Economics* [BFCM-3].
  NOTE: The title and author of this volume were an in-joke reference to Alex P. Keaton, a high school student with a passion for economics, from 1980s TV series* Family Ties, *portrayed by Michael J. Fox. However, an excerpt of* Family Ties *was shown on a television screen when Marty visited Café 80's in* BTF2. *This would seem to indicate that McFly, Fox and Keaton all existed in the same reality.

- A three-dimensional music television station called M-3D-TV debuts [BFCL-1].

- Emmett Brown visits Atlantis, an island mentioned in Plato's dialogues, *Timaeus* and *Critias*, and adds a travel sticker to his luggage bearing this fabled city's name [BFAN-9].
  NOTE: The name of the city—the existence of which has long been debated—appeared onscreen misspelled as "Atlalanta," but was corrected in a subsequent shot to "Atlantis."

- Doc Brown's Chicken, a restaurant at Universal Studios Hollywood claiming to serve "the finest chicken of all time" [REAL], showcases framed photographs of Emmett Brown holding up pieces of chicken at various worldwide landmarks and historical event sites [UNIV]. These include the U.S. Capitol Building, the Pyramids at Giza, Buckingham Palace, Stonehenge, the Eiffel Tower, the Taj Mahal, Hollywood and more [CHIC].

- Doc attends the Annual Convention of the Home Inventors and Mad Geniuses, where he presents his ELB Pediatric Policer—a helmet-mounted lie detector that determines if a child is engaged in wrongdoing, by measuring changes in skin temperature, blood pressure and pulse rate, and triggering alarms in the event of bad behavior [BFAN-26].

- Emmett Brown creates numerous innovations, including:
  —The ELB NightVision Prototype 85 helmet [BFAN-1]
  —The Thought-inducing Auto-pacer [BFAN-1]
  —Auto-Jog Mechanical Running Shorts [BFAN-1, BFAN-12]
  —Electro-guide boots [BFAN-3]
  —The Doc Brown Blackboard [BFAN-3]
  —Scratch 'N' Listen postcards [BFAN-4]
  —A three-dimensional holographic projector [BFAN-5]
  —The ELB Video Message Center [BFAN-6]
  —The Perpetual Motion Foot-Massage Unit [BFAN-7a]
  —The ELB Autogroom 5000 [BFAN-7b]
  —Magneto-sandals [BFAN-10]
  —The Ozone-Friendly Freon-Free Cooling Unit [BFAN-10]
  —Waterproof tennis shoes [BFAN-11]
  —The ELB Environmental Adjuster [BFAN-12]
  —The Magnascope 4000 [BFAN-15]
  —The Heat-Seeking Rat Trap [BFAN-15]
  —The ELB Lunchbox Burglar Deterrent [BFAN-15]
  —The Come-and-Get-It Lunchbox [BFAN-15]
  —The ELB Sunshine Umbrella for Rainy-Day Tans [BFAN-15]
  —The Fly Trap, Rehabilitation and Release Center [BFAN-15]
  —Full-Body Oven Mits [BFAN-15]
  —The Flashback-o-Matic [BFAN-17]
  —The ELB Aqua-Ammomatic [BFAN-18]
  —The ELB Life-on-the-Edge Facsimulator [BFAN-19]
  —Self-Watering Onion-Potatoes [BFAN-20]
  —The ELB Super-Sniffer Snout 4000 [BFAN-20]
  —A powered go-cart known as the Junkmobile [BFAN-21, BFAN-22, BFAN-26]

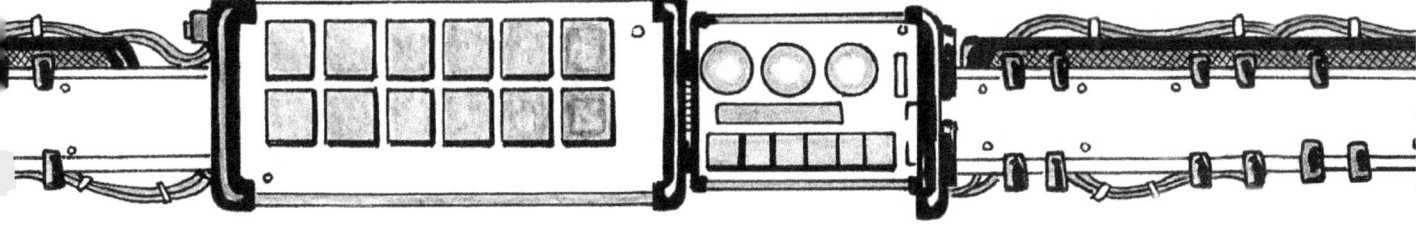

—The ELB Quick-o-Popper [BFAN-21]
—Super-Growth Mondo-Corn [BFAN-21]
—The ELB Hot-Diggity Dogger [BFAN-22]
—Super-Sudsy Soap [BFAN-22]
—ELB Yo-Bub No-Stub Folding Chairs [BFAN-22]
—The Megascreen TV large-screen television [BFAN-23]
—The Haircut Omatic [BFAN-25]
—Full-course Food Pellets [BFAN-26]
—The Electric Perpetual Portable Trampoline [BFCM-1]
—The Automatic Housecleaner [BFCM-1]
—The Dyno-Matic Spray Gun [RIDE]
—The Atmo-Processor [RIDE]
—The Canine Cafeteria [RIDE]
—The Agro-Waste Fuel Conversion System [RIDE]
—The Suc-o-Matic vacuum cleaner [RIDE]
—The Static-o-Matic Electric Hair Chair [RIDE]

> ***NOTE: Further information about the above inventions, and others, can be found in* A Matter of Time: The Unauthorized Back to the Future Lexicon, *available at hassleinbooks.com, amazon.com and bttf.com.***

Circa 1990s A.D.

• In the Biffhorrific timeline, Lorraine McFly-Tannen, fed up after years of abuse from her second husband, Biff Tannen, shoots and kills him [BTF2-d, GALE].

Sometime Between Friday, January 1, 1991 and Monday, April 1, 1991 A.D.

• Emmett and Clara Brown, their children Jules and Verne, and their dog Einstein settle in Hill Valley, bringing with them Doc's time-traveling DeLorean and the *Jules Verne Train*. Marty McFly, while attending junior college in Hill Valley, accompanies the Browns on many of their misadventures through time [BFAN-1 to BFAN-26, BFCM-1 to BFCM-4, BFCL-1 to BFCL-3, BFHM].

• Jules and Verne Brown enroll at Hill Valley Elementary School, where they greatly dislike the school administrator, Vice-Principal Strickland [BFAN-12, BFAN-26].

> ***NOTE: It's unclear whether this Strickland was the same man who worked at Hill Valley High School in the film trilogy.***

• In his home garage, Emmett Brown begins filming a series of video recordings to educate future scientists. These recordings contain Doc's recollections of his time-traveling adventures with Clara, Jules, Verne, Einstein and Marty McFly, and frequently include appended Video Encyclopedia entries illustrating various scientific principles, featuring scientist Bill Nye performing experiments, with Doc narrating [BFAN1 to BFAN26].

• Emmett Brown founds a think tank called the Institute of Future Technology (IFT) in order to advance scientific invention, as well as the further study of the space-time continuum. He serves as its chief inventive officer.

At the IFT, Doc establishes the Anti-Gravitic Laboratory, at which he produces a number of scientific innovations, including the Eight-Passenger DeLorean Time-Travel Vehicle. The lab creates a safety video for so-called "time-travel volunteers" using this vehicle, featuring a trio of crash-test dummies called Bender, Fender and Li'l Fender. In the video, the dummies bang their heads, have limbs severed by closing doors and are strangulated by cameras caught in a safety restraint, and also break rules regarding flash photography, eating and smoking, all to illustrate how not to behave while inside the eight-seat convertible.

Doc and a large team of scientists create a number of new scientific innovations at the institute, including the Timespan, a device utilizing holographic place/time projection; a personal time-travel suit known as the Timeman, complete with fusion-powered mag-lev hover boots; the Thru-Haul (model THV-4483/EX), an interdimensional large-item auxiliary transport vehicle "for time travelers on the move"; the Mr. Profusion, built

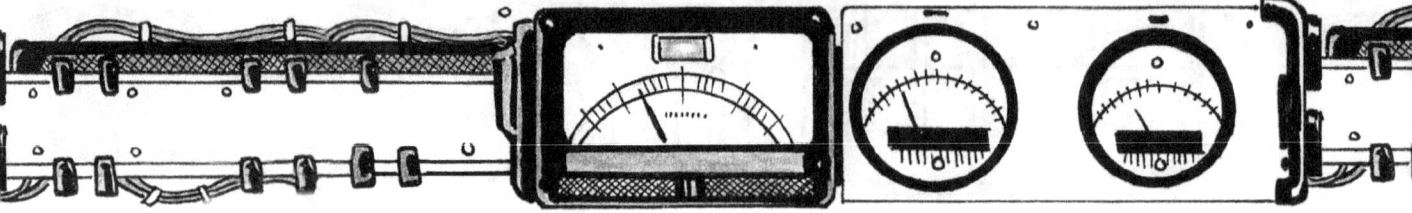

to provide safe, efficient fusion power for the home; the Digi-Chef, a digital food molecularizer that can combine various foods into a single substance (such as banana pizza) at the molecular level; and the Crash Repel and Avoidance System Hardware (C.R.A.S.H.), enabling those using the eight-seat DeLoreans to push off any other vehicles in danger of collision [RIDE].

> NOTE: These contraptions were described on signage at Universal Studios' Back to the Future: The Ride.

• Doc builds a new flying DeLorean able to fold up into a briefcase; convert into a stretch limousine [BFAN-1], zeppelin [BFAN-11] or covered wagon [BFAN-13]; and navigate underwater [BFAN-4]. He also invents a remote-controlled crane to carry the briefcase, and makes the car un-lockable only by his family's voice or Einstein's bark [BFAN-1]

> NOTE: The following pages chronicle the events of the animated series and its comic book spinoff. Each episode featured bookend sequences in which Doc discussed a particular adventure, but it becomes evident, when examining internal evidence (holidays, seasons and so forth), that these adventures were not told chronologically. As such, the following entries do not adhere strictly to airdate order.

• Emmett Brown adds a universal linguistics translator into the grill of his DeLorean, capable of translating any language—including that of evolved dinosaurs [BFAN-3, BFAN-5]. He also builds a smaller version to fit in a person's ear [BFAN-7a].

• Doc also builds a "stretch" version of the time-traveling DeLorean [BFAN-10].

• An argument over the Brown family computer with his older brother, Jules, leaves Verne Brown feeling unappreciated and overlooked. Eager to prove his worth,

despite his young age, Verne climbs into the DeLorean and takes it for a drive. Marty McFly, meanwhile, listens to a loud holo-teacher's reading of U.S. Civil War history, which causes the DeLorean's newly installed voice-activated time circuits to propel the vehicle back to February 11, 1864. Verne is thus catapulted into the past, on the eve of a bloody massacre. Upon discovering his disappearance, Jules, Marty and Doc all consider their role in making the boy feel inadequate, and vow to bring him back to the future. Thanks to a helpful clue discovered by Einstein, the quartet board the time train, bound for the Civil War era [BFAN-1].

• Einstein begins acting strangely, reacting violently to Marty's new key chain that contains many sound effects, including a cat's meow. Jules and Verne rescue Marty from danger, and Clara invites him to stay for supper. Einstein mistakes Doc's newest housecleaning invention as a threat and attacks it. Doc calms the dog down and, upon examination, discovers that Einie is suffering from what he describes as "cat-aracts," a rare disease causing lesions on both corneas. Doc develops a device that replicates what Einstein sees, and confirms his diagnosis—everything the dog sees, his brain interprets as a feline threat.

Doc prepares a cure made as a byproduct of fermenting juniper berries—a process that has not been performed in years. Using a rickety homemade distillery, Doc attempts to brew the medicine, but an explosion in the Brown garage claims the device. Clara, having caught herself up on the previous century by reading history books, reminds her husband that the kind of old-fashioned distillery they'll need in order to make the cure can be found in the Prohibition era of the 1920s. Doc removes the tarp from his rebuilt DeLorean, and he and Marty journey to 1927 to find a distillery. Returning one minute after they left, Doc and Marty give Einstein the juniper berry cure—freshly brewed at a Chicago brewery, circa 1927—for his cat-aracts. Einstein is instantly cured, wagging his tail in gratitude [BFCM-1].

CODE	STORY						
ARGN	BTTF-themed TV commercial: Arrigoni	BTF1	Film: *Back to the Future*	CITY	*BTTF*-themed music video: Owl City, "Deer in the Headlights"	HUEY	*BTTF*-themed music video: Huey Lewis and the News, "The Power of Love"
BFAN	*Back to the Future: The Animated Series*	BTF2	Film: *Back to the Future Part II*	DCTV	*BTTF*-themed TV commercial: DirecTV	LIMO	*BTTF*-themed music video: The Limousines, "The Future"
BFCG	*Back to the Future: The Card Game*	BTF3	Film: *Back to the Future Part III*	ERTH	*The Earth Day Special*		
BFCL	*Back to the Future* comic book (limited series)	BUDL	*BTTF*-themed TV commercial: Bud Light	GALE	Interviews and commentaries: Bob Gale and/or Robert Zemeckis	MCDN	*BTTF*-themed TV commercial: McDonald's
BFCM	*Back to the Future* comic book (monthly series)	CHEK	*BTTF*-themed music video: O'Neal McKnight, "Check Your Coat"	GARB	*BTTF*-themed TV commercials: Garbarino	MITS	*BTTF*-themed TV commercial: Mitsubishi Lancer
BFHM	*BTTF*-themed McDonald's Happy Meal boxes	CHIC	Photographs hanging in Doc Brown's	GETV	*BTTF*-themed TV commercial: GE	MSFT	*BTTF*-themed TV commercial: Microsoft
BTFA	*Back to the Future Annual* (Marvel Comics)		Chicken restaurant at Universal Studios				

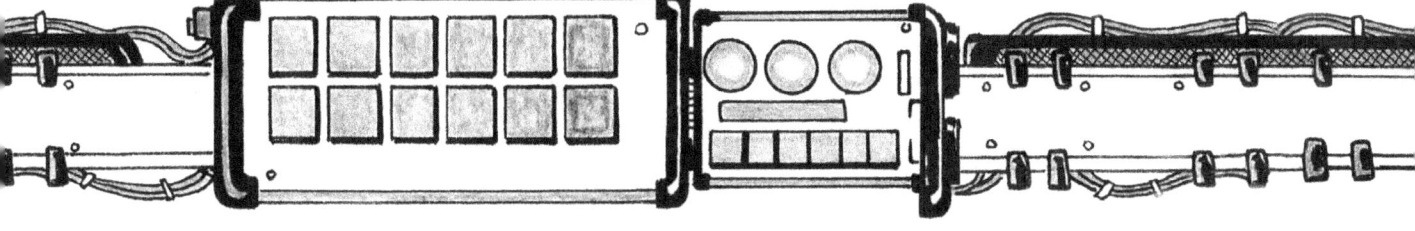

- Emmett Brown's latest experiment backfires, resulting in a blackout in the Brown family home. When his wife and sons bombard him with complaints, he realizes that despite their Old West origins, they have forgotten the simple pleasures of life and have become too consumed with modern technology. In an effort to distance his family from the luxuries of home, Doc decides to take them on vacation to the year 1367, during the Middle Ages. When that decision proves near-fatal for them all, Doc makes it up to his family by taking them to Super Splash Water World for a *real* vacation upon their return to 1991 [BFAN-2].

- Marty notices that his college grades are down, and also suspects Jennifer may be cheating on him with another student, a dim-witted jock named Kelp. Marty accuses her of having an affair, resulting in a fight. He visits Doc to talk things out, but finds the place empty. He then receives a postcard from the year 1692, containing a message from the scientist, requesting that Marty bring the DeLorean and a spare Flux Capacitor to September 23 of that year, where Doc is stranded in Salem, Massachusetts. After nearly being executed in that era as a witch, Marty escapes with Doc back to the present, where he apologizes to Jennifer for his earlier actions. She explains that she had been tutoring Kelp, and assures Marty that he has nothing to be jealous of [BFAN-4].

- Emmett Brown prepares to venture to ancient Rome, in the year 36 A.D., to return a batch of documents he had "borrowed" from scholars of that era. Marty volunteers to tag along, hoping to pick up some extra credit by writing an authentic essay about Caesar for history class. Jules and Verne ask to join them so they can visit the "arcades," but their father grounds them after they misuse his experimental Holographic Projector—intended to deceive potential burglars into thinking someone is home—in order to play a prank. Sullen, the boys agree to stay behind, though they secretly use the projector a second time, fooling their father into thinking

they remained in 1991, while they actually sneak into the DeLorean's back seat and follow Marty and Doc to 36 A.D. [BFAN-5].

- An evening of games takes a sour turn when Jules Brown teases Verne, convincing his little brother that he's adopted. Feeling confused and betrayed, Verne confronts his father to ascertain the truth. Doc utilizes one of his inventions—a machine able to sketch a photorealistic drawing of anyone in any era—to show Verne a picture of himself from when he was a baby. But before he can do this, the dinner alarm interrupts them. As Doc hungrily heads inside to eat, a fuming Verne leans against the sketching machine, overloading it with data. As a result, Verne's baby picture is drawn, but the sketch also depicts the previous entry, of inventor and philosopher Benjamin Franklin, leading Verne to incorrectly assume he is Franklin's son. Hoping to reunite with his "real" family, Verne steals the DeLorean and heads back to September 2, 1752. While in the past, he inadvertently causes Franklin to not discover the nature of electricity, and the world thus develops without electrical power. Realizing what has occurred, Doc journeys back to set things right and brings his son home [BFAN-6].

- Marty McFly, suffering from Athlete's foot fungus, implores Emmett Brown to help him alleviate his discomfort. Doc believes he can cure the ailment, but it will require them to travel to Peru, in the year 1532, to procure the sweat glands of the extinct *Bufo marinus* toad [BFAN-7a].

  NOTE: The Bufo marinus *species is not extinct in the real world.*

- Emmett Brown ventures into the Hill Valley Hardware Store, leaving Einstein snoozing in the DeLreaon's back seat. As Doc shops, two bank robbers, Sidney and Frankie, emerge from the Hill Valley Savings & Loan with their stolen loot. Having forgotten to bring a getaway vehicle, they steal the DeLorean, with Einstein inside. Frankie

					SUFFIX	MEDIUM			
NIKE	*BTTF*-themed TV commercial: Nike	**SCRT**	2010 Scream Awards: *Back to the Future*		**-b**	*BTF2's* Biff Tannen Museum video		**-s1**	Screenplay (draft one)
NTND	Nintendo *Back to the Future—The Ride*		25th Anniversary Reunion (trailer)			(extended version)		**-s2**	Screenplay (draft two)
	Mini-Game	**SIMP**	Simulator: *The Simpsons Ride*		**-c**	Animated series credit sequence		**-s3**	Screenplay (draft three)
PIZA	*BTTF*-themed TV commercial: Pizza Hut	**SLOT**	*Back to the Future* Video Slots		**-d**	Film deleted scene		**-s4**	Screenplay (draft four)
REAL	Real life	**TEST**	Screen tests: Crispin Glover, Lea Thompson		**-n**	Film novelization		**-sp**	Screenplay (production draft)
RIDE	Simulator: *Back to the Future—The Ride*		and Thomas F. Wilson		**-o**	Film outtake		**-sx**	Screenplay (*Paradox*)
SCRM	2010 Scream Awards: *Back to the Future*	**TLTL**	Telltale Games' *Back to the Future—The Game*		**-v**	Video game print materials or commentaries			
	25th Anniversary Reunion (broadcast)	**UNIV**	Universal Studios Hollywood promotional video						

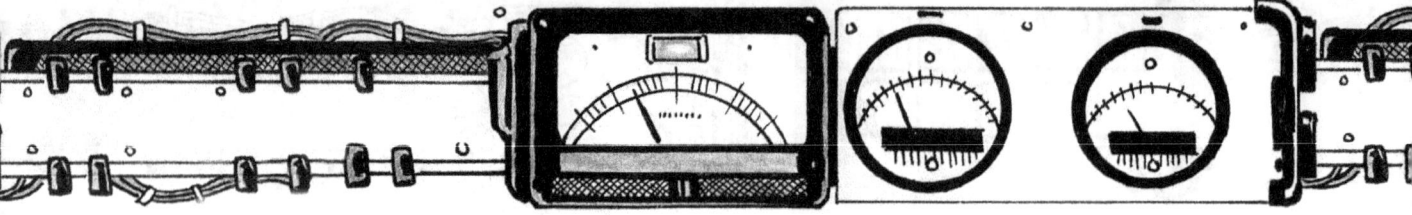

counts out their take, telling Sidney that they've scored $1,790—however, Doc's sensitive audio-controlled time circuits register the new coordinates for 1790, in Sydney, Australia. When Einstein awakens to find strangers in the car, he attacks. During the struggle, the DeLorean achieves 88 miles per hour, and the group is sent back to 1790. The trio eventually returns from the past, after spending time at an Australian prison colony. Relieved to be back in the 20th century, and away from the hard labor of prison warden Mungo P. Tannen, the criminals turn themselves in to Hill Valley authorities [BFAN-7b].

• A tabloid magazine called the *Enquisitor* publishes a story claiming the existence of a "Mutant Alien Two-Headed Elvis" [BFCM-4].

> *NOTE: Given that the* **Enquisitor** *was based on* **The National Enquirer,** *which has a reputation for fabricated stories, it's unlikely that the* **Mutant Alien Two-Headed Elvis**—*named after Elvis Presley—existed.*

• While attending college, Marty signs up for a music-appreciation course taught by Mister Babcock, known to students as "Old Buzzard." Marty does not do well in his class [BFAN-4].

Monday, April 1, 1991 A.D.

• An April Fool's Day joke perpetrated by Jules and Verne Brown damages Doc's Brain-Wave Analyzer and leaves him convinced that he's used up all but 0.01 percent of his brain power. Afraid to waste the last shred of his intelligence, Doc gives up his scientific pursuits and takes to lying around the house, crying over soap operas. Clara convinces him to do something with himself, and he spends the afternoon working at various part-time, menial-labor jobs around Hill Valley, including singing lounge music and playing piano at the Luau Lunch Hut.

Over time, Doc begins to worry that he's useless without his intellect, and so he runs away from home. Clara and Marty search for the scientist, failing to enlist the help of the Hill Valley Police Department. Doc soon discovers that even menial labor requires an ounce of intelligence—an ounce he doesn't believe he can spare—so he pilots the DeLorean back to a simpler time, the Pleistocene Period, when he will no longer be expected to think. The lack of scientific innovation in this era, however, tempts him to invent, so he instead returns to the present to attend Marty's rock concert [BFAN-12].

• The *Hill Valley Herald* publishes an article titled "Doc Brown Loses Mind" [BFCM-4].

• Marty, meanwhile, prepares for his performance with The Pinheads. He borrows the Environmental Adjustor from Doc's garage, intending to use it to create a dazzling lightning show to accentuate the group's rock-and-roll. Unbeknownst to him, the Brown boys had sabotaged that device as well. Concert promoter Ned the Fish introduces the band, but at the onset of the group's opening number, the Environmental Adjustor creates a deadly storm involving flash flooding, hail and tornados. Hill Valley is flooded, with residents seeking shelter in trees.

Caught in nature's upheaval, Clara and the boys turn to Doc for help in averting the impending catastrophe, and Jules and Verne admit to their tampering. Doc, his concern for his family overriding his fear of losing his mind, devises a complex scheme to disengage the malfunctioning Environmental Adjustor and save the day. In the process, he realizes that he has retained all of his intelligence [BFAN-12].

> *NOTE: This episode was adapted in the fourth issue of the Harvey Comics series.*

Thursday, May 2, 1991 A.D.—Before 12:37 PM

• The Institute of Future Technology selects a group of time-travel volunteers to take part in the maiden voyage of the Eight-Passenger DeLorean Time-Travel Vehicle. Their intended destination: one day forward in time. As they wait in the lobby, the volunteers receive a sub-ether transmission from Emmett Brown, their guide through

---

CODE	STORY						
ARGN	BTTF-themed TV commercial: Arrigoni	**BTF1**	Film: *Back to the Future*	**CITY**	BTTF-themed music video: Owl City, "Deer in the Headlights"	**HUEY**	BTTF-themed music video: Huey Lewis and the News, "The Power of Love"
BFAN	*Back to the Future: The Animated Series*	**BTF2**	Film: *Back to the Future Part II*	**DCTV**	BTTF-themed TV commercial: DirecTV	**LIMO**	BTTF-themed music video: The Limousines, "The Future"
BFCG	*Back to the Future: The Card Game*	**BTF3**	Film: *Back to the Future Part III*	**ERTH**	*The Earth Day Special*		
BFCL	*Back to the Future* comic book (limited series)	**BUDL**	BTTF-themed TV commercial: Bud Light	**GALE**	Interviews and commentaries: Bob Gale and/or Robert Zemeckis	**MCDN**	BTTF-themed TV commercial: McDonald's
BFCM	*Back to the Future* comic book (monthly series)	**CHEK**	BTTF-themed music video: O'Neal McKnight, "Check Your Coat"			**MITS**	BTTF-themed TV commercial: Mitsubishi Lancer
BFHM	BTTF-themed McDonald's Happy Meal boxes	**CHIC**	Photographs hanging in Doc Brown's Chicken restaurant at Universal Studios	**GARB**	BTTF-themed TV commercials: Garbarino	**MSFT**	BTTF-themed TV commercial: Microsoft
BTFA	*Back to the Future Annual* (Marvel Comics)			**GETV**	BTTF-themed TV commercial: GE		

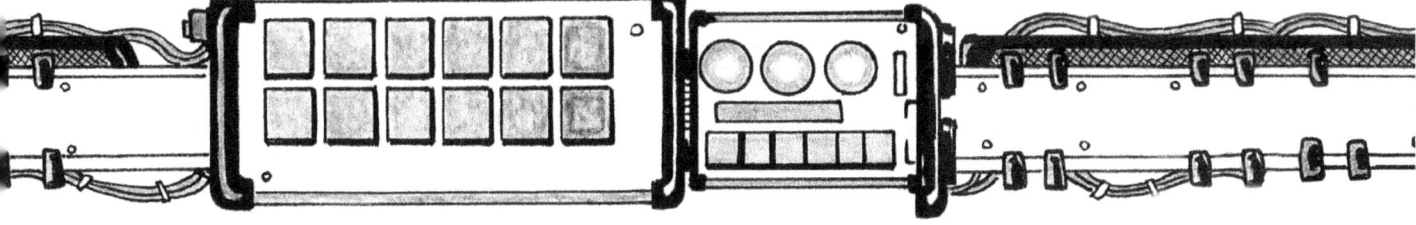

the space-time continuum. Doc communicates with the volunteers from October 21, 2015, while searching for teenage Biff Tannen, who has stowed away in another time machine in 1955 and is playing havoc with the timestream in Doc's era. Brown tasks the volunteers with keeping a lookout for the rogue teen at IFT.

Unable to locate Biff, Doc carries on with the experiment. While he prepares the volunteers for their one-day time-travel voyage, IFT security discovers Tannen running loose on the grounds. Biff breaks into Doc's laboratory and locks him in his office, then steals the hover-converted DeLorean and blasts off into the past. Trapped, a desperate Doc instructs the volunteers to give chase in the Eight-Passenger DeLorean Time-Travel Vehicle, which he will operate via remote-control, and to bump Tannen's car upon reaching 88 miles per hour. The activation of both Flux Capacitors, he says, will create a harmless time vortex, instantly snapping the two vehicles back to their 1991 point of departure [RIDE].

Thursday, May 2, 1991 A.D.—12:37 PM

• After receiving a brief tutorial on vehicle safety, the time-travel volunteers board the Eight-Passenger DeLorean Time-Travel Vehicle and prepare to leave the Institute of Future Technology. The vehicle activates, and they utilize its onboard Sub-Ether Time Tracking Scanner to locate Tannen in the stolen DeLorean [RIDE].

Thursday, May 2, 1991 A.D.—12:38 PM

• Emmett Brown provides some last-minute information to the time-travel volunteers, then launches the eight-passenger DeLorean and its occupants through time [RIDE].

Thursday, May 2, 1991 A.D.—12:34 to 12:35 PM

• After chasing Biff to the years 2015, 1,000,000 B.C. and 64,000,000 B.C., the time-travel volunteers catch up with their quarry and return him to the Institute

of Future Technology in 1991, where he is promptly apprehended by the staff and police [NTND]. Emmett Brown congratulates the group, thanking them for their service to science, and to the universe [RIDE].

> *NOTE: Strangely enough, the volunteers and Tannen returned to 1991 a full four minutes before their original departure time, conceivably able to alert their past selves and prevent Tannen's escape from occurring in the first place. Of course, if it never happened, then they couldn't return to warn themselves, thus creating a time paradox.*

July 1991 A.D.

• One hot summer afternoon finds the Brown family miserable and irritable. Even a visit from Marty McFly does little to ease the tense mood. Everyone is soon arguing, until Emmett Brown decides they need to go somewhere cool, and perhaps capture a little Christmas spirit. With Marty in tow, the Browns pile into the stretch DeLorean and take a wintry vacation in 19th-century London, England [BFAN-10].

• Jules Brown conducts a research project he dubs the "Which Came First Experiment," to determine whether the egg preceded the chicken, or vice versa. The extreme summer heat, however, causes the egg to hard-boil and the chicken to become lethargic, thoroughly botching the results [BFAN-10].

July to October 1991 A.D.

• Jules Brown invents the Robogriddle, a cooking contraption utilizing five robotic arms to automatically produce flapjacks at high speed, from batter-pouring to table service [BFAN-16].

• Verne Brown hones his video game skills, excelling at such games as *The Legend of Gruno* [BFAN-1], *Intergalactic Space Feud* [BFAN-13] and *BraveLord and Monstrux* [BFAN-19].

NIKE	BTTF-themed TV commercial: Nike	**SCRT**	2010 Scream Awards: Back to the Future
NTND	Nintendo Back to the Future—The Ride Mini-Game		25th Anniversary Reunion (trailer)
		SIMP	Simulator: The Simpsons Ride
PIZA	BTTF-themed TV commercial: Pizza Hut	**SLOT**	Back to the Future Video Slots
REAL	Real life	**TEST**	Screen tests: Crispin Glover, Lea Thompson and Thomas F. Wilson
RIDE	Simulator: Back to the Future—The Ride		
SCRM	2010 Scream Awards: Back to the Future 25th Anniversary Reunion (broadcast)	**TLTL**	Telltale Games' Back to the Future—The Game
		UNIV	Universal Studios Hollywood promotional video

SUFFIX	**MEDIUM**		
-b	BTF2's Biff Tannen Museum video (extended version)	**-s1**	Screenplay (draft one)
		-s2	Screenplay (draft two)
-c	Animated series credit sequence	**-s3**	Screenplay (draft three)
-d	Film deleted scene	**-s4**	Screenplay (draft four)
-n	Film novelization	**-sp**	Screenplay (production draft)
-o	Film outtake	**-sx**	Screenplay (Paradox)
-v	Video game print materials or commentaries		

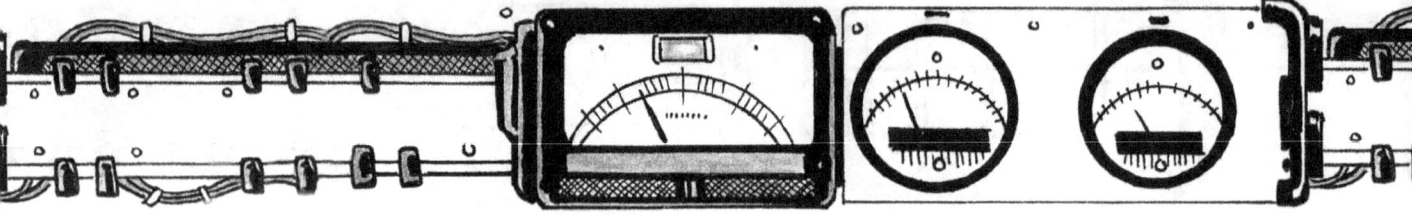

• Biff Tannen, jealous of his neighbors, decides to add a pool to his back yard. Enlisting the aid of his son, Biff Tannen Jr., Biff supervises while the boy digs. During the digging, the Tannens make a startling discovery: the deed to the Parker Ranch, signed over to Biff's great-great-grand-uncle, Thaddeus Tannen, in 1875. The two Biffs and Sheriff Andy Taylor drive out to Peter Parker's ranch, where Parker's granddaughter, Jennifer, is enjoying a meal with her family and her boyfriend, Marty McFly.

Biff presents the deed to the dumbstruck Parker family, and the sheriff authorizes it. Tannen plans to turn the ranch into a toxic waste dump, with a miniature golf course for his son on the side. As the bulldozers move in, Marty rushes to Emmett Brown's home, hoping to use the DeLorean to visit 1875 and intervene on the Parkers' behalf. Jules and Verne, however, inform him that their parents have taken the vehicle on a date to catch a showing of Shakespeare's *The Tragical History of Hamlet, Prince of Denmark* with its original cast, so Marty instead takes the time train [BFAN-16].

> ***NOTE: The cartoon series called Jennifer's paternal grandfather Pete Parker (in homage, perhaps, to Marvel Comics' Spider-Man), but the Telltale Games video game used the name Daniel Parker Sr.***

• Marty McFly returns from 1875 to find out if he has saved the Parker Ranch. Marty convinces the sheriff to take a closer look at the deed, which is now unsigned since Marty changed history by giving Thaddeus Tannen an invisible-ink pen. Since the deed is no longer valid, the ranch's ownership is restored to the Parkers [BFAN-16].

• Jules Brown creates the Cerebrum Observator, a device built from an otoscope—a medical instrument used to look into a person's ears—enabling him to view an individual's thoughts and dreams. He also devises the Uniview, comprising a helmet and lenses connected to a long tube, allowing a wearer to watch television without annoying others [BFAN-11].

• Verne Brown is dismayed when his father refuses to take him to the annual Hill Valley Father and Son Big Mouth Bass-off. When questioned about his hatred of fishing, Doc refuses to divulge the cause, leading Verne and Jules to take matters into their own hands. Utilizing a heavily modified otoscope, the boys peer into their father's thoughts while he sleeps, and discover that he has constructed an impenetrable wall around the date August 5, 1926. The brothers chip away at the memory block until uncovering the truth: As a small boy, their father once went fishing unsupervised and fell into a stream, causing him to become afraid of fishing. Determined to prevent this phobia from developing, the boys sneak out in the DeLorean. Marty McFly, visiting the family to retrieve his hoverboard, accompanies them [BFAN-11].

• One morning, Marty McFly plays baseball with Jules and Verne Brown. In response to Marty's lackluster skills at the bat, Emmett Brown quickly assembles a bionic exo-skeleton. The machine, designed to be a training module, will automatically hit the ball and train its user's muscles to react similarly during an actual game. Marty is impressed with the invention and, when Jules informs him that a Major League player named Pee Wee McFly had a failed baseball career in 1897, decides to take the exo-skeleton back in time to assist his predecessor. With the two youths in tow, Marty borrows the DeLorean and travels to September 1, 1897—the day before a humiliated Pee Wee retired from the sport [BFAN-8].

• During show-and-tell at school one day, Verne Brown becomes frustrated when rival classmate Roland Culver boasts of his grandfather having climbed a mountain, leaving Verne feeling inadequate. Marty McFly reminds the boy of his own family tree, and how Clara Clayton's parents—Verne's grandparents, pioneers Daniel Clayton and Martha O'Brien—fell in love and got married on the same day they met, while traversing the Oregon Trail. Excited by his heritage, Verne journeys with Jules back to that day—March 3, 1850—to meet his grandparents and bring back a photo worthy of bragging rights at the

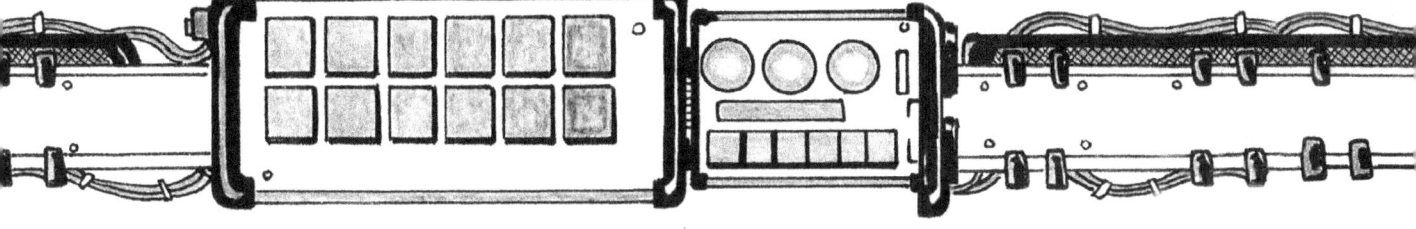

next show-and-tell. Marty, aware of the potential mishaps inherent in interacting with one's direct ancestors, accompanies the brothers on their voyage [BFAN-13].

Friday, August 2, 1991 A.D.—5:00 PM

• While conducting experiments in his garage, Emmett Brown is startled by an alarm, alerting him to the fact that it's time for dinner. Dropping everything, he hurries to the DeLorean and begins a whirlwind trip through the timestream, collecting his family and good friend Marty McFly to gather around the table for a warm meal. When they finally sit down to eat, Brown discovers that Einstein is nowhere to be found. Instead, the dog has commandeered the *Jules Verne Train* and streaked away into the evening sky and out of time, leaving twin trails of fire in his wake [BFAN-c].

> *NOTE: One can only guess where a dog with time-traveling capabilities would choose to go.*

Thursday, October 10, 1991 A.D.

• Upon the completion of his latest invention—the Proprietary Ultrasonic Subatomic Molecular Redistributor, a cyclotron that he hopes can be used to obliterate the Earth's overflowing garbage problem—Emmett Brown decides to test it out with his sons. Fearing a repeat of a botched testing in 1961 that left the Greater Hill Valley Medfield Basin window-less, Doc takes the boys three million years into the past [BFAN-3].

• Upon returning from 3,000,000 B.C., the Browns are stunned to discover that dinosaurs now rule the planet, having never become extinct. The creatures live in a "post-historic" age, in which they have developed civilization, technology, culture and the arts [BFAN-3]. This alternate version of Hill Valley is known as Dinocity [BFHM].

• Doc realizes that he has created an alternate timeline in which humans have not evolved. What's worse, the scientist calculates that in twelve minutes, the new timeline will catch up to the present, and the Browns will cease to exist as well. To set time right, Emmett prepares to return to the past, but the DeLorean is captured by two dinosaur law-enforcement officers. Jules comments that one of the dinosaurs, an *Allosaurus*, resembles Biff Tannen. Doc devises a quick plan to discharge electricity from the car's engine to its metal frame. The jolt loosens the dino-cop's grip on the DeLorean, allowing the vehicle to reach 88 miles per hour and travel back to the year 3,000,000 B.C.

The Browns return from the Cretaceous Period, where Verne left his *Pteranodon* friend "Donny" behind to die in the coming Ice Age. The child's spirits are lifted when a colorful parrot lands on his shoulder—a bird bearing a striking resemblance to Donny. Verne fancies that he's just met his old friend's descendant [BFAN-3].

> *NOTE: This episode was adapted in issue two of the Harvey Comics series.*

Sunday, December 15, 1991 A.D.

• As an anniversary gift for his parents, Jules Brown invents the J.E.B. Cross-time Headliner, which combines an old-style teletype machine with a Flux Capacitor, enabling him to print up newspaper pages from any desired era, in order to learn about history [BFAN-9].

> *NOTE: The cartoon set the couple's wedding date as December 15, while the card game cited September 15. It's unknown which is correct.*

• For his parents' 106th wedding anniversary, Jules Brown jury-rigs a Flux Capacitor to a credit card machine and purchases two tickets to McFly Space Cruises' inaugural flight to Mars, a century in the future. Ready to take their second honeymoon, Emmett and Clara kiss their children goodbye, and then set a course for the future. As soon as they leave, their children discover, via Jules' JEB Cross-Time Headliner, that one day after their parents' arrival, their solar sailship will be lost in space. Frantic, the brothers board the time train and race into the timestream to save their lives [BFAN-9].

NIKE	*BTTF*-themed TV commercial: Nike	**SCRT**	2010 Scream Awards: *Back to the Future*	**SUFFIX MEDIUM**		**-s1**	Screenplay (draft one)
NTND	Nintendo *Back to the Future—The Ride*		25th Anniversary Reunion (trailer)	**-b**	*BTTF2*'s Biff Tannen Museum video	**-s2**	Screenplay (draft two)
	Mini-Game	**SIMP**	Simulator: *The Simpsons Ride*		(extended version)	**-s3**	Screenplay (draft three)
PIZA	*BTTF*-themed TV commercial: Pizza Hut	**SLOT**	*Back to the Future* Video Slots	**-c**	Animated series credit sequence	**-s4**	Screenplay (draft four)
REAL	Real life	**TEST**	Screen tests: Crispin Glover, Lea Thompson	**-d**	Film deleted scene	**-sp**	Screenplay (production draft)
RIDE	Simulator: *Back to the Future—The Ride*		and Thomas F. Wilson	**-n**	Film novelization	**-sx**	Screenplay (*Paradox*)
SCRM	2010 Scream Awards: *Back to the Future*	**TLTL**	Telltale Games' *Back to the Future—The Game*	**-o**	Film outtake		
	25th Anniversary Reunion (broadcast)	**UNIV**	Universal Studios Hollywood promotional video	**-v**	Video game print materials or commentaries		

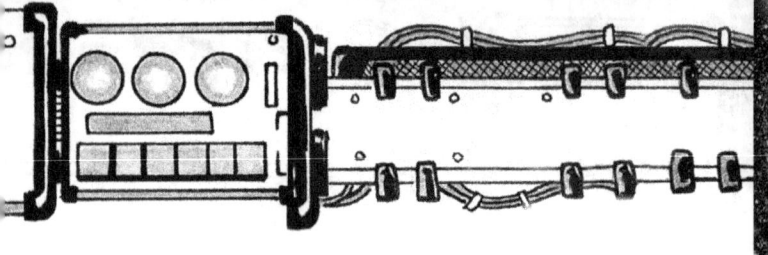

CHAPTER XIII:
1992 A.D.

Sometime in or Before 1992 A.D.

- While using a Geiger counter to search for buried money in the sand of the Hill Valley Beach and Unsynchronized Swimming Center, Emmett Brown loses his DeLorean keys and then spends the next week trying to locate them [BFAN-16].

- Books titled *Reflexology* and *How to Cook* are published. Emmett Brown obtains copies of both volumes for his personal library [BFAN-17]. Also published is a textbook about robotics, titled *Here Come the Robots* [BFCL-1].

- Biff Tannen befriends a man named Ralph, who shares his fondness for watching tractor-pulls, particularly on Founder's Day [BFAN-22].

- Issue #1 of a girl-centric comic book known as *Mega-Cindy, Slimy Worm of Doom*, is published. The first-edition printing of this issue soon becomes quite valuable [BFAN-18].

- Verne Brown begins watching *Major Dad*, an American sitcom on CBS starring Gerald McRaney, and mistakenly assumes the title character, Major John D. MacGillis, to be a real person [BFAN-15].

- The Hill Valley Dreamers, a local baseball team performing at the Hill Valley Stadium and Swap-Meet Grounds, develop a reputation for frequently losing games [BFAN-25].

- Children's television series *He-Boy Gladiator Show* debuts, and is broadcast on Hill Valley's Channel 92. Biff Tannen Jr. becomes a fan of this series [BFAN-26].
  > **NOTE:** *This series' title was based on that of the* **He-Man and the Masters of the Universe** *franchise.*

- *The Half Show* debuts on television. The show, featuring a cast of "juvenile martial-arts mutations," proves extremely popular with children [BFAN-20].
  > **NOTE:** **The Half Show** *was apparently similar to* **Teenage Mutant Ninja Turtles,** *the protagonists of which were often described as "heroes in a half-shell."*

- Emmett Brown subscribes to a scientific journal called *Acme Robotics*, which features a magazine centerfold

WALTER WISDOM AUCTIONS OFF THE STOLEN DELOREAN ON TV

of a robot striking an erotic pose [BFCM-1]. He also subscribes to a newspaper called *Atomic Science Weekly* [BFCM-3].

• Art's Yarn Barn begins sponsoring a team competing in a bowling league at the Hill Valley Bowl-o-rama [BFCL-3].

• The Hill Valley Theater shows the film *Back to the Future* [BFAN-22].

NOTE: Presumably, in* BTTF *continuity, the film did not feature the story of Marty McFly. (It's unknown whether actor Eric Stoltz played the lead role.)

• Conducting experiments to find water in Nevada's desert using a divining rod, Emmett Brown travels to the Hoover Dam and the Colorado River. There, he accidentally opens the reservoir and causes a power failure while attempting to fill his canteen from a water spout [BFAN-22].

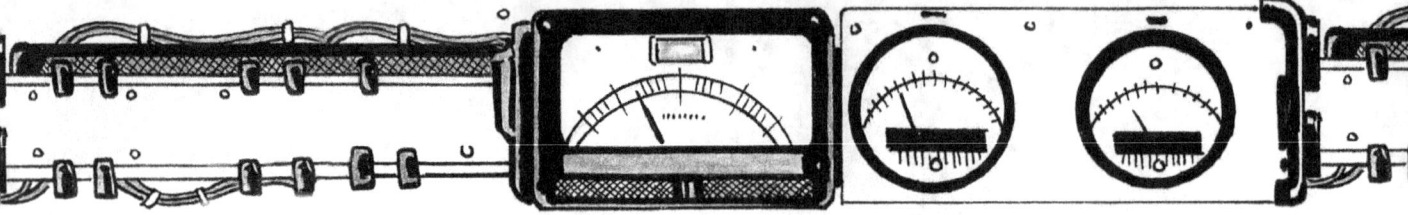

• Jules Brown invents a hovercase, utilizing hoverboard antigravity technology to enable a user to travel with a loaded briefcase without having to lift it [BFAN-20].

January to October 1992 A.D.

• Emmett Brown visits a McDonald's restaurant to record documentary footage of a new line of Happy Meal toys, including one depicting "some old guy" in his DeLorean. After careful consideration, Doc reasons that it's time to put away his camera and simply enjoy a meal [MCDN].
> *NOTE: The "old guy" was, of course, Doc himself.*

• Emmett Brown sails the Caribbean route that 17th-century buccaneer Sir Henry Morgan once used to search for Jamaica and long-forgotten buried treasure. Using ocean currents and trade winds, Doc sets sail in a small boat that he dubs the *S.S. Clara*, but having forgotten to bring along a compass, he ends up stranded on an island somewhere in the Caribbean. There, he fends off a band of pirates with a homemade cannon fashioned from a bell, vinegar and a large, round rock.

Back in Hill Valley, Marty McFly fails to procure tickets to a Walk DMC concert, as he had promised Jennifer Parker he would, and makes matters worse by lying to her about it. Fed up with his lies and irresponsibility, Jennifer ends their relationship. Meanwhile, Verne Brown feels stifled in his family. The young boy wants to get an earring to earn himself street credit with "the cool kids" who make fun of him for his out-of-style coonskin cap. Spurned by his parents' refusal to allow the piercing, Verne steals the DeLorean to visit the 1600s and sail with a band of pirates. There, he reasons, he'll be able to do whatever he wants—and get an earring, to boot. As he is leaving in the time machine, however, he comes across Marty, walking home after his fight with Jennifer. Marty asks for a ride and Verne agrees, saying Marty will first have to accompany him on an errand to the Caribbean Islands, circa 1697.

After tussling with pirates, Verne and Marty return to their own era. Marty vows never again to lie to Jen, who agrees to take him back. Verne has now changed his mind about getting an earring against his parents' wishes—though Clara is unhappy to discover a tattoo of a pirate ship on his stomach, and promptly removes it with the aid of one of Doc's inventions [BFAN-14].

• After receiving numerous complaints regarding television reception, a Hill Valley cable provider enlists Emmett Brown's assistance in fixing the problem. At the Hill Valley Space Center and Air-Sickness Clinic, Doc prepares to journey into outer space via the NASA space shuttle *Discovery* to give the cable company's satellites a complete overhaul. As payment for his services, Doc is rewarded with free cable, plus premium channels [BFAN-15].
> *NOTE: This may explain Doc's interest in DirecTV in a pair of 2007 commercials for the American direct broadcast satellite service provider and broadcaster.*

• Verne Brown is thrilled to hear that Walter Wisdom, one of his television heroes, will be making an appearance at Hill Valley's Lone Pine Mall. Doc, however, seems to have a bad history with the science show host. Marty McFly takes Verne to the mall to see the TV icon, but the duo receives only a sales pitch for Mr. Wisdom-related merchandise, rather than an actual meet-and-greet with the celebrity. Determined to meet the man himself, they sneak into the parking lot in which Mr. Wisdom's Big Brain Bus is parked. They trespass on the property, facing Wisdom's wrath until he realizes that Verne's father is Emmett Brown.

Claiming to be an old friend of Doc's, Wisdom convinces them to take him back to the Brown home. There, he peruses Doc's laboratory, a greedy eye on the radical inventions therein—the DeLorean, in particular. When Doc enters, he angrily evicts the TV personality, since he and Wisdom were once roommates and rival

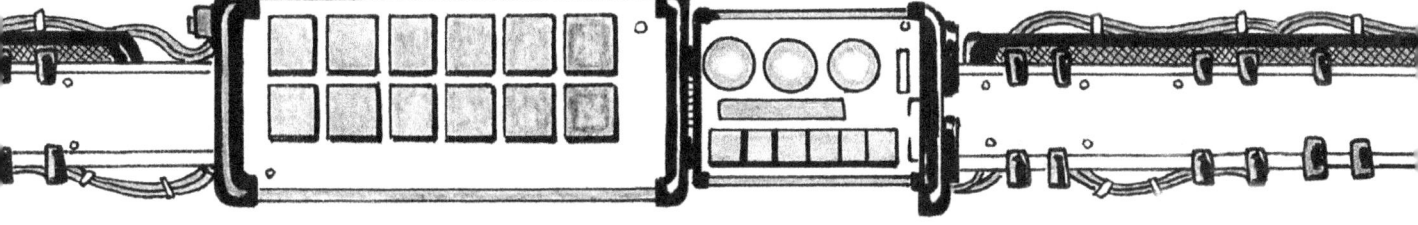

inventors at the American College of Technological Science & Difficult Math, back in the 1950s. Wisdom stole Doc's revolutionary Perpetual Motion Hula Hoop and entered it as his own creation in the Inter-Collegiate Science Invent-Off, winning first prize and parlaying his achievement into a contract with Clunko Toys, as well as his own television show. Verne is horrified to learn this, no longer a Mr. Wisdom fan.

Later that night, Wisdom breaks into the Browns' garage, loads a number of inventions into the DeLorean and speeds away. The Browns and Marty give chase in the time train, following the thief first to ancient Egypt, in the year 127 AD, and then to Krakatoa's volcanic eruption in 1883. When the locomotive crashes into the molten lava, Wisdom returns to 1992, leaving them for dead, and attempts to sell the DeLorean on a pirate broadcast for $999,995.

Wisdom's sales pitch is interrupted by the arrival of Marty and the Browns, who were spared a fiery volcanic death thanks to a heat-retardant suit. During the live broadcast, Doc challenges Wisdom to a contest of scientific intelligence. He easily bests the charlatan in intellectual combat by demonstrating his inventions. Wisdom has only the pilfered inventions to represent him, but Doc is far more familiar with his own creations. Wisdom attempts to activate Doc's Memory Archive Recall Indexer and Enhancer (M.A.R.I.E.), but is unaware that Doc has yet to work out all of the system's bugs, and the machine erases his memory instead of enhancing it. Wisdom is reduced to a gibbering vegetable, while Doc reclaims his reputation, his property and Verne's admiration [BFAN-15].

- After struggling for three weeks to learn the waltz from a cantankerous old woman at the Hill Valley Dance Academy, Verne Brown desperately wants to quit, but his mother refuses. Verne consults his father, who recalls an invention he made nearly fifty years prior: Fance-O-Dance Memorizing Shoes, which allow their wearer to perfectly execute a number of complicated dancing styles.

Doc demonstrates the cha-cha for his son, but years of disuse have rendered the mechanical shoes faulty, and they are soon destroyed. Unfortunately, Doc no longer has the blueprints to recreate them. In fact, the last time he had them was in 1944. Verne asks Doc to take him back in time to retrieve the paperwork, but the scientist reminds him that this could damage the space-time continuum. Verne turns to Marty McFly, offering to buy him a burger as compensation.

After befriending a young girl named Dorothy in 1944, winning a jitterbug competition and dodging a dim-witted U.S. soldier named Sergeant Frank Tannen, Verne Brown returns to 1992 with a new outlook on dancing. He no longer requires his father's Fance-O-Dance Memorizing Shoes, having gained confidence in his own dancing ability. Winning another trophy like the one he left Dorothy 50 years prior, Verne finds newfound passion for his waltz class at the Hill Valley Dance Academy. His cantankerous instructor is pleased to see his change in attitude. Upon hearing his goal of winning a trophy, she shows off a jitterbug trophy that she and a young boy won in 1944, and Verne suddenly realizes that his dance teacher *is* Dorothy [BFAN-17].

- While playing an all-boys baseball game in Courthouse Square, Verne Brown befriends a child named Chris, who proves to be an excellent pitcher. Impressed, Verne invites the youth to join the game. The two begin palling around, hanging out at a local comic book shop, where they come across a poster for a circus. Excited, they decide to attend the circus, but are disappointed to learn that the poster is dated 1933. Verne lets his new friend in on the "family secret"—his father's time-traveling DeLorean—and takes Chris back to 1933 so they can enjoy the event. Marty McFly, already in the car searching for something, goes along for the ride.

Verne and Chris later return to 1992 no longer on good terms, due to Verne discovering that "Chris" is actually a girl named Christine. But as he plays ball with other boys, Chris assists Verne from the sidelines.

BILL HILL OFFERS
HILL VALLEY'S
CITIZENS A LESSON
ABOUT FOUNDER'S DAY

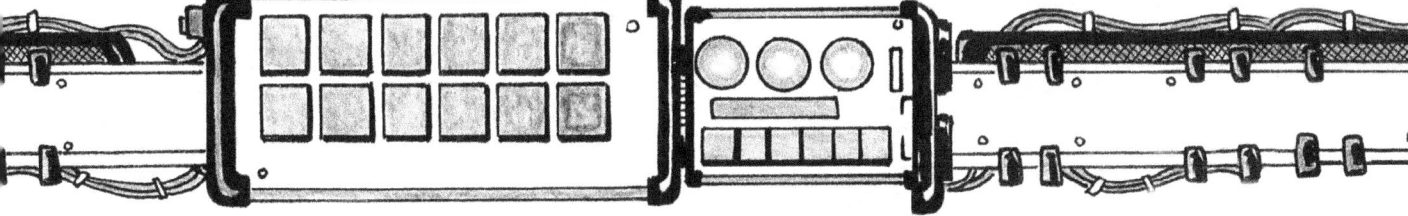

Thankful for the help—and realizing his own closed-mindedness—Verne invites his new friend onto the field to play ball, no longer prejudging her based on her gender [BFAN-18].

- Verne Brown, obsessed with playing the video game *BraveLord and Monstrux* at Super Mega Arcade World, begins letting his odd jobs around town fall by the wayside, all but forgetting about chores, promises made and extracurricular activities. After receiving complaints from Jörg Johannsen, a neighbor whose yard Verne was supposed to mow, the boy's parents suspect his video game hobby has become an addiction. Intervening, they ground Verne for a month, cutting him off from all video games.

  Verne grows desperate, suffering from coin-op withdrawal, and bribes Jules and Marty to help him, offering Jules a month of chores and Marty a baseball card collection for their assistance. Jules concocts a method of redirecting the video game feed from the arcade straight to Verne's bedroom. The experiment yields wholly unexpected results, however, when BraveLord (the game's barbaric warrior hero) and Monstrux (a tentacled demon able to endow inanimate objects with deadly intent) are birthed into the real world. Verne's father, meanwhile, is pulled into the digital realm.

  Monstrux wreaks havoc on Hill Valley, first turning Biff Tannen and his son into Brussels sprout-eating slaves, and then converting Super Mega Arcade World into a medieval fortress. The heroes believe their only hope of setting things right is to return to the arcade and reverse the video transfer device. Clara, stationed at the game in Verne's room, guides her husband through the bizarre realm of swords and sorcery, while Verne, Jules, Marty and BraveLord—who turns out to be more buffoon than barbarian—quest to Monstrux's lair. BraveLord loses his nerve and Monstrux reveals that Verne was the real bravery behind the video game hero. Though enticed by the idea of facing his greatest challenger, the demon easily outmatches the youth. BraveLord at last returns, ready to lay hold of the mantle of valiant defender, and together the two reverse the device. Monstrux and BraveLord are returned to the video game, while Doc is jettisoned from his digital imprisonment.

  Having defeated the game, as well as his video game addiction, Verne begins once more doing chores and performing odd jobs for neighbors, and even takes up soccer. Clara, however, has developed a newfound excitement for video games, and is first in line at Super Mega Arcade World the next morning, ready to play [BFAN-19].

- Jules Brown, tired of being excluded from other children's games due to his superior intelligence, grows to envy his younger brother Verne for his popularity and acceptance among neighborhood kids. With his social life dead, Jules devotes himself to cultivating a new breed of trees that produces leaves of various fabric patterns. When a disgruntled Verne fails to bum a few extra dollars from his father, the boy sarcastically suggests Jules figure out a way to make money grow on trees. Jules takes this thought to heart and does just that.

  News of Jules' money tree spreads throughout Hill Valley. Overnight, he is accepted at school, with everyone vying to be his friend. Fame and greed quickly go to the boy's head as he begins spending his blossoming fortune, buying friendships and taking his family on an extravagant shopping spree. He is also approached by *USA Hooray* regarding an exclusive article in the magazine's upcoming issue. Jules makes national headlines, drawing the scrutiny of FBI agents Smith and Jones, who suspect the child of making counterfeit money and thus launch an investigation into the Brown family.

  Meanwhile, Biff Tannen learns of the money tree and plans to steal it for himself. Fearing that his tree will be stolen, Jules hires Marty McFly to guard the tree. Marty falls asleep on watch, however, and Biff uproots the plant. When Jules discovers the theft, the Brown family unites to regain their fortune. A desperate chase ensues as Jules and Verne dangle from the flying DeLorean to retrieve the tree from Tannen's tow truck. The boys nearly lose their life in the process, leading Clara to realize what greed has done to their family. The Browns agree to let the money go, reminded that family is the greatest treasure of all.

  After using the money tree to purchase a trailer, Biff Tannen finds himself surrounded by the FBI task force. Fearing imprisonment, the bully snatches as many "leaves" off the tree as he can and makes a break for it—only to discover that, once pulled, the money withers into refuse. Seeing that the money is useless, the FBI calls off its investigation. Without his fortune, Jules loses many of his friends, but gains the respect of at least one girl: Franny Phillips, on whom Jules has a crush.

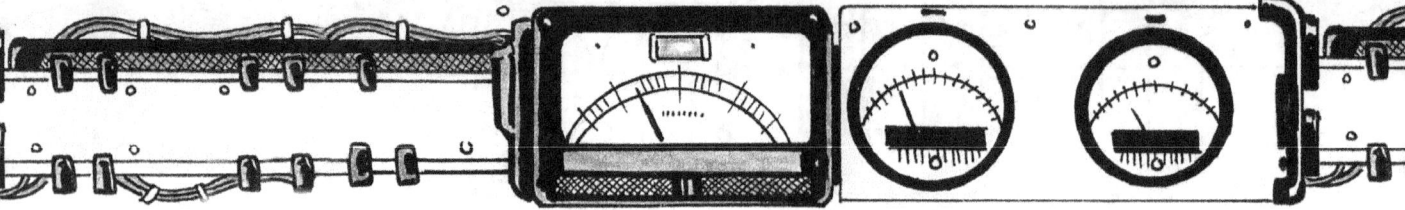

Doc Brown later tasks his son with cultivating a second money tree, which the scientist plants in the Amazon rain forest and experiments on in the hope of prolonging leaf life. His goal: to use the cash to ensure that he and Clara enjoy their Golden Years [BFAN-20].

• Upset that his name draws ridicule from school bullies, Verne Brown travels to France, circa the 1800s, to convince his namesake, science fiction author Jules Verne, to change his name. Hoping this will result in his own name changing, Verne enlists Marty McFly's assistance [BFAN-21].

• While tinkering with his ELB Hot-Diggety Dogger, to be used to distribute snacks at the upcoming Hill Valley Founder's Day Celebration, Emmett Brown inadvertently causes a massive blackout. The town is thrown into chaos, and the citizens of Hill Valley take out their frustrations on Doc's wife and sons. After being kicked out of his own home by Clara, Doc is later escorted out of town by Sheriff Andy Taylor, with the admonishment never to return, lest he be thrown in jail.

Regardless, Doc sneaks back into town and stays with Marty McFly. Utilizing a variety of disguises, Doc purchases the parts he needs at the Hill Valley Hardware Hut to construct a massive generator known as a Hydrolunarsolarwinderator, to restore the city's electricity. The gargantuan machine works, Doc is hailed as a hero and led home on the shoulders of his happy neighbors, and Clara welcomes him back into their home. Unfortunately, his generator produces too much power—lights will no longer turn off, while appliances run continually and out of control.

By morning, Hill Valley is once again up in arms, and Biff Tannen uses this opportunity to seize control of the people's goodwill, leading a mob to run the entire Brown clan outside the city limits. As a demonstration of his leadership, Biff throws soda on the generator, intending to destroy it and liberate the town from the electronic nightmare. This makes matters worse, as sparks shoot

from power lines and the generator is about to blow. Only Doc's quick intervention defuses the generator and saves the town.

Eventually, the electricity is restored to normal balance. In the meantime, the Founder's Day Celebration continues, though the town's spirits are low without power to operate their favorite Founder's Day games. Clara travels into the past and retrieves Hill Valley's *actual* founder, who tells the townsfolk what the original Founder's Day Celebration was like in his day. His speech inspires Hill Valley's citizens, who realize they don't need modern marvels to enjoy their time together. Newly invigorated, the town celebrates, while Clara safely returns the old-timer to the past [BFAN-22].

NOTE: Hill Valley's founder was unnamed in this episode, but the first draft of BTF2's screenplay gave him the name William "Bill" Hill.

• Jules and Verne Brown visit a shop called Wally's World of Wonderment with Marty McFly, to purchase a telescope in preparation for the passing of Comet Kahooey. There, they encounter Biff Tannen. Upon discovering that the comet is returning after its last visit a quarter-century prior, Biff becomes hysterical, claiming that he encountered an extraterrestrial when the comet last zoomed overhead, in 1967. That night has stayed with him ever since, and he stirs Hill Valley into a fright. Biff's paranoia grows when he discovers a downed spaceship in the woods. Emmett Brown, conducting an experiment in that area, claims the vessel as his own, and Biff creates a public panic that Doc is really an alien. Pandemonium reigns in the streets, and the National Guard are called in. Along with Sheriff Andy Taylor, the gunmen surround the Brown home to arrest the "alien."

Seeing their father in trouble, Jules and Verne decide to go back to 1967 and discern the truth about Hill Valley's close encounter, in order to clear their father's name. With Marty in tow, the brothers blast to the past, where the trio pose as aliens and scare Biff into remaining silent about what he saw. Upon returning to 1992, they

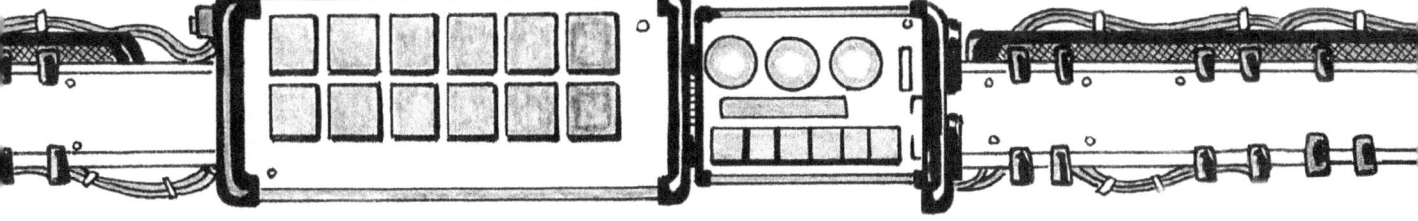

find that the town is no longer in an uproar, and Hill Valley no longer accuses Emmett of being from outer space. Comet Kahooey now passes peacefully overhead, sans public paranoia or panic [BFAN-23].

- Verne Brown hangs out one afternoon with a group of boys at Dead Man's Swamp, each child daring the others to swing across the bog from an overhanging tree vine, as an initiation into the Mega Muscleman Fan Club—inspired by their favorite comic book hero. Jackson, the club's self-appointed leader, taunts Verne into swinging, but the latter backs down, afraid to take the risk. Upset, Verne returns home to discover his father discussing his latest invention with Marty McFly: a pair of bright red booster boots. Doc encourages Verne not to give in to peer pressure, but the boy isn't convinced.

  Meanwhile, Jules cleans out some of his father's old belongings. The family learns that Doc had a very short-lived stint in the wrestling world as "Brainbuster" Brown, when he made front-page news during a Small Town Professional Wrasslin organization bout against champion Mad Maximus in 1952. Verne is impressed, though Doc admits he never went through with the fight. Verne decides that if he can change the past by ensuring that his father performs in the ring, then he will be able to impress Jackson and the other boys with his family's tough-man history.

  Verne later returns from the past, having learned a valuable lesson about following one's instincts in the face of taunts and jeers, and goes to Dead Man's Swamp to hang out with the Mega Muscleman Fan Club. Once more, Verne climbs the tree overlooking the swamp, and Jackson again bullies him into swinging across. Though he doesn't want to appear cowardly, Verne backs down from the challenge, believing it to be a bad move. Eager to show off, Jackson swings across—and splashes into the muck when the vine breaks. Jackson is humiliated in front of the other boys, and Verne knows he made the right decision not to give in to peer pressure [BFAN-24].

- While playing miniature golf with Jennifer Parker, Marty McFly is invited to a formal country-club dance by a wealthy debutante named Liz. After a fight with Jen, Marty agrees to go out with Liz, but can't afford a proper haircut. He visits Emmett Brown, correctly assuming the scientist will have a hair-cutting contraption. With the Brown family attending an outing at Mega Monster Mountain, Marty helps himself to Doc's Haircut-O-Matic. Unfortunately, Doc has not yet finished working out the machine's bugs, and Marty's hair takes on a metamorphic property, constantly cycling through outrageous hairstyles. Humiliated and pressed for time, Marty races to Mega Monster Mountain to seek Doc's help.

  At the amusement park—which costs one hundred dollars per ticket—the Brown family is divided. Jules and Verne enjoy modern rides, particularly the Spleen Splitter, while Doc and Clara prefer the simpler attractions of yesteryear. Frustrated at the exorbitant fees and flashy distractions of Mega Monster Mountain, Clara and Doc leave their children behind to indulge themselves, while the elder Browns visit the 1904 St. Louis World Exposition.

  Verne sets out to break the world roller-coaster records for the most times riding the Spleen Splitter, and the most times vomiting on co-passengers. Marty McFly finds the boys after they are thrown off the ride. Since Doc and Clara took the DeLorean to 1904, the three youths track them to the World's Fair using the time train.

  Marty finds Doc and Clara, who suggests that his wild hair is caused by an extreme case of static electricity. Clara instructs him to rub his feet on the carpet and discharge the static on the door knob. He does so, and his hair is instantly cured. Marty then takes the DeLorean to Liz's family's lavish estate to pick her up, but he has a change of heart, regretting his fight with Jennifer. Liz is fine with the news, however, having already made plans to go, instead, with Hill Valley's wealthiest bachelor, Milton Van Conrad III. Marty brings a pizza and some movies to Jen's house as a peace offering, and the two enjoy a nice evening together [BFAN-25].

					SUFFIX	MEDIUM			
NIKE	BTTF-themed TV commercial: Nike	SCRT	2010 Scream Awards: Back to the Future				-s1	Screenplay (draft one)
NTND	Nintendo Back to the Future—The Ride		25th Anniversary Reunion (trailer)		-b	BTF2's Biff Tannen Museum video	-s2	Screenplay (draft two)
	Mini-Game	SIMP	Simulator: The Simpsons Ride			(extended version)	-s3	Screenplay (draft three)
PIZA	BTTF-themed TV commercial: Pizza Hut	SLOT	Back to the Future Video Slots		-c	Animated series credit sequence	-s4	Screenplay (draft four)
REAL	Real life	TEST	Screen tests: Crispin Glover, Lea Thompson		-d	Film deleted scene	-sp	Screenplay (production draft)
RIDE	Simulator: Back to the Future—The Ride		and Thomas F. Wilson		-n	Film novelization	-sx	Screenplay (Paradox)
SCRM	2010 Scream Awards: Back to the Future	TLTL	Telltale Games' Back to the Future—The Game		-o	Film outtake		
	25th Anniversary Reunion (broadcast)	UNIV	Universal Studios Hollywood promotional video		-v	Video game print materials or commentaries		

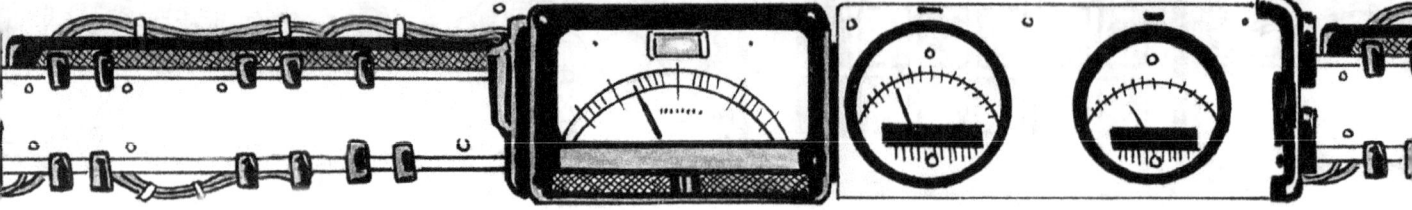

• Once again, Verne Brown attempts to "borrow" his father's time-traveling DeLorean for his own personal gain—but this time, Doc has built in an alarm system and is thus notified when his son tries to take the car without permission. Verne, scolded, reveals that he needed to go back in time to find something spectacular for his class show-and-tell at Hill Valley Elementary School. Doc understands his frustration, and gives the boy a rare, old arrowhead.

Verne excitedly takes the artifact to school—where it is promptly stolen by bully Biff Tannen Jr., who passes it off as his own, receiving his highest grade ever: a D+. Verne, meanwhile, is punished for coming to class empty-handed. The teacher gives him an ultimatum: Deliver a proper show-and-tell presentation the next day, or be drafted into the Drama Club's rendition of *Sleeping Beauty*, in which he will have to play Prince Charming and kiss fellow student Beatrice Spaulding. Grossed out, Verne vows to bring a great specimen to class. Enlisting Marty McFly's aid, Verne tricks his parents and takes the DeLorean with the intention of traveling to "one zillion B.C." to retrieve a genuine dinosaur egg [BFAN-26].

> *NOTE: Scientists place Earth's age at approximately 4.2 billion years, and "zillion" is not an actual number, making "1 zillion B.C." a fictional date in the planet's history.*

• After borrowing an unhatched *Apatosaurus* egg from the Jurassic Period, Verne Brown and Marty McFly return to 1992. Verne attempts to hide the egg until show-and-tell, but it hatches. Jules helps him keep the baby dinosaur a secret from their parents, but their plans are foiled when the creature—which they dub "Tiny"—escapes into Hill Valley.

Biff Tannen captures Tiny and sells the dinosaur to Walter Wisdom, a crooked TV science-show host and Emmett Brown's arch rival, for fifty thousand dollars. Wisdom schedules a local cable special so he can exploit the dinosaur before selling it to researchers for a considerable fortune. When Verne and Jules find out, Verne comes clean to his folks about stealing the egg. The Browns and Marty McFly hurry to rescue Tiny, and when the live television special begins, an empty-handed Wisdom is humiliated and labeled a fraud. Biff, also embarrassed in the process, fails to earn his hoped-for finder's fee.

The Browns use the time train to return Tiny to its mother in the Jurassic Period. Verne resigns himself to another show-and-tell period without a project—and to suffering the consequences of playing Prince Charming in *Sleeping Beauty*—until Tiny loses a baby tooth, which Verne keeps as a parting gift. Tiny is returned to his mother and, with a genuine dinosaur tooth to show his class, Verne is spared his acting debut—and the disgrace of having to kiss Beatrice Spaulding onstage [BFAN-26].

> *NOTE: Wisdom apparently regained his mental faculties after Doc left him a gibbering vegetable during their previous encounter in episode #15.*

October 1992 A.D.

• Upon learning that Verne—not known for his academic achievements—has earned an "A-" on a report about robots, Doc Brown rewards his son with a trip to 26th-century Hill Valley, to view the dawn of the Robot Age. Marty McFly accompanies the family on their trip to the future [BFCL-1]. This leads to a visit to 2,991,299,129,912,991 A.D., where Doc receives an electrical shock, leaving him stricken with amnesia [BFCL-2].

• Marty and the Browns return to 1992, where Doc's family rally around him in support, showing him his lab in the hope that it will restore his memory. They also reactivate one of Doc's old inventions—a psychiatrist robot called the Mechanical Psychoanalyst, designed to look and speak like Doctor Sigmund Freud. When that fails, Verne supposes that a second electrical shock might reverse the damage. Unfortunately, he puts the electrodes too close to Doc's Extra-dimensional Storage

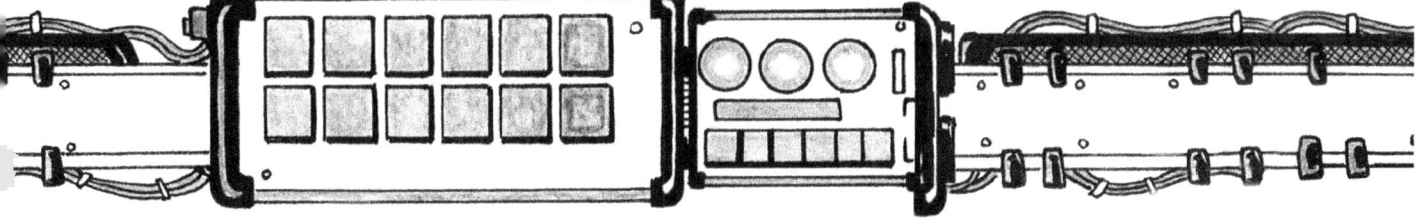

Closet, creating an explosion that inverts the space-time continuum.

Marty and the Browns become separated as reality comes unglued. The family briefly sojourns through several exotic locations, into multiple realities and back to November 8, 1955, before finally being reunited in Doc's shop. As they arrive, though, Clara slips back into the closet, lost to the void. Seeing her in mortal danger restores Doc's lost memory. Determined to set things right, he hooks the DeLorean to the shop, then flies into the closet, grabs his wife and speeds deeper into the void. His mind now fully functional, Doc realizes that the electric shock rendered the Extra-dimensional Storage Closet inside-out, and that by flying deeper into the continuum, with reality on the other side of the door chained to his vehicle, he can pull the universe right-side-out again. Thanks to Doc's ingenuity, Clara is saved, the world is returned to normalcy and the family rejoices [BFCL-3].

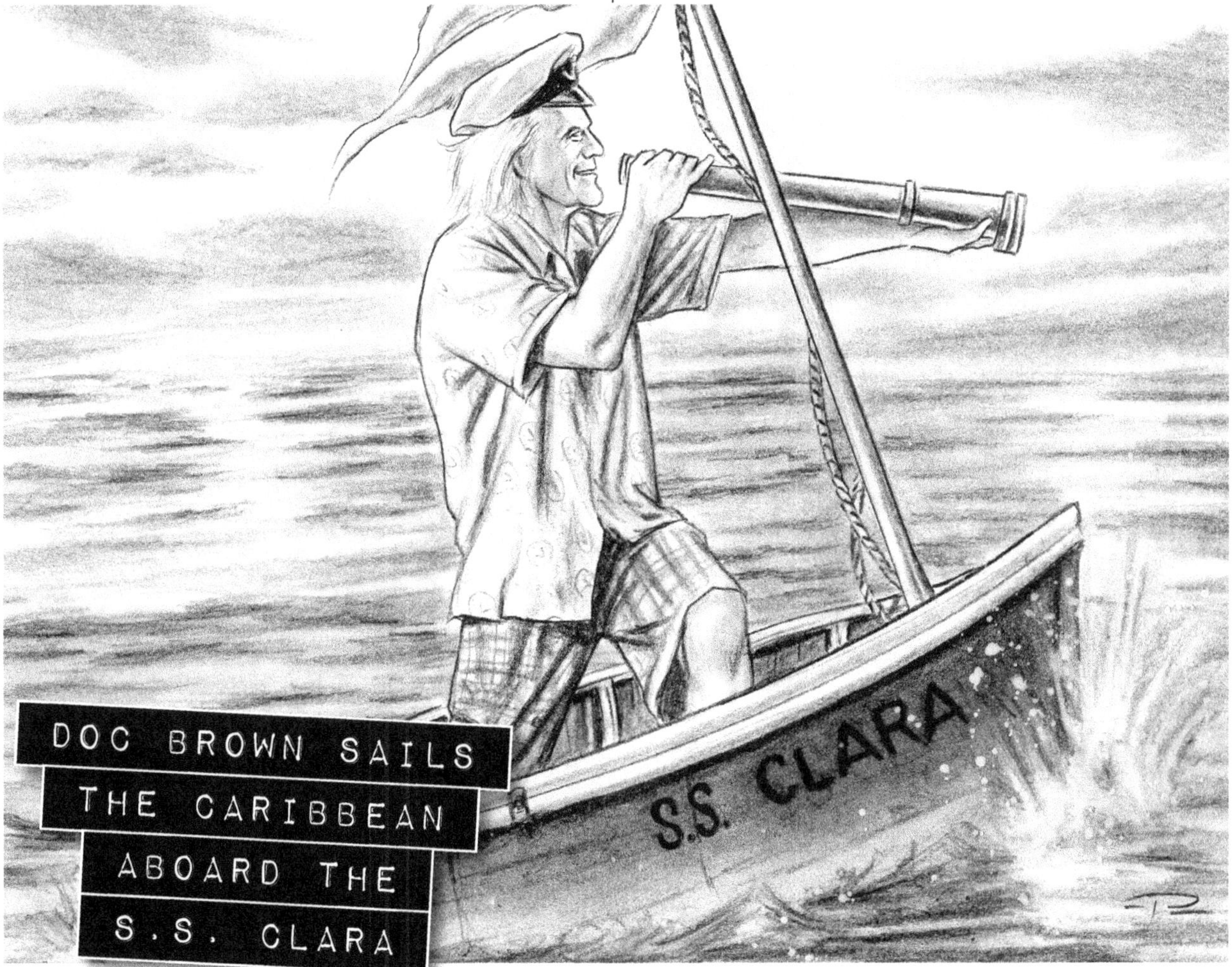

DOC BROWN SAILS THE CARIBBEAN ABOARD THE S.S. CLARA

MARTY AND JENNIFER GET MARRIED... AT THE CHAPEL O' LOVE?

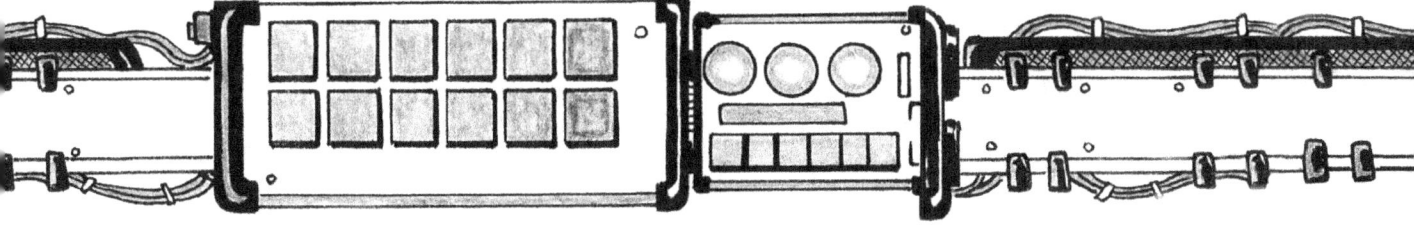

CHAPTER XIV:

1993 A.D. TO 2014 A.D.

Late 20th Century A.D.

• A series of nuclear conflicts breaks out, according to a 1955 prediction by Emmett Brown, which he dubs the Atomic Wars [BTF1].

> *NOTE: Doc's prediction was thankfully incorrect.*

Saturday, June 12, 1993 A.D.

• At space-time (S/T) coordinates 6-12-93-3, Dr. Steven Marble, a supervising scientist at the Institute of Future Technology, commences hoverbike testing in the facility's Anti-Gravitic Laboratory. The hoverbike's specialized Tandemonium maintains stability at a speed of 38 miles per hour [RIDE].

Sunday, May 1, 1994 A.D.—12:34 PM

• In one possible reality, in which a lapse in judgment results in Marty McFly's music career ending before it can begin, Marty marries Jennifer Parker in an informal ceremony at the Chapel O' Love, in Las Vegas, Nevada [BTF3, BFCG].

• In another potential timeline, after years of playing local battle-of-the-bands competitions, Marty McFly's band, Marty and the Pinheads, score their first big success with "Chapel of Love"—a cover of "Chapel O' Love," a 1964 hit by The Dixie Cups. Marty's version peaks at #11 on the charts [BFCG].

1995 to 2005 A.D.

• Marty and Jennifer McFly and their children, Marty Jr. and Marlene, enjoy a number of excursions during the kids' younger years. The couple captures their memories of these trips in a videobook labeled "Family Vacations—1995-2005" [BTF2-sx, BTF2-n].

> *NOTE: In the original script for BTF2, titled*

> *Number Two, Marty and Jen named their children Norman and Doris. This same draft also revealed that Lorraine had an aunt named "Doris," suggesting Marty may have named his daughter after her.*

1998 A.D.

• After meeting the Queen of Apocrypha and Tannen the Barbarian in 2,991,299,129,912,991 A.D., Doc and Marty return to 1992 in the recently damaged *Jules Verne Train*, "bouncing" off a number of other years along the way, including 1998 A.D. [BFCL-3].

2000 A.D.

• Earl Hays Publishing Co. publishes *Grays Sports Almanac: Complete Sports Statistics 1950-2000*, containing the results of five decades' worth of sporting events. Edited by Paul Grumrine, the book is compiled by Ben Flores, Tom Hoffarth, Sharon Jaeger, Norman Rubinstein and Mickey Bell [BTF2].

> *NOTE: The almanac's credits appeared on the actual film prop's title page. In BTF2's first-draft screenplay, the book was titled 2015 Sports Almanac: 50 Years of Sports Statistics 1965-2014; in the film's novelization, it was called Grey's Sports Almanac 1950-2000. In reality, Earl Hays is a prop-production firm specializing in mock product design and packaging. The names listed in the book were presumably those of the company's employees at the time of filming; Tom Hoffarth is still employed there as a sales representative.*

Friday, March 9, 2001 A.D.—1:03 PM

• Emmett Brown brings Microsoft senior vice-president Robert L. Muglia to Acme.com, in an attempt to help Muglia learn from Microsoft's past mistakes in its

---

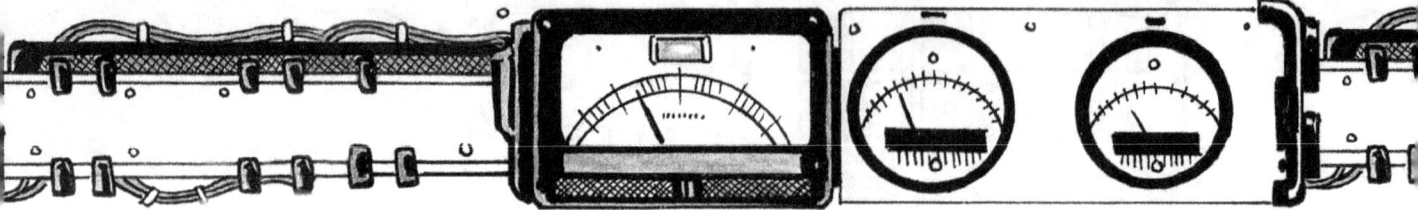

software promises. There, they spy TechFly, a down-on-his-luck IT technician who is frequently bullied by his supervisor, Mr. Biff, and is dealing with a number of software setbacks. Doc believes Muglia has more to learn from this encounter and whisks him away to 2003 [MSFT].

Saturday, April 12, 2003 A.D.—3:12 PM

• Emmett Brown brings Microsoft's Robert L. Muglia to 2003, where they find TechFly, Acme.com's beleaguered IT employee, being pressured by his boss, Mr. Biff, to use a failed Microsoft program. When TechFly fails to get the results Mr. Biff wants with his firm's limited apps, Muglia is tempted to intervene in the timeline to repair the situation, but Doc believes that such an act would result in catastrophe. To demonstrate, he takes Muglia to a parallel 2015, in which the senior VP makes a shocking discovery [MSFT].

Sometime Before 2004 A.D.

• Emmett Brown records a number of brief, humorous videos for a casino slot machine called Video Slots, encouraging users to bet money in the hope of winning a jackpot [SLOT].

2006 A.D.

• When the Institute of Future Technology falls on hard times financially, Emmett Brown seeks a loan from a banker named Mr. Friedman, to ensure that the institute will continue operating for many years to come. Suddenly, a DeLorean enters the timestream, striking and killing Friedman. The vehicle is driven by Professor John I.Q. Nerdelbaum Frink Jr., who, upon finding the institute closed in 2008, had traveled back in time to find out why Doc was unable to keep the IFT open, paradoxically causing that very event by killing Doc's financial backer. This leaves Doc with no choice but to sell the institute to another buyer: Herschel "Krusty the Clown" Krustofski, a cutthroat clown with aspirations of turning the scientific center into an amusement park. In need of a job, Doc offers to hang around and work at the park to supplement his finances [SIMP].

Monday, June 4, 2007 A.D.—10:03 AM

• Robert L. Muglia, Microsoft's senior vice-president, prepares to deliver a keynote speech at Tech-Ed 2007, when an unruly crowd, tired of unfulfilled promises and talks of "vision-casting," pelt him with tomatoes. He retreats backstage, flustered and humiliated, and receives an intervention from Emmett Brown, who arrives in his time-traveling DeLorean. Doc offers to show Muglia the dangers of empty talk of "visions," and teach him the importance of Microsoft following through on its technological promises [MSFT].

Monday, June 4, 2007 A.D.—10:07 AM

• After a harrowing, tech-heavy adventure through the IT department of Acme.com, Emmett Brown returns Microsoft senior VP Robert L. Muglia to Tech-Ed 2007. After what he's seen and learned, Muglia is ready to leave behind empty catchphrases such as "vision," often carelessly tossed about at such functions, and instead focus on his company's plan for the future. Doc accompanies him onstage and offers his own perspective during the presentation [MSFT].

2008 A.D.

• A bearded Emmett Brown visits O'Neal McKnight, a humble coat checker working at a nightclub. Doc is aghast to see his young friend not living up to his full potential, and decides a demonstration is in order. The wild-eyed scientist drags O'Neal to the year 2088, to help him discover who he is meant to be. When they return, O'Neal has a newfound sense of confidence—and style—and approaches an attractive woman at the club whom he'd been ogling moments before leaving. Meanwhile, Doc spins some records on a mean beat [CHEK].

Thursday, May 15, 2008 A.D.

• Professor John I.Q. Nerdelbaum Frink Jr. arrives at Emmett Brown's Institute of Future Technology, but discovers, to his horror, that a clown-themed Krustyland amusement park now rests in its place. Confused, Frink journeys back in time two years in a time-traveling DeLorean to discover what has happened to his friend, Doc Brown [SIMP].

2010 A.D.

- Doc Brown, while testing his time-traveling DeLorean in 1985, choses this date, 25 years in the future, for his maiden voyage. This plan is halted, however, when Libyan nationalists gun him down for stealing their plutonium [BTF1].

    NOTE: Doc eventually made his planned voyage, but instead visited 2015.

Tuesday, October 19, 2010 A.D.

- As Marty McFly drives the DeLorean to the 2010 Spike TV Scream Awards, a female pedestrian asks where he's headed, and he offers her a ride to the ceremony [SCRT].

Tuesday, October 19, 2010 A.D.—9:00 PM

- After showboating in front of a crowd of Loverboy fans in 1985, a time-traveling DeLorean, piloted by a mysterious figure in a radiation suit, arrives in the year 2010, crashing onto the front stage of that year's Spike TV Scream Awards [SCRM].

    NOTE: The "mysterious driver" turned out to be comedian and actor David Spade, the event's host.

2011 A.D.

- Emmett and Clara Brown, back in 1986, plan a trip to visit Marty and Jennifer McFly during this year [TLTL-1].

    NOTE: The reason for the visit was unspecified.

PROFESSOR FRINK KILLS THE IFT'S FUNDING

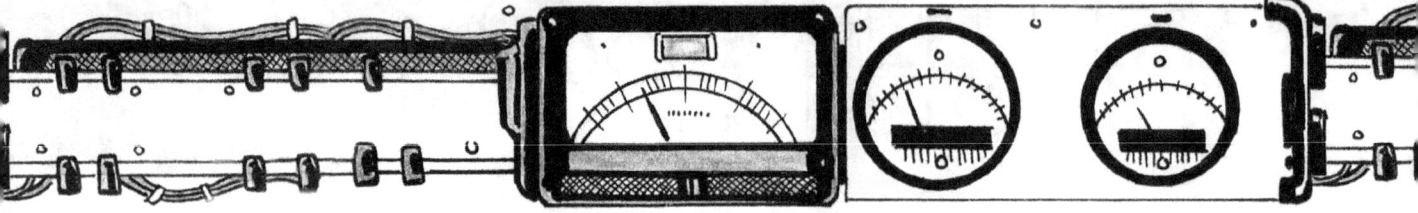

- After meeting the Queen of Apocrypha and Tannen the Barbarian in 2,991,299,129,912,991 A.D., Doc and Marty return to 1992 in the recently damaged *Jules Verne Train*, "bouncing" off a number of other years along the way, including 2011 A.D. [BFCL-3].

Thursday, January 13, 2011 A.D.—7:01 AM

- Emmett Brown arrives from March 23, 1983, and crashes into a Garbarino electronics store in Buenos Aires, Argentina, startling a young couple filming with a portable video device. Recovered footage from the amateur videographer shows Doc stumbling out of the store, surprised to find himself in the year 2011.

  Doc later holds a press conference for the Argentinean media, at which he answers questions about his time-traveling exploits, his dog Einstein, and whether he will immediately return to the past. The scientist informs the reporters that he might stay for a while and see some tango dancing [GARB].

May 25, 2011 A.D.

- One of Emmett Brown's DeLoreans—seemingly on auto-pilot—beckons with its headlights for a young skateboarder to hop in and take a ride. The temporal displacement has an adverse effect on the young man as he begins to see strange visions while driving, including jellyfish, cows and a *Tyrannosaurus rex*. Eventually, he stops for coffee at a gas station and envisions a deer walking the aisles, as well as a beautiful woman behind the counter. Still reeling with visions, he re-enters the DeLorean, punches in the coordinates for March 2015 and accelerates up to 88 miles per hour [CITY].

Sunday, July 17, 2011 A.D.—12:45 PM

- Two men in black suits and ties arrive on this date in a time-traveling DeLorean, after leaving from the year 2152. They immediately hit a Porsche head-on and are sent careening through the vehicle's windshield. As they

lay dying on the pavement, they ponder the futility of life and death [LIMO].

Friday, August 26, 2011 A.D.—2:59 AM

- Emmett Brown, now serving as Garbarino's new spokesperson, travels from this point in time to December 24 in a new time-machine sleigh he has invented for Santa Claus, to ensure that all presents will reach their intended recipients on time [GARB].

  NOTE: This would indicate that Santa Claus was an actual person in the Back to the Future *mythos.*

Tuesday, September 6, 2011 A.D.

- Garbarino hires Emmett Brown as the new face of its marketing campaign. This works out fine for Doc, as it provides him with access to numerous modern inventions—all of which he, at one time or another, failed to create himself [GARB].

Thursday, September 8, 2011 A.D.—10:04 PM

- While attempting to visit 2015 in order to purchase a pair of Nike shoes with power laces, Emmett Brown instead arrives in 2011. Visiting the Lone Pine Mall, he finds a shoe clerk presenting a brand new pair of light-up Nikes. These, however, do not yet have the power-lace function he seeks. Doc fears that his miscalculation could be the product of the time circuits malfunctioning, and promptly returns to his DeLorean to try again [NIKE].

Sunday, October 16, 2011 A.D.

- On Día de la Madre (Argentina's Mother's Day), Emmett Brown—still serving as the spokesperson for the Garbarino chain of Argentinean electronics stores—pays a special visit to his own mother, to thank her for always supporting him during his childhood. As a gift, Doc goes back into his own past and borrows a young version of

CODE	STORY						
ARGN	BTTF-themed TV commercial: Arrigoni	**BTF1**	Film: *Back to the Future*	**CITY**	*BTTF*-themed music video: Owl City, "Deer in the Headlights"	**HUEY**	*BTTF*-themed music video: Huey Lewis and the News, "The Power of Love"
BFAN	*Back to the Future: The Animated Series*	**BTF2**	Film: *Back to the Future Part II*	**DCTV**	*BTTF*-themed TV commercial: DirecTV	**LIMO**	*BTTF*-themed music video: The Limousines, "The Future"
BFCG	*Back to the Future: The Card Game*	**BTF3**	Film: *Back to the Future Part III*	**ERTH**	*The Earth Day Special*		
BFCL	*Back to the Future* comic book (limited series)	**BUDL**	*BTTF*-themed TV commercial: Bud Light	**GALE**	Interviews and commentaries: Bob Gale and/or Robert Zemeckis	**MCDN**	*BTTF*-themed TV commercial: McDonald's
BFCM	*Back to the Future* comic book (monthly series)	**CHEK**	*BTTF*-themed music video: O'Neal McKnight, "Check Your Coat"	**GARB**	*BTTF*-themed TV commercials: Garbarino	**MITS**	*BTTF*-themed TV commercial: Mitsubishi Lancer
BFHM	*BTTF*-themed McDonald's Happy Meal boxes	**CHIC**	Photographs hanging in Doc Brown's Chicken restaurant at Universal Studios	**GETV**	*BTTF*-themed TV commercial: GE	**MSFT**	*BTTF*-themed TV commercial: Microsoft
BTFA	*Back to the Future Annual* (Marvel Comics)						

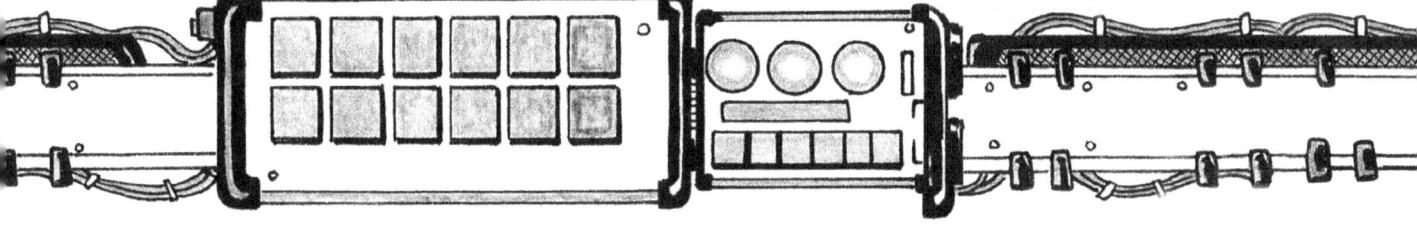

himself, then brings the child—and a complimentary bag of goodies from Garbarino—to visit his mother. The elder Doc is very moved by the temporal reunion [GARB].

> *NOTE: This strange episode in Doc's life opens a number of questions. His mother appeared to be a young woman, suggesting Doc visited her in the past. But, if that were the case, why would he bring a younger version of himself to a past version of his mother? There are also potential ramifications to such an action, including the fourth-dimensional shock that could result from a boy seeing his mother aged by several decades. Would this early journey through time lead to Doc pursuing time travel? And would he have pursued time travel if he had not already traveled through time? This entry assumes that Doc was celebrating Argentina's Mother's Day, since the video was made for an Argentinian brand. However, if he were celebrating the United States' observance of Mother's Day, the date would be May 8, 2011.*

Saturday, December 24, 2011 A.D.—11:30 PM

• As part of his duties as the spokesperson for Argentina's Garbarino's chain of electronics stores, Emmett Brown makes last-minute preparations on Christmas Eve before sending Santa Claus forward through time in a time-machine sleigh of Doc's invention [GARB].

Sunday, December 25, 2011 A.D.—12:00 AM

• Santa Claus arrives a half-hour in the future, thanks to Doc Brown's time-machine sleigh [GARB].

> *NOTE: It's unclear how traveling* forward *in time would have given Santa extra time to deliver the presents. The opposite would seem to be the case.*

February 2012 A.D.

• A time-traveling DeLorean arrives at an automotive garage for repairs. Four mechanics share Bud Light beers around the vehicle, speculating about what they would do if given the ability to travel through time. One man, Ali, boasts that he would invent fire—and then copyright it. Another, Kidus, says he would travel to the past and murder his own father. Suddenly, Kidus vanishes—erased from the timeline, the result of his pre-birth patricide. Shortly thereafter, the DeLorean disappears as well, and the three remaining workers quickly forget there was a fourth among them, or what they were even discussing moments prior [BUDL].

2013 A.D.

• In one possible timeline, George McFly passes away and bequeaths his writing fortune to Hill Valley Community Hospital. In this reality's March 1973, George had been critically injured in a car wreck nearby; were it not for the hospital's close proximity, he would have perished. Before dying, George requests that the sum of his riches be donated to the medical center for the construction of an emergency wing [BTF2-s1].

Thursday, September 5, 2013 A.D.—1:16 AM

• A flying DeLorean lands in the parking lot of the TransCanada building in Calgary, Alberta. Marty McFly steps out and replaces the vehicle's Mr. Fusion with a modern-day gas turbine from General Electric, capable of more easily generating 1.21 jigowatts. With the time machine now super-charged, Marty lifts off and jumps through time once more [GETV].

> *NOTE: Marty's face was not shown onscreen in this commercial, but the youth was wearing Marty's signature clothing from* **BTF1**.

GRIFF TANNEN'S GANG CRASHES THE COURTHOUSE MALL

CHAPTER XV

2015 A.D. AND BEYOND

Sometime Before 2015 A.D.

- Marlin Berry, a descendant of Chuck and Marvin Berry in one potential reality, is born [BFCG].

- Douglas J. Needles, Marty McFly's one-time high school rival, begins working at CusCo Industries, in charge of systems operations, under employer Ito T. Fujitsu. Marty also obtains a job at CusCo, and their old rivalry continues. Douglas marries a woman named Lauren Anne, and the couple raises two daughters, Roberta and Amy [BTF2].

- Darlene Needles, a relative of Douglas and Lauren Anne Needles in one possible reality, is born [BFCG].

- Clay Strickland, a descendant of Gerald Strickland, is born in one possible timeline [BFCG].

- Buffy Tannen, a descendant of Biff Tannen, is born in one possible timeline [BFCG].

- Clara Wilson, a descendant of Goldie Wilson, is born in one possible timeline [BFCG].

Sometime in or Before 2015 A.D.

- The Hill Valley Courthouse is converted into the Hill Valley Courthouse Mall. In addition, numerous businesses open in and around Courthouse Square, including 7-11/Compu-Vend; Blast From the Past; The Bot Shoppe; Bottoms Up; Cafe 80's; Flying High; Eclipse Contemporary & Traditional Lighting; Fusion Bar; GH; Hill Valley Gifts; the Hill Valley Museum of Art; the Hill Valley Surrogate Parenting Center; Hill Valley Transit; the Holomax Theater; Hyatas; Hydrators Unlimited; The Hydroponic Gardner; The Ice Cream Clone; Jet Burger; A Match Made on Earth; Mr. Perfect All-Natural Steroids; Pizza Go; Pizza Hut; Pontiac; Sal; Sight Sound & Mind; the Simulex Memory Center; Star;

Star Struck; State Farm; Tiny's; True Blues; Uniglobe Travel; Vid City; and World O' Transponders [BTF2, RIDE].

> *NOTE: It's unclear whether the Pontiac dealership, like prior automotive dealers, was owned by the Statler family. View the map on page 183 to see where each business was located.*

- Goldie Wilson Jr. follows in his father's footsteps by being elected the mayor of Hill Valley. His son, Goldie Wilson III, becomes a businessman instead of a politician, launching Wilson Conversion Systems, a company able to hover-convert any road car into a skyway flier for only $39,999.95 [BTF2].

- Marty and Jennifer McFly obtain a copy of *White Trash Cooking*, which they display in their kitchen [BTF2].

- An innovation called the vidphone, consisting of a large, wall-mounted screen enabling individuals to communicate over distances via video and audio, is introduced. Vidphones also double as a television capable of simultaneously showing multiple channels [BTF2-n].

> *NOTE: In essence, BTF2's writers accurately predicted not only wall-mounted large-screen televisions, but also voice-over-Internet-Protocol (VoIP) services, instant-messaging clients, and the integration of computers, phone service and television.*

- Vid Glasses, a type of headwear broadcasting up to two TV channels to a wearer's eyes, are invented. Similar headgear allows for phone service [BTF2].

> *NOTE: The glasses, unnamed in BTF2, were designated "Vid Glasses" on production sketches included on the film's Blu-ray release. In creating this device, the production team seemingly predicted Google Glass, a wearable, hands-free computer slated for commercial*

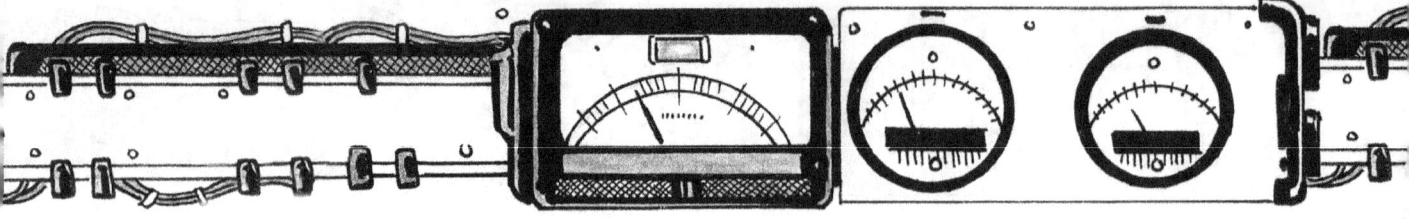

release in 2014, with an optical head-mounted display that provides information and can interact with the Internet via voice commands.

- US Air begins offering flights to Vietnam for surfers [BTF2].

- The uni-size form-fit patch is introduced, enabling clothing to be manufactured at large dimensions and then be shrunken or enlarged as necessary to fit a wearer [BTF2-n].

  NOTE: The Paradox screenplay used the term "un-size form fit" (a likely typo), which was corrected to the less nonsensical "uni-size form-fit" for BTF2's novelization.

- An innovation called ultra-thin paper enables books with thousands of pages to be printed at a manageable size [BTF2-s1].

- A mode of public transport called the Transrapid is developed, consisting of an escalator system able to carry pedestrians from one city to another [BTF2-s1].

- In the Biffhorrific timeline, Biff Tannen Jr. becomes a businessman like his powerful father, opening several franchises, including the Café 80's nostalgic restaurant [BTF2-s2].

- Suspended animation kennels become a popular business, enabling pet owners to leave their animals for extended periods of time [BTF2].

- An antigravity sport called slamball becomes popular, featuring players smacking each other with a ball while running around spherical courts, on walls and upside-down [BTF2-s2]. U.S. sportswear and equipment supplier Nike introduces a type of footwear known as grip-shoes, made specifically for slamball players [BTF2-s1, BTF2-s2].

NOTE: In an early-draft script for BTF2, Griff Tannen's gang chased Marty McFly into a slamball court, where Marty's Nike grip-shoes enabled him to run up curved walls and escape.

- Automotive businessman Earl Shieb IV begins advertising that he can hover-convert any vehicle for only $3,999 [BTF2-n].

  NOTE: Earl Scheib specialized in the repainting and collision repair of automobiles until his company's closing in 2010.

- The Scenery Channel, a scenescreen channel broadcasting beautiful outdoor views, 24 hours a day, is launched. The Scenery Channel creates the illusion of pleasant scenery outside a home's window, regardless of the surroundings [BTF2].

- The Privacy Act is passed, preventing anyone, including police officers, from using a citizen's thumb-activated identipad to access another individual's home without permission [BTF2-sx, BTF2-n].

- Emmett Brown invents the Ronco Aroma Amplifier, consisting of a funnel connected to an electronic box, and a hose running out the other side and attaching to a user's nose. The amplifier enables a wearer—such as Doc's dog, Einstein—to track a person based on scent [BTF2-s1].

  NOTE: Ronco, founded in 1964 by Ron Popeil, manufactures and sells a wide range of products, including kitchen devices. It's unknown whether Doc sold the device to the company.

- A device called a Portable Thumb Unit is introduced that identifies individuals, at the press of a thumb, for the purpose of automatic, electronic payments [BTF2-n].

- Pocket binoculars, a viewing device providing binocular vision when viewing distant objects, are invented. The

binoculars consist of a flat plastic card with two eyeholes [BTF2-n].

- An anti-gravity belt called an Ortho-lev, used to provide mobility to those with back injuries, is invented. The belt could be set to carry an individual either face-down or -up [BTF2].

- The creation of newsstand robots allows the automaton of kiosks selling newspapers and magazines. One such robot, in use in Hill Valley, is called Bernie [BTF2-s2].

- Several digital formats are introduced as an alternative to printed books, including Micro-C, Mini-C, ROM-Cart, ROM-D and Standard-C [BTF2-s1].

- McDonald's restaurants begin utilizing McWaiters, a tabletop touchpad menu for ordering, with pressure pads to scan a patron's thumbprint. Once an order is placed, a McWaiter delivers the food directly to that person's table [BTF2-s1].

- A wall-mounted food-preparation appliance called the Master-Cook is introduced for home use [BTF2].

- A professional runner named Marshall runs a three-minute mile [BTF2].
    NOTE: This event was reported in Doc's issue of USA Today.

- The Luxor Cab Co. begins using flying yellow taxis [BTF2].

- Hill Valley implements a series of mobile trash-collection robots known as Litter Bugs, which roam the streets providing a receptacle in which pedestrians can discard trash [BTF2, PIZA].

- Many houses are equipped with voice-activated home atmospheric controls, including a setting known as Lithium Mode [BTF2].
    NOTE: Lithium compounds are a standard treatment for bipolar disorder and related diagnoses, such as schizoaffective disorder and cyclic major depression. This may indicate that the Lithium Mode was used to calm an occupant's nerves.

- The P.K. Rata Recycling Center and other companies begin mass-recycling LaserDiscs, a now-obsolete home-video format popular in the 1980s and 1990s [BTF2].

- The Kirk Gibson Jr. Slugger 2000, an adjustable, red baseball bat, is released, and becomes a weapon of choice of thug Griff Tannen [BTF2].
    NOTE: Kirk Gibson was an outfielder for several Major League Baseball teams in the late 20th century. His son's name is Kirk Jr.

- Marty and Jennifer McFly compile a three-volume set of videobooks in their home, titled *The Kids: Marty Junior and Marlene, Vol. 1-3* [BTF2-sx, BTF2-n].

- A type of bookstore known as an infostore becomes popular, and one such store opens in Hill Valley, known as The Library. Unlike 20th-century book sellers, infostores display only covers, with computer terminals behind them [BTF2-s1].

- A professional football league called the IFL is established. Teams in this league include the Spacers and the Bears [BTF2-n].

- The Hill Valley International Vector Port, a mass-transit skyport serving Hill Valley and the surrounding area, is established [BTF2].

- Hilldale Waste Recylcing Station H 14 D is erected outside the entrance to Hill Valley's Hilldale housing development [BTF2].

NIKE	BTTF-themed TV commercial: Nike	**SCRT**	2010 Scream Awards: *Back to the Future*	**SUFFIX**	**MEDIUM**	**-s1**	Screenplay (draft one)
NTND	Nintendo *Back to the Future—The Ride* Mini-Game		25th Anniversary Reunion (trailer)	**-b**	*BTF2*'s Biff Tannen Museum video (extended version)	**-s2**	Screenplay (draft two)
		SIMP	Simulator: *The Simpsons Ride*			**-s3**	Screenplay (draft three)
PIZA	BTTF-themed TV commercial: Pizza Hut	**SLOT**	*Back to the Future* Video Slots	**-c**	Animated series credit sequence	**-s4**	Screenplay (draft four)
REAL	Real life	**TEST**	Screen tests: Crispin Glover, Lea Thompson	**-d**	Film deleted scene	**-sp**	Screenplay (production draft)
RIDE	Simulator: *Back to the Future—The Ride*		and Thomas F. Wilson	**-n**	Film novelization	**-sx**	Screenplay (*Paradox*)
SCRM	2010 Scream Awards: *Back to the Future*	**TLTL**	Telltale Games' *Back to the Future—The Game*	**-o**	Film outtake		
	25th Anniversary Reunion (broadcast)	**UNIV**	Universal Studios Hollywood promotional video	**-v**	Video game print materials or commentaries		

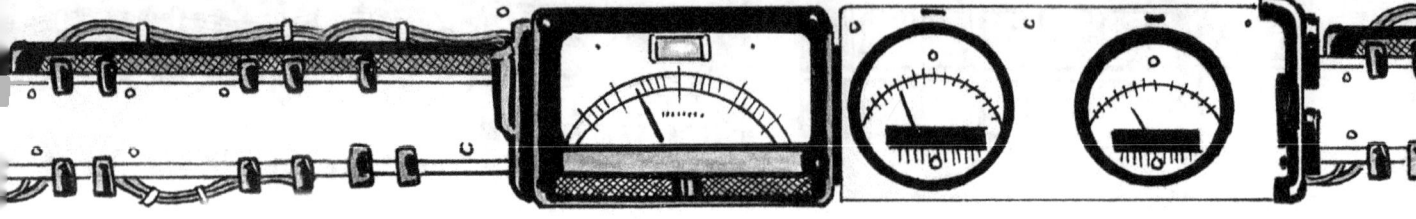

- Goldie Wilson, Hill Valley's former mayor, founds a company called Goldie Wilson, Inc., and rents billboard advertising space outside the store Blast From the Past [RIDE].

- The Garden Center, a floating fruit basket for home kitchen use, is introduced. Calling out "Fruit" or "Hey, fruit" summons the Garden Center to descend from the ceiling, offering a variety of fresh fruit items, while the command "Retract" causes the device to ascend out of sight [BTF2].

- Fusion Industries introduces its Mr. Fusion Home Energy Reactor [BTF2].

- Police officers Reese and Foley are assigned as partners in Unit N11-11. The two women rarely agree about anything, partly due to Reese's fanaticism regarding rules and regulations, and her belief that everything must be done entirely by the book, which Foley finds annoying. Foley, a rookie cop, often empathizes with those in poorer areas like Hilldale, and thinks Reese has lost her humanity after years spent on the job [BTF2-n].

- BMW releases a model of flying convertible car known as the 633CSI. Griff Tannen purchases one such vehicle [BTF2].

- Texaco's Hill Valley gas station begins offering aerodynamic kits as a service for flying vehicles. The station also provides adjustments to mag-levs—a transportation system utilizing magnetic levitation to suspend, guide and propel vehicles a few inches above a guideway surface—as well as robotic automotive fueling, with such fuel types as regular unleaded gasoline, Fusion Gold, Super X-Tra Fusion Plus, Liquid Nitrogen and Super Unleaded Plus [BTF2].

- Traditional vehicle license plates are replaced with bar-coded versions [BTF2].

- The Skyway system is created, providing a highway of hover lanes for flying vehicles [BTF2].

- An innovation known as the accu-lock is introduced, allowing drivers to tail other vehicles without letting those drivers known they are being followed [BTF2-s1].

- Several models of Freeway Flyer automobiles, hover-converted from classic cars, come into popular use, including the Six-Wheel Van, the '89 Mustang Converter, the '89 Firebird Converter and a type of pick-up truck [BTF2]. A flying version of the Ford Edsel is also released [BTF2-n].

  NOTE: The Freeway Flyers appeared in production materials included on BTF2's Blu-ray release.

- Douglas J. Needles, his wife Lauren Anne and their daughters, Amy and Roberta, move to 88 Oriole Road, A6TB-94 [BTF2].

- Rejuvenation clinics become popular, at which customers can restore their lost youth. One service offered at such clinics is an All-Natural Overhaul, consisting of skin-wrinkle removal, hair repair, blood changing, and the replacement of a person's spleen and colon, thereby adding 30 or 40 years to his or her life [BTF2].

- The Art Channel is introduced. The television broadcasts ever-changing images of famous paintings, serving as part of a home's décor [BTF2-sx, BTF2-n].

- American multinational telecommunications corporation AT&T, still operating telephone booths in Hill Valley, begins providing thumbprint ID systems for home security [BTF2].

  NOTE: In the real world, phone booths became largely obsolete by the early 21st century, thanks to the advent of mobile phone services.

CODE	STORY						
ARGN	BTTF-themed TV commercial: Arrigoni	BTF1	Film: *Back to the Future*	CITY	BTTF-themed music video: Owl City, "Deer in the Headlights"	HUEY	BTTF-themed music video: Huey Lewis and the News, "The Power of Love"
BFAN	*Back to the Future: The Animated Series*	BTF2	Film: *Back to the Future Part II*			LIMO	BTTF-themed music video:
BFCG	*Back to the Future: The Card Game*	BTF3	Film: *Back to the Future Part III*	DCTV	BTTF-themed TV commercial: DirecTV		The Limousines, "The Future"
BFCL	*Back to the Future* comic book (limited series)	BUDL	BTTF-themed TV commercial: Bud Light	ERTH	*The Earth Day Special*	MCDN	BTTF-themed TV commercial: McDonald's
BFCM	*Back to the Future* comic book (monthly series)	CHEK	BTTF-themed music video: O'Neal McKnight, "Check Your Coat"	GALE	Interviews and commentaries: Bob Gale and/or Robert Zemeckis	MITS	BTTF-themed TV commercial:
BFHM	BTTF-themed McDonald's Happy Meal boxes	CHIC	Photographs hanging in Doc Brown's	GARB	BTTF-themed TV commercials: Garbarino		Mitsubishi Lancer
BTFA	*Back to the Future Annual* (Marvel Comics)		Chicken restaurant at Universal Studios	GETV	BTTF-themed TV commercial: GE	MSFT	BTTF-themed TV commercial: Microsoft

- Hoverboards, a type of antigravity-based, wheel-less skateboards, become very popular among American youths. Styles of hoverboard include the Pit Bull, Rising Sun and No Tech models, as well as a bright-pink version for children. Manufacturers of such boards include Mattel [BTF2] and Attel [TLTL-5].

  Other innovations are also created incorporating hover technology, including hovercars and hover buses [BTF2], floating cameras known as hovercams [RIDE], levitating catering dollies called hovercarts [BTF2-s1], traveling briefcases known as hovercases [BFAN-20] and two-wheeled flying vehicles dubbed hovercycles [BTF2-d].

- The Auto-Chef, a type of robotic food-preparation device, is introduced. The ceiling-mounted appliance features the face of a rotund, smiling chef, as well as numerous attachments for automatically preparing a variety of meals—for example, a hotdog [BTF2].

  NOTE: This device appeared in sketches from early in BTF2's production.

- A model of hovering robot photojournalist is introduced, known as an automated droid fax-cam photographer, and is used by newspapers such as *USA Today* [BTF2-sx].

- Black & Decker markets its Hydrator, a device able to rehydrate pizza and other foods in mere seconds [BTF2].

- The term "bojo" becomes a popular insult, analogous to "idiot" [BTF2]. Other slang from this era includes "crag" (ass), "kirgo" (crazy), "numped" (beaten), "tranked" (tranquilized, as from narcotics), "lobo" (drug addict), "dead file" (dead duck) and ziphead (another term for drug addict) [BTF2, BTF2-sx, BTF2-n].

- Lawyers are abolished from the United States' legal system. Unfettered by the distractions of lawyers, the country institutes data-fax courts, in which defendants can be tried and convicted in an extremely short span of time [BTF2].

- Clothing manufacturers offer jackets with a Drying Mode, enabling wet clothing to dry itself in seconds by means of high-powered blasts of hot air, produced by fans hidden inside the garments [BTF2].

- Dust-repellant paper is invented, allowing books to remain free of the ravages of dust, thereby eliminating the need for paper dust jackets [BTF2].

- A home-security system called an Entry Identi-Pad is introduced, requiring a home's occupant to provide a thumbprint prior to admittance [BTF2].

- Express trams become a common mode of public transportation across both the Mid-Valley region and downtown Hill Valley [BTF2].

- The U.S. Postal Service launches its Facfax service, providing mailboxes able to fax a letter in half a second [BTF2].

- Ito. T. Fujitsu, Marty McFly's supervisor at CusCo Industries, marries a woman named Siva. The couple produces no children [BTF2].

- An automatic dog-walker is invented, consisting of a hovering, computerized dog collar, enabling a family to send their dog for a walk unaccompanied [BTF2-n].

2015 A.D.

- Two fun-loving teenagers, having stolen Doc Brown's DeLorean from the McFlys' home driveway in 1989, arrive in the year 2015. Upon arrival, the boys experience a craving for pizza. They drive to Domino's Pizza, only to discover that the Hill Valley branch has become Domino's Hardware. Discouraged, they ask a policewoman to direct them to a good pizza place, and she points them in the direction of Pizza Hut [PIZA].

  NOTE: Presumably, the two car thieves made their way back to 1989 after enjoying their slices.

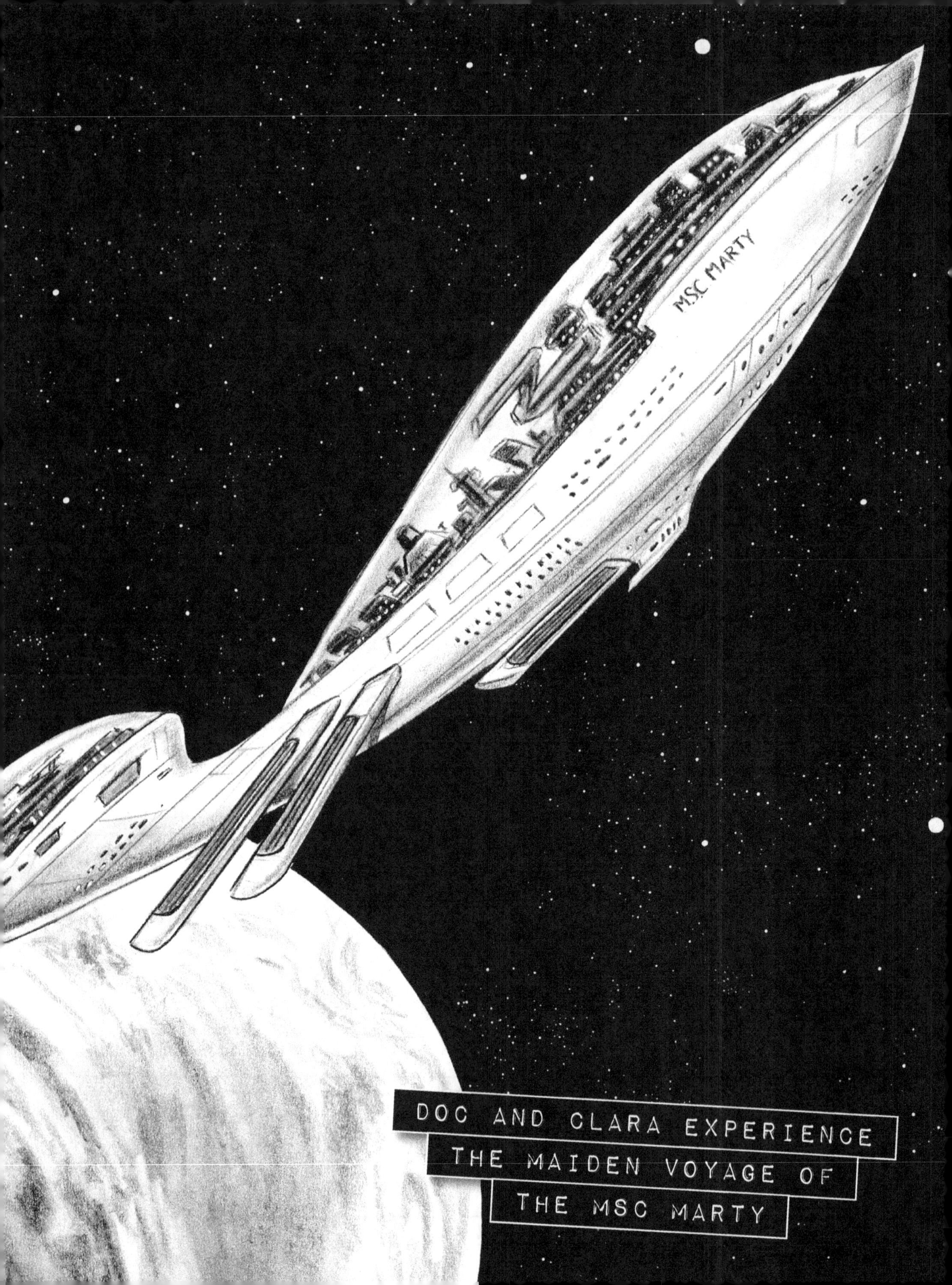

DOC AND CLARA EXPERIENCE
THE MAIDEN VOYAGE OF
THE MSC MARTY

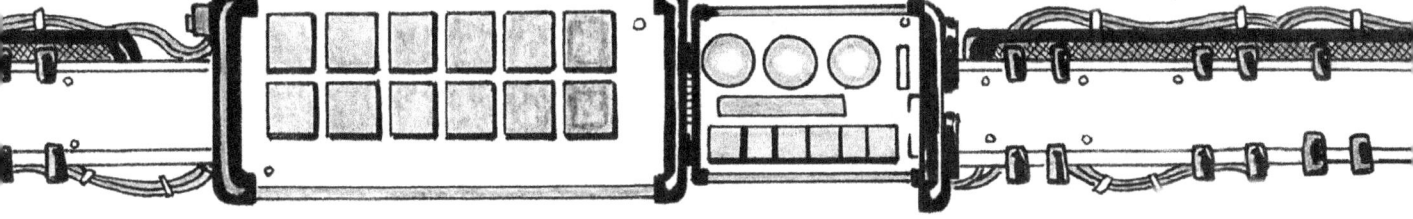

• The New York Yankees baseball team experiences a bad season, which the team's manager attributes to a bad start and inclement weather [BTF2].

• U.S. sportswear and equipment supplier Nike introduces Magnetic Anti Gravity (MAG) Sneakers, a style of self-lacing, LED-electroluminescent high-top footwear [BTF2].

• Hill Valley's local government issues Propositions 237 and 241, both of which are hotly debated by the town's citizens. The first pertains to the legalization of bionics, while the second proposes laws that some see as an invasion of privacy. In the meantime, a professional sports pitcher is suspended for using an uncalibrated bionic arm [BTF2].

• The Toronto Blue Jays baseball team fires its manager [BTF2].

• The Bears, a professional football team in a league known as the IFL, have their best season in 30 years, proving to the rest of the league that they are not the has-beens some have dubbed them [BTF2-n].
    NOTE: The Chicago Bears won Super Bowl XX in 1986.

• The Hill Valley Museum of Art offers an exhibit called "A Bellman Retrospective" [BTF2].

• The Bottoms Up plastic-surgery franchise advertises that its board-certified implant surgeons can provide a number of products, including the Super Inflatable "Tit" and Headlight "Tit" [BTF2].

• Scientists begin researching cholesterol as a possible cure for cancer [BTF2].

Monday, March 30, 2015 A.D.—12:00 AM

• A young skateboarder, after being picked up by a time-traveling DeLorean running on autopilot, takes a vision quest through the timestream. He eventually lands in 2015, where he almost runs over a spacesuited pedestrian. Both driver and pedestrian are unharmed [CITY].
    NOTE: It is unknown why the DeLorean approached this young man of its own accord,

or how it ultimately returned to Doc Brown's possession.

Tuesday, May 19, 2015 A.D.

• Time traveler Marty McFly finds himself the target of Griff Tannen and his gang of juvenile delinquents. Marty leads his pursuers in a hoverboard chase through the skylanes of Hill Valley. During the excitement, Griff leaves destruction of public property in his wake and, after losing control of his hoverboard, crashes into the Hill Valley sign. Marty loses the gang, and is intercepted by Emmett Brown, who has come back in time to collect him for dinner in 1991 [BFAN-c].
    NOTE: From Marty's perspective, this chase occured after he'd already run afoul of Griff Tannen in* Back to the Future II. *But for Griff, this was their first chronological encounter. While no context was provided for this scuffle in the cartoon's opening credits, Tannen likely believed he was chasing Marty's son, Martin McFly, Jr.

Wednesday, July 15, 2015 A.D.—12:03 AM

• In an effort to teach Microsoft senior vice-president Robert L. Muglia a lesson about what could happen in the future if his company follows through on its ill-conceived programming, Emmett Brown uses the voice-activated time circuits of his DeLorean to bring Muglia to an alternate 2015. There, the businessman finds himself in all-white digital space, where he is greeted by two Microsoft icons that were defunct in his timeline. Seeing that these programs continue to exist—and have achieved some level of artificial intelligence—Muglia reacts in terror. Doc quickly takes him back to 2007, so that he can properly adjust his keynote address at Tech-Ed 2007 and thus avoid this horrifying future [MSFT].

Sometime in or Before October 2015 A.D.

• *Jane's Book of Sunk Ships* releases a set of statistics regarding ships sunk by whales [BTF2].

• *Jaws 19*, a 3-D sequel to *Jaws*, is released in movie theaters, directed by Max Spielberg and produced by Ark Kline, Larry Hubbs and Paul Sonskoid. Its tagline: "This time it's really, really personal" [BTF2].

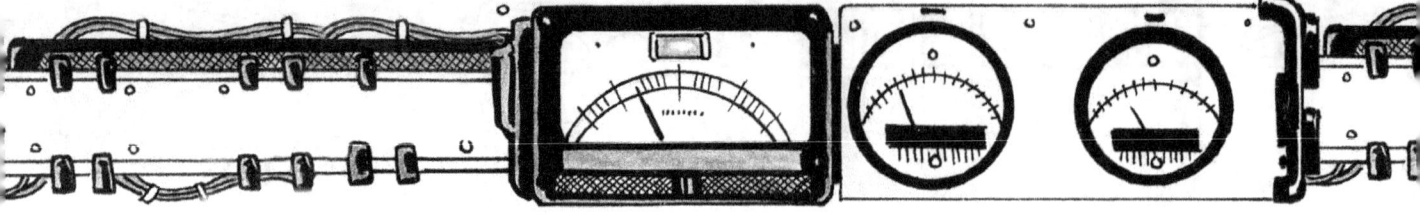

NOTE: *The slogan to this fictional movie was an in-joke homage to the tagline for* Jaws IV: The Revenge: *"This time, it's personal." The director (referring to* Jaws *director Steven Spielberg's son) was identified on a marquee at the Holomax Theater, while the producers' names appeared on a fake poster for the movie.*

October 2015 A.D.

• A group of outlaws known as thumb bandits go on strike following an amputation [BTF2].

    NOTE: *This strike was mentioned in a USA Today newspaper. The details of this strike, as well as the nature of the so-called thumb bandits, are unknown.*

• The annual slamball playoffs are held in Denver, Colorado [BTF2].

• Pollution in the South Pacific causes an increase in the price of kelp [BTF2].

• The Chicago Cubs win the World Series in five games against a Florida-based team [BTF2] known as the Miami Gators [GALE].

    NOTE: *When* BTF2 *was released in 1989, there was no Major League Baseball team in Florida. In 1993, however, the Florida Marlins—later renamed the Miami Marlins—were formed.*

• Britain's Queen Diana visits the United States [BTF2].

    NOTE: *This likely referred to Lady Diana Spencer, who, at the time of* BTF2*'s release, was the Princess of Wales and England's future queen consort. In the real world, Diana divorced Prince Charles Mountbatten-Windsor in 1996 and died the year after—events that the filmmakers could not have predicted—negating her ascension to the title.*

• Swiss terrorists become a dangerous threat to world peace [BTF2].

    NOTE: *The Swiss Confederation has a long history of armed neutrality, has not been in a state of war internationally since 1815 and is frequently involved in peace-building processes.*

Wednesday, October 7, 2015 A.D.

• In one possible timeline, Lorraine Baines McFly is among presenters at a dedication ceremony at Hill Valley Community Hospital's new George F. McFly Memorial Wing, named in honor of her late husband, a local author and humanitarian [BTF2-s1].

Wednesday, October 21, 2015 A.D.—4:29 PM

• Emmett Brown arrives from the year 1985, bringing Marty McFly and Jennifer Parker thirty years into the future to save their children, Marty Jr. and Marlene [BTF2].

    NOTE: *In the second film's first-draft screenplay, titled* Number Two, *the three time travelers were transported to October 7, 2015, at 3:30 PM.*

• The voice of air-traffic control issues forth from the DeLorean's dashboard, chastising Doc for making an unauthorized entry into commercial transport airspace. Doc bluffs that their transponder is on the fritz, and that they are descending into Hill Valley for repairs [BTF2-n]. This convinces Jennifer that she's been transported to the future, but when she asks too many questions about her life with Marty, Doc uses a sleep-inducing alpha rhythm generator to knock her unconscious until their mission is complete [BTF2].

    NOTE: *This played out much differently in the original script draft of* BTF2, *in which Doc did not put Jennifer to sleep. In that version, she remained an active part of Marty's 2015 adventure.*

CODE	STORY
ARGN	BTTF-themed TV commercial: Arrigoni
BFAN	Back to the Future: The Animated Series
BFCG	Back to the Future: The Card Game
BFCL	Back to the Future comic book (limited series)
BFCM	Back to the Future comic book (monthly series)
BFHM	BTTF-themed McDonald's Happy Meal boxes
BTFA	Back to the Future Annual (Marvel Comics)

BTF1	Film: Back to the Future
BTF2	Film: Back to the Future Part II
BTF3	Film: Back to the Future Part III
BUDL	BTTF-themed TV commercial: Bud Light
CHEK	BTTF-themed music video: O'Neal McKnight, "Check Your Coat"
CHIC	Photographs hanging in Doc Brown's Chicken restaurant at Universal Studios

CITY	BTTF-themed music video: Owl City, "Deer in the Headlights"
DCTV	BTTF-themed TV commercial: DirecTV
ERTH	The Earth Day Special
GALE	Interviews and commentaries: Bob Gale and/or Robert Zemeckis
GARB	BTTF-themed TV commercials: Garbarino
GETV	BTTF-themed TV commercial: GE

HUEY	BTTF-themed music video: Huey Lewis and the News, "The Power of Love"
LIMO	BTTF-themed music video: The Limousines, "The Future"
MCDN	BTTF-themed TV commercial: McDonald's
MITS	BTTF-themed TV commercial: Mitsubishi Lancer
MSFT	BTTF-themed TV commercial: Microsoft

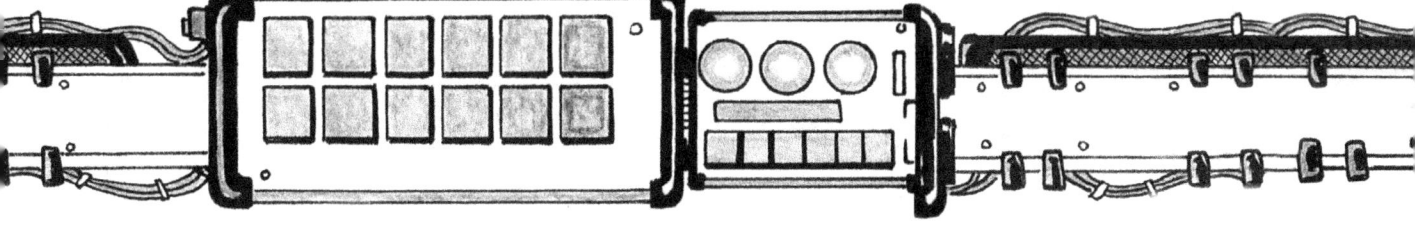

- Martin McFly Jr. becomes the victim of peer pressure from a bionic-enhancd goon named Griff Tannen, to help Griff and his gang—Rafe "Data" Unger, Leslie "Spike" O'Malley and Chester "Whitey" Nogura—rob the Hill Valley Payroll Substation. Nervous about breaking the law, Marty Jr. does not give an answer right away [BTF2].

- Hoping to prevent Marty Jr. from going to prison for helping Griff, Doc touches the DeLorean down in a back alley and prepares Marty for the task ahead. They hide Jennifer's sleeping form in the alley, and Doc dresses Marty in the typical teenage attire of 2015 so that he can impersonate his son. Doc reveals the reason for this charade, showing Marty the following day's *USA Today* issue depicting Marty Jr.'s arrest, which Doc says will ultimately drag the entire McFly family into turmoil. Marty must thus pose as his son, stand in for him at the crucial moment and refuse Griff's "job opportunity." Doc leaves Marty with instructions to rendezvous with Griff at the Café 80's and "just say no." Meanwhile, the scientist takes the DeLorean to intercept Marty Jr., putting him to sleep with the alpha rhythm generator to prevent him from interfering with their plan.

    Marty enters the Café 80's, where he encounters Biff Tannen, now a shriveled-up curmudgeon. Biff mistakes Marty Sr. for his son, and taunts him by telling him how his father (Marty) threw away his life—an inclination that Marty's future is not as bright as he'd imagined it would be. Before he can glean additional details, Biff's grandson Griff arrives. Griff drags Biff outside to reprimand him for not finishing the wax job on the teenager's cruiser [BTF2].

- While awaiting Griff's return, Marty overhears three teenage girls watching Huey Lewis and the News' video for "The Power of Love" on overhead monitors. To his dismay, they trash the music of the 1980s, relieved that they didn't have to grow up in that era [BTF2-n]. Feeling old and out-of-place, Marty demonstrates to two future children his skills at the 1980s arcade game *Wild*

Gunman—to no fanfare, as they consider it a "baby's game" since players must use their hands.

    While Marty's back is turned, his son wanders into the diner, having awakened too soon due to the sleep-inducer's charge being used up on Jennifer. Marty ducks behind the counter before his son can see him, and cringes as he hears Griff's gang bullying the fearful youth into joining their heist. When Marty Jr. resists the crime, Griff tosses him over the counter [BTF2].

Wednesday, October 21, 2015 A.D.—4:42 PM

- In one possible timeline, Marty McFly Jr. agrees to help Griff's gang rob the Payroll Substation [BFCG].

- To prevent this from occurring, Marty Sr. stands in for his dazed son. Rising un-intimidated from behind the counter, he refuses Griff's offer and prepares to walk away. However, when Griff accuses Marty of being a "chicken," the teen loses his cool. His manhood in question, Marty steps up to Griff, but soon realizes he's bitten off more than he can chew as the imposing cyborg increases his height by several inches. Utilizing a misdirect that worked on Griff's grandfather in the 1950s, Marty evades the hooligans and hurries out into the street [BTF2].

Wednesday, October 21, 2015 A.D.—4:48 PM

- In the timeline in which Marty McFly Jr. went along with the heist, the teen is arrested for theft and sentenced to fifteen years in prison [BFCG].

- Griff chases Marty Sr. through town. Marty snags a young girl's bright pink hoverboard and eludes his pursuers, leading them on a destructive rampage around Courthouse Square—and ending when Griff and his cohorts accidently crash into the Hill Valley Courthouse Mall. Marty escapes unharmed, watching from afar as the gang is arrested [BTF2].

NIKE	*BTTF*-themed TV commercial: Nike	SCRT	2010 Scream Awards: *Back to the Future*	SUFFIX MEDIUM		-s1	Screenplay (draft one)
NTND	Nintendo *Back to the Future—The Ride*		25th Anniversary Reunion (trailer)	-b	*BTF2's* Biff Tannen Museum video	-s2	Screenplay (draft two)
	Mini-Game	SIMP	Simulator: *The Simpsons Ride*		(extended version)	-s3	Screenplay (draft three)
PIZA	*BTTF*-themed TV commercial: Pizza Hut	SLOT	*Back to the Future* Video Slots	-c	Animated series credit sequence	-s4	Screenplay (draft four)
REAL	Real life	TEST	Screen tests: Crispin Glover, Lea Thompson	-d	Film deleted scene	-sp	Screenplay (production draft)
RIDE	Simulator: *Back to the Future—The Ride*		and Thomas F. Wilson	-n	Film novelization	-sx	Screenplay (*Paradox*)
SCRM	2010 Scream Awards: *Back to the Future*	TLTL	Telltale Games' *Back to the Future—The Game*	-o	Film outtake		
	25th Anniversary Reunion (broadcast)	UNIV	Universal Studios Hollywood promotional video	-v	Video game print materials or commentaries		

Back in Time: The Unauthorized Back to the Future Chronology

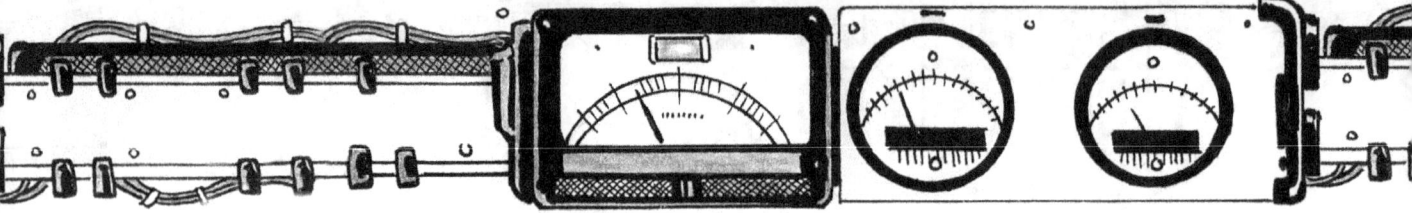

• With his mission accomplished, Marty enjoys some downtime and engages in small talk with an old-timer named Terry. While discussing sports, the old man (whom Marty had seen as a young mechanic back in 1955) mentions that he wishes he could go back in time and place a bet on the winner of the World Series—the Chicago Cubs, considered an underdog. Struck by the idea, Marty ventures into Blast From the Past, an 1980s-era antique shop, and purchases *Grays Sports Almanac: Complete Sports Statistics 1950-2000,* intending to take the book back with him to 1985 and use it to make a fortune at gambling [BTF2].

> *NOTE: In the first draft of BTF2's screenplay, the almanac's original dates were 1964 to 2014, consistent with the original premise of Marty visiting his parents in the 1960s.*

• Doc reunites with his young friend and witnesses the chase's aftermath. They retrieve the *USA Today* heralding the arrest of Marty's son, confirming that the future has now been changed. Marty Jr. remains innocent of any wrongdoing, while Griff is placed behind bars. With the future of the McFly family saved, Doc prepares to return Marty and Jennifer back to 1985, but discovers the *Grays Sports Almanac* in Marty's possession. The scientist chastises the teen for considering using such an important scientific breakthrough as time travel to further his own gain, and dumps the almanac into a nearby trash receptacle [BTF2].

> *NOTE: In the first draft of BTF2's screenplay, these events played out quite differently. Originally, Doc never informed Marty of his children's fate or tasked him with changing their destinies. In fact, as soon as they touched down in 2015, Doc, having not anticipated Jennifer coming along for the ride, immediately left to procure futuristic apparel for the young woman, before explaining why they were there. Unsupervised, the young lovers walked about Hill Valley, during which Marty fixated on the sports almanac, with Jen arguing that buying it would*

be a bad idea. In this version, Marty and Jennifer did see their son—named Norman—but did not intervene when Griff bullied the nerdy boy. What's more, Griff's gang mentioned that Marty had to borrow money from his daughter—here named Doris. His pride hurt, Marty purchased the almanac believing that if he were rich, he'd improve their lives and not raise a wimpy son.

• Two police officers, Reese and Foley, find Jennifer's unconscious form, mistake her for her older self from 2015, and bring to her home at 3793 Oakhurst Street, in Hilldale, assuming her to be intoxicated [BTF2-n]. Determined to retrieve the younger Jennifer before she can meet her future self and possibly create a galaxy-unraveling paradox, Doc and Marty return to the DeLorean and follow the cops [BTF2].

> *NOTE: In BTF2's novelization and early screenplay drafts, Doc noted that if Jennifer were to pass out from shock, she might accidentally bump her head and die. Were that to happen, she and Marty would never get married, Doc would never see their children in danger, he'd never come back to retrieve the couple, and Jen would never be killed by the shock of seeing her future self—a classic paradox.*

• Unbeknownst to them, Biff Tannen, standing nearby, overhears their discussion of the time-traveling DeLorean and the sports almanac. Biff grabs the discarded book and sets out to steal Doc's car so he can carry out Marty's plan for his own benefit [BTF2]. Hailing a flying taxi driven by a man named Fred—who travels with his pet parrot, Priscilla—Biff follows the DeLorean, waiting for an opportunity to make his move [BTF2-n].

**Wednesday, October 21, 2015 A.D.—
Approximately 7:00 PM**

• Officers Foley and Reese bring Jennifer to her home in Hilldale, where she recovers from Doc Brown's sleep-

---

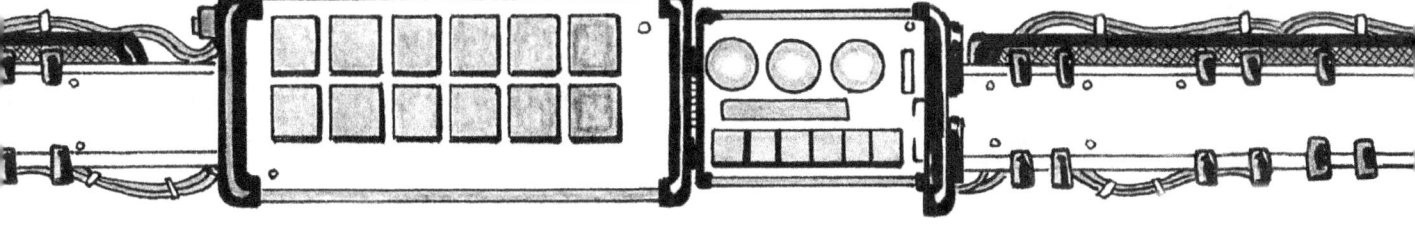

inducing alpha rhythm generator. The police help her inside and bid her a good evening, leaving Jen to come to grips with her bizarre situation. A quick look around the living room reveals that Jennifer's "dream wedding" to Marty was instead a simple ceremony at the Chapel O' Love. She soon realizes she's not alone in the house and hides inside a closet, barely avoiding being seen by her own future teenage daughter, Marlene [BTF2].

> *NOTE: In the original screenplay draft of* **BTF2,** *Marlene was named Doris, and was described as being obese, with a bad complexion. In that script, Jennifer visited her Hilldale home of her own accord, and was dismayed by her daughter's appearance. Meanwhile, Marty reunited with his own brother and sister—now in their early fifties—who mistook him for Marty's son and brought him to Hill Valley Community Hospital, where his mother, Lorraine McFly, was dedicating a new emergency wing in honor of her late husband, George McFly. Marty was confronted by Griff's gang at the ceremony, and used the hover-converted undercarriage of a food tray to surf away to safety.*

• George and Lorraine McFly, now senior citizens, arrive for dinner. George hangs upside down in an Ortho-lev harness, his back injured from a flying car falling from the sky and striking him on the golf course. Marty Jr. soon arrives, followed by Marty Sr.—now a 47-year-old corporate sellout.

Eavesdropping on her future family, Jennifer learns that Marty, having been called a "chicken," injured his hand in a car accident and had to give up his dreams of a musical career. Marty now shows signs of depression, and even Lorraine wonders if Jen only married him because she felt sorry for him. The phone rings, and Jennifer watches helplessly as Douglas J. Needles—a co-worker at CusCo Industries, and an old rival from high school—pressures Marty into taking part in an illegal business deal by calling him "chicken." Angrily, Marty throws his lot in with Needles, authorizing a financial transaction via thumbprint [BTF2].

Wednesday, October 21, 2015 A.D.—7:18 PM

• Mere moments later, however, Marty learns that Needles was entrapping him in order to get him fired by their boss, Ito T. Fujitsu. Marty loses his job via a fax proclaiming "YOU'RE FIRED" (which Jennifer pockets), utterly ruining his life [BTF2, BFCG].

> *NOTE: In the first draft of* **BTF2**'s *screenplay, Jennifer discovered even more disconcerting news—she and Marty were heading toward divorce. Her daughter, Doris, was a junk-food addict, while Marty worked as a valet attendant and older Jen was a security guard. In that version, Marty was unwilling to work and couldn't hold down a job for six months, instead chasing after get-rich-quick schemes and the lottery, bringing the family further and further into debt.*

• In a possible timeline in which Marty McFly is a successful musician, a greatest-hits album by Marty and the Pinheads, titled *Fired Up*, goes platinum and tops the charts [BFCG].

Wednesday, October 21, 2015 A.D.—After 7:18 PM

• After being stuck in traffic, Doc and Marty finally arrive at Hilldale. Fearing a paradox, Doc orders Marty to stay with the DeLorean while he discreetly retrieves Jennifer from the McFly home. Marty, however, can't help but wander down the street to get a peek at his future. While he's distracted, Biff Tannen arrives in a taxi and quietly steals the time machine, going back to 1955 to give his younger self the *Grays Sports Almanac*.

Doc finds Jennifer, but not before she encounters her older self. In shock, both Jennifers promptly pass out. Doc drags the unconscious teen back to Marty, just

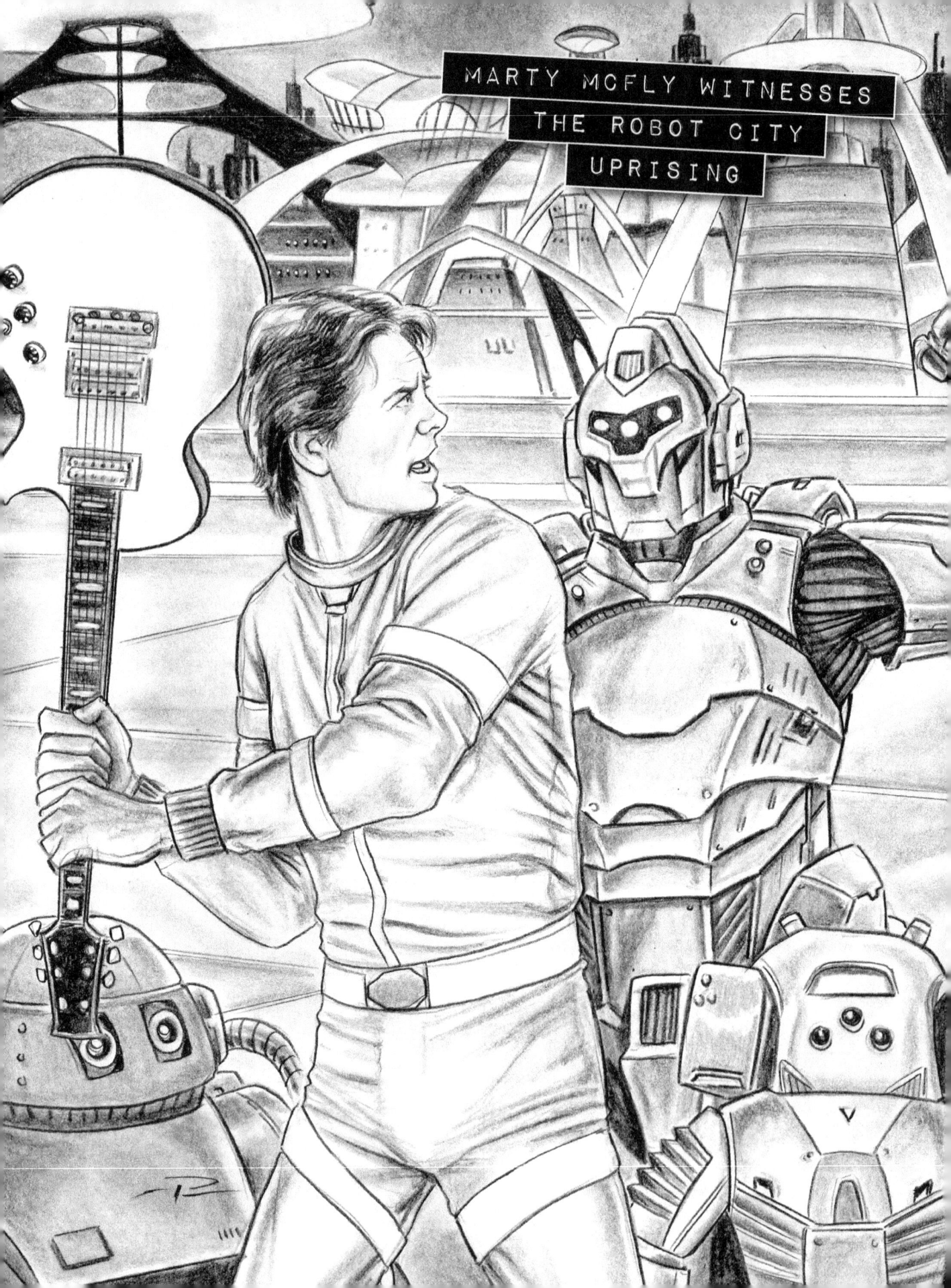

MARTY MCFLY WITNESSES THE ROBOT CITY UPRISING

as Biff returns with the DeLorean and hobbles away in pain. Oblivious to what Tannen has done, Marty helps Doc put Jen into the car, and the trio return to 1985 [BTF2]. Meanwhile, middle-aged Marty and his children discover the older Jennifer passed out in the living room and chalk it up to her having "tranked" herself again [BTF2-d].

> **NOTE: This may indicate that the future Jennifer had a substance-abuse problem.**

- Due to his temporal tampering, Biff has inadvertently erased himself from existence. He spends his last moments in great pain before simply vanishing from the space-time continuum [BTF2-d, GALE].

> **NOTE: An interview with Back to the Future scribe Bob Gale explained that this was due to Lorraine, in the Biffhorrific timeline, becoming fed up with Biff and shooting him in the 1990s, thereby negating his continued existence in 2015.**

Wednesday, October 21, 2015 A.D.

- Emmett Brown visits 2015 from the year 1991, searching for teenage Biff Tannen, who has stowed aboard a time-traveling DeLorean and come to the 21st century, and is now loose at Doc's Institute of Future Technology. Fearing what damage Biff could cause by running loose in the timestream, Doc searches for the delinquent. Utilizing a hovercam, Doc relays a message to 1991 via a sub-ether transmission, contacting a group of so-called "time-travel volunteers" to test out his Eight-Passenger DeLorean Time-Travel Vehicle on its maiden voyage. He informs the volunteers that he will return shortly, urging them to keep their eyes peeled for any sign of Tannen [RIDE].

Thursday, October 22, 2015 A.D.

- The front page of the Hill Valley edition of *USA Today* reads, "Youth Jailed—Martin McFly Junior Arrested for Theft," with a side article titled, "Youth Gang Denies Complicity." Emmett Brown, while exploring 2015, learns of these events and tracks the McFly family's troubles down to this one headline. Hoping to improve his friend's future, he returns to 1985 to recruit Marty's help in stopping his son from going through with the theft [BTF2].

> **NOTE: In the finished film of BTF2, Doc told Marty that his daughter, Marlene McFly, would try to break Marty Jr. out of jail and earn a prison sentence for herself in the process. However, the movie's novelization indicated that, following her brother's arrest, Marlene fell into a state of severe depression, with the implication that she would eventually commit suicide.**

- After Marty McFly intervenes in his son's destiny, future events are changed and reflected on the front page of *USA Today*'s Hill Valley edition. Whereas the headline once heralded Marty Jr.'s arrest, it now reads, "Gang Jailed—Hoverboard Rampage Destroys Courthouse," with a quote from gang leader Griff Tannen claiming he was framed [BTF2].

Sunday, October 25, 2015 A.D.—3:43 to 3:44 AM

- Young Biff Tannen, pursued by the Institute of Future Technology's time-travel volunteers, arrives in 2015. After spending a minute in this era, Biff activates the time circuits and evades his pursuers, the volunteers following him in an Eight-Passenger DeLorean Time-Travel Vehicle [RIDE].

Thursday, October 29, 2015 A.D.—3:20 AM

- In one possible timeline, Marlene McFly unsuccessfully attempts to break her brother, Marty Jr., out of jail, and is sentenced to 20 years' imprisonment [BFCG].

- After Marty McFly changes history by avoiding a drag race with Douglas J. Needles in 1985, his family is much happier, with Marlene following in his rock-and-roll footsteps by launching her own concert tour [BFCG].

Sometime After 2015 A.D.

- Martin McFly III, a grandson of Marty and Jennifer McFly in one possible timeline, is born [BFCG].

- Electra McFly, a descendant of Marty and Jennifer McFly in one potential reality, is born [BFCG].

- Jules McFly, a descendant of Marty and Jennifer McFly in one potential reality, is born [BFCG].

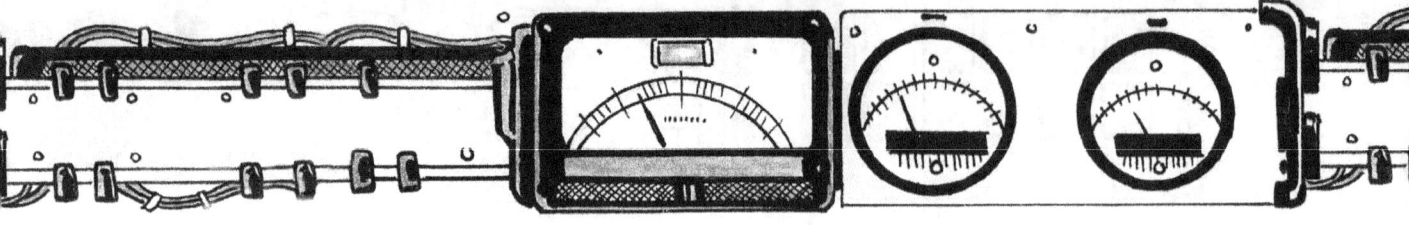

Circa 2020s A.D.

- Clara Brown considers sending her sons, Jules and Verne, to college in this decade, but her husband, Emmett Brown, favors the 1960s for the quality of that era's higher education [TLTL-1].

Sometime in or Before 2025 A.D.

- Griff Tannen is released from prison [TLTL-1].

2025 A.D.

- A duplicate time-traveling DeLorean suddenly appears from the past, having been created as a result of Emmett Brown's original time machine being struck by lightning in 1955, which transported the duplicate seventy years into the future. Doc finds the second vehicle in time to stop Griff Tannen from using it to damage the space-time continuum [TLTL-1].

Sometime in or After 2025 A.D.

- Griff Tannen is again sentenced to prison, where he remains until at least 2091 [TLTL-1].
    > *NOTE: The reason for Griff's re-incarceration is unknown.*

Friday, October 28, 2039 A.D.—6:30 PM

- A pair of Italian teenagers from the 1990s, visiting the future in a time-traveling DeLorean, are amazed not by the futuristic marvels awaiting them, but rather by an Arrigoni vending machine, at which they stock up on snacks and drinks before returning to their own era [ARGN].

2057 A.D.

- The last of the Earth's rainforests is destroyed. Upon learning of this development while visiting 2057, Emmett Brown travels back to 1990, hoping to alter the future by teaching mankind better environmental stewardship [ERTH].

2088 A.D.

- Emmett Brown brings O'Neal McKnight, a shy, young night-club coat-check attendant, to this year from 2008, in order to help the young man discover his true potential. McKnight's experience in this era inspires him to overcome his long-held shyness, enabling him to ask an attractive woman to dance [CHEK].
    > *NOTE: It's unknown what McKnight saw in the future that inspired such confidence.*

Sometime in or Before 2091 A.D.

- A newspaper called *Megabyte Daily* begins publication [BFAN-9].

- *Sabotage Weekly*, a publication exploring methods for damaging vehicles and installations, such as explosives, is launched. Among its readers is Ziff Tannen [BFAN-9].

- A region of Earth's solar system is defined as the Tri-Planet Area [BFAN-9].
    > *NOTE: Two of the planets were likely Earth and Mars, given the plot of the episode in question. The third world involved was unspecified.*

- Marty McFly impersonators become a popular musical profession. Impersonators often wear Marty facial masks and Elvis Presley-like jumpsuits, performing hit songs recorded by Marty's band during the late 20th and early 21st centuries [BFAN-9].

- Irving Infosystems builds a model of robot known as Irving. The large, airborne automaton, with a single eye, two arms, and a propeller at the bottom of its torso for locomotion, provides friendly service (such as driving directions) to those flying over Hill Valley [BFAN-9].

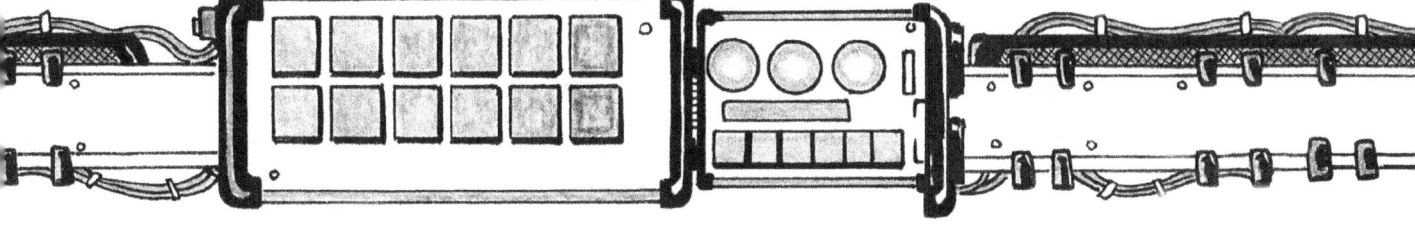

• The Tunnel Tubeway public-transit system is set up so that all vehicles entering the tubeway without first registering their destination will be automatically re-routed to the Violation Center—an exit tube into the Hill Valley Dump. A holographic robot known as Greta is created to welcome travelers to the Tunnel Tubeway, a form of high-speed public travel used in Hill Valley. Greta greets each car at the Tubeway's entrance and requests its destination, after which the system carries the vehicle to the proper coordinates in mere seconds [BFAN-9].

• The 24-Hour Cloning Shack opens in Hill Valley, not far from the McFly Space Center [BFAN-9].

• The McFly Museum of Aeronautics introduces Billy Spaceboy, a floating robot that greets group-tour visitors to the facilities. The mechanical tour guide sports a "B" on its chest and a warm, calming voice. All children visiting the museum who refrain from chewing plutonium spitwads while on site receive a free set of Billy Spaceboy Junior Cadet Wings [BFAN-9].

• McFly Space Cruises unveils the *MSC Marty*, its first passenger solar sailship, a type of clear-domed luxury space vehicle used to ferry travelers off Earth. The sailship is powered by booster rockets and large solar sails that act like a mirror, reflecting sunlight to propel the craft through space. The company also introduces its microstorage process of shrinking vehicles and luggage down to a tiny size, in order to accommodate travelers aboard such solar sailships. A polite model of droid called the Peter Park-It, resembling a human butler, is created to oversee the parking facilities at Hill Valley's McFly Space Center, using microstorage to shrink each parked vehicle down to a tiny size [BFAN-9].
    NOTE: This droid's name was a pun referencing Peter Parker, better known as Marvel Comics' Spider-Man—and also the name of Jennifer Parker's paternal grandfather.

2091 A.D.

• Comedian George Burns announces a comeback [BFAN-9].
    NOTE: Burns, still alive when the episode aired in 1991, died five years later, at age 100. Had he lived until 2091, he'd have been nearly two centuries old.

Saturday, December 15, 2091 A.D.

• McFly Space Cruises prepares to launch the *MSC Marty* to the planet Mars, which makes headlines in *Megabyte Daily*. Meanwhile, Emmett and Clara Brown arrive from 1991 to celebrate their 116th wedding anniversary, as their son, Jules, has bought them tickets for the *Marty*'s historic trip. The couple enjoy their second honeymoon, oblivious to the fact that Ziff Tannen—Biff's great-great grandson—has set out to avenge centuries of Tannen ridicule at the hands of the McFly family. Ziff, a Mission Control mechanic, sabotages the *Marty* by removing a vital sail support bolt.

    Not far behind their folks, Jules and Verne Brown emerge in the year 2091 via their family's time train. Soon after their parents' departure from 1991, Jules' J.E.B. Cross-Time Headliner—a printing press able to duplicate any newspaper headline past, present or future—revealed that on December 16, 2091, the *Marty* would be lost in space. The brothers hurry to the McFly Space Center to warn Doc and Clara, but are too late. Under the command of Marty McFly's great-granddaughter, Captain Marta McFly, the damaged solar sailship exits Earth's orbit on a course for Mars.

    Desperate to gain entrance to the *Marty*, the Brown brothers pose as students in Mrs. Phillips' fifth-grade class from Dan Quayle Elementary School, who are enjoying a field trip to the space center and the McFly Museum of Aeronautics. Blending in with the other kids, Jules and Verne sneak inside and find Mission Control. However, Ziff has tampered with the equipment to show things aboard the *MSC Marty* as running according to plan.

NIKE	*BTTF*-themed TV commercial: Nike	**SCRT**	2010 Scream Awards: *Back to the Future* 25th Anniversary Reunion (trailer)	**SUFFIX**	**MEDIUM**	
NTND	Nintendo *Back to the Future—The Ride* Mini-Game	**SIMP**	Simulator: *The Simpsons Ride*	-b	*BTF2*'s Biff Tannen Museum video (extended version)	
PIZA	*BTTF*-themed TV commercial: Pizza Hut	**SLOT**	*Back to the Future* Video Slots	-c	Animated series credit sequence	
REAL	Real life	**TEST**	Screen tests: Crispin Glover, Lea Thompson and Thomas F. Wilson	-d	Film deleted scene	
RIDE	Simulator: *Back to the Future—The Ride*	**TLTL**	Telltale Games' *Back to the Future—The Game*	-n	Film novelization	
SCRM	2010 Scream Awards: *Back to the Future* 25th Anniversary Reunion (broadcast)	**UNIV**	Universal Studios Hollywood promotional video	-o	Film outtake	
				-v	Video game print materials or commentaries	

-s1	Screenplay (draft one)
-s2	Screenplay (draft two)
-s3	Screenplay (draft three)
-s4	Screenplay (draft four)
-sp	Screenplay (production draft)
-sx	Screenplay (*Paradox*)

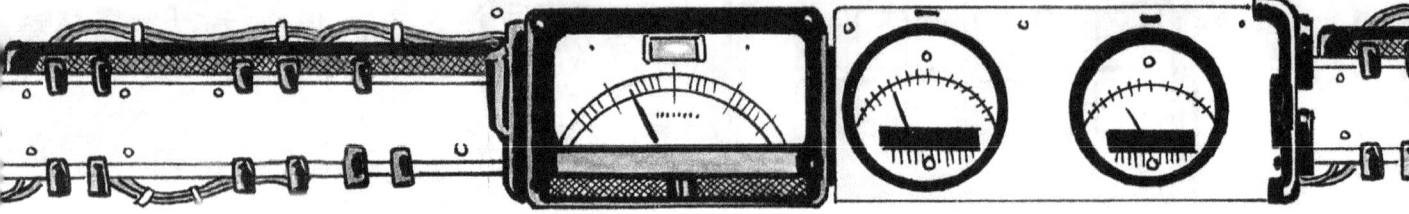

Ziff's plan works, causing one of the *Marty*'s sails to partially detach from the vessel. Captain McFly tries to maintain order among her passengers by distracting them with a Marty McFly impersonator, playing her ancestor's famous music. Clara volunteers her and Emmett's service, and the couple dons spacesuits to help fix the damaged spaceship. She soon realizes, however, that repairing such sophisticated technology is a bit more difficult than fixing a farm's water pump.

In Hill Valley, Jules and Verne expose Ziff as the saboteur. Strapping on a rocket pack, Tannen prepares a dramatic escape, but inadvertently dons the pack upside-down, causing him to crash-land in Hill Valley Prison—in the same cell as his grandfather, Griff Tannen.

Jules and Verne "borrow" a past relic hanging in the Aeronautic Museum: the *MSC Jennifer*, Earth's first passenger solar ship. With a little rigging, Jules makes the craft spaceworthy, after which he and his brother journey into space to recover the *MSC Marty* and tow it back to Earth [BFAN-9].

Sunday, December 16, 2091 A.D.

- A newspaper headline reports the *MSC Marty* as being lost in space during its maiden voyage, with sabotage suspected. After the intervention of Jules and Verne, however, the paper reports the *Marty*'s rescue and Ziff Tannen's arrest [BFAN-9].

2096 A.D.

- After meeting the Queen of Apocrypha and Tannen the Barbarian in 2,991,299,129,912,991 A.D., Doc and Marty return to 1992 in the recently damaged *Jules Verne Train*, "bouncing" off of a number of other years along the way, including 2096 A.D. [BFCL-3].

From 2091 to 2585 A.D.

- Humans come to completely rely on machines to perform all of their labor. As a result, mankind falls into a state of permanent relaxation and indulgence, forgoing exercise and creative endeavors. Programmed to look after humanity's well-being, a group of robots ignite the fires of rebellion, turning on their human masters to rattle them out of their sloth-like state and motivate them to become healthy, productive beings [BFCL-1].

Monday, January 3, 2152 A.D.—12:45 PM

- Two men in black suits and ties speed along a highway in a time-traveling DeLorean, passing bubbled cities and flying cars zipping along tracks of light stretching across a desert landscape. Once their sightseeing is completed, the men return to the year 2011, immediately suffering a fatal head-on collision with another vehicle [LIMO].

Sometime in or Before 2585 A.D.

- Mankind establishes a domed station in the Asteroid Belt of Earth's solar system, known as Robot City, in which hundreds of robots handle all manual labor so that humans can relax and watch holovision programs. Numerous companies open branches at Robot City, including Asterobotics, a provider of positronic brain units; Bostoid Pizza, which promises its robotic drivers can deliver an order within 30 seconds; The Entertainer, a video-rental business; the Robot Recycling Center, where mechanicals deemed old or out of style are sent to be crushed; and Taxi O'bot, a robotic taxicab business [BFCL-1].

  > *NOTE: The term "positronic brain" was coined by science fiction author Isaac Asimov in his* **Robot** *novels, and was later featured in the* **Doctor Who** *and* **Star Trek** *franchises, in regard to the Daleks and Data, respectively.*

- A type of plumbing robot called a Plumbot is introduced. The human citizens of Robot City often use Plumbots rather than performing plumbing tasks themselves [BFCL-1].

CODE	STORY						
ARGN	BTTF-themed TV commercial: Arrigoni	BTF1	Film: *Back to the Future*	CITY	*BTTF*-themed music video: Owl City, "Deer in the Headlights"	HUEY	*BTTF*-themed music video: Huey Lewis and the News, "The Power of Love"
BFAN	*Back to the Future: The Animated Series*	BTF2	Film: *Back to the Future Part II*			LIMO	*BTTF*-themed music video:
BFCG	*Back to the Future: The Card Game*	BTF3	Film: *Back to the Future Part III*	DCTV	*BTTF*-themed TV commercial: DirecTV		The Limousines, "The Future"
BFCL	*Back to the Future* comic book (limited series)	BUDL	*BTTF*-themed TV commercial: Bud Light	ERTH	*The Earth Day Special*	MCDN	*BTTF*-themed TV commercial: McDonald's
BFCM	*Back to the Future* comic book (monthly series)	CHEK	*BTTF*-themed music video: O'Neal McKnight, "Check Your Coat"	GALE	Interviews and commentaries: Bob Gale and/or Robert Zemeckis	MITS	*BTTF*-themed TV commercial: Mitsubishi Lancer
BFHM	*BTTF*-themed McDonald's Happy Meal boxes	CHIC	Photographs hanging in Doc Brown's Chicken restaurant at Universal Studios	GARB	*BTTF*-themed TV commercials: Garbarino	MSFT	*BTTF*-themed TV commercial: Microsoft
BTFA	*Back to the Future Annual* (Marvel Comics)			GETV	*BTTF*-themed TV commercial: GE		

- The Pedestrian Speed Way, a mode of travel carrying non-vehicle-based travelers across long distances at high speeds, is built, with exits at numerous cities, including Hill Valley [BFCL-1].

- A type of electronic entertainment media called holovision becomes popular in Robot City. Before long, the average human living in that city spends nearly 98 percent of his or her waking time watching holovision, with a Click-o-bot standing by to change channels via remote control [BFCL-1].

Friday, June 3, 2585 A.D.

- Proud of his son Verne for earning a high grade on a report about robots, Emmett Brown takes his family and Marty McFly on a field trip to 26th-century Hill Valley, to witness the dawn of the Robot Age. In that century, robots perform all menial labor, leaving their human masters to indulge in artistic and intellectual pursuits. Doc flies the time train into outer space, to a small asteroid housing Robot City, where automata are manufactured, salvaged and given orders for service on Earth.

  Much to their surprise, the time-travelers arrive in the midst of a robot uprising, with hundreds of machines attacking their human masters. During the carnage, the locomotive is struck by blaster fire, its Flux Capacitor rendered useless. Marty thwarts an attack by ordering the killer robot to stand down—which it does, without question. The time-travelers realize that the robots, bound by their programming, would have no choice but to cease their rebellion upon a single command from a human. Marty successfully quells the rebellion, enabling his group to assess the extent of the time-train's damage.

  Verne, oblivious to any potential danger, wanders off, hoping to see more robots. Jules accompanies him to keep his brother out of trouble. With a friendly mechanical as their tour guide, the boys soon learn the truth about the Robot Age: With machines to do their every bidding, humans have become lazy, spending all of their time watching holovision, getting massages,

eating junk food and laying about. Artistic and intellectual pursuits have fallen by the wayside, as mankind has become content being pampered. Since the robots were designed to help humans live better lives, the machines revolted in an effort to force their masters to exercise, eat better, and create artwork once more.

Jules and Verne visit the Robot Recycling Center, where automata must throw themselves into a grinder once they are no longer in style. Verne intervenes to save the robots, giving them one last command: not to obey any order that they consider "stupid."

While searching for the lost Brown brothers, Doc, Clara and Marty are apprehended and escorted to Governor Tannen, Robot City's overseer. Marty's victory over the wayward robots prompts Tannen to use the same tactic in order to stop the rebellion once and for all. As he makes this declaration, Jules and Verne arrive with an army of free-thinking robots. Tannen's commands no longer hold sway over the machines, who have made it their new mission to discipline humanity by making them do more chores for themselves, as well as exercise and eat better. As a token of gratitude, the robots give the Brown family the necessary parts to repair the Flux Capacitor. In the process of fixing the time train, however, Doc is involved in an electrical accident, causing him to lose his memory [BFCL-1].

- With Doc suffering from amnesia, the task of fixing the Flux Capacitor and getting everyone home falls to Jules Brown. The youth does his best to effect temporary repairs to the time-train, but his inexperience results in a slight miscalculation. When he enters 1992 into the time circuits, the train instead flies backwards, catapulting the vehicle carrying its occupants into the far future, to the year 2,991,299,129,912,991 A.D. [BFCL-2].

  NOTE: Many scientists believe Earth will cease to exist in approximately 7.6 billion years, with human life dying out within a billion years or so. This would effectively render a trip to the year 2,991,299,129,912,991 (1992 in reverse, repeated four times) impossible.

				SUFFIX MEDIUM			
NIKE	*BTTF*-themed TV commercial: Nike	SCRT	2010 Scream Awards: *Back to the Future*	**-b**	*BTF2's* Biff Tannen Museum video	**-s1**	Screenplay (draft one)
NTND	Nintendo *Back to the Future—The Ride*		25th Anniversary Reunion (trailer)		(extended version)	**-s2**	Screenplay (draft two)
	Mini-Game	SIMP	Simulator: *The Simpsons Ride*			**-s3**	Screenplay (draft three)
PIZA	*BTTF*-themed TV commercial: Pizza Hut	SLOT	*Back to the Future* Video Slots	**-c**	Animated series credit sequence	**-s4**	Screenplay (draft four)
REAL	Real life	TEST	Screen tests: Crispin Glover, Lea Thompson	**-d**	Film deleted scene	**-sp**	Screenplay (production draft)
RIDE	Simulator: *Back to the Future—The Ride*		and Thomas F. Wilson	**-n**	Film novelization	**-sx**	Screenplay (*Paradox*)
SCRM	2010 Scream Awards: *Back to the Future*	TLTL	Telltale Games' *Back to the Future—The Game*	**-o**	Film outtake		
	25th Anniversary Reunion (broadcast)	UNIV	Universal Studios Hollywood promotional video	**-v**	Video game print materials or commentaries		

Back in Time: The Unauthorized Back to the Future Chronology

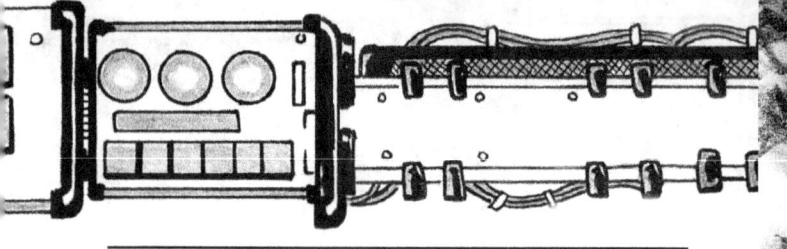

2737 A.D., 2995 A.D., 3749 A.D. and 8607 A.D.

- After meeting the Queen of Apocrypha and Tannen the Barbarian in 2,991,299,129,912,991 A.D., Doc and Marty return to 1992 in the recently damaged *Jules Verne Train*, "bouncing" off of a number of other years along the way, including these years [BFCL-3].

October 25, 8888

- *See entry for October 25, 64,000,000 B.C.*

Sometime Between 2585 and 2,991,299,129,912,991 A.D.

- A species of dragon evolves on the planet Earth [BFCL-2].

- Over the millennia, a number of primitive kingdoms arise throughout former North America, including Apocrypha (the largest of the empires), Calgon (containing a village called Hillvallia, once known as Hill Valley), Diatribe, Errata, Innuendo, Mundania, Oz, Paradise and Psuedonymia [BFCL-2].

2,991,299,129,912,991 A.D.

- Nearly three quadrillion years into Earth's future, technology has become nearly extinct, and the world has reverted back to the Dark Ages. Science is now regarded as magic, with "sorcerers" feared and persecuted. The kingdom of Apocrypha is now the largest empire on the planet, governed at this time by a queen.

  Marty McFly and the Brown family arrive from 2585, in desperate need of assistance. Jules deduces that in order to repair the damaged Flux Capacitor, he will require platinum—though he has no idea where to obtain it in such a desolate wasteland.

  The time travelers journey to a small, impoverished village and visit Oxen's Gore Tavern & Bed 'N' Breakfast. They attempt to buy a drink, but the barkeep is shocked to see a 20th-century credit card bearing a holographic image. He deems the strangers sorcerers, causing an uproar in the tavern, but Marty and Doc are saved by the unlikeliest of heroes—a warrior known as Tannen the Barbarian. Tannen calms the patrons, requesting the duo's help on a mission. He has been tasked with procuring the Ruby Begonia for the Queen of Apocrypha, and needs their "magic" to

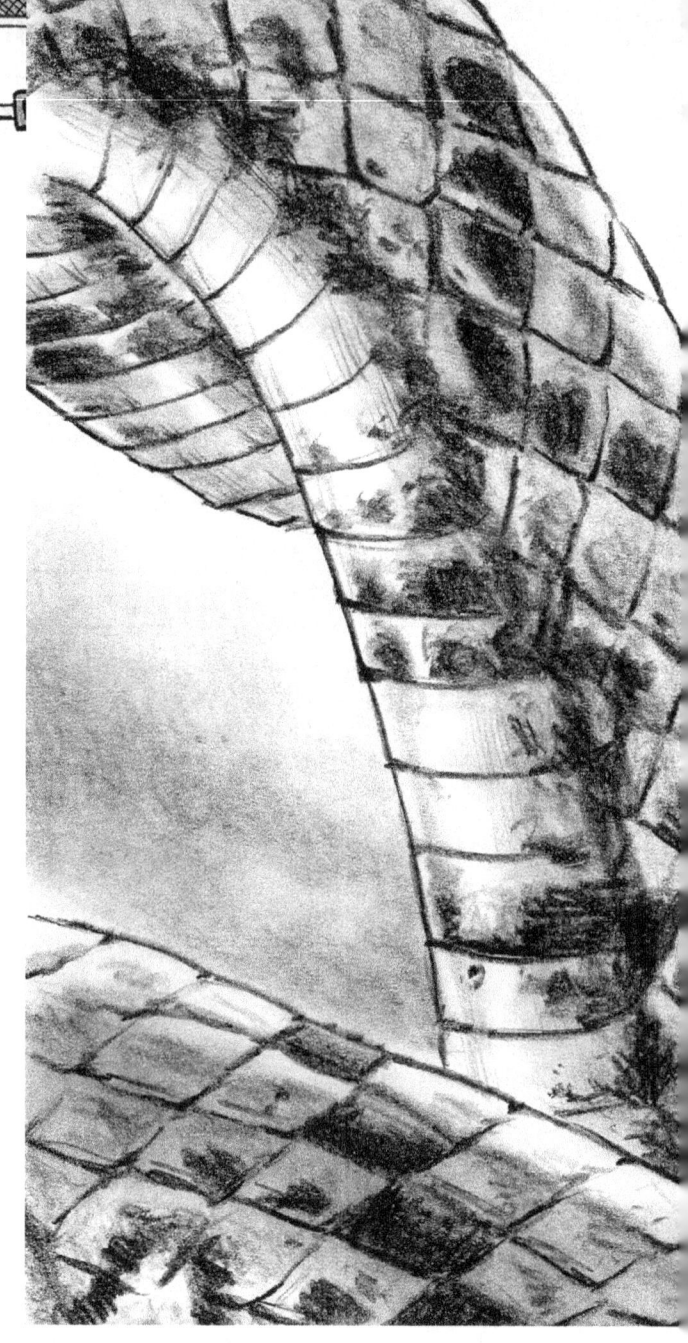

help him do so. Marty is reluctant to help, given Doc's mental state, but when Tannen reveals that Clara, Jules and Verne have all been captured by the Queen's guards, Marty readily agrees. Once they have secured the Queen's treasure, the barbarian vows to withhold it in exchange for Doc's family.

Tannen, Doc and Marty journey to a structure called the Enchanted Tower. The three adventurers reach the tower's peak and discover unbelievable riches within. Consumed by greed, Tannen forsakes his promises to both the Queen and Marty, believing that with his

newfound wealth, he can build his own kingdom, and thus no longer needs the monarch's favor. His plans are short-lived, however, as a fierce dragon—the gold's protector—attacks. The three barely escape the tower alive, and all of Tannen's treasure is left behind with the beast—all except for the Ruby Begonia that Marty swiped. His ambitions spoiled, Tannen agrees to fulfill his previous obligation.

The barbarian takes the two time-travelers to the Queen of Apocrypha, presents the treasure and asks for the Brown family's release in return. However,

the matriarch has already released her captives after befriending Clara, who has been teaching her how to cross-stitch.

Jules discovers that the Ruby Begonia is, in fact, made of platinum—the very component he needs to repair the Flux Capacitor. The queen allows the time-travelers to take what they need of the gem, and she and Tannen the Barbarian then bid farewell to the strangers from another time. With the Flux Capacitor repaired, Marty and the Browns pile into the *Jules Verne Train* and return to their home era of 1992 [BFCL-2].

Hill Valley: Then and Now (and Later)

By Greg Mitchell

"No McFly ever amounted to anything in the history of Hill Valley!"

—Gerald (S.S.) Strickland, *Back to the Future*

Introduction

By all rights, Hill Valley should be just like any other small, picturesque Californian town, with its Courthouse Square and the famous Hill Valley Clock Tower as its centerpiece. But this idyllic community with the prophetic, paradoxical name is home to a number of galaxy-shattering events, all stemming from the arrival of the von Braun family following World War I, and one von Braun in particular: inventor Emmett Lathrop Brown.

I. Humble Beginnings

In prehistoric times, Hill Valley was a barren wasteland, dominated by an active volcano and teeming with predatory lizards, such as the *Tyrannosaurus rex*. Long after the Ice Age reshaped the planet's geography, this patch of land (that would eventually turn into California's best-kept secret) would become a desert populated by breathtaking mesas and inhabited by the Pohatchee tribe of Native Americans. For centuries, the Pohatchee lived in relative peace, defending their lands from wild bears and other hazards of the desert. But that changed with the arrival of the White Man, who began laying siege to their home.

As happened across the continent, a bitter war erupted between the native tribes and the invading settlers. In the midst of this bloody conflict, William "Bill" Hill, an auspicious pioneer and powerful orator, founded the township of Hill Valley. The event was marked with celebration and games as the first settlers came together in a time of family and fun. More than a century later, Hill Valley would still hold such Founder's Day Celebrations in honor of "the Old Pioneer," commemorating the goodwill of those first few families who built the town.

During the U.S. Civil War, from 1861 to 1865, California joined the Union in its disapproval of slavery. Many of Hill Valley's own sons gave their lives for the cause of liberty. It was a dark time for America, but as the War ended, the settlement of Hill Valley had much reason to celebrate, as 1865 marked Hill Valley's incorporation into the state of California. By 1869, U.S. Marshal James Strickland would come to this town to serve as its moral backbone. A strict disciplinarian, Marshal Strickland kept the peace. While most townsfolk were a people of simple values and hard work, such as when the community rallied together to help Wendel Parker raise his barn, there have always been a contingent of Hill Valleyers who have bucked the authority of folks like Strickland. And most of these ruffians have belonged to the Tannen family.

Throughout its history, no single name has brought so much trouble to Hill Valley more than "Tannen." The family's roots are varied and complicated, as there have been Tannens on all continents throughout history, with similar physical descriptions and troublesome demeanors, from Rome's Bifficus Antanney and South America's Biffando de la Tanén to England's Lord Biffingham (the Earl of Tannenshire) and Australia's Mongo P. Tannen. While it's impossible to determine the exact origin of this thuggish brood, those who populated Hill Valley can perhaps be traced back to the witch-hunter Goodman Tannen, who lived in Salem, Massachusetts, during the late 1600s, and seems to have been the first recorded Tannen in the New World.

As the Tannen line multiplied, they also moved West, with the notorious criminal "Wild Bill" Tannen terrorizing caravans along the Oregon Trail. During the Civil War, General Beauregard B. Tannen led a Confederate regiment in Chattanooga, Tennessee. Eventually, the Tannens settled in Hill Valley, beginning with the Tannen Gang of brother-

sister outlaws Thaddeus and Hepzibah, along with cohort Ox McPhips. Perhaps it was the presence of existing Tannens that brought Beauregard to Hill Valley in 1876. The former general's introduction into the population brought an even greater influence and lasting change to the town's culture.

By July 1876, Beauregard oversaw construction of the Palace Saloon and Hotel. This would mark the beginning of a long relationship between the Tannen family and Hill Valley vice. Little is known of Beauregard's later life, though he may have been the father of infamous lawbreaker Buford "Mad Dog" Tannen—a man of mystery himself, also known as "Black Biff," who shot dead a newspaper editor in 1884 for printing an unfavorable story about him, ensuring that few journalists would again dare write about his exploits. Mad Dog and his outlaw band were responsible for robbing the Pine City Stage, and for the cold-blooded murder of Hill Valley's own Marshal James Strickland. A wanton rebel and ne'er-do-well, Mad Dog roamed about town, uncontained, ruling the streets at night with fear.

But all was not terrible in Hill Valley during the so-called "Wild West." The young town still boasted of limitless opportunity, drawing a number of immigrants, such as Ireland's McFly family.

1885 saw the construction of the Hill Valley Courthouse and its iconic Clock Tower. A town-wide celebration marked the occasion, but the night was not without tragedy, as Hill Valley was still mourning the loss of its new schoolmarm, Clara Clayton, who had perished in a buckboard accident down Shonash Ravine shortly after her arrival. However, with strong families, hard work and one eye on the future, Hill Valley continued to grow and prosper, expanding beyond, perhaps, even Bill Hill's vision, and came to California's aid during one of the state's darkest hours.

II. A Nice Place to Live

In the early hours of Wednesday, April 18, 1906, two miles off the California coast, a devastating earthquake ripped apart the San Andreas fault, laying waste to much of San Francisco in what would become one of the worst natural disasters in America's records—and the greatest loss of life in state history. Thousands of displaced refugees wandered from the rubble, lost and disheveled, looking to rebuild their shattered lives. Many of these victims found their way to Hill Valley, and the Courthouse was opened to the injured and needy. The town rallied together during this terrible time, overcoming differences in order to care for their fellow man. The love shown during these difficult weeks prompted many San Franciscans to remain in Hill Valley and join this compassionate community.

Elsewhere in the world, the shadow of the first World War stretched across the planet, but Hill Valley remained a place of hope and promise. German-born Erhardt von Braun followed his heart and, against his father's wishes, sojourned to America's borders, settling himself and his young wife Sarah in Hill Valley, and changing their surname to "Brown." Erhardt became a judge in 1916, taking a seat on the Hill Valley Criminal Court and administering justice with the vigor and fearlessness of early pioneer lawman Marshal Strickland. During his time in Hill Valley, Erhardt saw the birth of his only child—a son—whom his wife named "Emmett" after a ragdoll she had cherished as a child. It would be young Emmett who would have the most impact on the quiet town of Hill Valley.

Judge Brown's hard-nosed sense of right and wrong was much needed as the decades passed. By 1931, Irving "Kid" Tannen ran one of the largest bootlegging operations through hidden gin joints across town. Once again, the Tannen family brought corruption to their community. One staunch detractor of such rampant immorality was Edna Strickland, a young reporter and advocate of clean and sober living. However, Edna's zeal for righteousness resulted in her destructive behavior, when she set fire to Tannen's under-the-table establishments—a mystery that remained unsolved for decades hence. Tannen was eventually arrested for his varied criminal dealings, thanks in no small part to his accountant, Arthur McFly, but not without fathering a son: Biff Howard Tannen.

As the nations of the Earth entered the Second World War, Hill Valley did not leave the call to arms unheeded. While many young men enlisted to fight the Nazi Party, inventor Emmett Brown aided the Allied forces as well, assisting on the famed Manhattan Project that saw the creation of the first atomic bomb, while living in a tiny apartment above a gas station in Hill Valley. Brown's passion for inventing continued to thrive during this time and well into the 1950s—leading him to his greatest scientific discovery.

III. One Man's Revelation

Arguably, the most significant event in Hill Valley history occurred on a typical Saturday afternoon. At 4:20 PM, on November 5, 1955, Emmett Brown—now known locally as "Doc" Brown—was hanging a clock above his toilet. The porcelain was wet and Doc slipped, suffering a bump to the head. It was at this moment that Brown claims he had a revelation and saw, in his mind's eye, the inner workings of the Flux Capacitor, an invention he believed would make time travel possible.

It would take Brown thirty years and his entire family's fortune to realize that dream. During the interim, Hill Valley underwent a number of changes. The Vietnam War brought a time of social upheaval, dividing the community. Some, like Biff Tannen and Sam Baines, supported the war, while others chose to embrace peace. George McFly, son of Arthur, and his wife, Lorraine Baines McFly, joined the "flower power" movement and became active in their community, spreading a message of love and peace. They organized rallies and took strangers into their home, while raising their three children: David, Linda, and Martin. Also opposing the war effort was Hill Valley's future mayor (and one-time busboy), lawyer Muhammad Goldie Wilson.

The 1960s and 1970s passed, however, leaving scars on Hill Valley's once-picturesque Courthouse Square. Now occupied by pawn shops and adult bookstores, the town's heart turned dilapidated and seedy. Even the stately Hill Valley High School had been defaced by graffiti for years, with seemingly no one to care for its upkeep. The glory of the small California town had faded.

But one man sought to change this fate and to achieve greatness. After years of experimentation and failure, Emmett "Doc" Brown finally realized his dream and, in the early morning hours of October 26, 1985, successfully tested his modified DeLorean time machine, utilizing the Flux Capacitor he had envisioned so long ago. As of 1:20 that morning, Brown's dog Einstein became the world's first temporal traveler. Witnessing this event was 17-year-old Marty McFly, who had befriended the eccentric inventor after sneaking into Brown's garage-cum-lab years earlier, intrigued by wild stories he'd heard told about the man.

At last, excitement had come to Hill Valley that would revolutionize its place on the global stage. Yet, at just the moment that his future seemed brightest, Brown was gunned down by a group of Libyan nationalists, whom he'd swindled out of plutonium to power his time machine. Marty witnessed that, too, and, were it not for his speeding away in the DeLorean, the future rock star would have surely perished. Marty fled the terrorists, accidentally activating the Flux Capacitor and slingshotting to the year 1955—and Hill Valley was never the same.

IV. History Is About to Change

With Marty's insertion into Hill Valley's past, the town underwent far-reaching changes, both great and small. Within Marty's own family, his father George—once a shy, fearful man—learned confidence from his future son and became a successful science fiction author. Among the changes, the powerful Biff Tannen was humbled and opened up a car detailing shop, spending his life embittered and secretly resentful of the McFly family.

Meanwhile, Clara Clayton—the young schoolmarm who lost her life over Shonash Ravine in 1885—was spared that grisly fate, and eventually married Doc Brown, bearing him two sons, whom they named Jules and Verne. Brown, himself, was saved by Marty's time-traveling intervention, and survived his encounter with the Libyans in 1985. Yet, for all the lives that Marty changed and the people he helped, time-traveling did not come without its consequences, as he discovered on a trip to 2015.

There, old Biff stole the DeLorean and returned to 1955 to undo the work that Marty had begun, by giving himself an almanac enabling him to make millions of dollars betting on upcoming sporting events. As a result, Biff rewrote Hill Valley history, creating a dystopian "Biffhorrific" nightmare in which he ruled the town with greed, corruption and murder. In that parallel timeline, Hill Valley (nicknamed "Hell Valley") became a den of thieves—a dark, bleak industrial zone that boasted an endless array of adult entertainment, all leading to Biff's own Pleasure Paradise casino-hotel.

In a series of harrowing events, Marty and Doc were able to reverse the damage that had been done to the timestream, restoring Hill Valley, though not without making a pit stop in 1885, where Doc met and married Clara Clayton. At the end of their wild adventure, the DeLorean was destroyed, and Doc began questioning the dangers of time travel. Perhaps the world was not yet ready for such an invention.

Doc, Clara and their sons avoided modern Hill Valley for a number of years by seeing the world aboard the *Jules Verne Train*, another time-traveling vehicle of the scientist's design. By 1991, they returned to Hill Valley and purchased a home. Doc became a fixture in the local community, and gained a new temporal-defying DeLorean. He also founded the Institute of Future Technology and continued to successfully invent new modern conveniences.

During this time, Doc was reunited with Marty, who visited the Brown home often and spent a great deal of time with young Jules and Verne. Together, Marty and the Browns carried on their time-traveling exploits, for educational—and sometimes entertainment—purposes. During the early 1990s, they saw numerous sights and encountered many historical figures and events, though they were much more careful this time in how they interacted with the past. As a result, Hill Valley remained largely unaffected by their temporal tampering... with three notable exceptions:

After rescuing Doc from being gunned down by Kid Tannen's gang in 1931, Marty returned to 1986 to find that he'd changed history so that Kid never went to prison. In this new reality, Kid fathered two brothers for Biff, named Cliff and Riff, and the four Tannens terrorized Hill Valley—in particular, the McFlys—for years, earning a reputation as the fifth most dangerous crime family in California.

Marty managed to avert this outcome, but made things worse in the process by spawning yet another alternate timeline, one in which Hill Valley was an Orwellian police state. All citizens dressed uniformly and lived under an uncompromisingly conservative code of conduct in this pristine but sterile Hill Valley, their every action closely monitored by a dictatorial mayor—namely, First Citizen Emmett Brown. In this reality, Emmett had married the repressed Edna Strickland, who'd perverted his scientific brilliance to create a society fearfully conforming to her values regarding discipline. Crime and vice had been all but eliminated—but at great cost to personal freedoms.

Again, Marty prevented this skewed version of Hill Valley. But five years later, time travel again had disastrous results—this time not only for Hill Valley, but for the entire planet. After traveling back to the year 3,000,000 B.C. to test his Proprietary Ultrasonic Subatomic Molecular Redistributor, Doc inadvertently prevented the mass-extinction event that killed all dinosaurs, thereby eliminating humanity's rise up the evolutionary ladder. As a result, upon returning to his own era, he discovered a vastly different Hill Valley—now known as Dinocity—filled with massive buildings and inhabited by a technologically advanced society of sapient dinosaurs.

Thankfully, Doc managed to put things right. And in the ensuing years, despite the inherent dangers posed by altering history, Hill Valley flourished, an era of prosperity and technological advances leading the town to a new golden age of progress.

V. Hill Valley Beyond

By 2015, Hill Valley saw incredible leaps in technology. From hovercars to complete blood transfusions that could add thirty years to a person's life, the future was, indeed, bright—and very colorful. Perhaps it is no coincidence that such advancements were achieved in a town that was home to the famed Institute of Future Technology—which closed its doors in the early 21st century—and its chief inventive officer, Emmett Brown. Beneath its shiny veneer, the Hill Valley of the future was not without its problems, however. Street thugs—such as Biff's own grandson, Griff Tannen—and illegal drugs became rampant in the seedier parts of town, including the Hilldale subdivision. What's more, the corporate greed of the 1980s was still alive and well, and bizarre high fashion and consumerism were at a peak, laying the groundwork for a dark time that would not fully manifest for another five hundred years.

During the late 21st century, Captain Marta McFly, Marty's great-granddaughter, named a solar sailship after her progenitor: the MSC *Marty*. The McFly name would become synonymous in Hill Valley with space exploration by 2091, thanks to the McFly Museum of Aeronautics and Marta's own dock, McFly Space Cruises. It was an exciting time for science, as civilians were able to book passage on sailships like the MSC *Marty* and visit the stars themselves for short vacation trips, rather than years-long missions. Bad blood remained between the Tannens and McFlys, however, as Ziff Tannen unsuccessfully sought to sabotage Marta's efforts. The Tannens remained a thorn in Hill Valley's collective side, but their greatest threat still loomed in the distance.

Hill Valley's meteoric technological rise carried on well into the 26th century, giving birth to the Robot Age. By that time, many humans gave up all forms of work—as well as all forms of art and creation—opting instead to vegetate in luxury, growing corpulent and dulling their minds with visual entertainment. In outer space, a small asteroid housed Robot City, where automata were manufactured, salvaged and given orders for service on Earth. Seeing their human masters slowly destroying themselves with sloth, robot servants instigated a devastating rebellion. By choosing to become the enemy, the automata also became humanity's savior. With their slave labor force in open revolt, the humans had no choice but to care for themselves, compelled to exercise and eat healthier in order to combat the robot hordes. By 2585 A.D., the war against the machines was in full swing.

Eons passed. Mankind had long since quelled the robot uprising, reclaiming their dominion over the Earth and their lives. Epochs began and ended and, by the year 2,991,299,129,912,991 A.D., technology had altogether become the stuff of myth and legend, as widely feared as sorcery. Hill Valley was redubbed Hillvallia, a small village in the kingdom of Calgon, in the land of Apocrypha. Hill Valley, a town once famed for its marvelous inventions, was now a primitive landscape of farming, barbarism and simple life. Ironically enough, one man roamed the lands, serving as a protector to some, a villain to others: a warrior known only as "Tannen the Barbarian."

VI. Legacy

Throughout its life, Hill Valley was home to one of the most brilliant minds in human history, and rested in the epicenter of progress. However, during its final days, Hill Valley ended much as it began, as a quiet patch of desert, where ambitious souls traveled to follow their dreams and to forge their own paths. Perhaps that, rather than the role Hill Valley played in advancing the sciences, is the unsuspecting Californian town's greatest legacy.

Courthouse Square:
The More Things Change…

By Rich Handley and Paul C. Giachetti

"Please excuse the crudity of this model. I didn't have time to build it to scale or paint it."
—**Dr. Emmett L. Brown,** *Back to the Future*

Courthouse Square—the center of Hill Valley's daily activities, from the town's founding right on through the generations. Marty McFly and Doc Brown explored multiple iterations during their temporal travels, in numerous eras across divergent timelines. The face of Courthouse Square evolved over time, as businesses changed hands and tradition gave way to the latest trends and technological innovations. But no matter what year the time-travelers visited, the square's architecture remained eminently recognizable, with the Hill Valley Courthouse and its majestic Clock Tower residing at the center of it all.

Sometimes, that evolution demonstrated a consistent pattern (banks replacing banks, automotive dealers begetting other automotive dealers, and so forth), while other shops completely changed their nature over time, such as a jewelry store becoming a brokerage firm, and later a Pizza Hut.

This contrast was a large part of Courthouse Square's small-town charm. Every town's main street has its reliable mainstays, stores that seem to have always been in business, no matter the decade or the economy—but there's always one space that constantly changes hands, from one failed business to another, with frequent bouts of non-occupancy along the way. In Hill Valley's case, there were several such locations.

A number of online sources have charted this evolution, but most contain inaccuracies and overlook store names. *Back to the Future* fans searching for a breakdown of Courthouse Square's historical layouts may thus find themselves frustrated by inconsistencies from one map to the next. To

that end, the following pages present an atlas of all known Courthouse Square storefronts, from each era seen in the films, amusement-park ride, video game, animated series and comic books. It wasn't easy to compile, requiring *many* hours of painstakingly examining and re-examining… and re-re-examining… and re-re-re-examining… every single scene ad nauseam. But the end result is fascinating to peruse.

Rather than presenting a different chart for each year—1955, for instance, versus 1985—this map integrates the square's entire known history onto a single template, with all businesses for each location presented on a corresponding key, in ascending year order. Thus, you can choose a particular space and discover that spot's evolution throughout the years. This presented a bit of a challenge when it came to charting the Old West, from *Back to the Future Part III*, as the town's layout didn't quite match those of other eras, with fewer buildings, more widely spaced apart and not forming a perfect square. For that period, placements are thus approximated as closely as possible.

This evolution was sometimes quite humorous. For example, 1885's Palace Saloon and Hotel gave way to the Sisters of Mercy Soup Kitchen by 1931, Lou's Café by 1955, Lou's Aerobic Fitness Center by 1985, War Zone in Biffhorrific 1985, the SoupMo restaurant in Citizen Brown's 1986, Café 80's in 2015 and Oxen's Gore Tavern & Bed 'N' Breakfast in 2,991,299,129,912,991 A.D. In all eras, the store remained an eatery or bar—except for in the 1980s, when U.S. citizens became exercise-conscious instead of overeating, and in Biff Tannen's vice-corrupted reality, in which the business satisfied a very different type of hunger.

Those unfamiliar with the amusement-park ride, comics and cartoons may be confused by portions of the map showing stores not visible in the film trilogy. Footage from the ride featured the DeLorean flying outside Courthouse Square in 2015, offering a tantalizing glimpse of the shops located on the blocks behind Blast From the Past and the Holomax Theater. What's more, the cartoons and comics briefly showcased the square's layout in 1933, 1944, 1991, 1992 and 2585, as well as, astoundingly, three quadrillion years into the future.

Unfortunately, the cartoons' "present" (1991 and 1992) proved too problematic for mapping purposes, as Courthouse Square was drawn radically different than how it appeared in the movies, with buildings of entirely different architectures and inconsistent store names—which changed from one episode to the next, and sometimes even from scene to scene within the same episode. In fact, most scenes set in 1991 or 1992 appeared not to occur in Courthouse Square at all, given the existence of skyscrapers, narrow roadways with stores on both sides, houses, farms and other incompatible features.

Thus, although the animated series featured a wide variety of Hill Valley shops and other businesses (such as the Luau Lunch Hut, the Hill Valley Hardware Store and the Big Apple Bakery), most regrettably could not be incorporated onto the map. Those that are listed for 1991 and 1992 appeared on an interactive board game of Hill Valley, from the episode "Go Fly a Kite"—ironically, the only time in the cartoon in which Courthouse Square matched the look of the film trilogy. That board game, incidentally, contained a surprising inclusion: CusCo Industries, Marty's 2015 employer.

Finally, a note about dating: 1985A and 1986A both refer to dystopian timelines that were eventually prevented. 1985A is the "Biffhorrific" timeline, from *Back to the Future Part II*, in which Biff Tannen ruled a Hill Valley corrupted by gambling, pornography and other vices. 1986A, meanwhile, is the Citizen Brown timeline, from Telltale Games' video game, in which Doc Brown presided over a vice-free version of the town as its prudish dictator. Although several other timelines were shown throughout the *Back to the Future* mythos, only these two offered alternate versions of Courthouse Square.

Map Key

A

1885: Hill Valley Courthouse *(under construction)*
1931: Hill Valley Courthouse
1933: Hill Valley Courthouse
1944: Hill Valley Courthouse
1955: Hill Valley Courthouse
1985: Hill Valley Courthouse/Department of
    Social Services
1985A: Biff's Pleasure Palace/Biff Tannen's Pleasure
    Paradise/Biff Tannen Museum
1986: Hill Valley Courthouse
1986A: Hill Valley Courthouse/Mayoral Office/
    Decycling area *(basement)*
1991: Hill Valley Courthouse
1992: Hill Valley Courthouse
2015: Hill Valley Courthouse Mall *(including
    World O' Transponders and Hydrators Unlimited)*
2585: Hill Valley Courthouse *(with digital clock)*

B

1885: Hill Valley Festival *(including booths for El Sapo
    Coin Toss, Colt's Patent Firearms Manufacturing
    Company and R. Nelson Photographic Art Studio)*
1931: Public grounds *(with gazebo)*
1944: Victory Garden
1955: Public grounds *(with War Memorial)*
1985: Parking lot
1985A: Parking lot
1986A: Public grounds *(with Citizen Brown statue)*
1991: Public grounds *(with Old Pioneer statue)*
1992: Ball park/Old Pioneer statue
2015: Reflecting pool

B1

1885: Mayoral Clock Dedication
1931: Salvation Station
1985: Save the Clock Tower
1986A: Citizen Plus Program

C

1955: Statler Motors Studebaker
1985: Statler Toyota
1985A: Pig Mart
2015: Pontiac
2585: Acme Anti-Gravity Inc.

D

1885: Wells Fargo & Co.
1955: Ruth's Frock Shop
1985: Goodwill Industries
1985A: Tanya Exotic Sex Goddess
2015: Hyatas

E

1955: Orson and Tillich, Attorneys at Law
    (Jacobson & Field, Attorneys at Law)[1]/
    U.S. Army Recruitment Office
1985: Attorneys (closed)
1985A: Bad Rap Bail Bonds
2015: Simulex Memory Center

*[1] In BTF1, this business was called Orson and Tillich,
Attorneys at Law, but in BTF2—set on the same day—it had
inexplicably changed to Jacobson & Field, Attorneys at Law.*

F

1931: Eastern Auto Stores
1955: Western Auto Stores
1985: Goldie Wilson Campaign HQ
1985A: Bondage
1991: Bobs
1992: Bobs
2015: The Hydroponic Gardner/Hill Valley Gifts/
A Match Made on Earth

G

1885: Apaline's
1931: Majestic Arms Inn
1955: Blue Bird Motel
1985: Blue Bird Motel *(closed)*
1985A: Peep Show/Video All Nude Hardcore Movies/Pawn Shop
1986A: Ministry of Tourism
2015: Sight Sound & Mind

H

1885: Signs
1931: O'Malley & Sons Barber Shop
1955: Elite Barber Shop
1985: Elite Barber Shop *(closed)*
1985A: Bangkok Sauna & Asian Massage
1986A: The Combformist
2015: Mr. Perfect All-Natural Steroids

I

1885: Marshal's Office
1931: Hill Valley Stationers
1955: Hill Valley Stationers
1985: Cupid's
1985A: Hell Hole XXX
1986A: The Combformist
2015: Flying High/Eclipse Contemporary & Traditional Lighting

J

1931: Speakeasy *(burned down)*
1955: Zales Jewelers
1985: Abram's Brokerage Corp.
1985A: Hard X Core
1986: Valley Video
1986A: E. Brown Industries
2015: Pizza Hut

K

1931: Lamont's House of Ermine
1955: J. D. Armstrong Realty
1985: Loans on Anything of Value
1985A: Peeparama
1986A: Citizen Reading Room
2015: True Blues

L

1931: Law Offices of Gale, Zemeckis, & Fine
1955: Ask Mr. Foster
1985: Ask Mr. Foster
1985A: Naughty and Naked
1986A: Stemmles's Staycations
2015: Uniglobe Travel

M

1885: Gen'l Mercantile/Cha's Fees/Post Office
1931: Bank of Italy
1955: Bank of America
1985: Bank of America
1985A: Naughty XXX
1986A: All Citizen's Bank
2015: Hill Valley Transit

N

1876: Palace Saloon and Hotel *(under construction)*
1885: Palace Saloon and Hotel
1931: Sisters of Mercy Soup Kitchen/El Kid/
Kid's Ice Cream
1955: Lou's Cafe
1985: Lou's Aerobic Fitness Center
1985A: War Zone
1986A: SoupMo
1991: Karen
2015: Cafe 80's
2,991,299,129,912,991:
Oxen's Gore Tavern & Bed 'N' Breakfast/
Ye Oxen's Gore Tavern & Dinner Theater

O

1931: Hill Valley Police Station
1955: Roy's Records
1985: The Third Eye
1985A: Time to Shoot
1986A: Hill Valley Bureau of Discipline
1991: CusCo Industries
2015: Blast From the Past

P

1931: Hill Valley Police Station
1955: Texaco
1985: Texaco
1985A: Wrecking Yard
1986A: Hill Valley Bureau of Discipline
2015: Texaco *(top)* 7-11/Compu-Vend *(bottom)*

Q

1885: Livery & Feed Stable/Blacksmith
1931: Hill Valley Police Station
1955: Hal's Bike Shop
1985: Hog Heaven
1985A: Abandoned building
1986A: Hill Valley Bureau of Discpline
2015: The Bot Shoppe

R

1955: Lawrence Building
1985: Lawrence Building
1985A: Sin
2015: Bottoms Up

S

1955: Broadway Florist
1985: Broadway Florist
1985A: French Fantasies
2015: Hill Valley Surrogate Parenting Center

T

1885: Building under construction
1931: Essex Theater[2]
1955: Essex Theater
1985: Essex Theater
1985A: Hill Valley Theater of Live Sex Acts
2015: Holomax Theater

U

1931: Valley Bakery
1955: Gaynor's Hideaway
1985: Gaynor's Hideaway
1986: A1 Liquors
1985A: Dee Dee's Delight/Bath House
1991: Jamie's Bakery
2015: Fusion Bar

V

1885: *Hill Valley Telegraph*
1931: Hill Billiards *(downstairs)*/Hill Valley Apartments *(upstairs, including Kid Tannen's safe house)*
1955: Apartment building
1985: Apartment building
1985A: Toxic Waste Reclamation Plant
1986: Starbase Zero *(downstairs)*/Apartments *(upstairs, including Edna Strickland's flat)*
1991: Dave's The Variety Store

W

1885: Hill Valley Hook & Ladder
1985: Allstate Insurance
1985A: Biff Springs
1986: Public notice wall
1991: The Roxy
1992: The Roxy
2015: State Farm
2585: The Roxy

X

1955: Sherwin-Williams
1985: Sherwin-Williams
2015: The Ice Cream Clone

Y

1931: Town Theater
1955: Town Theater
1985: Assembly of Christ
2015: Hill Valley Museum of Art
2585: Asimov Library

Z

1955: Holt's Diner
1985: Elmo's Ribs
2015: Hill Valley Museum of Art
2585: Motel 6000

AA

2015: Sal

BB

2015: Pizza Go

CC

2015: Tiny's

DD

1885: Undertaking/T.L. Livingston, Cabinent Maker

EE

1885: M. Fennigot Millinery

FF

1885: Meat Market
2015: Jet Burger

GG

2015: Star Struck

HH

1885: Honest Joe Statler Fine Horses

II

1885: Bath House/Barber

JJ

1885: Fortune Teller

KK

1885: Mrs. M.W. Keen, Dress Maker

LL

1885: Fabrics, Buttons, Notions

MM

1885: Nicks Cantina–The Road to Ruin

NN

1885: W. J. Chang, Chinese Laundry

OO

1885: D. Merchant, Doctor *(top)*/Assay Office *(bottom)*

PP

2015: GH

QQ

2015: Vid City

RR

2015: Star

[2] *Although the Essex Theater's marquee was not shown in 1931, a poster advertised that the film* Shark *was playing there at the time. As such, it can reasonably be assumed that the Essex was at that same location in '31.*

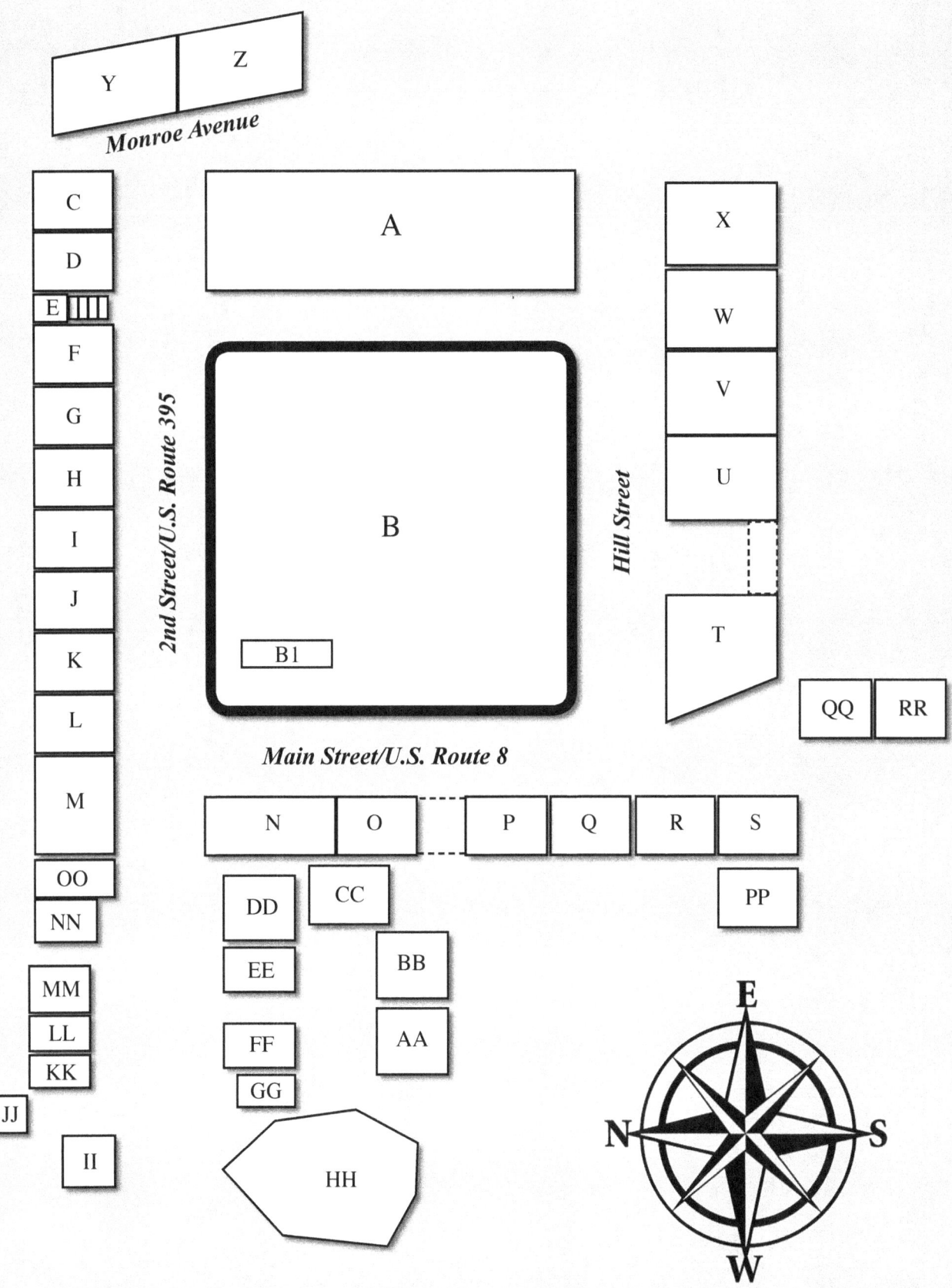

Y

Z

Monroe Avenue

C

D

E

F

G

H

I

J

K

L

M

2nd Street/U.S. Route 395

A

B

B1

Hill Street

X

W

V

U

T

QQ RR

Main Street/U.S. Route 8

N O P Q R S

OO

NN

MM

LL

KK

JJ

II

DD

CC

EE

BB

FF

AA

GG

HH

PP

E

N S

W

APPENDIX III

Make Like a (Family) Tree: Exploring Hill Valley Genealogy

By Rich Handley and Paul C. Giachetti

"Is there a Tannen in every century?"

—**Marty McFly,** *Back to the Future: The Animated Series*

Like many suburban areas, Hill Valley was home to numerous families with roots dating back to the city's origins, each with its own unique, recognizable physical and personality traits. From one generation to the next, it was a sure bet there'd be a Tannen bullying (and being outwitted by) a McFly... a Strickland maintaining strict order and discipline... a Peabody planting trees... a Statler selling vehicles... a Wilson in charge... and a Jones cleaning up the streets.

But with timelines frequently changing, it can be confusing to determine who was related to whom. With that in mind, the following charts will help you keep track of the recurring families featured in the *Back to the Future* films and their spinoff lore. When possible, birth and/or death dates are specified; otherwise, the year or era in which an individual is known to have been alive is provided.

Symbol Key

☐	**Character: male**	⋯⋯⋯	**Relationship: boyfriend or girlfriend (non-married)**
◯	**Character: female**	│	**Relationship: parent-child (vertical)**
◇	**Animal (or inanimate object beloved like a pet)**	─┼─	**Relationship ended: romantic break-up**
?	**Name (and gender if outside box or circle) unknown**	─✕─	**Relationship ended: death of person or animal**
─────	**Relationship: spouse (connected below) or sibling (connected above)**	─///─	**Relationship ended: nullified by timeline change**
-------	**Relationship: undetermined (connected above), engaged (connected below) or owner-pet (connected to a diamond)**		

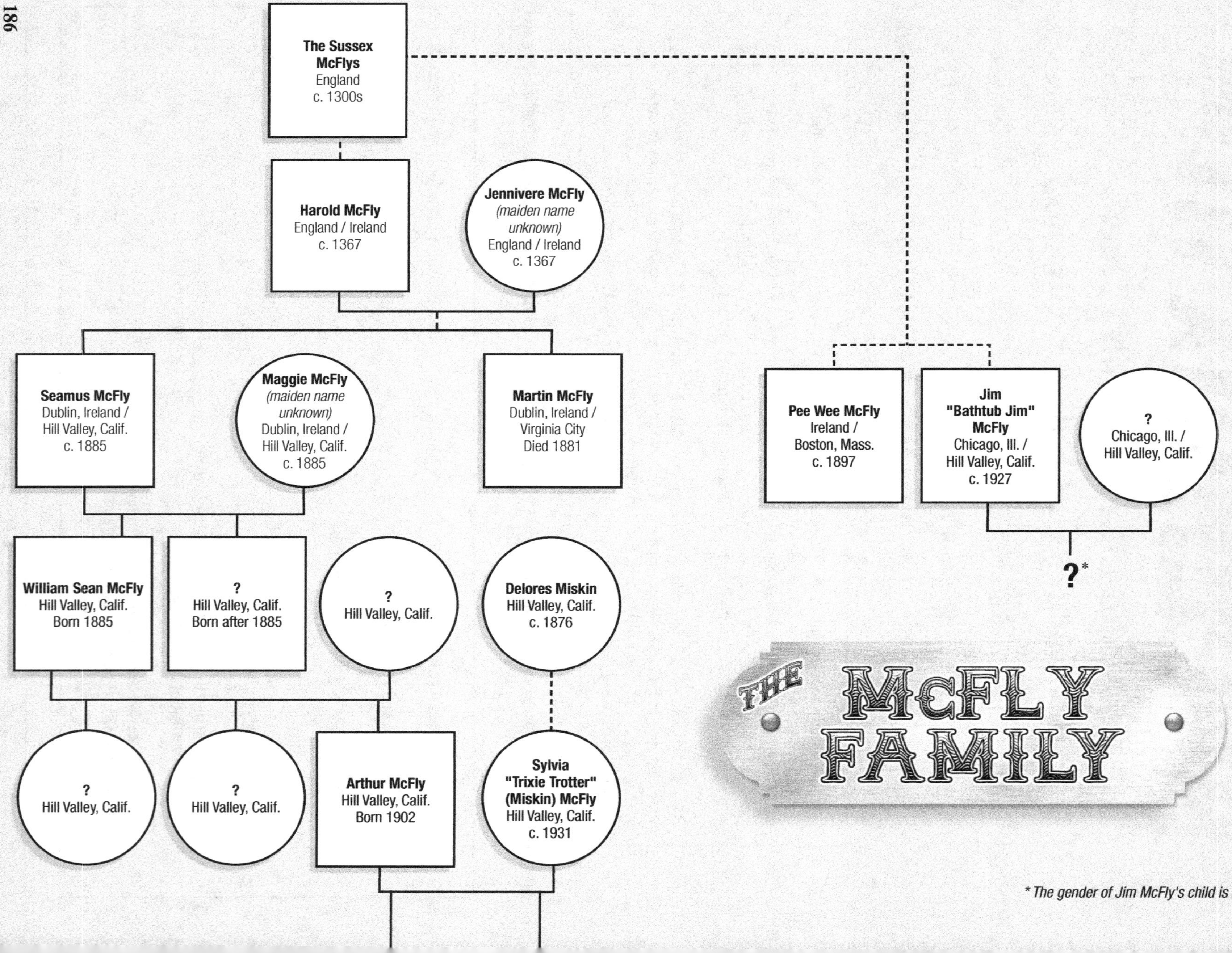

THE McFLY FAMILY

The Sussex McFlys
England
c. 1300s

Harold McFly
England / Ireland
c. 1367

Jennivere McFly
(maiden name unknown)
England / Ireland
c. 1367

Martin McFly
Dublin, Ireland /
Virginia City
Died 1881

Seamus McFly
Dublin, Ireland /
Hill Valley, Calif.
c. 1885

Maggie McFly
(maiden name unknown)
Dublin, Ireland /
Hill Valley, Calif.
c. 1885

?
Hill Valley, Calif.
Born 1885

William Sean McFly
Hill Valley, Calif.
Born 1885

?
Hill Valley, Calif.

?
Hill Valley, Calif.

?
Hill Valley, Calif.

Delores Miskin
Hill Valley, Calif.
c. 1876

**Sylvia
"Trixie Trotter"
(Miskin) McFly**
Hill Valley, Calif.
c. 1931

Arthur McFly
Hill Valley, Calif.
Born 1902

Pee Wee McFly
Ireland /
Boston, Mass.
c. 1897

**Jim
"Bathtub Jim"
McFly**
Chicago, Ill. /
Hill Valley, Calif.
c. 1927

?
Chicago, Ill. /
Hill Valley, Calif.

?*

The gender of Jim McFly's child is unknown.

186

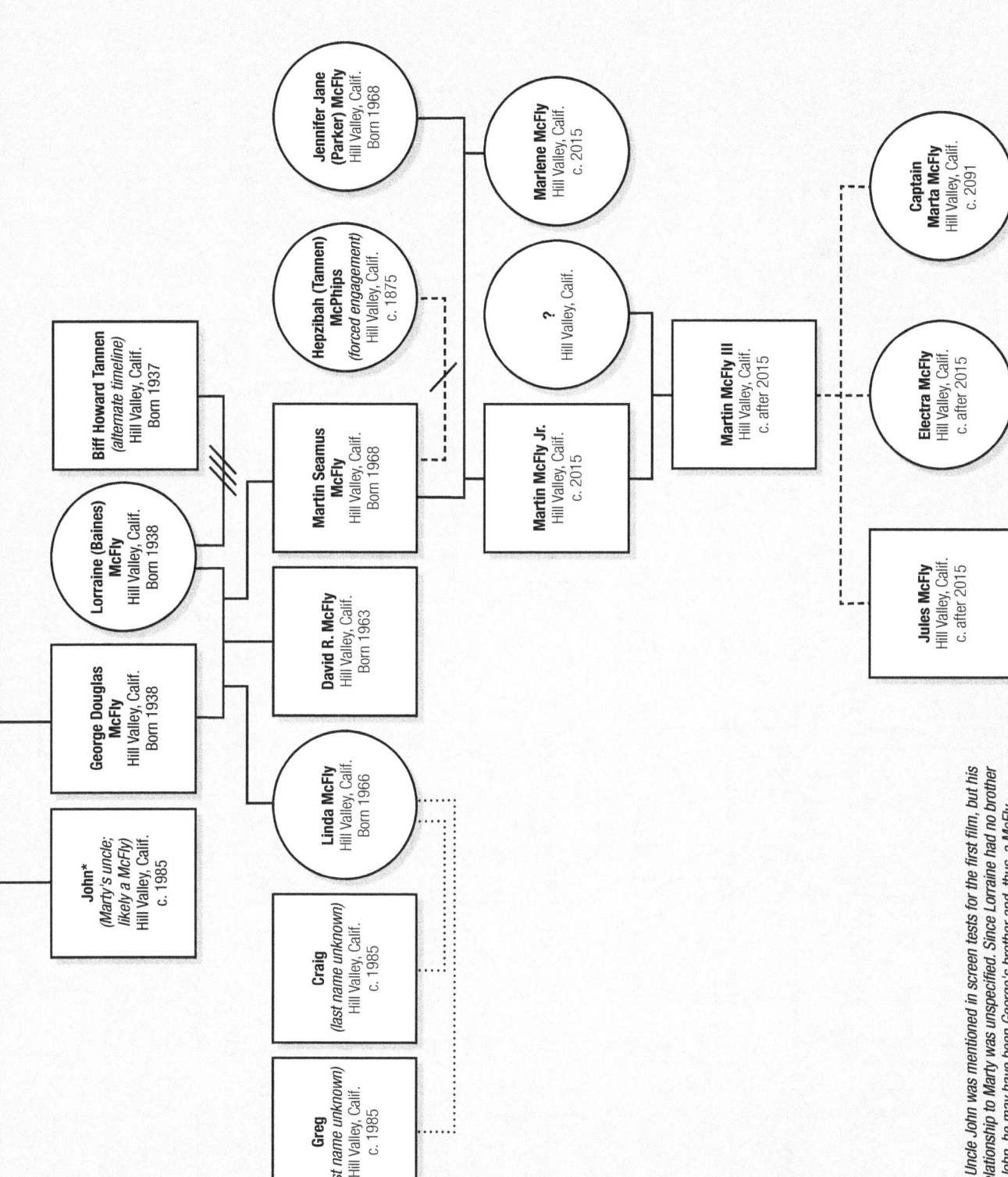

Biff Howard Tannen
(alternate timeline)
Hill Valley, Calif.
Born 1937

Lorraine (Baines)
McFly
Hill Valley, Calif.
Born 1938

George Douglas
McFly
Hill Valley, Calif.
Born 1938

John*
*(Marty's uncle;
likely a McFly)*
Hill Valley, Calif.
c. 1985

Jennifer Jane
(Parker) McFly
Hill Valley, Calif.
Born 1968

Hepzibah (Tannen)
McPhips
(forced engagement)
Hill Valley, Calif.
c. 1875

Martin Seamus
McFly
Hill Valley, Calif.
Born 1968

David R. McFly
Hill Valley, Calif.
Born 1963

Linda McFly
Hill Valley, Calif.
Born 1966

Craig
(last name unknown)
Hill Valley, Calif.
c. 1985

Greg
(last name unknown)
Hill Valley, Calif.
c. 1985

Marlene McFly
Hill Valley, Calif.
c. 2015

?
Hill Valley, Calif.

Martin McFly Jr.
Hill Valley, Calif.
c. 2015

Martin McFly III
Hill Valley, Calif.
c. after 2015

Captain
Marta McFly
Hill Valley, Calif.
c. 2091

Electra McFly
Hill Valley, Calif.
c. after 2015

Jules McFly
Hill Valley, Calif.
c. after 2015

* Marty's Uncle John was mentioned in screen tests for the first film, but his
exact relationship to Marty was unspecified. Since Lorraine had no brother
named John, he may have been George's brother and, thus, a McFly.

187

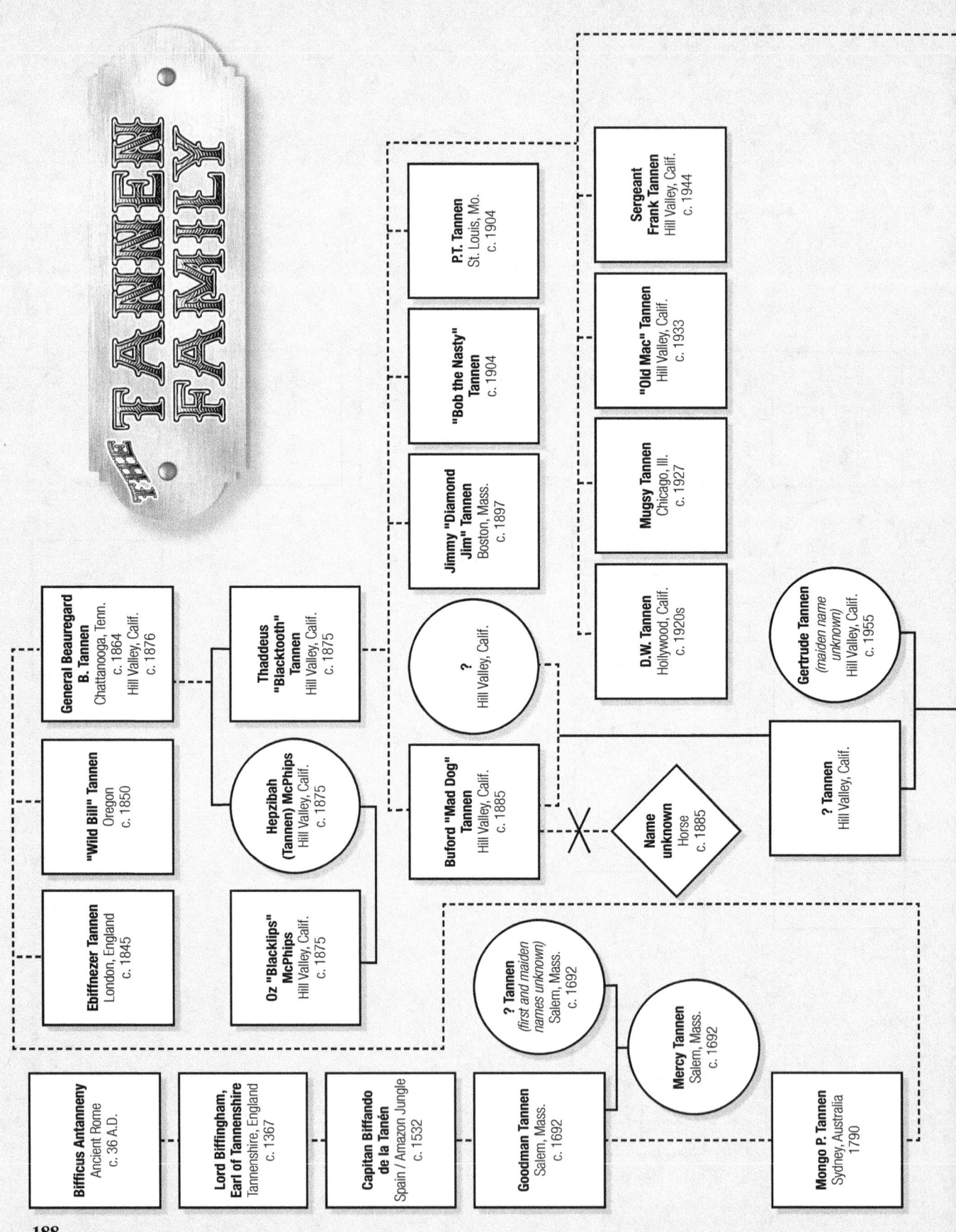

THE TANNEN FAMILY

General Beauregard B. Tannen
Chattanooga, Tenn.
c. 1864
Hill Valley, Calif.
c. 1876

Thaddeus "Blacktooth" Tannen
Hill Valley, Calif.
c. 1875

P.T. Tannen
St. Louis, Mo.
c. 1904

"Bob the Nasty" Tannen
c. 1904

Jimmy "Diamond Jim" Tannen
Boston, Mass.
c. 1897

Sergeant Frank Tannen
Hill Valley, Calif.
c. 1944

"Old Mac" Tannen
Hill Valley, Calif.
c. 1933

Mugsy Tannen
Chicago, Ill.
c. 1927

"Wild Bill" Tannen
Oregon
c. 1850

Hepzibah (Tannen) McPhips
Hill Valley, Calif.
c. 1875

?
Hill Valley, Calif.

D.W. Tannen
Hollywood, Calif.
c. 1920s

Gertrude Tannen
(maiden name unknown)
Hill Valley, Calif.
c. 1955

Ebiffnezer Tannen
London, England
c. 1845

Oz "Blacklips" McPhips
Hill Valley, Calif.
c. 1875

Buford "Mad Dog" Tannen
Hill Valley, Calif.
c. 1885

Name unknown
Horse
c. 1885

? Tannen
Hill Valley, Calif.

Bifficus Antanneny
Ancient Rome
c. 36 A.D.

Lord Biffingham, Earl of Tannenshire
Tannenshire, England
c. 1367

Capitan Biffando de la Tanén
Spain / Amazon Jungle
c. 1532

Goodman Tannen
Salem, Mass.
c. 1692

? Tannen
(first and maiden names unknown)
Salem, Mass.
c. 1692

Mercy Tannen
Salem, Mass.
c. 1692

Mongo P. Tannen
Sydney, Australia
1790

188

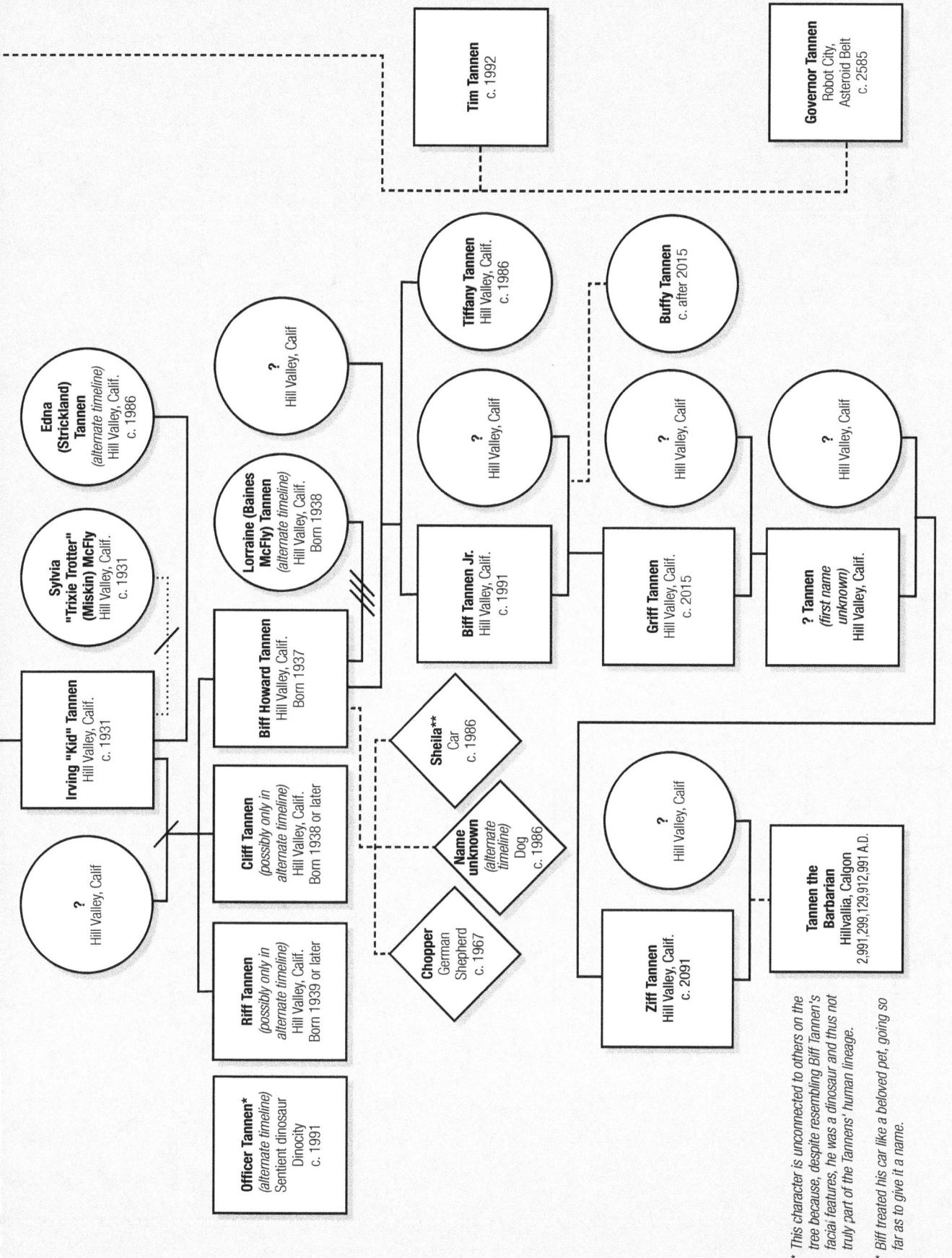

Tim Tannen
c. 1992

Governor Tannen
Robot City,
Asteroid Belt
c. 2585

Edna
(Strickland)
Tannen
(alternate timeline)
Hill Valley, Calif.
c. 1986

Sylvia
"Trixie Trotter"
(Miskin) McFly
Hill Valley, Calif.
c. 1931

Irving "Kid" Tannen
Hill Valley, Calif.
c. 1931

?
Hill Valley, Calif

?
Hill Valley, Calif

Lorraine (Baines
McFly) Tannen
(alternate timeline)
Hill Valley, Calif.
Born 1938

Tiffany Tannen
Hill Valley, Calif.
c. 1986

Buffy Tannen
c. after 2015

?
Hill Valley, Calif

?
Hill Valley, Calif

?
Hill Valley, Calif

Biff Howard Tannen
Hill Valley, Calif.
Born 1937

Biff Tannen Jr.
Hill Valley, Calif.
c. 1991

Griff Tannen
Hill Valley, Calif.
c. 2015

? Tannen
(first name
unknown)
Hill Valley, Calif.

Cliff Tannen
(possibly only in
alternate timeline)
Hill Valley, Calif.
Born 1938 or later

Sheila**
Car
c. 1986

Name
unknown
(alternate timeline)
Dog
c. 1986

Riff Tannen
(possibly only in
alternate timeline)
Hill Valley, Calif.
Born 1939 or later

Chopper
German
Shepherd
c. 1967

?
Hill Valley, Calif

Officer Tannen*
(alternate timeline)
Sentient dinosaur
Dinocity
c. 1991

Ziff Tannen
Hill Valley, Calif.
c. 2091

Tannen the
Barbarian
Hillvallia, Calgon
2,991,299,129,912,991 A.D.

* This character is unconnected to others on the
tree because, despite resembling Biff Tannen's
facial features, he was a dinosaur and thus not
truly part of the Tannens' human lineage.

** Biff treated his car like a beloved pet, going so
far as to give it a name.

189

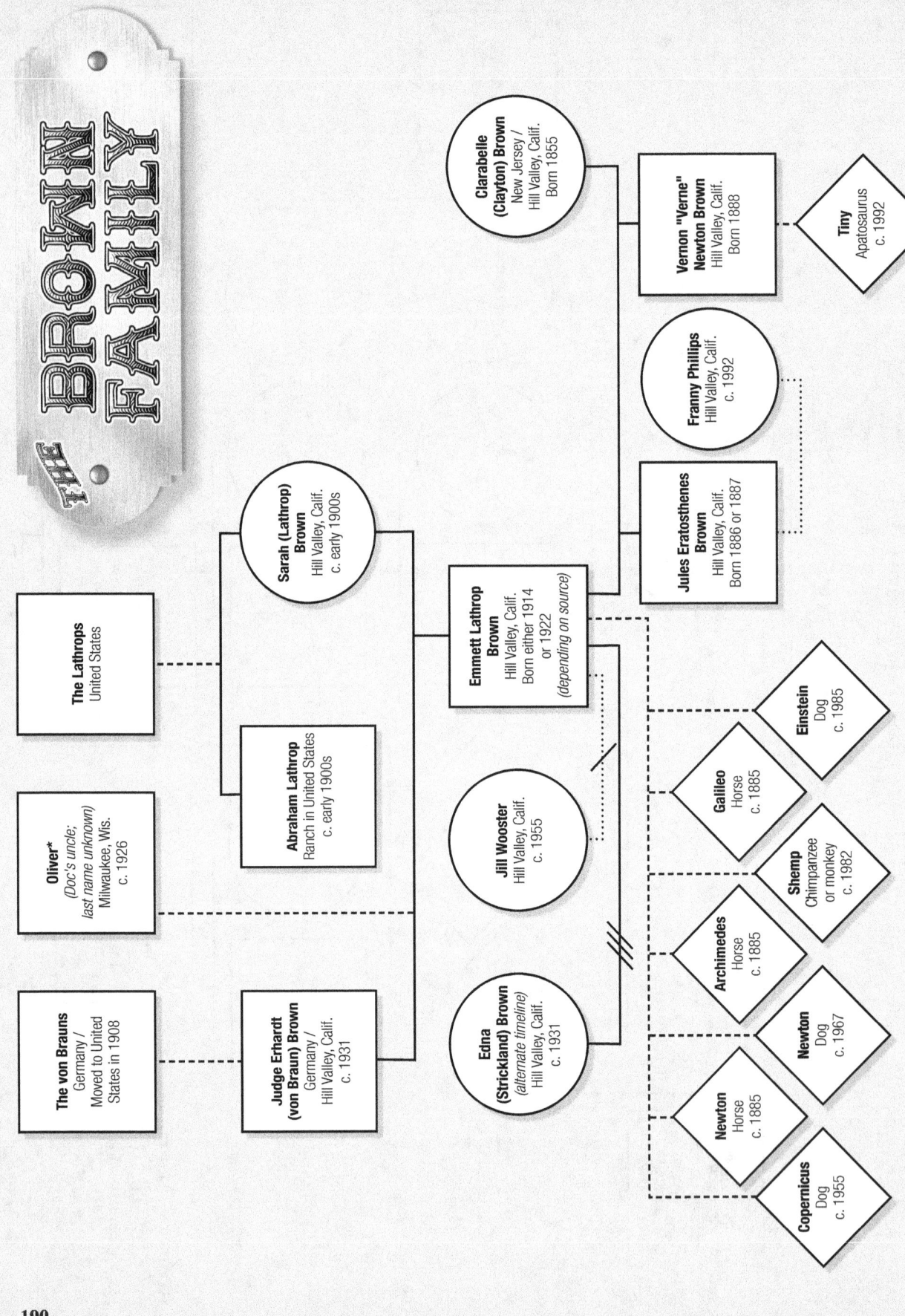

THE BROWN FAMILY

The Lathrops
United States

Oliver*
(Doc's uncle; last name unknown)
Milwaukee, Wis.
c. 1926

The von Brauns
Germany /
Moved to United
States in 1908

Sarah (Lathrop) Brown
Hill Valley, Calif.
c. early 1900s

Abraham Lathrop
Ranch in United States
c. early 1900s

Judge Erhardt (von Braun) Brown
Germany /
Hill Valley, Calif.
c. 1931

Clarabelle (Clayton) Brown
New Jersey /
Hill Valley, Calif.
Born 1855

Vernon "Verne" Newton Brown
Hill Valley, Calif.
Born 1888

Tiny
Apatosaurus
c. 1992

Franny Phillips
Hill Valley, Calif.
c. 1992

Jules Eratosthenes Brown
Hill Valley, Calif.
Born 1886 or 1887

Emmett Lathrop Brown
Hill Valley, Calif.
Born either 1914
or 1922
(depending on source)

Jill Wooster
Hill Valley, Calif.
c. 1955

Edna (Strickland) Brown
(alternate timeline)
Hill Valley, Calif.
c. 1931

Galileo
Horse
c. 1885

Einstein
Dog
c. 1985

Shemp
Chimpanzee
or monkey
c. 1982

Archimedes
Horse
c. 1885

Newton
Dog
c. 1967

Newton
Horse
c. 1885

Copernicus
Dog
c. 1955

* *It was never stated whether Oliver was related to Emmett Brown on the von Braun or Lathrop side of his family.*

190

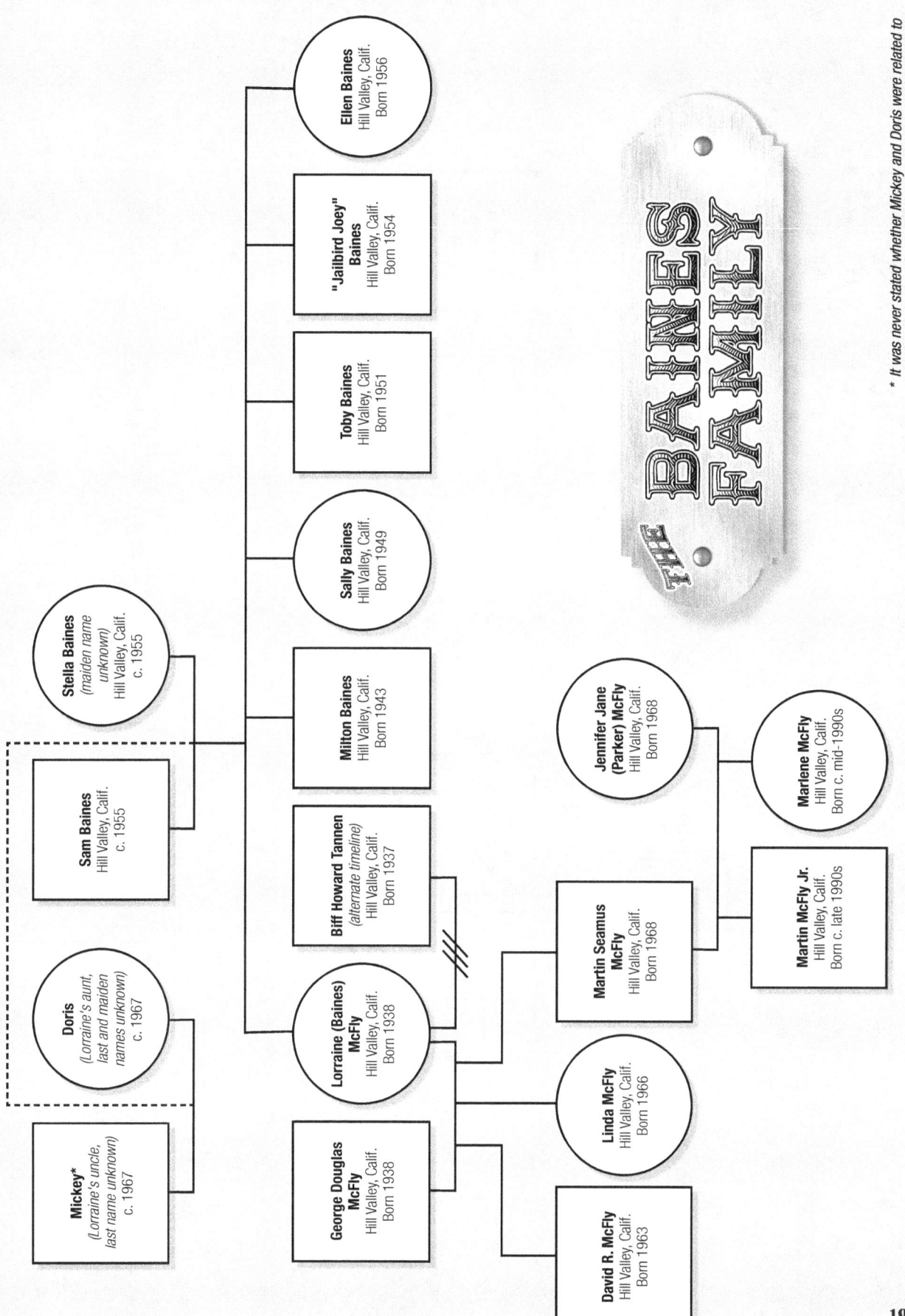

THE BAINES FAMILY

Ellen Baines
Hill Valley, Calif.
Born 1956

"Jailbird Joey" Baines
Hill Valley, Calif.
Born 1954

Toby Baines
Hill Valley, Calif.
Born 1951

Sally Baines
Hill Valley, Calif.
Born 1949

Stella Baines
(maiden name unknown)
Hill Valley, Calif.
c. 1955

Sam Baines
Hill Valley, Calif.
c. 1955

Milton Baines
Hill Valley, Calif.
Born 1943

Biff Howard Tannen
(alternate timeline)
Hill Valley, Calif.
Born 1937

Doris
(Lorraine's aunt, last and maiden names unknown)
c. 1967

Mickey*
(Lorraine's uncle, last name unknown)
c. 1967

Lorraine (Baines) McFly
Hill Valley, Calif.
Born 1938

George Douglas McFly
Hill Valley, Calif.
Born 1938

Jennifer Jane (Parker) McFly
Hill Valley, Calif.
Born 1968

Marlene McFly
Hill Valley, Calif.
Born c. mid-1990s

Martin Seamus McFly
Hill Valley, Calif.
Born 1968

Martin McFly Jr.
Hill Valley, Calif.
Born c. late 1990s

Linda McFly
Hill Valley, Calif.
Born 1966

David R. McFly
Hill Valley, Calif.
Born 1963

* It was never stated whether Mickey and Doris were related to Lorraine Baines on her father's or mother's side of the family.

191

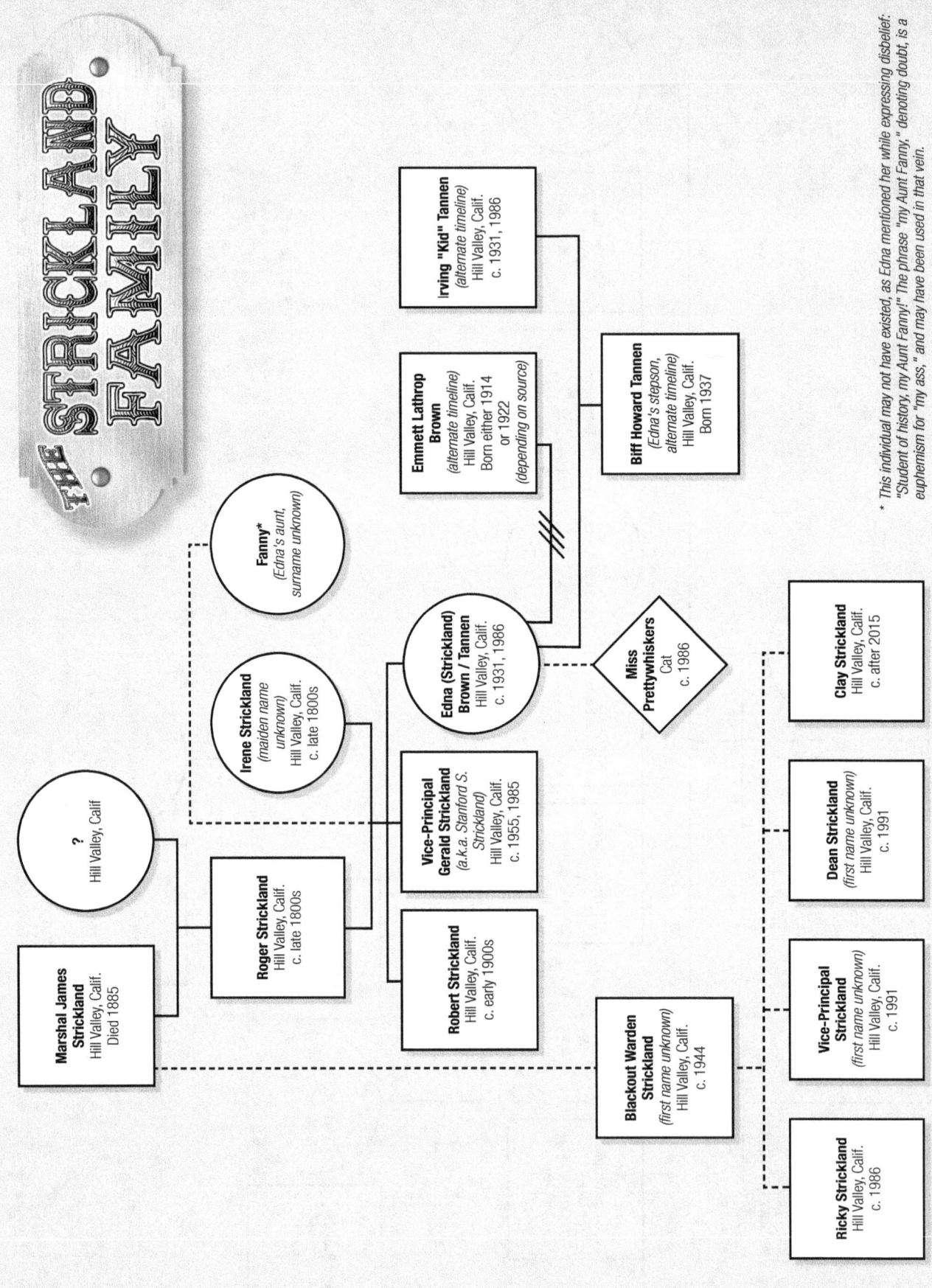

THE STRICKLAND FAMILY

Marshal James Strickland
Hill Valley, Calif.
Died 1885

?
Hill Valley, Calif

Roger Strickland
Hill Valley, Calif.
c. late 1800s

Fanny*
(Edna's aunt,
surname unknown)

Irene Strickland
(maiden name
unknown)
Hill Valley, Calif.
c. late 1800s

Emmett Lathrop Brown
(alternate timeline)
Hill Valley, Calif.
Born either 1914
or 1922
(depending on source)

Irving "Kid" Tannen
(alternate timeline)
Hill Valley, Calif.
c. 1931, 1986

Edna (Strickland) Brown / Tannen
Hill Valley, Calif.
c. 1931, 1986

Biff Howard Tannen
(Edna's stepson,
alternate timeline)
Hill Valley, Calif.
Born 1937

Vice-Principal Gerald Strickland
(a.k.a. Stanford S.
Strickland)
Hill Valley, Calif.
c. 1955, 1985

Robert Strickland
Hill Valley, Calif.
c. early 1900s

Miss Prettywhiskers
Cat
c. 1986

Blackout Warden Strickland
(first name unknown)
Hill Valley, Calif.
c. 1944

Clay Strickland
Hill Valley, Calif.
c. after 2015

Dean Strickland
(first name unknown)
Hill Valley, Calif.
c. 1991

Vice-Principal Strickland
(first name unknown)
Hill Valley, Calif.
c. 1991

Ricky Strickland
Hill Valley, Calif.
c. 1986

* This individual may not have existed, as Edna mentioned her while expressing disbelief: "Student of history, my Aunt Fanny!" The phrase "my Aunt Fanny," denoting doubt, is a euphemism for "my ass," and may have been used in that vein.

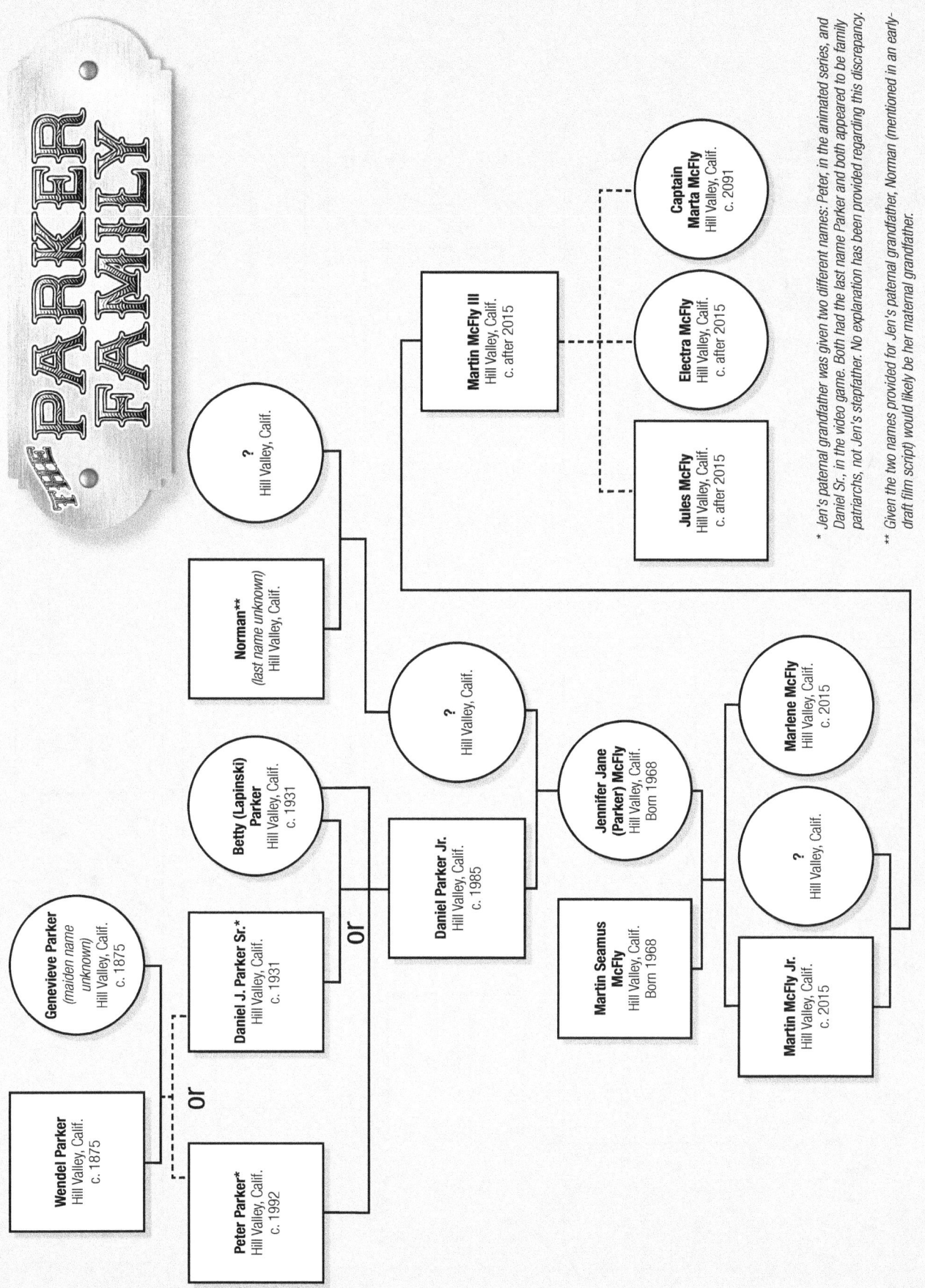

THE PARKER FAMILY

Wendel Parker
Hill Valley, Calif.
c. 1875

Genevieve Parker
(maiden name unknown)
Hill Valley, Calif. c. 1875

Daniel J. Parker Sr. *
Hill Valley, Calif.
c. 1931

or

Peter Parker*
Hill Valley, Calif.
c. 1992

Betty (Lapinski) Parker
Hill Valley, Calif.
c. 1931

?
Hill Valley, Calif.

Norman**
(last name unknown)
Hill Valley, Calif.

?
Hill Valley, Calif.

or

Daniel Parker Jr.
Hill Valley, Calif.
c. 1985

Jennifer Jane (Parker) McFly
Hill Valley, Calif.
Born 1968

Martin Seamus McFly
Hill Valley, Calif.
Born 1968

Marlene McFly
Hill Valley, Calif.
c. 2015

?
Hill Valley, Calif.

Martin McFly Jr.
Hill Valley, Calif.
c. 2015

Martin McFly III
Hill Valley, Calif.
c. after 2015

Jules McFly
Hill Valley, Calif.
c. after 2015

Electra McFly
Hill Valley, Calif.
c. after 2015

Captain Marta McFly
Hill Valley, Calif.
c. 2091

* Jen's paternal grandfather was given two different names: Peter, in the animated series, and Daniel Sr., in the video game. Both had the last name Parker and both appeared to be family patriarchs, not Jen's stepfather. No explanation has been provided regarding this discrepancy.

** Given the two names provided for Jen's paternal grandfather, Norman (mentioned in an early-draft film script) would likely be her maternal grandfather.

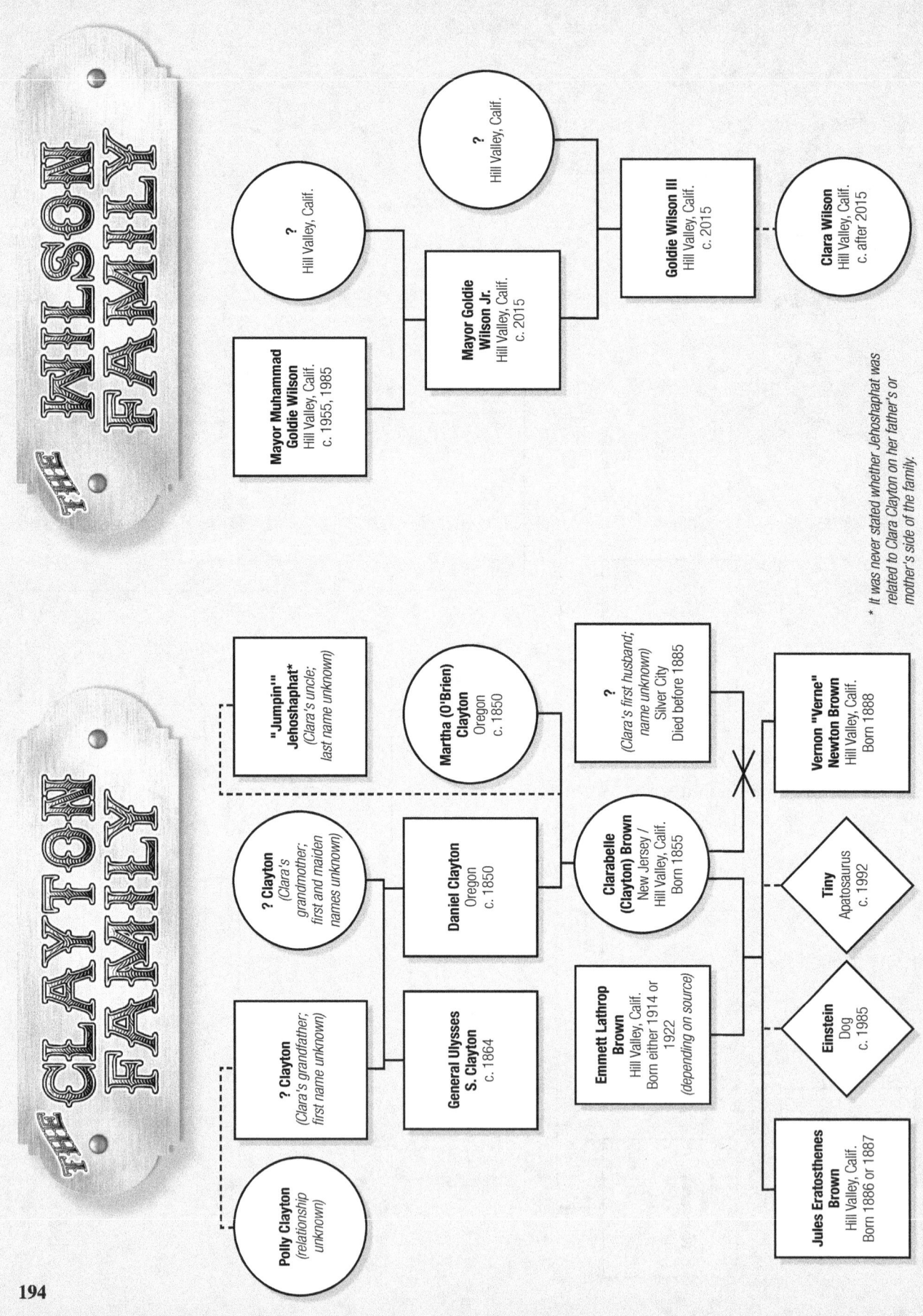

THE WILSON FAMILY

Mayor Muhammad Goldie Wilson
Hill Valley, Calif.
c. 1955, 1985

?
Hill Valley, Calif.

Mayor Goldie Wilson Jr.
Hill Valley, Calif.
c. 2015

?
Hill Valley, Calif.

Goldie Wilson III
Hill Valley, Calif.
c. 2015

Clara Wilson
Hill Valley, Calif.
c. after 2015

THE CLAYTON FAMILY

"Jumpin'" Jehoshaphat*
(Clara's uncle;
last name unknown)

Martha (O'Brien) Clayton
Oregon
c. 1850

? Clayton
(Clara's
grandmother;
first and maiden
names unknown)

Daniel Clayton
Oregon
c. 1850

? Clayton
(Clara's grandfather;
first name unknown)

General Ulysses S. Clayton
c. 1864

Polly Clayton
(relationship
unknown)

?
(Clara's first husband;
name unknown)
Silver City
Died before 1885

Clarabelle (Clayton) Brown
New Jersey /
Hill Valley, Calif.
Born 1855

Emmett Lathrop Brown
Hill Valley, Calif.
Born either 1914 or
1922
(depending on source)

Vernon "Verne" Newton Brown
Hill Valley, Calif.
Born 1888

Tiny
Apatosaurus
c. 1992

Einstein
Dog
c. 1985

Jules Eratosthenes Brown
Hill Valley, Calif.
Born 1886 or 1887

* It was never stated whether Jehoshaphat was
related to Clara Clayton on her father's or
mother's side of the family.

194

THE PEABODY FAMILY

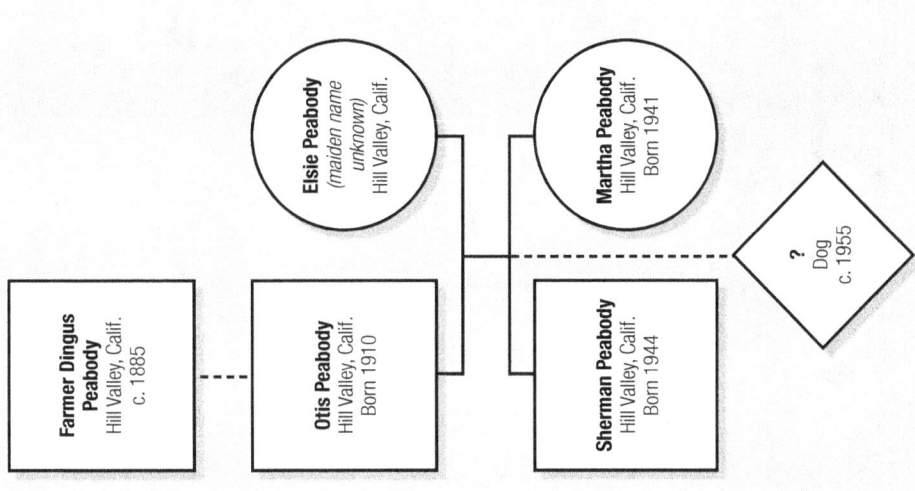

Farmer Dingus Peabody
Hill Valley, Calif.
c. 1885

Otis Peabody
Hill Valley, Calif.
Born 1910

Elsie Peabody
(maiden name unknown)
Hill Valley, Calif.

Martha Peabody
Hill Valley, Calif.
Born 1941

Sherman Peabody
Hill Valley, Calif.
Born 1944

?
Dog
c. 1955

THE NEEDLES FAMILY

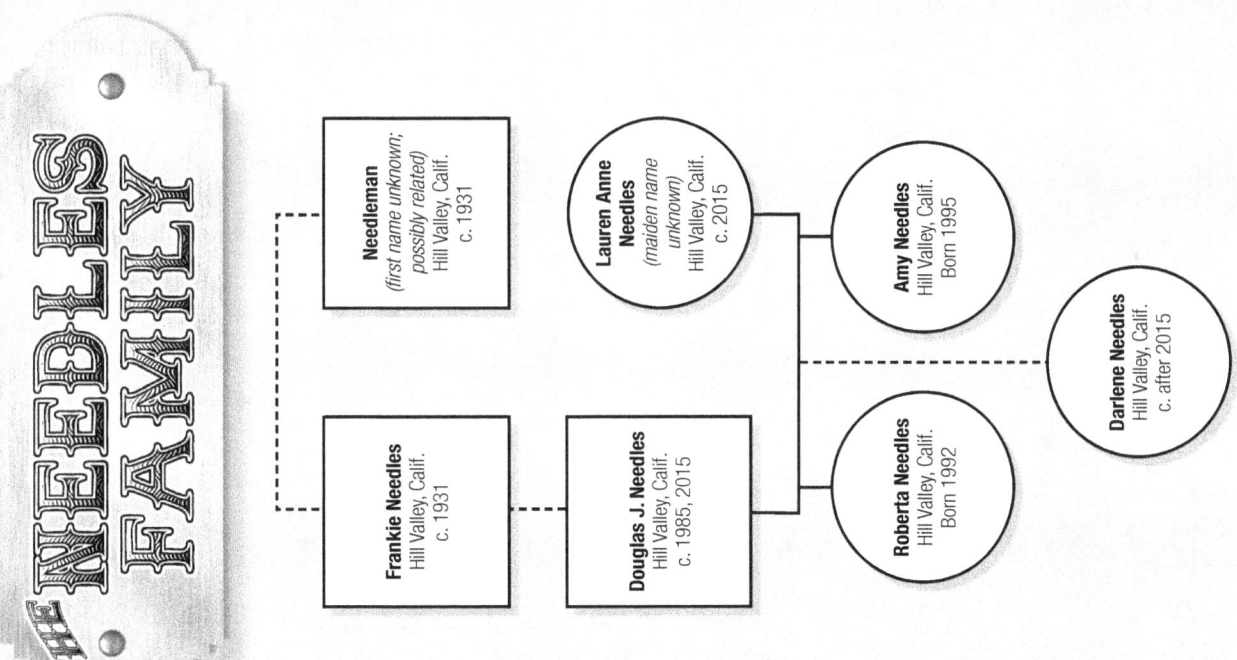

Needleman
(first name unknown; possibly related)
Hill Valley, Calif.
c. 1931

Frankie Needles
Hill Valley, Calif.
c. 1931

Lauren Anne Needles
(maiden name unknown)
Hill Valley, Calif.
c. 2015

Douglas J. Needles
Hill Valley, Calif.
c. 1985, 2015

Amy Needles
Hill Valley, Calif.
Born 1995

Roberta Needles
Hill Valley, Calif.
Born 1992

Darlene Needles
Hill Valley, Calif.
c. after 2015

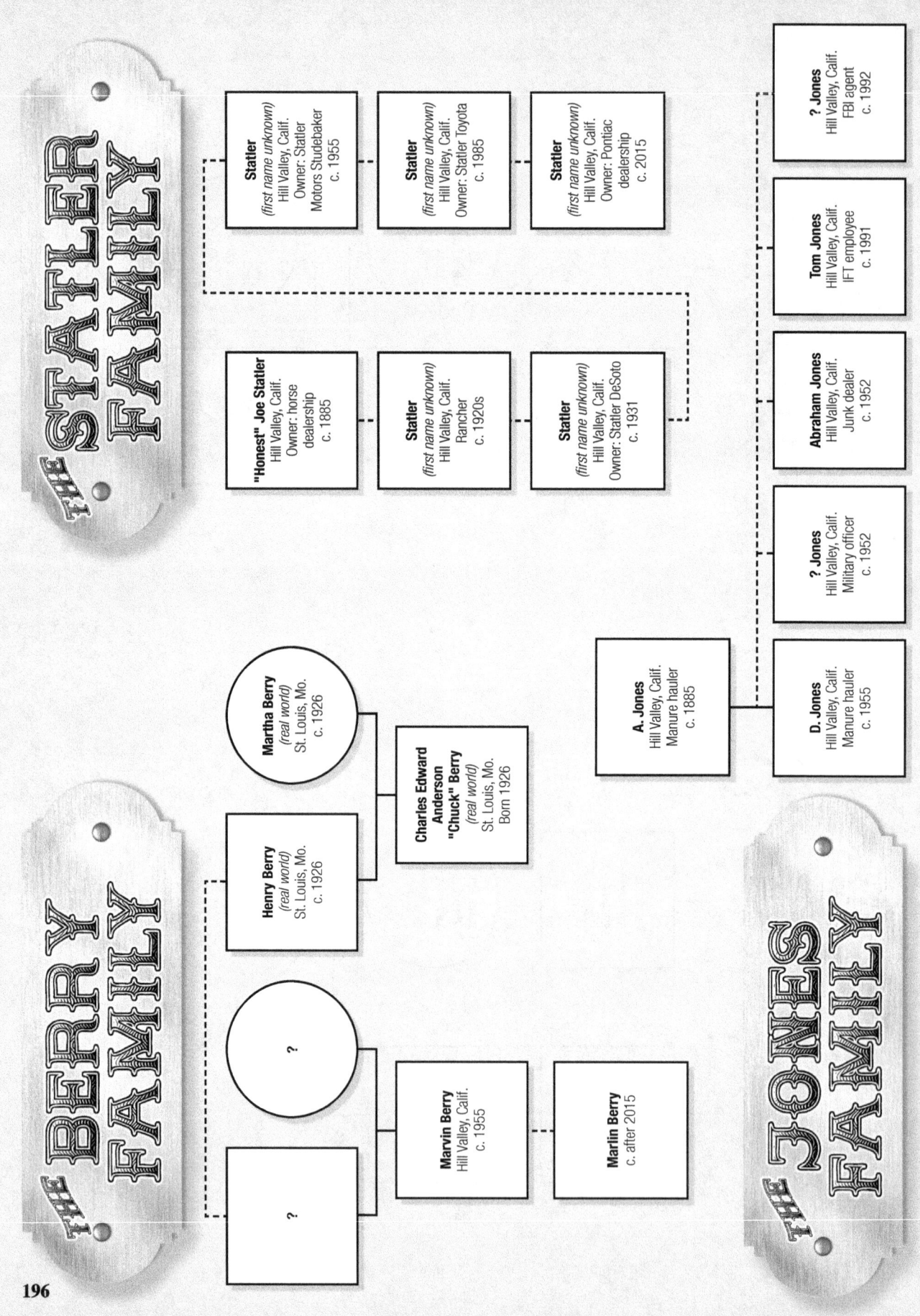

THE STATLER FAMILY

Statler
(first name unknown)
Hill Valley, Calif.
Owner: Statler Motors Studebaker
c. 1955

Statler
(first name unknown)
Hill Valley, Calif.
Owner: Statler Toyota
c. 1985

Statler
(first name unknown)
Hill Valley, Calif.
Owner: Pontiac dealership
c. 2015

"Honest" Joe Statler
Hill Valley, Calif.
Owner: horse dealership
c. 1885

Statler
(first name unknown)
Hill Valley, Calif.
Rancher
c. 1920s

Statler
(first name unknown)
Hill Valley, Calif.
Owner: Statler DeSoto
c. 1931

THE BERRY FAMILY

Martha Berry
(real world)
St. Louis, Mo.
c. 1926

Henry Berry
(real world)
St. Louis, Mo.
c. 1926

Charles Edward Anderson "Chuck" Berry
(real world)
St. Louis, Mo.
Born 1926

?

?

Marvin Berry
Hill Valley, Calif.
c. 1955

Marlin Berry
c. after 2015

THE JONES FAMILY

A. Jones
Hill Valley, Calif.
Manure hauler
c. 1885

D. Jones
Hill Valley, Calif.
Manure hauler
c. 1955

? Jones
Hill Valley, Calif.
Military officer
c. 1952

Abraham Jones
Hill Valley, Calif.
Junk dealer
c. 1952

Tom Jones
Hill Valley, Calif.
IFT employee
c. 1991

? Jones
Hill Valley, Calif.
FBI agent
c. 1992

APPENDIX IV ◀▊▊▊▊

All the Time in the World:
Charting the Path of Temporal Travel

By Rich Handley

"The appropriate question is, 'When the hell are they?'"

—Dr. Emmett L. Brown, *Back to the Future*

Doc Brown's DeLorean and other time-traveling contrivances have carried the characters throughout history, from the distant past to the far-flung future. Nearly every iteration of *Back to the Future* has involved time travel in one form or another, from the films, animated series and amusement-park ride to the comic books, card game, video game, music videos, commercials and even Happy Meal boxes. (The sole exceptions, for those interested, are cartoon episodes #19 and 20, in which no time travel occurred.)

Below is a listing of all known jumps through time, broken down by mode of travel. Note that the order of events in the animated series does not match airdate order. Since the cartoon was structured with Doc reminiscing about a different time-travel adventure each episode, only the framing sequences were in sequential order—the time trips themselves were presented randomly. This timeline attempts to put those adventures in a coherent chronological context, taking into account stated months or seasons, as well as holidays and other factors. For additional information about any particular time-jump, consult the main timeline.

Two of Doc's time-travel technologies not discussed below are the Timespan holographic place/time projection system and the Timeman personal time-travel suit, both described on signage at *Back to the Future: The Ride*. Since it's unknown whether Brown ever traveled through time with these inventions, there is no way to chart their temporal journeys.

ORIGINAL DeLOREAN

• **Oct. 26, 1985 A.D.**—Doc sends the DeLorean and Einstein forward in time; while in transit, they transform into a Mitsubishi Lancer and a robotic dog [MITS].
  NOTE: This commercial contradicts the first film's account of Einstein's maiden voyage.

• **Oct. 26, 1985 A.D.**—To test the DeLorean, Doc sends Einie one minute into the future [BTF1].

• **Oct. 26, 1985 to Nov. 5, 1955 A.D.**—Marty McFly escapes the Libyans by taking the DeLorean into the past [BTF1].

• **Nov. 12, 1955 to Oct. 26, 1985 A.D.**—A younger Doc helps Marty go back to the future by channeling lightning into the Flux Capacitor [BTF1, DCTV, BFAN-6].

• **Oct. 26, 1985 to 2015 A.D.**—Doc and Einstein explore the future, adding a hover-conversion kit and a Mr. Fusion power source [BTF1].

• **Oct. 21, 2015 to Oct. 22, 2015 A.D.**—Doc jumps ahead one day to read a newspaper account after Marty McFly Jr. is arrested for attempted robbery [BTF2].

• **Oct. 22, 2015 to Oct. 29, 2015 A.D.**—Doc jumps ahead another week and learns that Marlene McFly will also

---

receive prison time for staging Marty Jr.'s jailbreak [BTF2].

- **Oct. 29, 2015 to Oct. 26, 1985 A.D.**—Doc travels back to tell Marty about his kids' grim fates [BTF1].

- **Oct. 26, 1985 to Oct. 21, 2015 A.D.**—Doc brings Marty and Jennifer Parker to 2015 so Marty can save their future children [BTF1, BTF2].

- **Oct. 21, 2015 to Nov. 5, 1955 A.D.**—Biff Tannen steals the DeLorean and travels back to give his younger self a futuristic sports almanac to bet on [BTF2].

- **Nov. 5, 1955 to Oct. 21, 2015 A.D.**—Biff, having changed history, returns the DeLorean to his own era [BTF2].

- **Oct. 21, 2015 to Oct. 27, 1985 A.D.**—Marty and Doc return to 1985, to find Hill Valley hellish and Biff-controlled [BTF2].

- **Oct. 27, 1985 to Nov. 12, 1955 A.D.**—Doc and Marty go back to 1955 to retrieve the almanac from Biff [BTF2].

- **Nov. 12, 1955 to Jan. 1, 1885 A.D.**—The DeLorean, piloted by Doc, is struck by lightning and propelled back to the Old West [BTF2].

- **Nov. 12, 1955 to 2025 A.D.**—A temporal duplicate of the DeLorean, created during the lightning strike, is transported seventy years into the future [TLTL-1].

- **Jan. 1, 1885 to Nov. 12, 1955 A.D.**—Doc hides the DeLorean in an old mine for Marty to find, where it remains hidden for seventy years [BTF3].

- **Nov. 12, 1955 to Sept. 1, 1885 A.D.**—Younger Doc repairs the hidden car, which Marty uses to travel back and rescue older Doc [BTF3].

- **Sept. 7, 1885 to Oct. 27, 1985 A.D.**—Using a locomotive to push the car up to time-travel speed, Marty returns to the 1980s; Doc stays behind to be with Clara Clayton [BTF3].

- **Oct. 27, 1985 A.D.**—Moments after Marty's return, another train completely demolishes the DeLorean [BTF3].

DUPLICATE DeLOREAN

- **Nov. 12, 1955 to 2025 A.D.**—A temporal duplicate of the original DeLorean, created during a lightning strike, arrives seventy years in the future [TLTL-1].

- **2025 A.D.**—Griff Tannen tries to use the new DeLorean to vandalize the timestream, but Doc reclaims the car [TLTL-1].

- **Date Unknown to 1985 or 1986 A.D.**—While Doc attends a Huey Lewis and the News concert at a club called Charlie's, a young couple takes it for a spin [HUEY].

- **Date Unknown to 1931 A.D.**—Doc travels back with Einstein to conduct research about Marty's grandmother, Sylvia McFly [TLTL-5].

- **1931 to May 14, 1986 A.D.**—When Doc is arrested for burning down Kid Tannen's speakeasy, an automatic-retrieval function sends the car back to 1986 [TLTL-1].

- **May 14, 1986 to June 13, 1931 A.D.**—Marty journeys to 1931 to prevent Doc from being executed by Kid's gang [TLTL-1].

- **June 13, 1931 A.D.**—Marty travels back a few hours earlier to prevent Arthur McFly's murder [TLTL-2].

- **June 13, 1931 to May 15, 1986 A.D.**—Marty and Doc return to their present, to find Kid Tannen and his sons (Biff, Cliff and Riff) terrorizing Hill Valley [TLTL-2].

- **May 15, 1986 to Aug. 25, 1931 A.D.**—Doc and Marty go back to 1931 to make sure Kid is imprisoned and unable to establish the Tannen crime family [TLTL-2].

- **Aug. 25, 1931 to May 15, 1986 A.D.**—Returning from the past, Marty crashes the DeLorean into a billboard of Citizen Brown; the vehicle smashes onto the ground, demolished [TLTL-3].

CODE	STORY						
ARGN	BTTF-themed TV commercial: Arrigoni	**BTF1**	Film: *Back to the Future*	**CITY**	BTTF-themed music video: Owl City, "Deer in the Headlights"	**HUEY**	BTTF-themed music video: Huey Lewis and the News, "The Power of Love"
BFAN	*Back to the Future: The Animated Series*	**BTF2**	Film: *Back to the Future Part II*	**DCTV**	BTTF-themed TV commercial: DirecTV	**LIMO**	BTTF-themed music video: The Limousines, "The Future"
BFCG	*Back to the Future: The Card Game*	**BTF3**	Film: *Back to the Future Part III*	**ERTH**	*The Earth Day Special*	**MCDN**	BTTF-themed TV commercial: McDonald's
BFCL	*Back to the Future* comic book (limited series)	**BUDL**	BTTF-themed TV commercial: Bud Light	**GALE**	Interviews and commentaries: Bob Gale and/or Robert Zemeckis	**MITS**	BTTF-themed TV commercial: Mitsubishi Lancer
BFCM	*Back to the Future* comic book (monthly series)	**CHEK**	BTTF-themed music video: O'Neal McKnight, "Check Your Coat"	**GARB**	BTTF-themed TV commercials: Garbarino	**MSFT**	BTTF-themed TV commercial: Microsoft
BFHM	BTTF-themed McDonald's Happy Meal boxes	**CHIC**	Photographs hanging in Doc Brown's Chicken restaurant at Universal Studios	**GETV**	BTTF-themed TV commercial: GE		
BTFA	*Back to the Future Annual* (Marvel Comics)						

- **May 16, 1986 A.D.**—Citizen Brown tows the DeLorean to his lab near Clayton Ravine so he can fix it and help Marty eliminate this dystopian timeline [TLTL-4].

- **May 16, 1986 to November 1985 A.D.**—Once activated, the vehicle's time circuits send Citizen Brown back in time six months [TLTL-4].

- **November 1985 to May 16, 1986 A.D.**—Citizen Brown spends the next six months repairing the DeLorean, which returns to 1986 in real time [TLTL-4].

- **May 16, 1986 to Oct. 12, 1931 A.D.**—Brown and Marty head for Aug. 26, 1931, to stop Doc from marrying Edna Strickland, but a mis-calibration brings them to the wrong date [TLTL-4].

- **Oct. 12, 1931 A.D.**—Doc repairs the time circuits, then tests the system by traveling one minute into the past, but the malfunction instead carries him six hours back [TLTL-4].

- **Oct. 12, 1931 A.D.**—A second test jump sends Doc back nine hours and 37 minutes [TLTL-4].

- **Oct. 12, 1931 A.D.**—A third test jump displaces Doc by eight hours [TLTL-4].

- **Oct. 13, 1931 to June 13, 1876 A.D.**—Edna, distraught over her breakup with Emmett, steals the DeLorean and inadvertently propels herself back to the Old West [TLTL-5].

- **June 13, 1876 to Oct. 13, 1931 A.D.**—In one reality, the DeLorean slowly rusts out on Edna's farm for 55 years [TLTL-5].

- **July 17, 1876 A.D.**—Marty and Doc arrive in another DeLorean to find Edna; she tries to escape, but Doc takes remote control of her vehicle with his own [TLTL-5].

- **July 17, 1876 to Oct. 13, 1931 A.D.**—With the two DeLoreans synched, Doc returns them all to 1931 [TLTL-5].

- **Oct. 13, 1931 A.D.**—A temporal breakdown of Edna's stolen DeLorean makes the vehicle vanish entirely [TLTL-5].

ADDITIONAL DeLOREAN

- **June 13, 1986 to Oct. 13, 1931 A.D.**—Doc learns that Marty was stranded in the past after Edna Strickland stole the duplicate DeLorean, and goes back to find him [TLTL-5].
  NOTE: This third car's origin is unexplained.

- **Oct. 13, 1931 to July 17, 1876 A.D.**—Doc and Marty travel back to the Old West to find out how Edna erased Hill Valley from history [TLTL-5].

- **July 17, 1876 to Oct. 13, 1931 A.D.**—Marty and Doc stop Edna from burning down the town; Doc remotely takes control of her DeLorean and navigates both cars to 1931 [TLTL-5].

- **Oct. 13, 1931 to May 15, 1986 A.D.**—Marty and Doc return to 1986 [TLTL-5].

- **May 15, 1986 A.D. to Date Unknown**—When DeLoreans from three divergent futures arrive, each driven by an older Marty, Doc and young Marty blast off to make sense of it all [TLTL-5].

- **1988 to May 1, 1990 A.D.**—Doc travels two years into the future to help Universal Pictures' corporate executives document Universal Studios' planned Orlando theme park [UNIV].

- **May 1, 1990 to 1988 A.D.**—After videotaping various Universal exhibits, Doc returns to his starting point [UNIV].

- **1990 to 2057 A.D.**—Doc visits the future to learn the fate of Earth's rainforests [ERTH].

- **2057 to 1990 A.D.**—Doc rushes to warn mankind to take better care of the environment [ERTH].

- **1990 to 1631 A.D.**—Doc goes back in time again to examine the non-polluted Mississippi River [ERTH].

- **1631 to 1900 A.D.**—Doc visits Los Angeles' past to witness its clean sky and mountains [ERTH].

- **1900 A.D. to Date Unknown**—Doc makes several time jumps to Asia, Africa and Europe in the past, to study how the world was before man began polluting it [ERTH].

- **Date Unknown to 1951 A.D.**—Doc visits Kathmandu, Nepal, but returns without Einstein [ERTH].

- **1951 to 1990 A.D.**—Doc returns to his present, to urge humanity to visit libraries and learn how to fix Earth's environmental damage [ERTH].

- **1990 to 1951 A.D.**—After delivering his warning, Doc heads back to retrieve Einstein [ERTH].

- **1951 to 1990 A.D.**—Doc and Einstein head back to their present [ERTH].

- **May 2, 1991 to Oct. 21, 2015 A.D.**—Doc travels into the future and records a message for a team of time-travel volunteers at the Institute of Future Technology [RIDE].

- **Oct. 21, 2015 to May 2, 1991 A.D.**—Doc returns to the volunteers in 1991 [RIDE].

- **May 2, 1991 to Nov. 16, 1955 A.D.**—An IFT time-travel team visits 1955 [RIDE].

- **Nov. 16, 1955 to May 2, 1991 A.D.**—The time-travel team returns to the institute, unaware Biff Tannen has stowed away aboard the DeLorean [RIDE].

- **May 2, 1991 to Oct. 25, 2015 A.D.**—When Biff steals the DeLorean for a joyride, Doc sends the time-travel volunteers after him in an eight-passenger DeLorean [RIDE].

- **Oct. 25, 2015 A.D. to Oct. 25, 1,000,000 B.C.**—Biff escapes the volunteers by jumping back to the Ice Age [RIDE].

- **Oct. 25, 1,000,000 B.C. to Oct. 25, 64,000,000 B.C.**—Biff again evades his pursuers by fleeing to the time of the dinosaurs [RIDE].

- **Oct. 25, 64,000,000 B.C. to May 2, 1991 A.D.**—The eight-passenger vehicle bumps Biff's DeLorean, sending both cars back to the institute [RIDE].

- **June 4, 2007 to Mar. 9, 2001 A.D.**—Doc brings Microsoft's Robert L. Muglia to 2001, where Acme.com IT technician TechFly is experiencing software setbacks [MSFT].

- **Mar. 9, 2001 to Apr. 12, 2003 A.D.**—Doc next brings Muglia to 2003, where TechFly's boss, Mister Biff, is forcing him to use a failed Microsoft program [MSFT].

- **Apr. 12, 2003 to July 15, 2015 A.D.**—Doc shows Muglia an alternate 2015, an all-white digital space in which defunct Microsoft icons have attained sentience [MSFT].

- **July 15, 2015 to June 4, 2007 A.D.**—Doc returns Muglia to Tech-Ed 2007, where the executive changes his keynote address to lead Microsoft in a new direction [MSFT].

- **May 15, 2008 to 2006 A.D.**—John I.Q. Nerdelbaum Frink Jr. travels back to find out how the Institute of Future Technology became the Krustyland theme park [SIMP].

- **2008 to 2088 A.D.**—Doc brings O'Neal McKnight to the future to help the nightclub coat checker reach his full potential [CHEK].

- **2088 to 2008 A.D.**—McKnight returns to the present with newfound confidence and style [CHEK].

- **Date Unknown to Oct. 19, 2010 A.D.**—Marty McFly drives the DeLorean to the 2010 Spike TV Scream Awards [SCRT].

- **Date Unknown to Oct. 19, 1985 A.D.**—Comedian David Spade takes the DeLorean back to 1985 and stops at a Loverboy concert at Los Angeles' Greek Theatre [SCRM].

CODE	STORY						
ARGN	BTTF-themed TV commercial: Arrigoni	BTF1	Film: *Back to the Future*	CITY	BTTF-themed music video: Owl City, "Deer in the Headlights"	HUEY	BTTF-themed music video: Huey Lewis and the News, "The Power of Love"
BFAN	*Back to the Future: The Animated Series*	BTF2	Film: *Back to the Future Part II*			LIMO	BTTF-themed music video:
BFCG	*Back to the Future: The Card Game*	BTF3	Film: *Back to the Future Part III*	DCTV	BTTF-themed TV commercial: DirecTV		The Limousines, "The Future"
BFCL	*Back to the Future* comic book (limited series)	BUDL	BTTF-themed TV commercial: Bud Light	ERTH	*The Earth Day Special*	MCDN	BTTF-themed TV commercial: McDonald's
BFCM	*Back to the Future* comic book (monthly series)	CHEK	BTTF-themed music video: O'Neal McKnight, "Check Your Coat"	GALE	Interviews and commentaries: Bob Gale and/or Robert Zemeckis	MITS	BTTF-themed TV commercial:
BFHM	BTTF-themed McDonald's Happy Meal boxes	CHIC	Photographs hanging in Doc Brown's	GARB	BTTF-themed TV commercials: Garbarino		Mitsubishi Lancer
BTFA	*Back to the Future Annual* (Marvel Comics)		Chicken restaurant at Universal Studios	GETV	BTTF-themed TV commercial: GE	MSFT	BTTF-themed TV commercial: Microsoft

- **Oct. 19, 1985 to Oct. 19, 2010 A.D.**—Spade enters Nov. 5, 1955, on the time circuits, then changes the date to 2010, to host the Spike TV Scream Awards [SCRM].

- **Jan. 3, 2011 to Jan. 13, 2011 A.D.**—Doc jumps through time, crashing into a Garbarino electronics store in Buenos Aires, Argentina [GARB].

- **Jan. 13, 2011 to Mar. 23 1983 A.D.**—Doc travels back to two years before the DeLorean's maiden voyage [GARB].
  NOTE: The 1983 and 2011 dates were revealed on a behind-the-scenes photo of the car's time circuits at BTTF.com.

- **2011 to Early 20th Century A.D.**—Doc visits his own past to retrieve himself as a child [GARB].

- **Early 20th Century to Oct. 16, 2011 A.D.**—Doc visits his mother on Día de la Madre (Argentina's Mother's Day) so she can spend time with his younger self again [GARB].

- **Date Unknown to Sept. 8, 2011 A.D.**—Doc sets out for 2015 to purchase Nike MAG shoes with power laces, but miscalculates and arrives in 2011 [NIKE].

- **Sept. 8, 2011 to Sept. 8, 2015 A.D.**—Doc checks the time circuits and makes a second attempt to reach 2015 [NIKE].

FOLDABLE DeLOREAN

- **1991 to Feb. 11, 1864 A.D.**—Verne runs away from home, taking the foldable DeLorean back to the era of the Civil War, in Chattanooga, Tennessee [BFAN-1].

- **Feb. 11, 1864 to Early 1991 A.D.**—Verne's family follows in the time train and convinces him to come back to the future [BFAN-1].

- **Early 1991 to Jan. 18, 1927 A.D.**—Marty and Doc travel back to the Prohibition era, in Chicago, Illinois, to find a cure for Einstein's cat-aracts affliction [BFCM-1].

- **Jan. 18, 1927 to Early 1991 A.D.**—After distilling a cure with help from "Bathtub Jim" McFly, Doc and Marty return to the future [BFCM-1].

- **Early 1991 to 1367 A.D.**—Doc brings his family back to a simpler time, to remind them not to be so reliant on technology [BFAN-2].

- **1367 to Early 1991 A.D.**—After a run-in with Lord Biffingham, the Earl of Tannenshire, the Browns return to their own era [BFAN-2].

- **Early 1991 to Sept. 23, 1692 A.D.**—Marty heads back to rescue the Browns when they become stranded in the era of the Salem witch trials [BFAN-4].

- **Sept. 23, 1692 to Early 1991 A.D.**—Marty and the Browns return to their own year [BFAN-4].

- **Early 1991 to 36 A.D.**—Doc visits ancient Rome and borrows the notations of several early historians [BFAN-5].

- **36 to Early 1991 A.D.**—Doc returns to the future with those notes and updates his files [BFAN-5].

- **Early 1991 to 36 A.D.**—Doc goes back to ancient Rome with Marty to return the notations to their rightful owners; Jules and Verne stow away in the back seat [BFAN-5].

- **36 to Early 1991 A.D.**—Doc, Marty and the boys return to their own era [BFAN-5].

- **Early 1991 to 36 A.D.**—Doc goes back to ancient Rome a third time and records a video of himself eating pasta [BFAN-5].

- **36 to Early 1991 A.D.**—Doc returns to his own time period once more [BFAN-5].

- **Early 1991 to Sept. 2, 1752 A.D.**—Verne steals the DeLorean to find his real father, whom he believes to be Benjamin Franklin; Doc and Marty pursue in the *Jules Verne Train* [BFAN-6].

- **Sept. 2, 1752 to Early 1991 A.D.**—Marty, Doc and Verne return to the future after Emmett convinces Verne that he's the boy's father [BFAN-6].

- **Early 1991 to 1532 A.D.**—Doc brings Marty to ancient Peru to find a rare *Bufo marinus* toad, to craft a cure for Marty's Athlete's foot fungus [BFAN-7a].

- **1532 to Early 1991 A.D.**—After encountering conquistador Biffando de la Tanén, Doc and Marty return to their era with a *Bufo marinus* [BFAN-7a].

- **Early 1991 to 1790 A.D.**—Bank robbers Frankie and Sidney steal the DeLorean as a getaway car and end up in an Australian prison in 1790, with Einstein asleep in the back [BFAN-7b].

- **1790 to Early 1991 A.D.**—Einie rescues the would-be thieves from warden Mungo P. Tannen and escorts them back to the present [BFAN-7b].

- **Apr. 1, 1991 to Pleistocene Period**—Doc, the victim of a practical joke to make him think his brain is full, decides to live a simple life among proto-humans [BFAN-12].

- **Pleistocene Period to Apr. 1, 1991 A.D.**—Doc returns to the present day to attend Marty's Pinheads rock concert [BFAN-12].

- **July 1991 to Dec. 24, 1845 A.D.**—When the summer heat becomes unbearable, Doc takes his family to enjoy Christmas in 19th-century England [BFAN-10].

- **Dec. 24, 1845 to July 1991 A.D.**—After an encounter with Ebiffnezer Tannen, the Browns return to their own era [BFAN-10].

- **Aug. 2, 1991 to May 19, 2015 A.D.**—Doc and Marty visit 2015, where Marty has a run-in with Griff Tannen and his gang [BFAN-c].

- **May 19, 2015 to June 10, 1885 A.D.**—Marty and Doc return to the Old West and save Clara from being hurt in a gunfight between Buford Tannen and another gunslinger [BFAN-c].

- **June 10, 1885 A.D. to Between 85,000,000 and 65,000,000 B.C.**—Doc, Clara and Marty travel back to rescue Jules and Verne from being eaten by a large, red *Tyrannosaurus rex* [BFAN-c].

- **Between 85,000,000 and 65,000,000 B.C. to Aug. 2, 1991 A.D.**—Marty and the Browns return to 1991 [BFAN-c].

- **Late 1991 to Aug. 5, 1926 A.D.**—Marty and the Brown boys explore Doc's youth in Milwaukee, to prevent him from developing a fear of fishing [BFAN-11].

- **Late 1926 to Late 1991 A.D.**—After eliminating Doc's childhood trauma, the boys and Marty return to the present [BFAN-11].

- **Late 1991 to Sept. 1, 1897 A.D.**—Marty, Jules and Verne go back to save the baseball career of Pee Wee McFly [BFAN-8].

- **Sept. 2, 1897 to Late 1991 A.D.**—After helping Pee Wee become a baseball hero instead of a failure, the boys and Marty head back home [BFAN-8].

- **Late 1991 to Mar. 3, 1850 A.D.**—Verne, Jules and Marty travel back to photograph pioneers Martha O'Brien and Daniel Clayton for Verne's show-and-tell; the DeLorean is trampled by a herd of buffalo [BFAN-13].

- **Mar. 4, 1850 to Late 1991 A.D.**—Doc follows his sons back in the time train, retrieving the stranded youths and the crumpled DeLorean [BFAN-13].

- **Oct. 10, 1991 A.D. to Oct. 10, 3,000,000 B.C.**—Doc and his sons journey back to the Cretaceous Period to test Doc's Proprietary Ultrasonic Subatomic Molecular Redistributor [BFAN-3].

- **Oct. 10, 3,000,000 B.C. to Oct. 10, 1991 A.D.**—The Browns return to their own era, but realize they've inadvertently caused dinosaurs to evolve instead of humans [BFAN-3].

- **Oct. 10, 1991 A.D. to Oct. 10, 3,000,000 B.C.**—Doc and the boys go back to prehistoric times once more, to ensure the dinosaurs' extinction [BFAN-3].

CODE	STORY						
ARGN	BTTF-themed TV commercial: Arrigoni	**BTF1**	Film: *Back to the Future*	**CITY**	*BTTF*-themed music video: Owl City, "Deer in the Headlights"	**HUEY**	*BTTF*-themed music video: Huey Lewis and the News, "The Power of Love"
BFAN	*Back to the Future: The Animated Series*	**BTF2**	Film: *Back to the Future Part II*	**DCTV**	*BTTF*-themed TV commercial: DirecTV	**LIMO**	*BTTF*-themed music video: The Limousines, "The Future"
BFCG	*Back to the Future: The Card Game*	**BTF3**	Film: *Back to the Future Part III*	**ERTH**	*The Earth Day Special*		
BFCL	*Back to the Future* comic book (limited series)	**BUDL**	*BTTF*-themed TV commercial: Bud Light	**GALE**	Interviews and commentaries: Bob Gale and/or Robert Zemeckis	**MCDN**	*BTTF*-themed TV commercial: McDonald's
BFCM	*Back to the Future* comic book (monthly series)	**CHEK**	*BTTF*-themed music video: O'Neal McKnight, "Check Your Coat"	**GARB**	*BTTF*-themed TV commercials: Garbarino	**MITS**	*BTTF*-themed TV commercial: Mitsubishi Lancer
BFHM	*BTTF*-themed McDonald's Happy Meal boxes	**CHIC**	Photographs hanging in Doc Brown's Chicken restaurant at Universal Studios	**GETV**	*BTTF*-themed TV commercial: GE	**MSFT**	*BTTF*-themed TV commercial: Microsoft
BTFA	*Back to the Future Annual* (Marvel Comics)						

- **Oct. 10, 3,000,000 B.C. to Oct. 10, 1991 A.D.**—Returning to their own era, the time-travelers find it no longer dino-controlled [BFAN-3].

- **Dec. 15, 1991 to Dec. 15, 2091 A.D.**—Doc and Clara visit the future to enjoy a second honeymoon on McFly Space Cruises' inaugural flight to Mars [BFAN-9].

- **Dec. 15, 2091 to Dec. 15, 1991 A.D.**—The couple return home after Ziff Tannen's sabotage of the flight cuts their honeymoon short [BFAN-9].

- **1992 to 1697 A.D.**—Marty accompanies Verne to the Caribbean Islands so Verne can get an earring [BFAN-14].

- **1697 to 1992 A.D.**—After an encounter with pirate king Mac the Black, Verne and Marty return home [BFAN-14].

- **1992 to 127 A.D.**—Walter Wisdom steals the DeLorean and travels back to ancient Egypt; Doc, Marty, Jules and Verne pursue in the time train [BFAN-15].

- **127 to 1883 A.D.**—Wisdom escapes Doc by jumping to 1883, where the train is nearly enveloped by Krakatoa's volcanoes [BFAN-15].

- **1883 to 1992 A.D.**—Thinking Doc and the locomotive destroyed, Wisdom returns to 1991 and tries to auction off the DeLorean on TV [BFAN-15].

- **1992 to Sept. 27, 1944 A.D.**—Verne brings Marty back with him to World War II, to find the blueprints for Doc's Fance-O-Dance Memorizing Shoes [BFAN-17].

- **Sept. 27, 1944 to 1992 A.D.**—Retrieving the lost documents, Marty and Verne head home again [BFAN-17].

- **1992 to Apr. 7, 1933 A.D.**—Verne brings his friend Chris back in time to see the now-defunct Bob Brothers All-Star International Circus [BFAN-18].

- **Apr. 8, 1933 to 1992 A.D.**—After saving the circus from landlord Mac Tannen, Verne and Chris return to the 1990s [BFAN-18].

- **1992 to 1881 A.D.**—Verne and Marty attempt to convince Jules Verne to change his name so Doc and Clara will give Verne a different name in his honor [BFAN-21].

- **1881 to Oct. 29, 1888 A.D.**—When Jules Verne refuses to cooperate, the youths visit the day of Verne's birth, to convince Clara and Doc to choose a better name [BFAN-21].

- **Oct. 29, 1888 to 1992 A.D.**—Verne returns to 1992 after witnessing his own birth and deciding he likes his name after all [BFAN-21].

- **1992 to Late 19th Century A.D.**—When Doc causes a power outage on Founder's Day, Clara Clayton goes back in time to find city founder Bill Hill [BFAN-22].

- **Late 19th Century to 1992 A.D.**—Clara brings Hill to the future so he can help her calm the angry masses [BFAN-22].

- **1992 to Late 19th Century A.D.**—After Hill reminds everyone that Founder's Day predated electricity, Clara returns the Old Pioneer to his own era [BFAN-22].

- **Late 19th Century to 1992 A.D.**—Clara returns to 1992 to enjoy the celebration [BFAN-22].

- **1992 to 1967 A.D.**—When Biff Tannen convinces others that Doc is an extraterrestrial, Marty, Jules and Verne go back in time and use the DeLorean as a spaceship to scare Biff Tannen into keeping his conspiracy theories to himself [BFAN-23].

- **1967 to 1992 A.D.**—With the "alien Doc" problem thwarted, Marty and the boys return to 1992 [BFAN-23].

- **1992 to Feb. 15, 1952 A.D.**—Marty takes the boys back to witness Doc's stint as professional wrestler "Brain Buster" Brown [BFAN-24].

- **Feb. 15, 1952 to 1992 A.D.**—The Brown boys return home, having learned a lesson from their father's exploits [BFAN-24].

- **1992 to June 29, 1904 A.D.**—Doc and Clara attend the 1904 St. Louis World Exposition; Marty and the boys follow in the time train when Marty experiences haircut issues [BFAN-25].

- **June 29, 1904 to 1992 A.D.**—Marty and the Browns eventually return to the present [BFAN-25].

- **1992 A.D. to 150,000,000 B.C.**—Verne and Marty go back to what will later be Chattanooga, fetching an *Apatosaurus* egg for Verne's school show-and-tell [BFAN-26].

- **150,000,000 B.C. to 1992 A.D.**—Marty and Verne return to the present, where the boy names the hatched dinosaur Tiny [BFAN-26].

- **October 1992 A.D.**—When Doc's Extra-dimensional Storage Closet turns reality inside out, he chains the DeLorean to the closet's pan-dimensional generator and pulls the invention—and, thus, the universe—right-side-out again [BFCL-3].

EIGHT-PASSENGER DeLOREAN

- **May 2, 1991 to Oct. 25, 2015 A.D.**—When Biff steals the DeLorean for a joyride, Doc sends a team of time-travel volunteers after him in his eight-passenger version [RIDE].

- **Oct. 25, 2015 to Oct. 25, 1,000,000 B.C.**—Biff escapes the time-travel volunteers by jumping back to the Ice Age; the eight-passenger model follows [RIDE].

- **Oct. 25, 1,000,000 B.C. to Oct. 25, 64,000,000 B.C.**—Biff evades his pursuers by fleeing to the time of the dinosaurs; the time-travel volunteers again pursue him [RIDE].

- **Oct. 25, 64,000,000 B.C. to May 2, 1991**—The eight-passenger vehicle bumps Biff's DeLorean, sending both cars back to the institute in 1991 [RIDE].

UNIDENTIFIED DeLOREAN(S)

- **1989 to 2015 A.D.**—Two young men steal the DeLorean from Marty McFly's driveway and explore Hill Valley's future, where they dine at a Pizza Hut [PIZA].

- **Circa 1990s to Oct. 28, 2039 A.D.**—A pair of Italian teenagers take a DeLorean into the future and stock up on Arrigoni vending machine products [ARGN].

- **Oct. 28, 2039 to Circa 1990s A.D.**—The Italian teens return to the 1990s to share their future booty with their mother [ARGN].

- **May 25, 2011 to Mar. 30, 2015 A.D.**—A DeLorean on auto-pilot lures a skateboarder to go for a ride, then takes him to the future, nearly hitting a space-suited pedestrian [CITY].

- **Jan. 3, 2152 to July 17, 2011 A.D.**—Two black-suited individuals ride a DeLorean through a desert lined with domed cities, then travel into the past [LIMO].

- **July 17, 2011 A.D.**—The DeLorean immediately hits a Porsche head-on, sending the two men in black through the windshield and into out-of-body experiences [LIMO].

- **Date Unknown to February 2012 A.D.**—A DeLorean visits an automotive garage as four mechanics ponder how they'd use time travel; the car's presence causes one man to erase himself from existence upon deciding he'd kill his own father [BUDL].

- **February 2012 A.D. to Date Unknown**—The DeLorean then jumps to an unknown destination, causing the remaining mechanics to forget their co-worker existed [BUDL].

- **Sept. 5, 2013 A.D.**—Marty stops at TransCanada's parking lot to replace a DeLorean's Mr. Fusion with a G.E. gas turbine [GETV].

- **After 2015 A.D.**—Marlin Berry, Verne Brown, Electra McFly, Jules McFly, Marty McFly III, Darlene Needles, Clay Strickland, Buffy Tannen, Tiffany Tannen and Clara Wilson each attempt to steal the DeLorean and alter each other's fates [BFCG].

CODE	STORY						
ARGN	BTTF-themed TV commercial: Arrigoni	BTF1	Film: *Back to the Future*	CITY	BTTF-themed music video: Owl City, "Deer in the Headlights"	HUEY	BTTF-themed music video: Huey Lewis and the News, "The Power of Love"
BFAN	*Back to the Future: The Animated Series*	BTF2	Film: *Back to the Future Part II*	DCTV	BTTF-themed TV commercial: DirecTV	LIMO	BTTF-themed music video: The Limousines, "The Future"
BFCG	*Back to the Future: The Card Game*	BTF3	Film: *Back to the Future Part III*	ERTH	*The Earth Day Special*		
BFCL	*Back to the Future* comic book (limited series)	BUDL	BTTF-themed TV commercial: Bud Light	GALE	Interviews and commentaries: Bob Gale and/or Robert Zemeckis	MCDN	BTTF-themed TV commercial: McDonald's
BFCM	*Back to the Future* comic book (monthly series)	CHEK	BTTF-themed music video: O'Neal McKnight, "Check Your Coat"			MITS	BTTF-themed TV commercial: Mitsubishi Lancer
BFHM	BTTF-themed McDonald's Happy Meal boxes			GARB	BTTF-themed TV commercials: Garbarino		
BTFA	*Back to the Future Annual* (Marvel Comics)	CHIC	Photographs hanging in Doc Brown's Chicken restaurant at Universal Studios	GETV	BTTF-themed TV commercial: GE	MSFT	BTTF-themed TV commercial: Microsoft

- **Date Unknown**—A middle-aged Marty McFly from one possible reality has several temporal encounters with his "evil twin" from another timeline [TLTL-5].

- **Date Unknown**—A second middle-aged Marty (the first's "evil twin") eliminates the other's timeline, then makes five more time jumps in a blue-painted DeLorean [TLTL-5].

- **Date Unknown**—This second Marty also alters the timeline of a third, grittier middle-aged Marty during several more time jumps [TLTL-5].

- **Date Unknown to May 15, 1986 A.D.**—All three middle-aged Martys travel to 1986 to elicit Doc's help in protecting their individual realities [TLTL-5].

JULES VERNE TRAIN

- **After 1885 to Oct. 27, 1985 A.D.**—Doc and Clara bring their sons to the future to retrieve Einstein and briefly visit Marty and Jennifer [BTF3].

- **Oct. 27, 1985 A.D. to Date Unknown**—Doc's family blast off in the time train [BTF3].

- **1986 to 2025 A.D.**—Doc travels to 2025 and finds a temporal duplicate of the original DeLorean, created when that car was struck by lightning in 1955 [TLTL-1].

- **Date Unknown to 1991 A.D.**—Doc and his family settle down in Hill Valley, bringing the *Jules Verne Train* with them [BFAN-1].

- **1991 to Feb. 11, 1864 A.D.**—When Verne runs away in the DeLorean, Doc, Jules and Marty follow him to the Civil War era, in Chattanooga, Tennessee [BFAN-1].

- **Feb. 11, 1864 to 1991 A.D.**—Stowing the DeLorean in a compartment at the back of the train, Marty and the Browns return to the future [BFAN-1].

- **Early 1991 A.D. to Circa 1000 B.C.**—Doc and his family visit ancient Egypt [BFAN-4].

- **Circa 1000 B.C. to Late August 1692 A.D.**—The time train is damaged as the Browns leave Egypt, causing the train to end up at the time of the Salem witch trials [BFAN-4].

- **Sept. 23, 1692 to Early 1991 A.D.**—With Marty's help, the Browns return to their own year [BFAN-4].

- **Early 1991 to Sept. 2, 1752 A.D.**—When Verne runs away to find his real father (whom he believes to be Ben Franklin), Doc and Marty follow in the time train [BFAN-6].

- **Sept. 2, 1752 to Early 1991 A.D.**—Marty, Emmett and Verne return to the future after Doc convinces Verne that he's the boy's father [BFAN-6].

- **Aug. 2, 1991 A.D. to Date Unknown**—Einstein takes the time train on a solo adventure [BFAN-c].

- **Summer 1991 to 1875 A.D.**—Marty travels back to stop Biff Tannen from stealing Jennifer Parker's family ranch [BFAN-16].

  NOTE: This episode aired during season 2, but was said to occur the previous summer.

- **1875 A.D.**—Jules and Verne jump the train a moment ahead in space-time to avoid killing Genevieve Parker, tied to train tracks by Thaddeus Tannen [BFAN-16].

- **1875 to Summer 1991 A.D.**—After thwarting Tannen's attempt to seize the ranch, Marty and the Brown boys return to 1991 [BFAN-16].

- **Late 1991 to Mar. 3, 1850 A.D.**—Doc travels back to rescue his sons and Marty after they become stranded while meeting Martha O'Brien and Daniel Clayton [BFAN-13].

- **Mar. 4, 1850 to Late 1991 A.D.**—Loading the buffalo-trampled DeLorean in the back of the train, Marty and the Browns head back to 1991 [BFAN-13].

- **Dec. 15, 1991 to Dec. 15, 2091 A.D.**—Jules and Verne rush to protect their parents, lost in space during McFly Space Cruises' inaugural flight to Mars [BFAN-9].

- **Dec. 15, 2091 to Dec. 15, 1991 A.D.**—The reunited Browns return home [BFAN-9].

- **1992 to 127 A.D.**—Doc, Marty, Jules and Verne use the train to stop Walter Wisdom from stealing the DeLorean [BFAN-15].

- **127 to 1883 A.D.**—The time train follows Wisdom back to 1883, where it is nearly enveloped by Krakatoa's volcanoes [BFAN-15].

- **1883 to 1992 A.D.**—Surviving the eruption in giant oven-mitts, Marty and the Browns return to 1992, in time to stop Wisdom from selling the DeLorean on TV [BFAN-15].

- **1992 to June 29, 1904 A.D.**—Marty follows Doc and Clara back to 1904 to seek the scientist's help, after Marty's hair grows out of control due to Doc's invention [BFAN-25].

- **June 29, 1904 to 1992 A.D.**—Marty and the Browns return to the present [BFAN-25].

- **1992 A.D. to 150,000,000 B.C.**—When Biff Tannen and Walter Wisdom steal Verne's pet dinosaur, Verne returns Tiny to its natural habitat in the train's box car [BFAN-26].

- **150,000,000 B.C. to 1992 A.D.**—Verne returns to his own era [BFAN-26].

- **1992 to June 3, 2585 A.D.**—Doc brings his family and Marty to see future Hill Valley [BFCL-1].

- **June 3, 2585 A.D.**—Marty and the Browns take the train to Robot City, a domed station in the Asteroid Belt; there, the train is damaged during a robotic revolution [BFCL-1].

- **June 3, 2585 to 2,991,299,129,912,991 A.D.**—A damaged Flux Capacitor propels the train into the far distant future, where the group encounters Tannen the Barbarian [BFCL-2].

- **2,991,299,129,912,991 to October 1992 A.D.**—The repaired *Jules Verne Train* heads back to its own era, "bouncing" off the years 4, 6, 8, 12, 18, 267, 328, 1998, 2011, 2096, 2737, 2995, 3749 and 8607, before finally arriving in 1992 [BFCL-3].

MINIATURE MAIL TRUCK

- **Sept. 23, 1692 to Early 1991 A.D.**—While stranded in the era of the Salem witch trials, Doc builds a miniaturized time machine to alert Marty in the future [BFAN-4].

WOODEN BARREL

- **Aug. 5, 1926 A.D.**—Jules fits a cask with a spare Flux Capacitor, enabling Verne to survive a waterfall plunge by jumping through space-time on the way down [BFAN-11].

CHRISTMAS SLEIGH

- **Aug. 26, 2011 to Dec. 24, 2011 A.D.**—Doc travels into the future and gives Santa Claus a time-traveling sleigh to help him deliver his gifts on time [GARB].

- **Dec. 24, 2011 to Dec. 25, 2011 A.D.**—Doc sends Santa one half-hour into the future, to the start of Christmas at midnight [GARB].

- **Dec. 25, 2011 A.D.**—Santa uses the sleigh to deliver presents to children worldwide [GARB].

MODE OF TRAVEL UNSPECIFIED

- **Circa 1991 to Before Oct. 18, 1931 A.D.**—Doc travels back to meet Thomas Edison and have him autograph an electric light bulb [RIDE, BFAN-11].

- **Circa 1991 to Dec. 17, 1903 A.D.**—Doc witnesses the first controlled powered flight of Orville and Wilbur Wright, in Kitty Hawk, North Carolina [RIDE].

CODE	STORY						
ARGN	BTTF-themed TV commercial: Arrigoni	BTF1	Film: *Back to the Future*	CITY	*BTTF*-themed music video: Owl City, "Deer in the Headlights"	HUEY	*BTTF*-themed music video: Huey Lewis and the News, "The Power of Love"
BFAN	*Back to the Future: The Animated Series*	BTF2	Film: *Back to the Future Part II*	DCTV	*BTTF*-themed TV commercial: DirecTV	LIMO	*BTTF*-themed music video: The Limousines, "The Future"
BFCG	*Back to the Future: The Card Game*	BTF3	Film: *Back to the Future Part III*	ERTH	*The Earth Day Special*		
BFCL	*Back to the Future* comic book (limited series)	BUDL	*BTTF*-themed TV commercial: Bud Light	GALE	Interviews and commentaries: Bob Gale and/or Robert Zemeckis	MCDN	*BTTF*-themed TV commercial: McDonald's
BFCM	*Back to the Future* comic book (monthly series)	CHEK	*BTTF*-themed music video: O'Neal McKnight, "Check Your Coat"	GARB	*BTTF*-themed TV commercials: Garbarino	MITS	*BTTF*-themed TV commercial: Mitsubishi Lancer
BFHM	*BTTF*-themed McDonald's Happy Meal boxes	CHIC	Photographs hanging in Doc Brown's Chicken restaurant at Universal Studios	GETV	*BTTF*-themed TV commercial: GE	MSFT	*BTTF*-themed TV commercial: Microsoft
BTFA	*Back to the Future Annual* (Marvel Comics)						

- **Circa 1991 to Before Apr. 18, 1955 A.D.**—Doc attends a presentation by Albert Einstein [RIDE].

- **Circa 1991 to Between Jan. 20, 1969 and Aug. 9, 1974 A.D.**—Doc attends a speech delivered by U.S. President Richard Nixon [RIDE].

- **Circa 1991 to Feb. 7, 1964 A.D.**—Doc witnesses the Beatles' arrival at New York's Kennedy Airport during their first visit to the United States [RIDE].

- **1991 A.D. to 3,000,000 B.C.**—Doc travels back to prehistoric days and witnesses a fight between two dinosaurs [BFAN-3].

- **1992 to 1940s A.C.**—Doc goes back in time to enter a jitterbug competition [BFAN-17].

- **1992 to Soon After 1892 A.D.**—Doc and Clara travel back to Hill Valley's frontier days and visit the Hill Valley General Store [BFHM].

- **Late 20th Century A.D.**—Doc travels the world, enjoying fried chicken at numerous landmarks, including the U.S. Capitol building, in Washington, D.C.; the ancient Pyramids of Egypt's Giza Necropolis; England's Buckingham Palace and Stonehenge monuments; France's Eiffel Tower; India's Taj Mahal; and Hollywood, California [CHIC].

  NOTE: It's unclear whether time travel was required for the above trip.

			SUFFIX MEDIUM		
NIKE	*BTTF*-themed TV commercial: Nike	**SCRT** 2010 Scream Awards: *Back to the Future* 25th Anniversary Reunion (trailer)		**-s1**	Screenplay (draft one)
NTND	Nintendo *Back to the Future—The Ride* Mini-Game		**-b** *BTF2's* Biff Tannen Museum video (extended version)	**-s2**	Screenplay (draft two)
		SIMP Simulator: *The Simpsons Ride*		**-s3**	Screenplay (draft three)
PIZA	*BTTF*-themed TV commercial: Pizza Hut	**SLOT** *Back to the Future* Video Slots	**-c** Animated series credit sequence	**-s4**	Screenplay (draft four)
REAL	Real life	**TEST** Screen tests: Crispin Glover, Lea Thompson and Thomas F. Wilson	**-d** Film deleted scene	**-sp**	Screenplay (production draft)
RIDE	Simulator: *Back to the Future—The Ride*		**-n** Film novelization	**-sx**	Screenplay (*Paradox*)
SCRM	2010 Scream Awards: *Back to the Future* 25th Anniversary Reunion (broadcast)	**TLTL** Telltale Games' *Back to the Future—The Game*	**-o** Film outtake		
		UNIV Universal Studios Hollywood promotional video	**-v** Video game print materials or commentaries		

APPENDIX V ←))))

Hill Valley Hall of Fame:
Historical Meetings and Celebrity Encounters

By Rich Handley

"Chuck! Chuck, it's Marvin. Your cousin, Marvin Berry! You know
that new sound you're looking for? Well, listen to this!"

—**Marvin Berry,** *Back to the Future*

> **A**s Doc and Marty repeatedly traversed time, it was inevitable that their adventures would lead to their meeting people of historical significance, including a few of their own idols—and even, oddly enough, a few individuals from other franchises. In so doing, they sometimes reshaped the course of human history. The following pages present a collection of the characters' known brushes with fame. Additional information about particular individuals can be found in the main timeline, as well as in the companion volume, *A Matter of Time: The Back to the Future Lexicon.*

HISTORICAL INDIVIDUALS OR GROUPS

Baltimore Orioles and Boston Beaneaters
Marty encountered the two National League baseball teams in 1897—and even played pro ball with the Beaneaters, under manager Frank Gibson Selee—after traveling back in time to help Pee Wee McFly win a crucial playoff game. Prior to his intervention, the Orioles beat the Beaneaters, due to gangster Jimmy "Diamond Jim" Tannen coercing Pee Wee to strike out, but Marty changed history by convincing his cousin to stand up to Tannen and instead play honorably [BFAN-8].

> *NOTE: "Boston Beaneaters" was the name by which the Atlanta Braves were known during that era. In 1897, the team won the league pennant against the Orioles.*

Dr. Thomas Alva Edison
Doc Brown greatly admired the scientist, who was known for his many inventions, including a phonograph and a long-lasting electric light bulb. Emmett, in fact, kept a framed photo of the man on his fireplace mantle [BTF1]. During a trip to the 1920s, Doc met his idol and asked him

to autograph a bulb. To Brown's delight, Edison wrote, "To Doc, The best! Thomas" [BFAN-11, RIDE].

Dr. Albert Einstein
Doc also admired the German theoretical physicist, known for his General Theory of Relativity. He even named his dog after the Nobel Prize winner [BTF1]. During one trip through time, Brown had an opportunity to meet his idol, and brought Einie along for the ride so the mutt could meet his namesake [RIDE].

Dr. Benjamin "Ben" Franklin
The author, printer and politician—and inventor of bifocal lenses, lightning rods, printing presses, a metal-lined fireplace and more—was another of Doc's idols [BTF1]. Emmett met the U.S. Founding Father in 1752, when Verne erroneously convinced himself that Franklin was his real father. Doc inadvertently wrecked the man's furniture, causing a chair to land on a pair of barrel staves, and thereby inspiring Ben to invent the rocking chair [BFAN-6].

Builders of the Great Pyramid of Giza
Doc visited ancient Egypt during the construction of the

largest of the three pyramids in Egypt's Giza Necropolis. At the time, the builders were erecting the structure to balance point-down, with its width increasing with elevation. When Emmett knocked over the upside-down pyramid after bumping into it with the *Jules Verne Train*, however, the structure flipped over and landed point-up—a design that pleased the architect more than the original concept [BFAN-15].

David Llewelyn Wark "D. W." Griffith

While visiting Hill Valley in 1885 to rescue Doc from being shot by Buford Tannen, Marty met the seven-year-old future film director, whose works would later include *The Birth of a Nation* and *Intolerance*. Griffith, having witnessed Marty defeating Tannen in a duel by using a stove door as a shield, asked Marty how he came up with the idea. Marty replied that he'd seen it in a movie, inspiring in the boy a desire to become a filmmaker [BTF3-sx, BTF3-sp, BTF3-sn].

> *NOTE: Since Griffith was born in 1875, his age at the time of* BTF3 *does not jibe with actual history.*

Original Cast of William Shakespeare's *Hamlet*

Doc and his wife Clara traveled back to watch the debut performance of Shakespeare's famous play, which the Bard wrote sometime between 1599 and 1601 [BFAN-16].

James Riddle "Jimmy" Hoffa

In the Biffhorrific timeline, Biff Tannen was photographed with the American labor union leader at several teamster events [BTF2-b].

> *NOTE: Hoffa vanished in 1975 under unknown circumstances, and is purported to have been related to organized crime, his death the result of foul play. It's unknown if this was his fate in the alternate universe, as well as whether Biff was involved in the disappearance.*

Manhattan Project Scientists

Emmett Brown worked as a private contractor for the U.S. Defense Department during World War II, aiding in military efforts against Nazi Germany [BFAN-17]. During this era, he joined the Manhattan Project, a research and development program under the direction of Major General Leslie Groves of the U.S. Army Corps of Engineers, and helped to create the world's first atomic bomb [GALE].

Charles Peter McColough

In 1952, Doc's friend and colleague, Charles, tried to convince him to become a major stockholder and employee of his fledgling company, Xerox Corp. Convinced that the firm had no future, since few would know how to pronounce its name—Doc mispronounced it "X-rox"—the scientist turned down the offer, missing out on a hugely profitable investment opportunity [BTF1-s1].

Robert L. Muglia

When the Microsoft executive delivered a keynote address at Tech-Ed 2007 regarding his vision for the future, attendees tired of unrealized promises pummeled him with vegetables. Therefore, Doc brought Muglia back in time to witness how faulty Microsoft software caused setbacks for users in the early 2000s, enabling him to avoid his firm's past mistakes—and thus deliver a more successful keynote [MSFT].

Emperor Tiberius Julius Caesar Augustus

In 36 A.D., Doc offended one of Caesar's officers, Bifficus Antanneny, who challenged Marty to a chariot race at the Circus Maximus. Realizing Bifficus had to win in order for Caligula's rise and the Empire's fall to occur as recorded, Doc instructed Marty to lose the race [BFAN-5].

> *NOTE: The emperor was not named onscreen, but historically, the Empire's leader in that year—and Caligula's predecessor—was Tiberius Julius Caesar Augustus (who, in busts of his likeness, appeared quite different from his cartoon portrayal).*

Mark Twain (born Samuel Langhorne Clemens)

Sometime before 1885, the author and humorist, whose works included *The Adventures of Tom Sawyer* and *Adventures of Huckleberry Finn*, visited Hill Valley. While there, he told a number of tall tales to the patrons of the Palace Saloon and Hotel, including Chester the bartender [BTF3-sp, BTF3-n]. Doc once went frog-hunting with Twain in Calaveras County [BFAN-7a].

> *NOTE: Doc's frog-hunting adventure would seem to indicate that the events of Twain's short story, "The Celebrated Jumping Frog of Calaveras County," actually occurred in* BTTF *history.*

CODE	STORY						
ARGN	BTTF-themed TV commercial: Arrigoni	BTF1	Film: *Back to the Future*	CITY	*BTTF*-themed music video: Owl City, "Deer in the Headlights"	HUEY	*BTTF*-themed music video: Huey Lewis and the News, "The Power of Love"
BFAN	*Back to the Future: The Animated Series*	BTF2	Film: *Back to the Future Part II*	DCTV	*BTTF*-themed TV commercial: DirecTV	LIMO	*BTTF*-themed music video: The Limousines, "The Future"
BFCG	*Back to the Future: The Card Game*	BTF3	Film: *Back to the Future Part III*	ERTH	*The Earth Day Special*		
BFCL	*Back to the Future* comic book (limited series)	BUDL	*BTTF*-themed TV commercial: Bud Light	GALE	Interviews and commentaries: Bob Gale and/or Robert Zemeckis	MCDN	*BTTF*-themed TV commercial: McDonald's
BFCM	*Back to the Future* comic book (monthly series)	CHEK	*BTTF*-themed music video: O'Neal McKnight, "Check Your Coat"	GARB	*BTTF*-themed TV commercials: Garbarino	MITS	*BTTF*-themed TV commercial: Mitsubishi Lancer
BFHM	*BTTF*-themed McDonald's Happy Meal boxes	CHIC	Photographs hanging in Doc Brown's Chicken restaurant at Universal Studios	GETV	*BTTF*-themed TV commercial: GE	MSFT	*BTTF*-themed TV commercial: Microsoft
BTFA	*Back to the Future Annual* (Marvel Comics)						

Creator of the Venus de Milo

While visiting Rome in 36 A.D., Jules and Verne Brown inadvertently broke the arms off the statue—believed to depict Greek goddess Aphrodite—while its sculptor was creating it. Though initially angered, the artist was pleased upon seeing how the statue looked armless [BFAN-5].

> *NOTE: The Venus de Milo is thought to have been sculpted between 130 and 100 B.C.—more than a century before the Browns witnessed its creation in the animated series.*

Jules Gabriel Verne

The French author of *A Journey to the Center of the Earth*, *Twenty Thousand Leagues Under the Sea* and *Around the World in Eighty Days* was a favorite writer of both Emmett Brown and Clara Clayton. As such, the couple named their sons Jules and Verne [BTF3]. Young Verne hated his name and asked Marty to help convince the author to rename himself so Verne's identity would be changed as well. Among their suggested alternates were Bill, James Bond, Charles Dickens, Frank, Hammer, Luke Perry, Raphael, Bart Simpson, Dr. Seuss and Mark Twain. The attempt failed [BFAN-21].

Orville and Wilbur Wright

Doc Brown witnessed the brothers' first successful powered airplane flight near Kitty Hawk, North Carolina, in 1903, while visiting his personal heroes on their dates of historical significance [RIDE].

CELEBRITIES

The Beatles

Doc had a close encounter with the British rock-and-roll band in 1964, photographing the group during a press conference welcoming them to the United States. Snapping a picture from the front row, the scientist happily commented, "Let it be" [RIDE].

> *NOTE: Let It Be was the final studio album released by The Beatles, in May 1970. Apparently, the record's name may have been inspired by Doc's utterance.*

Chuck Berry

Though Marty never actually met the famed rock-and-roll singer and guitarist, he did influence the man's career. Chuck's cousin, Marvin Berry, was the front man of Marvin Berry and the Starlighters. When that band performed at the Enchantment Under the Sea Dance in 1955, Marty joined them on guitar, playing Chuck's song "Johnny B. Goode" three years prior to its release. Amazed, Marvin called his cousin, who was looking for a new sound at the time [BTF1].

> *NOTE: Thus, Marty introduced Berry to his own music—played on the same Gibson guitar with which the singer often performed. In essence, Berry then stole the song… from himself.*

Brett Morgan Butler

The Los Angeles Dodgers centerfielder appeared in an instructional video that Doc filmed to explain the Magnus effect and the physics of throwing a curveball [BFAN-8].

Huey Lewis and the News

Doc attended a Huey Lewis concert in 1985, at a nightclub called Uncle Charlie's. While he was at the show, a young couple, fascinated with his DeLorean, took the vehicle for an unauthorized joyride [HUEY].

> *NOTE: Lewis portrayed a Battle of the Bands judge in BTF1, dismissing The Pinheads' performance as being "too darn loud." The band was originally slated to appear in BTF2 as 60-year-old versions of themselves in 2015, but this did not come to pass.*

Jayne Mansfield (born Vera Jayne Palmer)

In the Biffhorrific timeline, Biff Tannen dated the beautiful actress, nightclub entertainer and *Playboy* Playmate—known for her roles in *The Girl Can't Help It*, *The Wayward Bus* and *Too Hot to Handle*—prior to marrying Lorraine Baines McFly [BTF2-b].

O'Neal McKnight

Doc met McKnight while the youth worked as a nightclub coat-check clerk, and brought him forward to the year 2088 so the future musician could see what he was meant to be. McKnight discovered his potential as a club dancer and ladies' man, while Doc took a turn spinning records in a D.J. booth [CHEK].

Marilyn Monroe (born Norma Jeane Mortensen Baker)

In the Biffhorrific timeline, Biff Tannen dated the actress,

NIKE	*BTTF*-themed TV commercial: Nike	**SCRT**	2010 Scream Awards: *Back to the Future*	**SUFFIX MEDIUM**		**-s1**	Screenplay (draft one)
NTND	Nintendo *Back to the Future—The Ride* Mini-Game		25th Anniversary Reunion (trailer)	**-b**	*BTF2's* Biff Tannen Museum video (extended version)	**-s2**	Screenplay (draft two)
		SIMP	Simulator: *The Simpsons Ride*			**-s3**	Screenplay (draft three)
PIZA	*BTTF*-themed TV commercial: Pizza Hut	**SLOT**	*Back to the Future* Video Slots	**-c**	Animated series credit sequence	**-s4**	Screenplay (draft four)
REAL	Real life	**TEST**	Screen tests: Crispin Glover, Lea Thompson	**-d**	Film deleted scene	**-sp**	Screenplay (production draft)
RIDE	Simulator: *Back to the Future—The Ride*		and Thomas F. Wilson	**-n**	Film novelization	**-sx**	Screenplay (*Paradox*)
SCRM	2010 Scream Awards: *Back to the Future*	**TLTL**	Telltale Games' *Back to the Future—The Game*	**-o**	Film outtake		
	25th Anniversary Reunion (broadcast)	**UNIV**	Universal Studios Hollywood promotional video	**-v**	Video game print materials or commentaries		

model, singer and sex symbol—known for her dalliances with John F. and Robert Kennedy, as well as for her work in the films *Gentlemen Prefer Blondes*, *How to Marry a Millionaire*, *The Seven Year Itch*, *Bus Stop* and *Some Like It Hot*—prior to marrying Lorraine Baines McFly [BTF2-b].

William Sanford Nye
(a.k.a. "Bill Nye, The Science Guy")
The science educator, comedian, mechanical engineer and TV host helped Doc create a Video Encyclopedia database for students, in which Nye demonstrated various science principles while Brown provided accompanying narrations [BFAN-1 to BFAN-26].

FICTIONAL INDIVIDUALS

Judah Ben-Hur
While visiting Rome in 36 A.D., Marty and the Brown family met Judah Ben-Hur, a well-muscled slave whose master often beat him with a whip. When Jules and Verne saved Judah from one such beating, the slave expressed his gratitude by helping them find their father [BFAN-5].

>*NOTE: Judah Ben-Hur was a fictional character in Lew Wallace's 1880 novel,* **Ben-Hur: A Tale of the Christ,** *and the 1959 Charlton Heston film,* **Ben-Hur,** *based on that book. The* **BTTF** *version adopted Heston's appearance and speaking pattern.*

John I.Q. Nerdelbaum Frink Jr.
Doc was a colleague of the socially inept professor. When the Institute of Future Technology was replaced by the Krustyland theme park, Frink traveled two years back in time to find out why. In so doing, he inadvertently killed a banker about to loan Doc the money necessary to keep the IFT afloat, thereby ironically causing Emmett to sell the facility to Krusty the Clown [SIMP].

>*NOTE: Frink, a character from* **The Simpsons,** *appeared in queue footage in* **The Simpsons Ride** *as an in-joke reference to Universal Studios Florida's replacement of* **Back to the Future: The Ride** *with that attraction. Christopher Lloyd reprised the role of Doc for that footage.*

Krusty the Clown (born Herschel Shmoikel Pinchas Yerucham Krustofski)
After failing to secure a loan to keep the facility open (thanks to Frink's inadvertent temporal meddling, noted above), Doc sold the Institute of Future Technology (IFT) to the cynical, burnt-out television personality, and worked for a time as the clown's chauffeur [SIMP].

>*NOTE: Krusty also appeared in* **The Simpsons Ride's** *queue footage.*

Dr. Douglas "Doogie" Howser
Doc met this child prodigy (who became a physician at age 16) when a physical manifestation of Mother Nature became gravely ill. Traveling to the future, Emmett learned that it would be grim if she could not be saved. He then returned to the past to warn Howser, who was treating Mother Nature's illness at a hospital [ERTH].

>*NOTE: Howser, portrayed by Neil Patrick Harris, was the title character of* **Doogie Howser, M.D.,** *which aired on ABC from 1989 to 1993. This unusual crossover occurred in Time Warner's 1990 video,* **The Earth Day Special.**

ABOUT THE AUTHORS ◀▥

GREG MITCHELL

Greg Mitchell is a screenwriter and novelist, and the author of the faith-versus-fear series *The Coming Evil Trilogy* and the sci-fi/action-adventure *Rift Jump*. His short stories have appeared in *Bigfoot Terror Tales Vol. 2*, two editions of *The Midnight Diner*, *Underground Rising*, and the occult detective anthology *A Cat of Nine Tales*. He's released two e-books—the zombie love story *Flowers for Shelly*, and *The Coming Evil: Lengthening Shadows*. Previously he's been a frequent contributor to the sci-fi shared universe *Avenir Eclectia*, where he's chronicled the exploits of Dressler, the giant-bug hunter. In film, he wrote the screenplay for *Amazing Love: The Story of Hosea*, starring Sean Astin from *The Lord of the Rings Trilogy*. He has contributed to The Official *Star Wars* Blog and previously served on board the team at HalloweenComics.com, where he developed original tie-in fiction for John Carpenter's horror classic *Halloween*, including the online exclusive short story *Halloween: White Ghost*. He lives in Northeast Arkansas with his wife and two daughters, and is still waiting for his very own hoverboard. Keep him company at www.thecomingevil.com.

RICH HANDLEY

Rich Handley is the editor and co-founder of Hasslein Books, the managing editor of *RFID Journal*, and a frequent contributor to *Bleeding Cool Magazine*, StarWars.com and TrekWeb.com. This is his fourth book, following *Timeline of the Planet of the Apes*, *Lexicon of the Planet of the Apes* and *A Matter of Time: The Back to the Future Lexicon*. Rich has penned various articles and short fiction pieces for the licensed *Star Wars* universe, assistant-edited Realm Press' *Battlestar Galactica* comic book line, co-wrote Archaia Publishing's novel *Conspiracy of the Planet of the Apes* and helped Ed Gross update his popular reference book *Planet of the Apes Revisited*. A columnist and reporter at *Star Trek Communicator* magazine for several years, he assisted GIT Corp. compile its *Star Trek: The Complete Comic Book Collection* and *Star Trek Movie Comic Book Collection* DVD-ROM sets. More recently, he wrote the introductions to IDW's *Star Trek* newspaper strip reprint books and contributed an essay to the Sequart Research & Literacy Organization's upcoming *Star Trek* comic book anthology.

ABOUT HASSLEIN BOOKS ◀▥

Hasslein Books (hassleinbooks.com), co-founded by Rich Handley and Paul C. Giachetti, is a Long Island-based publisher of reference guides by geeks, for geeks. The company is named after Doctor Otto Hasslein, a time-travel expert portrayed by actor Eric Braeden in the film *Escape from the Planet of the Apes*. Our lineup of unauthorized genre-based reference books includes *Timeline of the Planet of the Apes*, *Lexicon of the Planet of the Apes*, *A Matter of Time: The Back to the Future Lexicon* and *Back in Time: The Back to the Future Chronology*, with future volumes slated to feature *Red Dwarf*, James Bond, *G.I. Joe*, *Alien vs. Predator*, *Battlestar Galactica*, *Doctor Who*, *Ghostbusters*, Universal Monsters and *The Man From U.N.C.L.E.* "Like" us on Facebook (facebook.com/hassleinbooks), follow us on Twitter (twitter.com/hassleinbooks) and frequent our blog (hassleinbooks.blogspot.com) to stay informed regarding all upcoming projects.

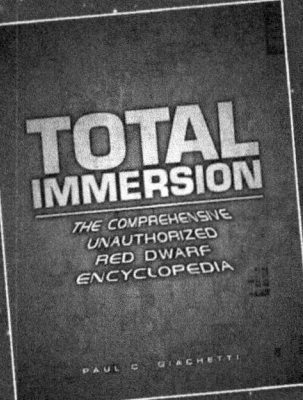

www.ingramcontent.com/pod-product-compliance
Lightning Source LLC
Chambersburg PA
CBHW080958020726
47505CB00009B/2244